# Me and My Shadow

## A novel of the Silver Dragons

## About the author

Award-winning *New York Times* bestselling author Katie MacAlister has a passion for mystery, a fascination with alpha males, and a deep love of history that qualifies her perfectly for the fiction she writes. She lives with her husband and dogs in the USA.

www.katiemacalister.com

### Also by Katie MacAlister

*The Dark Ones*
A Girl's Guide to Vampires
Sex and the Single Vampire
Sex, Lies and Vampires

*The Silver Dragon*s
Playing With Fire*
Up in Smoke *
Me and My Shadow

* available as Hodder paperbacks from March 2010

# Katie MacAlister

# Me and My Shadow

A Novel of the  Silver Dragons

**HODDER**

First published in Great Britain in 2009 by
Hodder & Stoughton
An Hachette UK company

1

Copyright © Marthe Arends

A CIP catalogue record for this title is available from the British Library.

ISBN 978 0 340 99300 2

Typeset in Bembo
Printed and bound by Clays Ltd, St Ives plc

Hodder & Stoughton policy is to use papers that are natural, renewable
and recyclable products and made from wood grown in sustainable forests.
The logging and manufacturing processes are expected to conform to the
environmental regulations of the country of origin.

Hodder & Stoughton Ltd
338 Euston Road
London NW1 3BH
www.hodder.co.uk

To my friend Brian Murphy, for making me laugh,
teasing me mercilessly, and letting me rant
without once telling me to suck it up, buttercup.

# Chapter One

"Off with her head!"

I looked over my laptop screen at the man who stood in the center of the sitting room, pointing with a fine dramatic flair at a woman in the doorway.

"I demand that you punish that . . . that . . . dragon for insubordination!"

"Oh, yeah, like *that's* gonna happen," a voice muttered from the floor.

Magoth narrowed his eyes on the dog lying in a patch of sunlight, reading through a stack of near-pornographic graphic novels. "I have not given you permission to speak in my presence, demon."

"Here's a news flash for you—you're not a prince anymore, so I can say what I like. Right, May?"

I was about to nod, but thought better of giving the demon in doggy form carte blanche to do as it willed. My experience with Jim might not have been great, but it had been sufficient to give me pause. "No, you can say what Aisling told you was allowable to say when she sent you to stay with us. And if I recall, the words 'Don't lip off to anyone, for any reason, anytime, ever' were included in her instructions."

Jim, whose full demon name of Effrijim was deemed too girlie by its owner to be used in anything but formal ceremonies, grinned, not an easy task considering it bore the form of a large, shaggy black Newfoundland dog. "Actually, I think she said if I pissed you off, she'd banish me to the Akasha until the baby was old enough to vote, but everyone knows doppelgangers don't get pissy easily, so it's all copacetic."

"Were we in Abaddon at this moment," Magoth told the demon, the words coming out as a growl, "you would be on your belly begging for my mercy. It would be a useless gesture—nonetheless, I would allow you to continue begging, while writhing in torment so great you would plead for destruction, until such time as I grew tired of your screams of absolute, utter, endless agony."

"Yeah, yeah," Jim said, turning back to its graphic novel. "Been there, done that, have the 'My demon lord torments me for fun' T-shirt."

Magoth puffed himself up until I thought he was going to explode. I considered whether the cleaning bill would be worth the entertainment value to be found therein, but decided against it. "What's the problem, Maata?" I asked instead, shifting my gaze to the woman who stood at the door, watching us with noticeable amusement in her silver eyes.

She held on to a placid expression. "Magoth—"

"Prince of Abaddon Magoth, to you, dragon," the man in question said. "Or Lord Magoth. Or even, His Unholy Highness Magoth."

"Magoth," Maata repeated, "tried to get into the basement. *Again.*"

I raised one eyebrow at the exiled demon lord, former silent-film star, and bearer of a (literally) cursed penis as he stormed around the room in impotent rage.

Being born an incredibly handsome man in possession of sultry looks that had women throwing away their better judgments (and sometimes souls) over the centuries, Magoth had no reason to adopt a form other than his natural one. Not, I noted silently to myself, that he could now if he wanted.

"You see how I am treated? This is intolerable, wife! I insist that you lesson this minion! I will not be told by a mere slave what I may or may not do! She threatened me with violence! *Me!* She deserves a lengthy and inventive punishment for daring to treat me in such an insupportable manner!"

"It was my fault. He used my bathroom break to get past me to the entrance of the lair," Maata said, apology rich in her voice. "He won't do so again."

"It was the merest of coincidences that I was in the basement at the exact moment the slave was out of the room," Magoth sniffed, adopting a self-righteous expression that I didn't for one moment buy.

"You sneaked past me when I was in the bathroom," Maata accused.

"I am a demon lord! I do not sneak!" he said, outraged.

"One," I said, ticking it off on a finger, "you're no longer a demon lord. At least not technically. Two, Maata is one of Gabriel's elite guards, not a slave, and you will treat her with the respect due her. And three, I'm not your wife, so stop calling me that."

"You're my consort," he insisted, his eyes narrowing on me.

"You de-consorted me when you found out you'd been kicked out of Abaddon, remember?"

"I spoke in the heat of the moment. You know full well that I have not conducted divorce proceedings. Until it pleases me to remove you from that position"—he smiled, and I thanked my stars that we weren't in Abaddon, or I might have lost a few bits of my soul to that smile—"or until you die, you will remain my consort."

"Thank you for that reiteration of demon lord protocol." Inside me, deep inside my chest, the shard of the dragon heart that I bore stirred, triggered as always by any threat or strong emotion. I clamped down hard on it, practicing the control I'd been working so hard to wield. I smiled at Gabriel's bodyguard. "Thanks, Maata. I'll take care of this."

"Better you than me," she answered with a wry smile as she left.

"You want me to rough him up a little?" Jim asked, rising and walking slowly toward Magoth. "I'd go straight for his noogies, but that curse gives me the willies. Ha! Willies! Get it?"

"Go ahead and try," Magoth said, his eyes glittering with an unholy light.

Jim paused, shooting me a worried look. "You said he doesn't have any powers here, right?"

"He's without about ninety-five percent of his power, yes," I answered.

Jim froze. "Oh, man! I thought you said *all* of his power was gone!"

"It is. Well, all but about five percent, as best as we can figure."

"Five percent? Geez, May! We've got to have a little talk about the difference between a demon lord without any power, and one with enough to squash flat a sixth-class demon!"

Magoth smiled again. A little black tendril of power snapped at Jim.

The demon yelped and backed toward the door. "Fires of Abaddon, can't you take a joke? I was just funning, Your Imperial Dark and Twisted Majesty. Er . . . I think *Hart to Hart* is on that retro-TV-show channel.

You know how I love me some Stefanie Powers. Catch ya later, Your Eminence of Unholy Darkness."

I gave Magoth my full consideration as the door shut behind Jim. It was true that over the last six weeks while Magoth had lived with us, Gabriel and I had determined that the demon lord had retained only a tiny fraction of his powers, but you don't become a prince of Abaddon without picking up a few tricks.

"You know the basement and areas below are off-limits until the workmen are done, Magoth. We explained that to you when they started building the lair."

His expression shifted from outrage to sullen discontent. "As the mortals say, you are not the boss of me."

"Perhaps not, but you are here on sufferance, a fact I am obliged to point out yet again. Irritating Gabriel by attempting to force your way into his lair is going to do nothing but give him due cause to boot your butt out into the street."

He oiled his way around the desk at which I sat, and trailed a finger up my arm as he moved behind me. I fought the urge to shiver, his touch so cold it leeched the heat from the air around me. "Ah, but you wouldn't allow your scaly boyfriend to do that, would you, my sweet, sweet May?" He brushed a quick, frigid kiss on the back of my neck. Beneath the desk, my hands tightened into fists, pain pricking my palms. I knew without looking that my fingers had changed into long, scarlet talons. The dragon shard urged me to shift, enticing me with mental visions of Magoth lying dead on the floor at my feet.

I was sorely tempted to give in to the shard, but I reminded myself that once I gave myself up to it, there would be no going back. Much as I loved Gabriel, as happy as I was being the mate to a powerful—not to mention witty, urbane, and incredibly sexy—wyvern, I did not want to spend the rest of eternity as a dragon.

"You've been warned about touching me," I managed to say in a neutral voice. The dragon shard fought hard to dominate me, but I hadn't survived as Magoth's slave for almost a hundred years without learning how to control my emotions.

His cold breath touched my neck for a moment longer before wisdom evidently got the better of him. He pushed aside my laptop and lay on top of the desk in a seductive pose, one hand languidly gesturing toward his body. "You want me."

"I want Gabriel," I said, struggling inwardly as the dragon shard once again threatened to overwhelm me.

He smiled again, but this was a smile of seduction, not promised retribution. "Your dragon may satisfy your doppelganger needs, but the animal within you wants me, sweet May. I can feel it."

"I am not an animal," I said, my voice taking on a rough tone. I cleared my throat, determined to keep my usual unflappable demeanor with him, no matter how much he provoked me.

He leaned forward slightly, his eyes half-lidded. I recognized the signs—heaven knew I'd been the recipient of his seduction attempts often enough. If I just let him work himself through the worst of it, eventually I'd be able to distract him with some other interesting mental tidbit. Magoth was always attracted by shiny things, be they tangible or intangible.

"Tell me you don't feel it, as well," he said, his gaze attempting to draw me into the seduction. He didn't have enough power to put a thrall on me—a full-fledged sexual enchantment of sorts—so it was simply a matter of distracting him with a suitably interesting conversational offering.

To my surprise, shock, and utter horror, instead of passing along a benign bit of Abaddon gossip, I found myself leaning forward until my lips brushed his.

The dragon shard swamped me with emotions, hot and foreign, and suddenly out of the confusing mass came a burning desire to mate with him.

"No," I gasped, shoving myself away from the desk, away from Magoth. Horror crept up my flesh. Never once since I'd met Gabriel had I considered Magoth with anything but loathing and irritation. What was going on that I was now responding to him?

I pulled up a mental picture of the man I loved with all my heart, remembered the warm latte-colored brown skin, the dimples that made my knees go weak, the flash of mercurial silver eyes, the fires he alone stirred in me, making me burn for him. *Only* for him.

I stamped out the tiny little flame that appeared on the floor.

"You see? The beast you bear says yes, sweet one. Give in to it. Let me show you what exquisite pleasure I can bring you."

I had to force my legs to back up. The need was great in me to take just what he offered, so great it almost had me casting common sense to the wind. "It's not a beast. It's one-fifth of the dragon heart, and it does not rule me. You can stop trying to seduce me, because it simply won't work. And must I remind you what Gabriel said he'd do to you the last time he caught you trying to make love to me?"

"I don't make love. I make ecstasy," he answered, but his hands twitched protectively toward his groin before he stopped them. "No matter how much you protest, my adorable one, the fact remains that we both know the honeymoon with your dragon is over, and it's me you truly want." He slid off the desk and stalked toward me.

"Stop trying to get a look at Gabriel's lair, stop getting in Maata's way, and stop trying to seduce me," I said, backing toward the door. I jerked it open and was through it before he could answer, although the sound of his mocking laughter followed me as I raced down the hall to the stairs that led down to the basement.

Maata was sitting on a chair at the bottom of the stairs, reading a book. She glanced up as I leaped down the last couple of stairs, her eyebrows going up at the sight of my flushed face. Since I was normally a calm, possessed person, I knew she recognized signs that the shard was driving me to distraction.

"Where is he?" I asked.

She knew exactly whom I was talking about. "Examining the lock. They got the door up."

"Thanks." I didn't wait to chat, just bolted for the hole that was cut into the cement floor, clattering down the metal ladder set into the wall until I reached the rocky bottom. Lights hung drunkenly from the ceiling, a dank, earthy smell heavy in the air. It wasn't surprising, given that the workmen had just excavated this subterranean lair over the last month, digging deep into the earth to create a series of tomblike passages that ended in a large room where Gabriel would keep his most precious items.

Two guards appeared as I jumped the last few feet to the earth and stone floor. They smiled as I fled past, scattering greetings behind me as I dodged another three silver dragons who were lounging around on various packing crates.

My unseemly haste was cause for amusement, I knew, but none of that mattered at the moment. Gabriel's people—now mine—might be amused by the fact that I couldn't control the dragon shard, but they understood well what drove me.

Another metal ladder down to a lower, almost oppressively deep level, and the entrance of the lair rose before me. The door was metal, such as those found on large bank vaults, ponderously heavy, impervious to explosives and other devices intended to breach its thickness. Three high-tech locks and a retina scanner kept even the most proficient of safecrackers at bay. The spells that would be woven into the door would come later, I knew, ensuring safety from those beings who possessed skills beyond those of the mortal world.

I skidded to a stop at the door, seeing only one dragon present.

"Gabriel?" I asked Tipene, the second of Gabriel's elite guard.

He tipped his head toward the door. "They're testing the security system."

I considered whether I would be able to last the ten minutes or so it would take before Gabriel and the security experts would emerge. I knew the answer even as I leaned in to allow the retina scanner to examine my eyes before I moved directly in front of the door, my eyes on the lock.

Tipene watched me with interest as I shook out my hands, trying desperately to clear my mind enough so I could "talk" to the lock.

"I've never understood why doppelgangers can do that," he commented as I laid my hands on the lock, closing my eyes to concentrate.

"I have no idea, either. I'm just grateful I can do it."

"I don't think you're going to have much luck. This is a MacGyver 512 titanium carbon magnetic electron lock, calibrated on the atomic level. It's absolutely top-of-the-line, not even released to the public yet. I know you can open most locks, but I doubt if even you will be able to get through it, May."

"We'll see." I persuaded the lock to open a few of its secrets up to me, probing its depths, noting with interest just how intricate and well made it was. Most locks allowed me to open them with nothing but a token resistance, but this one was different. It didn't respond at all to the usual persuasions, making me resort to brute strength. As I worked my way through the many levels of the lock, I made a mental note to tell Gabriel that there were some cases where overdesign was not to the good.

The last of the tumblers finally gave way under the force of my will, allowing the steel rods to withdraw smoothly into the body of the lock. I flung a quick smile at Tipene's goggling when I jerked the door open.

"How—?" he started to say, but I didn't wait around to gloat.

At the sound of the door opening, the three men who stood in the vault consulting a clipboard turned to look at me.

I ignored two of them, flinging myself on the third.

"Little bird!" Gabriel's voice, arms, and presence wrapped themselves around me, making me feel as if I'd come home after a long journey.

With blatant disregard for both dragon etiquette and mortal manners, I kissed him, needing the reassurance that only he could provide me.

"I don't believe it," one of the two men said as I dug my fingers into Gabriel's soft dreadlocks, tugging on them to make him give me what I wanted. "She didn't just open that lock. It's impossible. It's just impossible. No one can open that lock. Maybe we didn't close it properly. . . ."

"Fire," I whispered into Gabriel's mouth.

His dragon fire spun through me, setting me ablaze with his molten heat.

"It was closed," the second man said, censure in his voice. "And as you can see by the fact that the silver mate is right here, I think it's all too clear that the lock is not as impossible to defeat as your company has claimed. If I've told one dragon, I've told a hundred—the best security system in the world won't do any good so long as the door is easily breached."

"My locks are not easily breached," the first man snarled. "This has to be an anomaly."

"What's wrong?" Gabriel asked, finally disengaging his tongue from mine.

"We have got to get rid of Magoth." I didn't want to say more in front of the other men. Gabriel trusted them to construct his lair, but neither one of them was a dragon, and I wasn't sure how far his trust went.

"Hey, May, just thought you'd like to know that Magoth found your wallet again, and is on the phone with your MasterCard in his hand. Hey, Gabe, how they hangin'? Oooh. Nice lair. Is that a MacGyver 512 you got there? Drake has one on order." Jim stepped around the two security experts and cast an interested eye around at the work in progress.

"István dropped it off a couple of days early," I explained at Gabriel's surprised expression. "Evidently Drake feels that since Aisling's due date has come and passed, everyone would be more comfortable without Jim making references to her exploding like an overripe peach."

"The word was actually 'pimple,' but yeah, Drake threatened to chop me up into demon chow if I didn't get out of the way," Jim said with absolute nonchalance. "But it's all good, because Ash made May my temporary boss while she's busy popping out that baby, and May loves me. Right, May?"

Gabriel's quicksilver eyes flashed from the two men, now arguing over the relative merits of wards versus banes (the latter being weakish curses that were nonetheless extremely powerful, and very difficult to break). "What has Magoth done now?"

"We just have to get rid of him," I said in a low voice, hoping he could read the message in my eyes. "Immediately."

"Right, May?" Jim repeated, a little more forcefully. "Ya love me, right? I'm da man?"

Gabriel examined my face. "Has he touched you?"

I sighed, holding up my hand. Rather than normal, slightly freckled fingers, it was made up of long, elegant silver digits tipped with scarlet claws. "The dragon shard isn't working correctly. It seems to be confused. And the sooner Magoth is gone, the sooner I can straighten it out."

"Who's your daddy? That's right—incredibly handsome, and manly in a furry sort of way, Jim is! I'm all yours, sweet cheeks, duly authorized by Ash to submit to your every whim and desire, especially the ones that involve giving me food and belly scratches."

"You don't mean . . ." Gabriel's eyes opened wide.

I nodded.

"I'll kill him."

The words were spoken softly, and in Gabriel's normal velvety tones, but the underlying threat was so great it made my blood grow cold.

"Whoa, now! No offense intended," Jim said, backing away. "If you don't want May giving me belly scratches, I can get them elsewhere. Word of advice, though, Gabe— you may wanna think about switching to decaf."

"You can't," I said sadly, the dragon shard, content at having stirred things up, subsiding into silence as reason returned to me. "He's still immortal, and there's a chance we can unload him back into Abaddon."

A thin little curl of smoke escaped his nose. For some reason, that always charmed me. I leaned in to give him a quick lip nibble and kiss.

"Oh, yeah, now, that's what I'm talkin' about," Jim said from the foot of the metal ladder.

I shot the demon a glare, and pointed. "Leave!"

"I was just—"

"Leave!" I ordered again. "Go tell Magoth if he orders just one more item from that high-end sex shop,

I'll stick his twelve-inch glow-in-the-dark spiked dildo where the sun don't shine."

Jim gave me a wounded look before it obeyed my command. "And I thought you were going to be fun. You've been hanging around Aisling too much—you really have."

"Come in here," Gabriel said, pulling me deeper into the coolness of the semifinished lair. Steel- and iron-lined to minimize the effectiveness of any magical attacks against it, the lair resembled a small wine vault, with long, gleaming shelves waiting for the placement of treasure he held in England. "Are you sure, little bird? You were not thinking of me, and the shard reacted to that?"

I smiled and kissed the tip of his nose. "I like the fact that you don't for one moment think I really was attracted to Magoth."

*"Tch."* He made a dismissive gesture. "You love only me. I know that you could never be attracted to him."

I didn't enlighten him to the fact that Magoth had, previous to my meeting Gabriel, come very close to seducing me. "Much as thinking about you does stir the dragon inside me, in this case, it wasn't due to that. And yet, I don't think it was really reacting to him, either. It was as if . . ." I paused, trying to sort through the unfamiliar emotions to form them into some semblance of sense. "It was as if the shard was reacting to what he represented—a dark, dangerous power. I've never felt like that around Magoth before, so I can only assume that, for some reason, the shard is suddenly wanting power."

"That doesn't make sense," Gabriel said, shaking his head so his shoulder-length dreadlocks trembled. "The shards of the dragon heart hold power themselves. They would not seek more."

"It doesn't make sense to me, either. I'm just telling you what it felt like, and that I'd really like to see the last of Magoth. Maybe I should send Bael another e-mail—"

"No." Gabriel leaned forward and kissed me swiftly, his lips demanding and aggressive. "I would prefer you not becoming involved with Abaddon."

"I'm consort to an ex-prince of Abaddon," I pointed out gently, touching the frown between his brows. "I don't see how much more involved I can become. When he kicked Magoth out of Abaddon, Bael said he'd finalize Magoth's expulsion in two months, and that deadline is almost upon us. Perhaps I could prompt Bael into reinstating Magoth. I can live with being his servant, Gabriel, but I can't live with myself if the shard makes me do something we'll all regret."

"We cannot remove the shard from you without bringing the other shards together to re-form the dragon heart," he said, his voice rich with distress. He touched my cheek, gently tucking a strand of hair behind my ear. "And you cannot do that without having a proper lair in which to do so. The shards are the most valuable relics of dragonkin, little bird."

"I know." I leaned into his palm for a moment, trying to remember what it felt like to just love him without the distraction of the shard trying to force me into a dragon state.

"Once the lair is functional, then we can go about locating the last shard, and the ceremony can commence to withdraw the one you bear—"

"Hey, May? There's someone at the door for you."

Jim's voice interrupted Gabriel, causing us both to turn and glare at the furry demon.

"Jim, I realize that Aisling allows you great freedom, but you are interrupting a private conversation. Frankly, I don't care who—"

"I think you're going to want to see this guy," Jim said with a knowing look.

I frowned. "See who?"

"That thief taker who nailed your ass and dragged you to the committee."

"Savian?" I asked, the sudden memory of the charming, if more than a little roguish, Englishman coming immediately to mind. "What's he doing here?"

"Dying," Jim said succinctly.

# Chapter Two

It's amazing how fast dragons can move when they are driven to it. The words had no sooner left Jim's mouth than Gabriel and Tipene were gone, the faintest of blurs caught out of the corner of my eye the only indication that they had been present. I didn't wait to ask Jim what Savian was doing dying on our doorstep; I shadowed, and raced out of the lair, skidding to a halt when I finally made it to the front steps.

"Is he dead?" I asked, slipping out of the shadows.

Tipene was in the process of lifting a lifeless body from the steps. Blood pooled beneath it, stark against the white stone, little crimson trails of it snaking their way down the steps toward the street. Gabriel wasn't surprised to see me, but Maata, who was holding the door open, jumped when I emerged from the shadows right next to her.

"I keep forgetting you can do that," she said, giving me a weak smile. "It's a bit unnerving seeing you suddenly materialize out of nothing."

"I was just hidden from your sight, not dematerialized," I said, peering over her shoulder to see Savian.

At the sight of the bloodied, battered body, I wished I hadn't.

"He's not dead," Gabriel answered. "Tipene will take care of him until I can see to his injuries. Maata, come with me. Little bird, can you see any signs of who left him here?"

"How could she see signs that we can't?" Maata asked.

"Things look different in the shadow world," I said, glancing around.

She frowned. "I'm confused. You just said that shadow walking meant we couldn't see you. Why would something look different? Oh, wait—are you talking about going into the Dreaming?"

"The beyond, the Dreaming, the shadow world . . . different words for the same thing. It's just an alternate reality, but only a few people can access it, and yes, that's what I'm talking about. When I'm in the shadow world, I can see signs that aren't visible in our world. Gabriel?"

The sun was out, shining brightly on the front of the house. Although there weren't a lot of people out, I didn't particularly want one of the noontime passersby to see me disappear into nothing. Gabriel and Maata moved immediately to block my view of the street, allowing me to slip into the shadow world unnoticed.

The street where we lived looked more or less the same in the shadow world, although angles were slightly off, giving the buildings a somewhat skewed appearance. Other than that obvious difference, I didn't see anything out of the ordinary . . . until I glanced down. "Oh, we are in so much trouble."

"What is it?" Gabriel asked when I bent to touch a spot on the sidewalk, his shadowy image standing next to me.

I smiled as I stood up and showed him my hand. "I'm so glad your mother taught you how to access the shadow world, even if you're incorporeal here. It's arcane residue."

"Arcane? From a mage?"

"Possibly. Dragons shed dragon scales, elemental beings leave traces of their primary element, demons leave little splotches of demon smoke, and theurgists leave arcane residue." I glanced around a wider area, my eyes searching for any other signs.

"Which means it could be anyone who uses arcane power. A mage?"

"It could be a mage, yes. Other theurgists use arcane power, too—oracles and diviners, for instance. Goetists like necromancers and summoners can tap into arcane power, as well. It could be any of them."

"And dragon scales?" Gabriel asked as I followed the arcane residue down the street.

"Lots of them, but they're a few hours old, so I assume they're from the silver dragons. I don't see any fresh ones, if that's what you're asking. Damn." I stood up from the crouch I'd adopted to follow the fading residue trail. "It's gone already. Elementals and theurgists are the hardest beings to track because their traces fade so quickly. I'm sorry, Gabriel. I can't tell you anything other than—"

"May, come back to me."

I glanced over to where Gabriel stood next to me. His voice, although somewhat muffled by the projection of himself into the shadow world, held a distinct note of command, a circumstance that was unusual enough for me to take notice. "What?"

"Come back to me." His eyes glittered like mercury against black velvet. "Come back to where my body is."

"We're just a couple of blocks from home, and I'd like to look around some more." I waved toward the sidewalk. "There's a slight chance that not all of the residue has disappeared."

His image faded before my eyes, his voice an echo on the air. "There is another dragon in the Dreaming."

I spun around, instantly reaching for the dagger I wore strapped to my ankle, even though I knew the weapon would do nothing against the only dragon known to be able to enter and exit the shadow world at will. "Baltic?"

A distant voice, tinged with amusement, drifted over to me. Judging by the somewhat ethereal nature of the sound, I gathered the very dangerous former wyvern, once thought dead, but evidently very much alive, was at some distance from me. "Ah, it is the silver mate who speaks. A doppelganger, my assistant tells me, which explains how your wyvern got around the curse. How very clever of Gabriel to think of mating himself to a woman who was not technically born."

"Annoyed that you hadn't thought of that eventuality when you cursed the silver dragons never to have a mate born to them?"

I felt a familiar presence next to me, but separated by realities. Gabriel's voice was distant, however, when he demanded I return to the real world.

"You have a quick tongue, I see," Baltic answered, his voice somewhat nearer now. I knew it was folly to keep bandying wits with him, but I didn't want to lose this opportunity to find out what I could about the mysterious dragon who seemed to be responsible for so many problems plaguing us. "Perhaps Gabriel tolerates such, but I will not."

A mist passed in front of me, resolving itself into the form of an angry man. He paused just long enough to shoot me a look that promised retribution later before he took up a protective stance before me. "Threatening my mate again, Baltic? You didn't succeed in taking her from me last time; I don't know why you believe you will fare any better now."

There was a moment of startled silence before the mysterious dragon answered, "Your shaman mother must be indebting herself greatly to manage repeatedly buying you an entrance into the beyond, Gabriel." Neither one of us corrected Baltic's false impression that Gabriel was present in a physical form. "Nonetheless, the time will come when you cannot cling to her for help."

Beside me, Gabriel stiffened at the insult, but said only, "Your bait is insufficient. Did you have something more, or was that your sole offering?"

Baltic's laugh echoed down the shadow world's empty street. I was more than a little interested to note that he sounded no closer. Obviously, he had thought twice about tangling with Gabriel and me together. "You have almost as sharp a tongue as your mate. It is regretful that both will be silenced when I retrieve my shard."

Gabriel made a low, growling noise that warned he was about to lose his temper.

"*Your* shard?" I called out, hoping to distract him. "You gave it to Kostya. I think that relinquishes any claim you might have on it."

"I would not give mud from my boots to that murderous whoreson," the voice snarled. "That fool thief taker thought he could blackmail me."

"Savian?" I asked, confused for a moment before I remembered the dead thief taker Gabriel and I had found a few months before. "Or Porter?"

"Do not think that because you found a way around the curse, you will succeed," Baltic said in a now almost inaudible voice. "For you will not. The days are numbered, wyvern. I intend to have your mate and the shard she bears. Enjoy both while you still possess them."

"Is he gone?" I asked in a whisper a moment later.

The shadowy form of Gabriel nodded. "It was not wise to engage him, little bird."

"I knew you were only a couple of blocks away, and it was obvious he wasn't close. Besides, I'm tired of guessing. It's time we got a few answers to the hundred or so questions we have about him. I didn't get to ask him outright if he was Baltic, though."

Gabriel disappeared, and I ducked into what was an alley in the real world, returning to our reality without anyone but him seeing me; I took the hand he offered, hurrying homeward with a thousand questions buzzing through my brain.

"He didn't deny either his identity or being the source of the curse, though."

I glanced at him as we ran up the front stairs, avoiding the spilled blood. "You don't think he's Baltic? Just because he took the form of a white dragon when you came to save me in Abaddon?"

Gabriel shrugged. "I think it's clear who he is. But that is less important than what he is. He's far more powerful than he should be, and that leaves me concerned for your safety, especially now, when you bear the shard. I do not want you to meet him alone."

"You're cute when you go protective and Drake-like on me, but I assure you it's not necessary. I can hold my own against him."

"Yes," Gabriel said as he opened the door to one of the spare rooms. "That's just what I'm afraid of."

An hour later, I did my duty as a wyvern's mate.

"Hello, beautiful. I take it I'm not in the underworld?"

The man before me looked like he'd taken a beating. His face was bruised and still swollen, although the spot where his cheek had been torn open was now closed, and healing. His voice was hoarse and cracked, his lips red and rough, but his eyes held a sort of wary amusement that told me Savian must be feeling a whole lot better.

"I haven't been there, but I would imagine it looks something like Abaddon, and not at all like the best guest room in a large house in the middle of London," I answered.

He tried to smile, grimaced at the pain, and settled for just one side of his mouth quirking up. "I gather you healed me?"

I shook my head, nodding toward the man on the other side of the bed. "Gabriel did, thanks to his magic silver dragon healing saliva."

Savian groaned and closed his eyes for a moment. "Please tell me he didn't lick me."

Gabriel laughed.

"Don't get me wrong—I'm very grateful you didn't let me die—but the thought of being licked by anyone but a naked, supple woman sitting astride me . . ."

"You needn't get yourself into a dither," I said lightly. "If it makes you feel better, Gabriel used a salve as opposed to going to the source. What happened to you? You look like you were hit by a Mack truck."

"I feel like it," he answered, struggling to pull himself to an upright position.

Gabriel moved quickly to help him while I adjusted pillows behind him. He sighed with pleasure as he leaned back.

"It's not a what that hit me, but a who. Now I know why they told us at the thief taker's academy not to tangle with goetists."

"Who?" Gabriel asked.

I sat on the edge of the bed, careful not to jostle the thief taker too much.

Savian didn't answer immediately, giving Gabriel an odd look.

"Go ahead," the latter told him, to my surprise. "She would have found out soon anyway."

"She being me, I suppose. What would I have found

out? And just why are you keeping secrets from me?" I
asked, wondering if I should be outraged.

"I don't know the woman's name, although I suspect
she's the one they call Thala."

"Thala?" I searched my memory but came up blank,
turning to Gabriel to see if he knew it.

He shook his head. "I do not recognize the name,
either."

"She's pretty. Very pretty. Deceptively so," Savian
said, frowning and wincing at the same time. "No woman
ought to look as pretty and frail as she did and be able to
take me down without even breathing hard."

"What did she look like?" I asked.

"Little taller than you, not so petite, stacked. Brown
eyes, and the most glorious red hair I've ever seen."

"Red hair?" I glanced at Gabriel. "The woman with
Baltic who Cyrene and Maata and I saw at Fiat's house
had red hair, and the rest of the description fits her. I
thought she was a dragon, but Maata said she was of
mixed blood."

Gabriel looked thoughtful for a moment. "How was
she connected with the one you sought?" he asked
Savian.

"Companion. Bodyguard. Lover, wife, girlfriend—I
have no idea. She was there where you said I'd find him,
so I gather she has some sort of a close relationship with
him. All I know for sure is she doesn't like being surprised, she knows more ways to disable a man than a
mortal could, and she had more than a passing familiarity with arcane power," he answered, gently touching his
face. "I think she tried to blow my head off with some
sort of a spell, and when that didn't work, she settled for
taking a two-by-four to me."

"I'm surprised you didn't subdue her," I said, thinking of the time he hauled me to Paris to stand trial.

He made another half grimace, half smile. "It's all I

could do to keep her from killing me. Where she had her training is beyond my conception, but I sure as hell wouldn't mind spending a couple of years there, myself."

"A spell," Gabriel said slowly. "Was she a mage?"

"I doubt it. Her power felt ... different. Not pure. The half-dragon thing fits, if she's the woman May saw. She certainly had strength beyond what's normal for mortals."

"If the woman I saw is this Thala, then that means you were doing a job involving Baltic." I gave Gabriel my blandest look. "Care to explain?"

He grinned, blast his delicious hide. Although I tried very hard not to let him know just how affected I was by the sight of his dimples, somehow he knew, and I had no doubt he was using them deliberately to weaken me. The dragon shard knew, too, but it cared even less than I did. It demanded I jump his bones right then and there. "You knew I had to find that last shard."

"Yes, but I expected that we'd try to find it together," I answered, laying emphasis on the last word. "If I didn't know better, I'd say you have been taking lessons from Drake on how to be an annoying wyvern. Spill."

Gabriel's grin took a wry twist as he nodded again at Savian. "Her every wish is my every command. Spill."

"All right, but I'd prefer not having anyone angry at me." Savian paused for a moment; then he, too, grinned at me. "Unless there's a chance it'll tick you off enough that you dump the boyfriend and hook up with me?"

Gabriel's quicksilver eyes narrowed with deadly intent.

The dragon shard considered Savian's question. I told it to knock it off, and simply gave him a look that warned him he should know better.

"Can't blame a man for trying," Savian said with a mock sigh as he readjusted his position.

"Oh, I believe I can," Gabriel said softly.

The threat just made Savian smile for a moment before he rearranged his expression to be one of businesslike focus. "Here follows my report for the past week. Per your instructions, I checked locations in Berlin, Paris, St. Petersburg, and Riga. There were no signs of activity by the individual in question in any of the cities but the last one."

"Riga," I mused, digging through my brain for any information on the location of the city. "Russia?"

"Latvia," Savian corrected.

"I think I know where that is," I said, nodding. "But why are you trying to hide the identity of the person Gabriel sent you to find? I assume that's what all this is leading to—that you were sent to track down Baltic?"

Savian looked uncomfortably at Gabriel, who made a little gesture of unhappiness. "We both know how important it is to find the shard. I just took the most expedient method of doing so."

I eyed him for a moment, ignoring the shard's demand that I do inappropriate things to him with scarlet-tipped claws, and a decidedly unforked tongue. "Agreed, but why did you feel it necessary to pursue this without involving me?"

"You are involved, little bird. You are more involved than just about anyone else I could name," Gabriel said dryly. "I simply asked the thief taker to locate the missing shard."

"Which led him to Baltic."

Gabriel pursed his lips, obviously about to add the usual rider he felt was necessary whenever I named the mysterious dragon.

"You said it was clear who he was, Gabriel. I think the time has come to move past any remaining identity questions. He *is* Baltic."

To my surprise, he nodded. "I agree. I have not yet

fathomed how he was resurrected—dragons are not like mortals, easily returned to life, and wyverns more so. As a rule, once we are dead, we stay dead—but it was not that statement I wish to dispute. We have no proof that Baltic still holds a shard. It's my belief it is no longer in his possession, and was given to Kostya. Or rather, its location was made known to him."

"Why do you believe that?" I asked, intrigued enough to be sidetracked momentarily from Savian's report. "You know how Kostya is about the shard we took from him—he was ready to wipe out all the silver dragons to get it back, and I can't see him acting like that, risking all-out war with not only us but the green and blue dragons, as well, if he already had a shard tucked away."

"I do not mean he possesses the Modana Phylactery already. Baltic, as he himself stated, was not the type to give up something so valuable to a mere heir. But Kostya was recognized by him as being such, and that means Baltic must have entrusted to him the location of his lair, and given him the means to access it."

"An interesting thought," I said slowly. "It makes you wonder why Kostya didn't go after Baltic's lair when Baltic was killed. Assuming he actually was killed, and later resurrected by some means, and not just gravely wounded."

"What makes you think he didn't?" Gabriel asked.

Savian's head had been swiveling back and forth between us, as if he were watching a tennis match. He interrupted, rubbing his head as he did so. "I wish you would both stand on one side. I'm getting motion sickness."

We both ignored that complaint.

"You think Kostya got into Baltic's lair?" I asked.

"Makes sense to me," Savian grumbled. "A visit to my boss's lair would certainly be number one on my list of things to do once I took over as head dragon."

"But Kostya was imprisoned for a century in the aerie

in Nepal." I thought for a moment, trying to remember what Aisling had told me of Kostya's spotted history. "Gabriel, didn't you say he was nearly dead when you found him?"

"Emaciated and wounded, but not as close to death as you think. I told you before, little bird, it takes a concerted effort to kill a dragon, especially a wyvern. But that is not the point—Kostya retreated to the aerie after the fall of Baltic in order to lick his wounds and dream darkly of a return to power. He was not imprisoned until recently, a few years ago at the most."

"By Baltic," I said, trying to get the facts straight in my woefully confused mind.

Gabriel gave me an odd look. "If Kostya had breached his lair, do you think Baltic would have contented himself with simply confining Kostya?"

"He'd have been toast," Savian said, nodding.

"Point taken. So you sent Savian after what, then? The location of the lair? The shard? Or Baltic himself?"

"All three if possible," Savian answered, rubbing the back of his head again. I felt guilty enough to move to the other side of the bed, perching on the foot of it. "But it was the lair I was to find at all costs."

"And you found it in Latvia?"

"I found where it used to be, yes. That is, I found Baltic's stronghold. The one he held before he ... er ... was toppled."

"Dauva," Gabriel said, a distracted expression on his face. "You found Dauva. Many have sought it, but all traces of it have long since disappeared."

Savian gave another half smile, half wince. "Most dragons don't have the skills necessary to see through the layers of protection that were woven over the remains. To be honest, even I didn't find it the first time I searched the location. But going by the records you gave me, I knew it had to be there, so I kept looking for signs, and two days ago, I found one."

"An entrance to the lair?" I asked, every hair on my body standing on end at the thought of gold. The dragon shard, never subtle in its attempt to turn me into a dragon, swamped me with a sudden, overwhelming physical need for Gabriel. I looked at him in mute appeal, my hands gripping the blankets on the bed to keep me from throwing myself on him.

"Mate," he responded, his eyes flashing with silver heat, his voice deepened by arousal. It swept along my sensitized skin like silk. I moaned.

"Am I de trop?" Savian asked, amusement evident in his voice.

"It's the shard," I ground out through clenched teeth, still fighting with my body and the dragon shard to regain control. "Don't mention gold."

"I didn't. Oh, the lair?" He shook his head. "I didn't find it, let alone any go—er . . . that shiny substance that acts like an aphrodisiac to dragons. I think I was close to the lair, but before I could pursue a very intriguing scent, that she-devil with the red hair found me. After that, the only thing I was concerned with doing was keeping my skin where it belonged."

Savian's calm, matter-of-fact voice dampened my ardor somewhat. Gabriel, with an effort, stopped stripping me with his eyes, and settled his gaze on Savian. His jaw was tense, however. I knew all I'd have to do was reach out with one silver-scaled, scarlet-tipped finger, and his control would snap.

"Mayling," he warned, keeping his eyes on Savian.

"People who read other people's minds can't complain about what they find there," I said, making a heroic effort to get control of my rampant emotions.

Savian laughed. "Even I knew what you were think-

ing, May. And if I didn't think a limb or two might drop
off if I got out of bed, I'd leave you two alone, although
I would like to point out again that I am currently
available."

One of Gabriel's fingers flicked. Savian's hair caught
on fire.

"What the . . . I take it back! I'm not available. Ow.
Could you . . . ?"

I gave Gabriel a look of gratitude for the distraction before glancing back at Savian, who was slapping
madly at his head. "You should know better than to bait
a dragon."

"May!"

I put out Gabriel's fire. "I will, but only because I
want to hear the end of your tale. So this woman beat
you up in Latvia? How did you end up in London?"

He gave his head a couple more exploratory pats before glaring at me. "I just got my hair cut, too."

"Latvia?" I prodded.

"I wasn't beat up there. What sort of a thief taker do
you think I am that I'd allow someone to get the jump on
me in an unfamiliar place? If I was that green, I'd have
been dead decades ago. By the time I was done unravel-
ing all the bind runes, I was well aware that the only one
who could have woven such an intricate protection was
a goetist, and a pretty powerful one at that."

I glanced at Gabriel. "Do dragons normally engage
goetists to protect their lairs?"

"No. Most dragons use banes, which can be drawn by
anyone, although sometimes demons are used to break
them."

"That's right. I remember Aisling telling me she'd
used some demons to break the bane on Fiat's lair. But
why bind runes for this lair?"

Gabriel looked as confused as I felt. Practitioners of
magic, as any member of the Otherworld will tell you,

are divided into only two camps: goetists and theurgists. Goety refers to the dark magic used by those with connections to Abaddon, and individuals who draw power from the dead, such as Guardians, and vespillos, whereas theurgists—mages and diviners—draw their power from sources in the mortal world. Others, like necromancers, utilize both sources.

"Dragons gain their power from theurgistic sources," I mused, watching Gabriel. "So why would Baltic use a goetist to seal his lair?"

"It doesn't make sense," he answered, confusion giving way to a thoughtful look that he turned on Savian. "Dark power is less effective on dragons than it is on mortals."

"Everyone knows that," Savian said, picking bits of ash from his hair.

"It's just one more confusing piece of a puzzle that I'm starting to think we'll never solve," I complained before gesturing to Savian. "What happened after you found the lair?"

He grimaced. "Unfortunately, one of the bind runes was a trap, and it no doubt alerted the redhead to my presence. By the time I realized what had happened, she was close by. I thought it was more prudent to leave the area and try another time, but by the time I made it back to Riga, I realized two things."

We both waited.

One side of his mouth lifted in a wry smile. "The first was that she wasn't going to be thrown off my trail by the simple methods I'd used. She was almost on me by the time I made it back to the hotel. It was only through the sheerest luck I happened to take a back entrance rather than the front, and saw her before she did me."

"And the second thing?"

Savian gingerly touched the still-healing wound on his neck. "She wasn't alone."

"Baltic?" Gabriel asked.

"No. At least, I don't think so. You said this wyvern was imbued with arcane power, and the dragon who helped the she-devil pursue me across the whole of Latvia, Germany, and parts of France didn't have any scent of magic about him. I shook him off my trail in Paris. I thought I'd given both of them the slip, but the redhead jumped me just before I could reach you. I figured I was dead, but she stopped just short of killing me, dumping me in an alley nearby."

"How very odd," I said. Gabriel said nothing, but I knew his expression of puzzlement matched mine.

"No, no, it's all in a day's work. No need to thank me for almost dying while undertaking a commission for you. The most grievous and painful of injuries such as I have received are the merest nothing compared to your gratitude. A bonus hazard-pay reward isn't at all necessary. Don't even mention it." Savian leaned back against the pillows, his eyes closed as he waved a wan hand vaguely toward me.

"I'm sure you're being well paid for the chances you take," I said, getting off the bed. "And as for your grievous injuries, they are mostly healed, and will be completely so in a few hours. You'll be just fine to go back to Latvia."

His eyes shot open at that. "Back to Latvia?"

"Of course." I smiled at Gabriel, who took my hand and curled his fingers through mine.

"We must have the shard," he told Savian. "And it's obvious that we can't wait for Kostya to get around to finding it. We will have to take action."

"Get the shard ourselves, you mean?"

Gabriel nodded.

"I suspect Kostya isn't going to be happy at the idea of us poking around his lair," I pointed out.

"Then we will bring him with us."

"You don't think he already has it?" I asked.

Gabriel shook his head. "Not now. The question of the bind runes aside, for there to be so great an effort made at concealing Dauva itself tells me the lair must still be there, and intact. There would be no other reason to hide the ruins otherwise. And according to your experiences with Kostya's lair, he uses a different type of protection altogether."

"Yes." I remembered the bane drawn into the door to Kostya's lair. It was exactly what I expected to find—theurgistic in origin. "That's a very good point. So off to Latvia we go."

"I'm too weak to travel anywhere," Savian protested as I smiled at him. "I was almost killed!"

"Almost, but not quite. Get your rest," I said, patting the blanket-clad foot nearest me before allowing Gabriel to draw me out the door. "We'll leave for Latvia in the morning."

# Chapter Three

"Heya, István. Miss me? Has Ash popped yet? I don't hear any screaming. She's not gushing out baby juice and blood and guck, is she? 'Cause I'm going straight back to Gabriel's pad if she's in labor."

"Jim," I said, feeling obligated to chastise the demon dog even if it was my charge only temporarily. "That's not very supportive. I've heard that childbirth can be a very frightening time for a woman. I'm sure Aisling would appreciate your empathy rather than your burning desire to escape what is an exciting time for her and Drake."

"Lawdy, Miz Scarlett, I don't know nuthin' about birthin' babies, and I don't want to know, either," Jim answered, marching past István, one of Drake's personal guards, as he stood holding the door for us.

"That'll be enough out of you, prissy," I said, frowning at the demon. "And no more *Gone with the Wind* DVD. I take it everything is all right?"

The last question was addressed to István, who nodded as we entered the house. "Aisling threatened to go home to her uncle to have the baby. Drake swore he would tie her down to a couch if she kept insisting on doing things like walking and moving around. Nora and Pál had an argument over whether Aisling should be allowed to go to the bathroom by herself, and they aren't speaking to each other. René has been teaching Aisling how to swear in French, which she does with frequency."

"So all is normal," Gabriel said with a little flash of his dimples.

"As normal as it gets around here," István said with a wave toward doors that I knew led to a large sitting room. "Me, I'm staying out of Aisling's way. She put a binding ward on Drake this morning that left him mad enough to burn down half the master bathroom before he escaped it."

"Oh, man, I missed seeing that? Sucksville." Jim's eyes narrowed in speculation. "What did he do to piss her off so much, and do you think I could get him to do it again?"

I pulled out a small piece of paper from my pocket and showed it to Jim. "I have here the exact steps needed to banish a demon within my command to the Akasha. Would you like to go now, or later?"

"Geez! I was just teasing! No one can take a little joke anymore! Man, Gabe, I don't envy you a life spent with a doppelganger without a sense of humor."

"Now would be good," István said from behind us.

Jim cast the dragon a look over its shoulder as it opened the door to the sitting room. "*Et tu*, István? Hey, Ash! Lookin' good there, babe. Wow, I didn't think you could get any fatter, but you did. You're not going to, like, pop, are you?"

I sighed and wondered if Aisling would mind me banishing her demon less than twenty-four hours after it had been given into my care.

"Aisling, what a pleasure it is to see you again," Gabriel said, his hand on my back as we entered the room. He took both her hands in his as he pressed a kiss to her knuckles. I stifled the urge to smack him on the back of his head, chalking up the sudden spurt of jealousy to the dragon shard. "You are glowing, as you should be. You do not mind that May and I have dropped in to see you?"

"No, not at all." She was lying on the couch, a thick blanket over her legs and bulging midsection. "I'm delighted to have someone sane to talk to. Here, let me move so you can sit with me, May."

She struggled to sit upright. Gabriel, with one hand behind her, the other on her arm, gently assisted her. Or he started to.... A sudden roar from the doorway, followed immediately by a fireball that shot past me and hit Gabriel with enough force to fling him backwards a few feet, ended his attempt at help.

"Now, that's what I'm talking about," Jim said with satisfaction as it plopped its big butt down next to Aisling. "Action at last!"

"Hello, Drake. He wasn't really touching her; he was just helping her sit up," I said as the green wyvern, and Aisling's very attentive, very jealous husband, stormed into the room, his emerald eyes spitting fury at Gabriel.

Drake never took his eyes off Gabriel as he helped Aisling into a sitting position, carefully tucking the blanket around her before narrowing his gaze on the love of my life. I was a bit surprised to see Gabriel grinning in return. Although he had a much less volatile temper than Drake, he didn't take kindly to being pushed around, especially by another wyvern.

"Well, I can see I'm not going to have to break up a fight between you two, at least," I said, moving nonetheless to stand between the two men.

"Aisling is near her birthing time. It is natural that

Drake should be intolerant of other males around her while she is vulnerable," Gabriel said, his hand sliding around to my waist as he made a little bow to Drake. "Had I known he was right outside the room, I would have allowed you to assist Aisling."

Drake looked like he wanted to pick a fight with Gabriel, smoke issuing in little puffs from his nose, but Aisling put a hand on him and tugged him down onto the couch next to her. That seemed to do the trick, for his gaze left Gabriel for the first time, and he acknowledged my presence with a nod.

"May, you are welcome here. Aisling will enjoy your company."

The exclusion of Gabriel in the welcome was pointed, but luckily amused him.

"We are not here for a social visit, although of course it is always a delight to see Aisling," Gabriel said, turning the power of his dimples on her.

I nudged him with the tip of my toe, perhaps harder than was necessary, because he laughed and pulled a chair forward for me, taking another one just beyond my reach.

"And I thought Ash was jealous. Whew. Glad my Cecile isn't like you two," Jim muttered.

Both Aisling and I gave it a glare. It took the point and rolled over onto its back. "Belly rubbles, Ash? Pwetty pwease?"

"You are here on weyr business?" Drake asked as Aisling, with a little roll of her eyes, scratched Jim's hairy belly.

"No. Our business involves Kostya. I could not reach him at his house, and thought you might be able to help us locate him."

"He's been away," Drake said slowly, his expression unreadable. "But I expect him back at any time."

"Assuming the *sárkány* he called is still scheduled for

two days from now, I would expect that he would be in town making preparations for it. Where has he been?"

Drake's gaze shifted an infinitesimal amount. "St. Petersburg, I believe."

St. Petersburg ... just a hop, skip, and a jump plane-wise from Riga, and Baltic's ruined stronghold. I slid a glance toward Gabriel, but his face was as impassive as Drake's. His emotions, however, weren't quite so subdued. A sense of quickening excitement nudged at my awareness, prodding the dragon shard to wake up and take in the surroundings.

"We will speak with him later today, then, when he arrives back in England."

"He should be back by now," Aisling said, glancing at the clock.

Drake shot her a warning look.

"What?" she asked him.

He made an aborted gesture.

"Oh, for Pete's sake ... Gabriel and May are our friends. They know Kostya called the *sárkány* in order to get the black dragons recognized as a sept. It's not going to be any shock to them to know he's been trying to find Baltic's lair so he can properly take over as wyvern."

Drake sighed, the fingers of one hand stroking her knee. "This is a serious matter, *kincsem*. Circumspection should be uppermost in your mind at all times."

"Circumspection, my aunt Fanny," she snorted. "I'm not going to play games with our friends."

"Mate, I insist—"

"And that's another thing," she said, rounding on him as best she could considering her bulk. "You've turned into Mr. Bossy Pants these last few weeks, and I'm really getting tired of it. I'm pregnant, Drake. I'm not made of glass, I'm not going to burst into labor if I do things for myself, and my mind is just as strong as it ever was. Jim, so help me god, if you say just one thing, I'll have

May banish you to the Akasha for the next two hundred years."

"Hey, all I was going to say is that I wouldn't be bragging about the state of your mi—"

"Silence," I told Jim.

It shot me a glare, huffed to itself, and plopped down with a disgusted air.

Aisling and Drake were frowning at each other.

"If I correct you, it is because you are outside the bounds of weyr etiquette," Drake told her.

"It's just Gabriel and May!" she answered.

"A wyvern, and a wyvern's mate."

"They are our *friends*," Aisling said, waving her hand toward us. "I feel perfectly within my right to say what I think in front of them, no matter what position they hold."

"They are also opposed to my brother receiving the recognition he seeks," Drake countered, his eyes flashing with annoyance.

"Your brother," Aisling said, breathing heavily, "is almost as annoying as you are. *Almost!*"

Gabriel's lips twitched. I was having a similar problem keeping a straight face, but knew it would just make things worse if I laughed outright.

"You are being emotional because of the impending birth. I would remind you again that such outbursts are not conducive to the calming environment you seek for the event itself," Drake said with maddening serenity.

Aisling gasped. "Are you calling me unhinged?"

"No, of course not—"

"You are!" She struggled to her feet, slapping off his helping hands, clutching the lap blanket to herself as she squared her shoulders and leveled him a look that should have dropped him dead on the spot. "That's it! I'm de-mating you! I'm filing for a divorce! I'm going to go back to Uncle Damian and have the baby there, where people think I'm sane and competent and don't tell me what to do every minute of the day. Jim, heel! You can come home with me."

She stormed out of the room without a look toward us, Jim, still bound by my command to silence, trailing behind her. Drake, a martyred expression on his face, paused in the act of following her, saying, "She's a little emotional right now. You will no doubt forgive her."

"The baby is only a few days overdue, I believe?" Gabriel asked.

Drake nodded. "The midwife has confirmed that all is well, but the strain of waiting is beginning to take its toll on Aisling."

I kept the comment to myself that Aisling wasn't the only one being affected.

"You will excuse me. I must see to soothing her ruffled feathers before she books another flight to the US."

"Another one?" I couldn't help but ask, trying not to smile.

Drake sighed again as he opened the door. "She threatens to return home daily now. It is becoming tiresome to explain to the airlines that the reservations must be canceled. If you wish to remain here for Kostya, you are welcome to do so. He is expected for dinner. I thought it would distract Aisling."

I gave in at the expression of suffering on his face, although I waited for him to close the door before I laughed out loud. "Poor man," I said.

Gabriel grinned. "It is unkind of me, I know, but I cannot help but think Drake has made his bed, and is finding it not quite so sweet to lie upon."

I was about to agree with him when it struck me that perhaps he didn't mean it in the way I thought. "Aisling is putting up with a lot from him, too, you know.

That overprotective act can be wearing to the nerves, and I can only imagine how annoying it would be to be treated as if one was made of glass."

"And just how would you like to be treated?" Gabriel asked, walking behind me. His voice was rich with innuendo, causing my back to stiffen with sudden arousal. The dragon shard in me knew exactly what he was doing—he was flirting, teasing me, fulfilling a dragon's need to play with its prey. He walked in a circle, not touching me, but his eyes glittered with a quicksilver heat that left me short of breath.

"How do I want to be treated?" I asked, struggling to hold on to myself, the true part of me, not the dragon-tainted bits that were slowly, insidiously taking over my sense of self.

"Yes." He pathed around behind me again, causing me to shiver with anticipation. The dragon shard stopped insisting I pay attention to it, and simply took over, allowing my body to shift and stretch and transform into a silver-scaled form that was so foreign to me, and yet so familiar.

"I want to be treated like this," I said in a sultry voice I almost didn't recognize, and whipped my tail around one of his legs, jerking it toward me so he fell backwards onto the floor. Before he could protest, I was on top of him, licking him with fire, tasting him, wanting him, needing him to complete the self that waited so impatiently.

He growled deep in his chest, a mating sound that skittered along my body like a static charge. He, too, started to shift, but a noise at the door was followed by a soft voice saying in French-inflected English, "I have returned, although I could not find the pickle-flavored crisps you . . ."

I struggled to my feet at the sight of the man in the doorway who held a shopping bag from a prestigious store. "Er . . . hello."

"René, is it not?" Gabriel asked, completely composed despite the fact that a strange man walked in just as I was about to have my dragonly way with him. I fought the dragon shard for control, slowly, inch by inch returning my body to normal. The man named René greeted Gabriel pleasantly enough, but he watched me with a decidedly wary look as the last of the silver scales shimmered into my normal skin color.

"It is a pleasure to see you again," René said, his eyes flickering to me again.

"This is my mate, May. Little bird, this is an old friend of Aisling's, a daimon who has been of much assistance to her."

Daimons were fates, I knew. I'd never actually met one before, although I thought it was interesting that they were occasionally assigned to individuals who they felt needed a little help.

"Including as a purveyor of hard-to-find delectables," René answered, holding up his bag with a grin. "Drake, he refuses to leave her side, so it is up to me to bring the so-charming Aisling the food she craves most."

"I thought pregnancy cravings were over by the time birth was imminent?"

He shrugged, a loose-shouldered gesture that made me think of smoky bars in Marseille filled with slinky women in loud-print dresses. "It depends on the woman, *hein*? I have seven little ones myself, and when the *maman* desires something, it is better to humor her, I have found. With my wife, it was macaroons. Always the macaroons. At all hours, she must have macaroons. Aisling, she has a passion for crisps of the most repulsive flavors, but it is not for me to deny her when she most desires them. I find the crisps just as I found the macaroons for my Brigitte. Did you say 'mate'?"

Gabriel grinned as René gave me a thorough visual inspection. "Despite the curse, yes, she is."

"But I thought . . . you are not a dragon, then?"

"To be honest, I don't know quite what I am any-more," I answered with more than a touch of despair.

Gabriel took my hand, his fingers warm and strong, offering comfort. "Do not fight the shard, May. Control it as we discussed, but do not fight it. I will not allow it to consume you."

René's eyebrows went up. "A shard? You do not mean . . ."

"I'm technically known as the Northcott Phylactery, yes," I said, giving Gabriel's hand a squeeze to let him know I appreciated the support. "I'm a doppelganger, really."

"A shadow walker? How very interesting. I have only ever met one other of your kind."

"Ophelia?"

"*Oui*. You know her?"

I shook my head. "Not really. I gather she's having a rough time being on her own, but other than one or two conversations on the phone with her, I have no contact with any other doppelgangers. We tend to stay pretty much on our own."

"Ah, you were not born," René said, nodding his head as he figured out how we had gotten around the curse put on the silver dragons by the dread wyvern Baltic. "Very clever. And now you are here to help Aisling with the birth, Gabriel?"

"I would be happy to act as midwife, but Drake, I believe, would rather birth the child himself than let me near his mate."

"Dragons," René said, nodding, adding in an aside to me, "They can be very protective."

"So I gather. Perhaps you can answer a question for me. Are daimons assigned to particular individuals, or can you be hired? I know Gabriel will feel otherwise, but I certainly feel as if we could use a helping hand—"

A racket exploded from the entrance of the house, a woman's shouts carrying loud and clear over a more masculine rumbling.

"*Cabrón!* Do you think I will be kept from seeing my grandchild? Move aside before I have my son throw you into the gutter where you belong!"

"Who on earth—?" I started to ask, but I asked it to an empty room, Gabriel and René immediately racing from the room. I followed, pausing at the door to take in the sight of a tall, olive-skinned, dark-haired woman chewing up István, who was probably double her weight, not to mention built like a truck. To my intense surprise, István was backpedaling madly as the tall Spanish woman yelled, her hands gesticulating wildly.

"Where is my Drake? Where is my grandchild?" She punctuated her sentences with blows to István's chest. "Stop running from me and fetch—"

The woman caught sight of us from the corner of her eye. She stopped hitting István and rounded on Gabriel, her black expression suddenly turning sly and sultry. "Gabriel!" she all but cooed.

Hackles I didn't know I possessed went up at the sight of her as she sauntered toward Gabriel, brushing past René as if he didn't exist, her hips swaying with an unmistakable message. My fingers lengthened into claws, but I curled them up, refusing to give in to the shard's demand that I deal with the brazen hussy who was going to be one very sorry person if she so much as laid a finger on my mate.

"I did not know you were here," she continued, her voice a blatant invitation.

I don't remember moving, but somehow, I found myself standing in front of Gabriel, my hands clenched as I thought for a few seconds of how nice she would look unconscious on the entryway floor. "Hello. I'm May."

"This is my mate, Catalina," Gabriel said, laughter

obvious in his voice as he snaked his hand around my waist, gently pulling me over to his side. "Mayling, you have heard me mention Drake's mother, yes? This is doña Catalina de Elférez."

"Mate." She said the word as if it were rancid, her dark eyes scrutinizing me for a moment.

I am no stranger to piercing looks, or the importance of presenting a placid expression even when my brain is screaming to run away, so it was not much of an effort to smile at her. "It's a pleasure to meet you."

Her expression changed from hostility to wariness. "You have a mate. Is she . . . ?" She hesitated for a moment, then gestured vaguely toward me. "Is she mentally damaged?"

I gaped at her in surprise. "I beg your pardon?"

She leaned close toward Gabriel, her gaze resting on me with obvious curiosity, as if I was some sort of a bizarre sight she'd never come across. "Resurrection, if not done properly, can often lead to damage of the brain."

"Resurrection?" I gaped a little more before turning to look at Gabriel.

His dimples were fighting to show, but he merely tightened his arm around me, and reassured Catalina that I was not the equivalent of a mental squash. "I did not resurrect her in order to bypass the curse."

"No, no, I would never suggest that you did such a thing, since we both know that resurrection without sanction is very much disallowed in the weyr." Her gaze was still wary on me as I mustered up once again the same smile that had soothed many of Magoth's temper tantrums. "But, my darling Gabriel, you must take some steps to cover up this horrible tragedy. Just look at her. Look at that grimace. That is not a grimace of a sane person."

"It's a smile," I said through my teeth, holding on to the blasted thing for all I was worth. "I'm smiling, not grimacing."

"Yes, of course you are smiling," she said loudly, patting my arm as she gave Gabriel a sympathetic look. "You are very good to stand by her despite the failure of your experiment. I will, naturally, not breathe a word to anyone what I have noticed about her. Your secret is very safe with me."

"I have not been resurrected!" I said rather louder than was probably necessary.

She waved a hand toward a mountain of black leather luggage that a driver was still bringing in. "I have some pretty toys I brought for my grandchild, but your poor, sweet mate shall have her pick of them. They will no doubt amuse her, and keep her happy for many days. Now, my darling Gabriel, you must promise me you will do everything in your power to rescue my innocent grandchild from that she-devil's clutches. Do you know that my Drake refused to allow me to be here when the child was being born? It was *her* doing, naturally, but I am nothing if not an excellent mother, and I did as he bade me, no matter how cruel it was."

She snaked her hand through Gabriel's other arm and tugged him away from me, toward the room we'd just left.

I looked at René. He grinned at me.

"The baby is not yet born," Gabriel said, casting me a look over his shoulder, part embarrassment, part reluctance, as she dragged him toward the sitting room.

"No? Well, there is time for us to save the poor little one before it is tainted by that demon lord my darling Drake insists on calling mate. Come, now, tell me all that has happened since I have last seen you, although naturally we will not discuss the tragic result of your attempt to find a mate." She paused and glanced toward us, then inclined her head to him. "Will your mate be all right if she is left alone? She does not have suicidal tendencies? I knew a resurrected mage who seemed perfectly normal, but any sound of a bell would set him to rending his clothing and pulling out his hair. It was very tragic. Your mate will be fine left alone? Yes? Excellent. You must tell me everything while my rooms are being made ready."

The door shut behind them, leaving René, István, and myself alone in the hallway, Catalina's taxi driver having deposited the last few cases before he hurried out.

"Drake's mother," I said to them.

István made a face. "She was not supposed to come. Drake told her not to come. Aisling will not be happy."

René gave another of those loose shrugs and said, "There is no use in trying to tell Catalina anything. She does as she pleases."

"I don't look deranged, do I?" I asked, touching my face and wishing for the millionth time I could see my reflection.

"You look worried, but not deranged," René told me kindly.

"Thank you," I said, not much buoyed, but willing to take what I could get. I cast a glance toward the closed door to the sitting room. "I think I'll go fetch Jim from Aisling. I'm sure Drake has calmed her down by now, and Jim is probably making a pest of itself."

The demon wasn't, in fact, in the way, but only because it had evidently been kicked out of Aisling's bedroom. I found it lying on the floor on its back.

"You can talk now," I told it, averting my sight from its nether regions.

"Geez, hanging around Magoth really taught you how to torment demons, didn't it? I thought you'd never come up here to get me!" Jim rolled over and got to its feet, shaking itself in a way that left a corona of black hair on the floor around it. "Gotta be dinnertime. Let's go eat."

"Is everything OK in there?" I asked, nodding toward the door.

"Yeah, yeah, Drake started in with Ash about how he can't survive the ages without her, and all that crap, and she fell for it just like she always does." The demon shook its head disgustedly as it marched past me toward the stairs. "Women. Can't live with 'em, can't live with 'em."

"I'm sure I can see to it that you don't live at all," I said sweetly, which merited an annoyed look from Jim as it went down the stairs. "By the way, Drake's mother has arrived."

Jim did an about-face. "Fires of Abaddon! You almost let me get within blasting range! And me just getting my coat to maximum fabulousness. Sheesh, May. I expected better of you."

"Where do you think you're going?" I asked as it headed back toward Aisling's room.

"Gonna go warn Ash. She's going to hit the roof, and I want to be there to see the fireworks."

"Effrijim—" I started to say.

"Oh, man!" it whined, slumping to a halt. "Not you, too?"

"By the powers vested in me by your true overlord, I hereby charge, demand, and otherwise order you to leave Aisling alone unless she expressly desires your company, or if her life is in danger."

Jim hesitated at the door.

"A visit from her mother-in-law does not constitute a threat to her life," I warned, knowing exactly what it was thinking.

It raised an eyebrow. "You don't know Catalina very well, do you?"

"Come on," I said, gesturing toward the stairs. "Let's go wait for Kostya to arrive. I'm sure, given his temper, there will be fireworks aplenty when he sees Gabriel and me."

"There'd better be! That's all I'm sayin'!"

In that belief, I was wrong, and evidently I had my twin to thank.

"Mayling!" Cyrene squealed when Jim and I arrived in the hall after spending an hour paddling around Drake's basement pool. Since the silver dragons weren't overly fond of water, it not being their element, they tended to view things such as showers as merely unpleasant experiences to be endured as quickly as possible. Although Gabriel's house in Manukua had a pool, it was more or less for visitors, which made it difficult to find time for a pleasure swim. As Jim and I padded up the stairs from the pool, Cyrene spotted us and rushed across the hall, where Kostya was being greeted by his mother, with Gabriel and Drake in a wing formation behind her.

"You've been swimming?" Cyrene's pupils dilated slightly, as was common whenever water was mentioned in her presence. As a water elemental, she had an affinity for freshwater sources such as springs and lakes, but she loved any form of water, and was known to take hour-long baths. "Drake has a pool?"

"Yes, but it's not polite to arrive at someone's house and demand to go swimming," I said, grabbing her as she started past me toward the stairs to the basement. "You should at least say hello to Aisling."

"Drake said she's resting and will be down later," Cyrene said, pouting just a bit before turning a smile on me. "You look happy. Has Magoth stopped hitting on you?"

"Oh, like that could happen," Jim said, snuffling Cyrene's hand until she fondled its ears and scratched its neck. "The day he stops hitting on babes is the day I give up being a demon and go back to spriting. Oh yeah, baby, right there. *Urng.*"

Jim's eyes rolled up a bit as Cyrene's long fingernails found a particularly itchy spot.

"Have you ever known Magoth to *not* have sex on his mind?" I asked.

"Oh, yes," Cyrene surprised me, nodding. "But only when he's torturing someone. And even then . . . well, we won't go into that. At least he hasn't been granted his powers."

"No," I said slowly. "And that actually worries me. I would have thought that as soon as Bael tossed him out of Abaddon, he would have given Magoth back his powers in order to unleash him on the mortal world. But he hasn't done anything, yet. Magoth has petitioned him to be reinstated, but Bael hasn't even responded to that except to say it's under consideration."

"Well, you have bigger things to worry about than that," Cyrene said with blithe indifference to the idea of a demon lord being free to run amok among the mortals. "Kostya needs our help."

My gaze moved from her to the man in question. Although Kostya was Drake's older brother, a weird quirk of genetics had left the two men wyverns of different septs . . . or it would have, if Kostya was recognized by the weyr as such. "What does he need help with now? I thought he had the requisite number of black dragons to formally apply for recognition? Isn't that what the meeting is all about?"

"It is, but not everyone supports sweet, adorable Kostya." Her eyes narrowed into little sapphire slits as she looked at Gabriel.

"Sweet, adorable Kostya has tried to kill Gabriel more than once and, until the last month, has been hell-bent on destroying the silver dragons by forcing them to join his sept, so you'll have to forgive us if we're a bit jaded," I pointed out.

Cyrene waved away the survival of the silver dragons

as trivial. "Oh, that's all in the past. He's been the model of dragonhood since you came back from Abaddon."

"That, I'm afraid, has less to do with the fact that he's seen reason, and more because he realized he is going to need friends should Baltic take it into his head to reclaim his sept."

"That is *not* Baltic," Kostya said loudly, interrupting his mother. I had forgotten for a moment how good dragons' hearing was.

"Hello, Kostya," I said politely, summoning up a brief smile.

To my surprise, he bowed. The dragons, I'd found, habitually used what I thought of as old-world manners, including being able to make bows that, on them, escaped looking silly and just looked elegant and courtly. Even Gabriel, whose manners were more open and casual than the other wyverns', could summon up a really world-class bow when he felt the need. I wondered for a moment if it was something genetic in dragons. "I beg your pardon. I am remiss in greeting you in my haste to speak with my mother. You look well, May."

I wanted to goggle at his change in attitude.

"Thank you," I said, a little stunned. By this point, I expected Kostya to be screaming for vengeance, or ranting about the past as he was wont to do.

"I trust the shard is not giving you any grief?" he inquired politely.

My eyes widened as I glanced toward Gabriel. He grinned at me and winked.

"Er . . . not unduly so, no. Thank you for asking." I was prompted by the knowledge that formalities must be preserved even in informal situations to add, "You are well?"

"I am," he said, inclining his head. "Cyrene and I took a little trip to my homeland. It is most pleasant at this time of year."

"I'm sorry," I said, finding the whole conversation too bizarre to let pass without comment. "Are you chitchatting with me?"

"Yes, he is. Isn't he doing it wonderfully?" Cyrene asked, blowing him a kiss.

Gabriel laughed and moved over to stand next to me, his arm loosely around my waist. "It is quite amazing, is it not?"

Kostya smiled at Cyrene, and for a second, I was aware on a primal level of the charm that had attracted her to him. But although my acquaintance with Kostya had not been of a lengthy nature, it had been violent enough to leave me wary of such a benign appearance, even despite the dragon shard's interest.

"Incredibly so," I said, knowing my twin would completely miss the sarcasm in my voice.

Jim didn't. The demon choked. I eyed it, about to forbid it to speak if it looked like it was going to say anything inappropriate. Catalina leaned toward her eldest son, whispering furiously as she gestured an elegant hand toward me. He looked at her for a minute before turning an astonished gaze on me.

"I am not mentally deficient," I announced, just in case he believed his mother.

Jim snorted again and opened its mouth to speak.

I pulled out my dagger and spun it around my fingers before flinging it to the floor about half an inch in front of Jim's toes. It leaped backwards. "All right, all right, I get the point! Man! I'm telling Ash you're pulling weapons on me!"

"Do not say anything about it," Catalina finished speaking to Kostya in what she no doubt imagined was a whisper. "It is best if you do not dwell on the sad situation. Her kind gets so upset."

I smiled and slipped just a smidgen the normally tight rein I held on the dragon shard. It purred with satisfaction, sending silver scales shimmering up my arms, my fingers lengthening and turning crimson at the claws. I waggled them at Kostya. "Your mother has sage advice. And speaking of people who were resurrected, why do you think Baltic isn't really Baltic?"

"He could not be," Kostya said with a familiar stubborn set to his jaw. "Dragons are not easily resurrected."

"Gabriel said that, as well, but his mom seems to think otherwise."

"She's never tried to resurrect a dragon," Kostya replied with a glance at his mother.

"It is true, what my darling Kostya says," Catalina said with a dramatic sigh. "I tried to have Toldi resurrected, but alas, he came back . . . less."

"Less than what?" I asked, curious about the odd tone in her voice.

She cast me a sympathetic glance, nodding slightly toward me. "Just . . . less. It was a kindness to put him out of the way. Again. Which I did, naturally, because I was nothing if not a good mate."

An odd sort of choking noise emerged from Jim. I picked up my dagger, noting that the demon's eyes widened as I twirled it around my fingers. "'Again' as in you killed him before?"

"Oh yes. He was not a nice man, Toldi. He murdered most of my family, you know, in order to get me to accept him as mate. Which I did, but only because I knew I would be able to destroy him easily when I chose." Catalina picked an invisible bit of fluff off Kostya's arm, speaking with a nonchalance that would have been more at home in a psychopath.

I slid a quick look at Gabriel. One of his dimples appeared.

Drake sighed and gestured toward the sitting room, having cast a quick glance up the stairs. "If you insist on having this discussion, brother, perhaps you will do so out of Aisling's hearing. If she thinks we are having a counsel regarding Baltic, she will want to be present, and it is her rest time."

Jim made a whipcrack noise as it passed Drake on the way into the sitting room. I said nothing as Drake glanced at the dog, setting its tail on fire for a good ten seconds before the demon noticed. By that time, we'd all trooped back into the sitting room.

"So you killed him twice?" I asked Catalina, ignoring Jim's hysterics as it ran around the room yelling at the top of its lungs until Drake put out the fire.

"Fires of Abaddon, Drake! I mean, literally fires of Abaddon!" it bellowed, pungent smoke trailing behind it as it marched over to where we sat.

"Sit down and be quiet unless you have something helpful to say," I ordered it.

"Such a very odd demon," Catalina remarked, watching as Jim obeyed my orders albeit with ill grace and no little amount of glaring. "And yes, my dear, I had to kill Toldi a second time. I couldn't leave him . . ." She paused and gave me yet another pitying look that had me grinding my teeth. "But we have agreed not to speak of such unfortunate things. I just hope that Gabriel has the strength to do what is necessary when the time comes."

She brushed off my look of utter disbelief with a smile at Gabriel before taking Kostya's arm. "Come, my darling Kostya. Tell Mama what you have been doing these last one hundred and thirty years."

"I have no time for talk, Mother," Kostya said with a glance at his watch. "I have a sept meeting in less than an hour. I simply wished to tell Drake . . ." He hesitated a second, very pointedly not looking at either Gabriel or me. ". . . tell Drake that our trip was fruitful."

Catalina demanded to see him at the first opportunity, and went off to oversee the unpacking of her luggage.

"You found the lair, then?" Gabriel asked after she left.

Kostya stared at him for a second, then sharpened his gaze into a glare and pointed it at his brother. "You told them where I was going?"

Drake shrugged one shoulder. "It concerns them."

"They are not black dragons! The location of Baltic's lair does not concern them!"

Kostya shook off Cyrene's hand on his arm, and stormed over to his brother, clearly about to launch into yet another diatribe, but he remembered in time that he was watching his p's and q's. With an effort, he bit back what he was about to say, forcing a smile to his lips as he looked at Gabriel and me.

"It's killing you to be nice to us, isn't it?" I asked, leaning into Gabriel.

"Yes."

Cyrene punched him in the arm.

His strained smile grew larger until I could see each and every one of his teeth. "No, of course it isn't. I have realized the error of my intention to re-form the sept to its original glory, and have resigned myself to the fact that the si-silv—that you are happy on your own."

"He can't say it," Jim said to me in a volume that was not at all sotto voce. "He was practicing last week, and he couldn't actually get the words out."

"Sil-ver," Cyrene coached Kostya, giving his arm a squeeze. "Come on, punky, you said it on the plane. You can say it now. Sil-ver dragons."

A shudder shook his body.

Gabriel rolled his eyes. "If the comedy hour is over, perhaps Kostya could give us a few minutes to discuss the issue of the Modana Phylactery."

"What is there to discuss?" Kostya asked, his eyes narrowing. "I agreed to let your mate use the shard to re-form the dragon heart if you supported my sept within the weyr. That was our agreement. You gave me your word. You cannot change the terms now."

"I do not intend to do so. But I am curious as to whether or not you found the phylactery when you found the lair. Do you have it?" Gabriel asked, his lovely voice as smooth as oiled silk.

Kostya's gaze slid to his brother for a second. "Not yet. But I will."

"Which means you, too, found Dauva."

Silence filled the room for a moment as Kostya absorbed Gabriel's words. Smoke wisped out of Kostya's nose as he took a step toward us. "I might have known you would try to violate the agreement."

"I've done nothing of the kind," Gabriel answered, his expression and voice pleasant, but beneath my hand, his muscles were tense. "I'm simply ensuring that we don't have to wait years for you to get around to bringing the shard to May."

Kostya looked like he was about to burst, but evidently he was more in control of his emotions than he had been in months past. "So you found the lair, as well?" he asked through gritted teeth.

"We know of its location, yes," Gabriel said.

I decided a little defusing wouldn't hurt the situation. "Gabriel's agent didn't enter the lair. He couldn't. So if you're worried about us running off with all sorts of black dragon goodies, you can relax. Not that Gabriel would, anyway. I assume there's some sort of rule about wyverns stealing from other wyverns."

Silence filled the room as Gabriel, Drake, and Kostya all looked away.

"You're kidding me," I said, noting that no one bothered to agree with me. "You guys steal from each other?"

Once again, they avoided my eye.

I raised an eyebrow at Drake. "Are you telling me

that if you had the chance, you would take stuff from Gabriel's lair?"

"The green dragons are particularly adept at ... liberating ... items," Drake said, somewhat defensively, I thought.

I turned to Gabriel. "You'd steal something from Drake?"

"Drake is one of my oldest friends," he said smoothly, taking my hand so he could rub his thumb over my knuckles. "Of course I wouldn't steal from my friend."

"Nor would I steal from him," Drake said quickly, not to be outdone on the altruism front.

"I value his friendship over anything," Gabriel said.

"It is unthinkable to imagine I could steal from him," Drake agreed.

"Completely unthinkable."

"Utterly out of the question."

I eyed the two of them.

"Unless it was gold," Drake admitted.

"Yes, of course. Gold is another thing entirely," Gabriel said, nodding. The other dragons nodded with him.

"If you're willing to steal from your oldest and dearest friends, then how did you get anyone to agree to let us use their dragon shards?" I asked, wondering if I'd ever get used to dragon society.

"That's different," he said with a little shrug. "The dragon heart is the most powerful thing known to dragonkin."

"Then shouldn't it be harder for you to get the shards brought together?" Cyrene asked before I could.

"It would be suicide to attempt to use the dragon heart," Drake answered.

"It is too dangerous," Gabriel said, nodding. "There is no dragon alive who possesses the ability to wield the heart—for which you should be thankful, little bird, since the use of it would have far-reaching repercussions."

"How far-reaching?" I asked.

Gabriel looked thoughtful for a moment. "Think destruction of at least half of the mortal world."

"And a piece of that is inside me?" I said, clearing my throat when my voice came out a squeak.

Gabriel's fingers tightened on mine. "Do not fear, May. To use the dragon heart, you must have two things: the power to control it, and its goodwill. Because of that, we do not live in fear of destruction. Wyverns in the past have tried to re-form the heart and use it, but their attempts were disastrous. We have learned from their losses. The only reason the heart will be re-formed is to shard it into proper receptacles."

"You might want to tell Baltic that, 'cause I'm willing to bet he's got other plans," Jim said, and I had to admit I was thinking the same thing.

"Baltic would not be so foolish," Drake said at the same time Kostya frowned and said, "That is not Baltic."

"Pumpernickel, I think you're going to have to get into the groove," Cyrene told him, hugging his arm and pressing a little kiss on his earlobe. "Everyone seems to agree that it's Baltic. I think we ought to go with the flow here and say it's Baltic, too."

"It can't be him. I'd know," Kostya said stubbornly.

"We shall see, won't we?" Gabriel said with a smile that didn't quite go to his eyes. "Now that we know the location of the lair, we can lend our assistance in opening it."

Kostya shot Gabriel a suspicious look that was answered by a more genuine smile.

"We wouldn't want the phylactery damaged in the process of opening the lair," Gabriel added.

"That won't be necessary. I am perfectly capable of retrieving the Modana Phylactery on my own, without damaging it," Kostya insisted. "Your presence in Latvia will not be required."

"Regardless, I feel for May's sake it would be prudent to be there."

"Latvia?" a voice said from the doorway, a delighted purr that sent cold chills down my back. "We're going to Latvia? What an excellent idea! I haven't been there since . . . ooh, since the black plague."

Dismay filled my stomach as Magoth sauntered into the room, one of Drake's bodyguards behind him, gesturing toward the bane of my existence as he said, "He demanded to see May."

"I told you to stay put," I said, frowning at Magoth, who was mouthing what looked to be obscene suggestions to Cyrene.

His attention immediately switched back to me. "An amusing attempt to be dominant, but as you know, sweet May, I prefer to be the one on top." He looked around the room with obvious delight. "And just look what I would have missed! A trip to the Baltics. How—you will excuse the expression—divine. I have many fond memories of the area—death and famine and disease so thick it seeped into the land like blood dripping from a dismembered corpse. Now, that was a time to remember. There's much to be said for the old ways, you know. This trip will be just what I need! When do we leave?"

# Chapter Four

"I just hope you know what you're doing." Cyrene released the tree branch before I could grab it. It smacked me wetly dead center in the face. I rubbed my stinging cheek and glared at the back of the head of my twin, not an easy feat given the thick fog that lay sluggishly over the forest. The faint patter of water sliding off damp leaves to the thick, springy ground below was muffled but constant.

"Bringing a demon lord out to a dragon's lair—it's not the brightest idea you've ever had, Mayling."

I caught the branch she released that time, mentally uttering retorts to her comments as I plodded after her, my gaze alternating between watching for more face-slapping branches and examining the terrain in an attempt to figure out where we were in relationship to the nearest town.

"Kostya is not at all happy that he's here," Cyrene added, turning to give me a stern look before hopping over a fallen tree. She slid down an embankment, her head disappearing from sight, but her voice still able to reach me. "Not happy at all."

"That doesn't surprise me. Kostya is never happy," I muttered as I made my way over the log, slipping on the soft earth. Tendrils of damp hair clung to my cheeks.

Ahead of us, Gabriel, Kostya, and Savian were deep in conversation. Magoth followed them, the four men plowing a path through a murky, forested area that would have been a perfect setting for an atmospheric gothic movie, vines snaking off the densely packed trees, and moist, springy moss clinging to every surface.

It was oddly quiet, as well, no sounds of civilization managing to penetrate the thick cotton-wool fog that wrapped around us. Only the occasional whine of a mosquito broke the pat-pat-pat of dripping water.

One of the little bugs landed on the back of Cyrene's exposed neck. I shuffled forward through earthy-smelling leaf residue, and slapped the back of her neck.

She spun around, her mouth opened in surprise.

"Mosquito," I explained.

Her eyes narrowed. "Oh, you'd like me to think that, wouldn't you? But I know the truth—you're just peeved because Kostya is angry with you because you insist on bringing Magoth, and you're taking it out on me."

I gave her a little shove forward when Magoth, clad in expensive hiking garb that I suspected owed its orgins to my credit card, disappeared behind a clump of scrubby fir trees. "I don't give a hoot if Kostya is angry. And if you don't want to end up lost in the wilds of rustic Latvia, I'd advise you to get moving."

Cyrene *hrmph*ed and started forward. "I just wanted to point out that if Kostya is in a grumpy mood, you have no one but yourself to blame. He's very unhappy about having you and Gabriel out here, but when you said Magoth had to come, too, I thought he'd never calm down."

"Magoth being here wasn't my choice," I pointed out, smacking at a mosquito that landed on my arm. "He invited himself, as you know, and since I have no way of making him do what I want him to do, we figured it would be easier to just bring him along where we could keep an eye on him, rather than have him follow us and get up to who knew what sort of trouble."

"*Hrmph.* Kostya doesn't like Magoth."

I took a deep breath and held it for a moment, then said only, "I'd be surprised if Kostya liked *anything*."

"He does, too, like things! He likes lots of things," Cyrene said, deliberately releasing a tree frond early.

I glared at her again before saying, "Such as?"

She marched on for a moment in silence while she tried to find something that would satisfy me. "Well, I can't think of anything at the moment, but there are any number of things. Oh ... oral sex! He likes oral sex a lot!"

Jim, who had been off sniffing what it said was an imp trail, shambled up behind me, catching the last bit of the conversation. "There's not a male alive who doesn't," it said, spitting out a tiny little boot. "If I couldn't lick my own package—"

"Enough!" I said hastily, not wanting to hear more.

Jim cast me a hurt look. "I was just going to say I would have picked a human form if I couldn't. Sheesh. Some people have dirty, dirty minds."

"A dirty mind is the sign of a healthy libido, say I," Magoth said, popping up from behind a large cluster of rocks. "What are you ladies doing back here? Are you engaging in wild lesbian urges? We could have a quick threesome if you like."

He waggled his eyebrows at Cyrene, who just rolled her eyes and pushed past him.

"You could have a Magoth sandwich! One of you could start at the top, while the other started at the bottom, and you could meet in my center," he suggested.

Something inside me stirred.

"That's not even funny," Cyrene told him.

"It is a bit self-centered having both of you pleasuring me, I admit. How about this—you and your twin can make love, and I will watch and give pointers?"

The hairs on the back of my neck stood on end.

Cyrene spun around to give him a tight look. "I told you before—I'm Kostya's mate."

"I suppose he could join us, too, although it's not so much fun with two males," Magoth said thoughtfully. "Mind you, there are ways. I haven't indulged in an all-out orgy in, oh, at least a week. No, ten days. But if you have your heart set on it, I suppose I could oblige."

I gritted my teeth and scooted past Magoth, giving him a wide berth. "You are not a dragon's mate, Cy."

Magoth turned to leer at me as I passed. I realized at that moment that the dragon shard was responding not only to Magoth but to the location. It liked it here; it liked the primal feeling of the area, the earthy sense of power that seemed to flow around us in intangible streams between ground and living things and air. My feet stopped as the shard zapped me with a sudden, overwhelming wave of emotion.

"Get Gabriel," I gasped to Cyrene, wrapping my arms around myself as I struggled to control the power of the dragon within me.

"What?"

"Oh, man. That's not good," Jim said, studying me. "You're going to do the nasty with Magoth, aren't you? Right out here in the open where Gabriel can see? Wait! Let me get out my cell phone. Ash is going to want pictures of this. . . ."

Magoth looked startled for a moment, then slipped into his normal suave, seductive persona. "I knew the day would come when you gave in and—"

"Shut up," I snarled, doubling over as I fought the

transformation. "Cy, for the love of all that's aquatic, get Gabriel!"

"What is wrong with you?" she demanded to know, marching over to me. Doubled up as I was, all I could see was her feet. "Is this an attempt at garnering some sympathy? Because if it is—"

Silver shimmered up my arms and legs, my back arching as my body lengthened and stretched into a shape that was not normal for a doppelganger.

Cyrene took two steps backwards, her hand to her mouth in surprise. "I'll get Gabriel," she said, still backing up.

I snarled something unintelligible at her as I spun around to face Magoth.

He watched me with pursed lips and a thoughtful expression. "You prefer to do it in dragon form, eh? I can't say that I've indulged in that before, dragons being strangely averse to visiting Abaddon, but if you insist on it, I'm sure we can make it work."

"Oh man, oh man, oh man," Jim said, trying to hold a cell phone in its mouth and use one of its paws to take a picture of me. "This is great. I'm going to make millions off of this video."

I flicked my tail at it, sending the cell phone arcing through the air into the dense undergrowth.

Jim's lips formed an O of astonishment. "That was Aisling's phone!"

I narrowed my eyes at the demon and breathed fire. "Do you want to follow it?"

"Hurry with Gabriel!" Jim bellowed after Cyrene, keeping its eyes fixed firmly on me. "May's gone feral!"

*Feral.* The word resonated within me as I stretched, relishing the power to be had in this form. I was feral. I was dragon, and this place was mine.

Magoth shimmied forward toward me, his clothes dripping off him with each step until he stood before me stark naked. He put one hand on his hip and gave me a knowing look. "Shall we begin?"

I smiled, and sent a plume of fire onto his penis, which was waving jauntily at me.

Magoth's jaw dropped for a moment. Then he grabbed my head with both hands and planted his mouth on mine.

"May!" Gabriel's voice sounded distant and faint, as if he were at a great distance, not just a few hundred yards ahead.

"I don't suppose you have a digital camera in your bag? I'll just check, OK?" Jim said.

I let Magoth kiss me for a moment, the dragon shard analyzing the sensation. The differences in the shapes of our mouths made him less effective than I knew he was with a human, but it wasn't that that ended up causing me to reject his advances.

It was the place. It was the land around us that called to me, not Magoth. I pushed him away just as Gabriel burst from a dense clump of ash trees, Savian hot on his heels. Kostya and Cyrene pulled up behind them, all four watching with startled expressions as my tail whipped out, catching Magoth in the midsection, flinging him a good thirty yards backwards until he smacked into a large tree.

"Wow, nice one. That's gotta be at least a bronze medal for demon lord flinging," Jim said, watching with interest as Magoth fell out of the tree to the ground.

"Thanks, but no, thanks," I yelled to Magoth before turning my attention on Gabriel. The dragon shard hummed happily inside me at the sight of him, and I thought seriously for a moment of pouncing on him. I knew he would like that—it was a dragon mating game, and something told me that he would respond to it.

"Yes, I would, but that's not what *you* want," he said, reading my mind again.

I made a little pouty dragon face.

"My darling!" Magoth staggered into view, still naked, but now covered with dirt and lichen, with bits of tree clinging to his hair. "My sweet, powerful May! Your idea of foreplay is most pleasing to me. Do it again?"

I flicked my tail again, and he went flying, squealing with delight that was stopped only by the sound of his body smashing into yet another tree. He cooed gently to himself as he slid down the trunk.

"Silver medal. I think you should go for the gold," Jim said.

"May, why have you shifted?" Gabriel asked, stroking his hand down the elongated curve of my neck.

I shivered at his touch and leaned my head into his chest, bathing him in a light sheen of fire. "I don't know. Chase me?"

"What is going on?" Kostya asked, pushing between Savian and Gabriel to look at me.

I licked Gabriel's neck.

"Oh, that's what's going on. Er ..." Kostya glanced at Gabriel.

"No, this is not normal. May does not embrace the dragon within," he answered the unasked question. "May?"

"I just felt like it," I said, twining my tail around his leg. "It's this place. It feels right here, like I've come home after a long, long journey. It feels like a place we should play."

"Play?" Gabriel looked around us.

"What does she mean, play?" Cyrene asked, frowning at me. "May, honestly! Should you be sucking his ear like that in front of Magoth?"

"I'm fine! Don't worry about me!" Magoth called from the distance. The only part of him visible was one hand waving out of a dense bank of ferns. "I think I'm in love."

"Dragons use play as part of their mating," Kostya explained as he, too, started examining the area around us.

"Really?" Cyrene transferred her frown to him. "You never play with me when we make love."

"That's different. You're human."

"I am not! I'm a naiad!"

"You look human," he pointed out.

"Well, so does May. Most of the time."

Magoth tottered toward us, dirt speckling the front of him, twigs now added to the leaves and lichen and moss that clung to his head, a small leafy shrub evidently stuck to his foot. His hands waved in the air as he approached. "Once more, my sweet—"

The whipcrack of my tail as it hit him was followed almost immediately by the sound of Jim whistling. "That's got to be an Olympic record right there. Nice going, May. I think you knocked him out."

Magoth's unresponsive body tumbled from the tree to the ground, hitting with a muffled thud.

"I'll go rescue lover boy, shall I?" Savian said, giving me a long look as he headed off to where Magoth had fallen into a thick patch of what looked to be poison ivy.

"Mayling, tell me what you feel," Gabriel said, his hand on my neck again.

I looked deep into his eyes and let my emotions show.

"No, not that." His dimples threatened to burst to life. "I know that. What do you feel about this place?"

I sighed and tried to clear my mind of the lustful images of me twined around Gabriel in an erotic dragon dance. "It's . . . right. It's a good place. I feel happy here."

"Do *you* feel happy, or does the dragon shard?" he asked.

I tried to sort through the emotions that swamped me, picking out those sensations that were native to me. "It's the shard. It likes it here."

Gabriel and Kostya exchanged glances; then both turned to look at a rocky outcropping that was about ten yards away. The rocks jutted out of the earth like angular, flinty fingers, softened over the centuries by moss and plants and the detritus of the forest around them.

"The lair?" Gabriel asked Kostya.

He nodded. "Has to be."

"What do you mean, the lair? We found the lair already," Cyrene said. "Or we found where it should be. It's over there." She pointed to the south.

"It's a false entrance," Kostya explained.

"Set up to fool anyone who was searching for it," Gabriel added, nodding to himself. "Very clever. I would have done the same, although I'm not sure I would have gone to the trouble of rune binds."

"You have to admit it was convincing," Kostya said as both men strolled toward the rocks.

Savian emerged, dragging a limp Magoth. He deposited him in a heap, looking over at Gabriel and Kostya as the two men climbed over the outcropping, clearly searching it. "What did I miss?"

I hummed to myself and tapped my claws on the ground, visions of Gabriel chasing me through the woods keeping the dragon shard occupied. "They think this is the entrance to Baltic's lair."

"You're kidding. This?" Savian looked around, his eyes carefully searching the outcropping of rock. He shook his head. "I don't see it. Where?"

"I'd show you, but I'm currently occupied," I said.

He pursed his lips as he glanced back at me.

"I'm keeping the dragon shard distracted while I try to shift back," I answered the question in his eyes. "If I get near Gabriel, it will demand I jump him, so I'm letting it have all sorts of fantasies about being chased through the woods. Ooh. That one was really good."

I was distracted for a moment by the vision the shard

provided to me, but gently eased myself out of it, focusing my attention on my body as I slowly, inch by inch, urged the dragon form to withdraw back into my normal one. Savian nodded, and went to help the others examine the rocks for the entrance.

"Half-babe, half-dragon, and me with no camera," Jim sighed as it plopped its big hairy butt down on Magoth's still form. "Life sucks. There's just no two ways about it."

"He's not dead, is he?" I asked, nodding toward Magoth.

Jim snuffled Magoth's dirt-splattered face. "Naw, just knocked out."

"Good."

"May, we need you," Gabriel called.

"Sorry, can't right now. I've only got one leg done, and almost a whole arm," I answered, waving my mostly human arm at him.

"We need you in dragon form."

"You do? Why?" The shard stopped imagining hot, steamy, dragon-form sex with Gabriel under a moonlit sky, and focused on him again.

"There she goes. Bah. Nothing exciting about seeing a dragon in its natural form," Jim said with a disgusted snort.

"The shard you bear was Ysolde's. She has a tie to this place because of her relationship with Baltic. If you are in dragon form, you will be able to utilize the power of the shard easier."

I let the shard take over as I marched over to Gabriel. "You're both dragons. Why can't you do whatever it is that you want done?"

His grin warmed me to my toes. "Ah, but we don't have the same delectable dragon shape as you."

I gave him a look.

He laughed. "Neither Kostya nor I can detect the opening of the lair, but the shard might let you find it."

"It is well hidden, even from me," Kostya agreed, scowling at the stones.

"I still say you're barking up the wrong tree. I'd feel it if this was the opening to a lair," Savian said, shaking his head.

"Fine. But if I can't shift back, and end up staying like this, I'm not going to be happy," I grumbled as he stepped out of the way so I could scramble up the rocks.

"How do you feel?" Gabriel asked, watching me carefully.

The dragon shard wanted to dance with happiness.

"Right now?" I paused for a moment, gathering my inner strength, both my own and the strength of the dragon within me, allowing the two to merge for a moment before I brought my tail down onto the rocks with a force that knocked the people around backwards several feet just as if they were made of paper. The stones crashed inward with a muffled explosion, dust and debris swirling around me in a whirlwind that blocked my vision for a moment. As the air cleared, a black, gaping hole slowly became visible at my feet. The dragon shard celebrated, the teasing, heady scent of gold drifting out of the darkness. "Right now I feel great."

Gabriel was first to his feet, but Kostya, with a snarl, flung himself forward over the hole into the lair. "It is mine!"

"Gold," I crooned, stretching sensuously at the thought of it.

"Mine!" Kostya bellowed.

"We outnumber you," I pointed out.

Cyrene, who had been grumbling as she dusted herself off, hurried over to stand with Kostya. "Oh no, you don't!"

"We have Jim and Savian," I pointed out as Gabriel, his eyes lit with familiar lust, took a step toward the hole, his breathing deepening. I knew the gold scent had hit him, as well.

"The agreement was for the shard," Kostya yelled. "You will get use of the shard until May can re-form the heart and reshard it. That is all! The rest of the lair belongs to the black dragons!"

"Yeah!" Cyrene said.

I slipped down the edge of the rock, back to the almost-invisible pathway where Magoth lay gently snoring.

Gabriel watched me for a moment.

"Kostya's right," I told him, overriding the shard's demand that I take it to the gold. I separated my mind from it, and started the process of shifting back to my own body again. "Much as I would love to see the gold that smells so very nice, we did agree to the shard only in exchange for our support with the weyr."

Gabriel sighed heavily, but jumped off the stones and returned to my side, waving one hand at Kostya. "I bow to my mate's demands. I will not challenge you for the lair so long as you let us use the Modana Phylactery."

Kostya wasn't happy over the idea of letting the shard go, even temporarily, but he had agreed to the terms, even if he was now regretting them. He nodded curtly at Gabriel and, grasping a convenient bit of vine, swung himself over the edge of the hole into the yawning darkness. Cyrene started to follow, stopping when his head popped back up, a familiar scowl on his face.

"This is my lair, Cyrene. Only black dragons may gaze upon its treasures."

"I'm your mate," she said, trying to shove his shoulders aside so she could climb into the hole.

He sighed heavily, casting me a plaintive look.

"You made this particular bed," I told him, wrestling with the shard to regain control over my body. "I'm afraid you're going to be lying on it alone. Dammit, Gabriel, the smell of gold is too much for me. I can't shift back to my normal form here. I'm going to have to do it somewhere else."

"I am so your mate! Well, all right, not technically, but I'm mate lite, so that counts."

"Then we will go somewhere you feel more comfortable," Gabriel said immediately, pushing a branch out of my way. I knew he would prefer remaining to take charge of the phylactery that Kostya would retrieve from the lair, but he selflessly escorted me up the almost-invisible path.

"No, it doesn't count," Kostya said as we left. "You are not a black dragon, Cyrene. I appreciate your help and support—"

"Oh! I like that! You string me along and now you dump me just when things are going good? Well, I have a few things to say about that, Mr. Dragon!"

Luckily, we moved out of earshot of Cyrene's harangue. It took a good five minutes before we were out of the range of the scent of gold and I was able to catch my mental breath and take charge of myself again.

Savian and Jim followed along after a few minutes.

"Sorry. Don't mean to intrude," Savian apologized as Gabriel stood gently stroking my back while I pushed the dragon form back into a more familiar one. "But your twin is a little . . . er . . ."

"Bitchy," Jim said, snorting when the last of the silver scales disappeared into beige-ish skin.

"Vehement," Savian corrected with a smile at me.

"'Vehement' doesn't threaten to drown someone in their lair. 'Bitchy' is all over that," Jim pointed out.

"*Agathos daimon,*" I swore softly to myself, glancing at Gabriel. "If she's threatening him with water, she's really pissed. I suppose I should go back and intervene."

"You'll shift again," he pointed out. "I'll go."

"I don't think she'll listen to you," I said as he started back the way we had come.

"Does she ever listen to anyone?" Jim quipped.

"Quiet, beast," I told it, about to go after Gabriel

when Cyrene appeared, hauling a befuddled-looking Magoth after her.

"That's it!" she yelled as she caught sight of us. Her free hand gestured wildly. "I've had it! I've totally had it with that . . . that . . ."

"Dragon?" I offered as she pulled up to a stop in front of me. She let go of the hold she had on Magoth, who collapsed to the ground with a particularly fatuous leer toward me.

He was still naked, although no longer aroused, and had managed to lose the small shrub on his foot, but he wore a coronet apparently made up of an ancient, un-used bird's nest, dirty spider silk, and a small clump of leaves sprouting from the region of his left ear.

"There you are, sweet May. Was it as good for you as it was for me?" Magoth asked.

"Better," I said, letting myself smile just a little.

Gabriel gave me a look that let me know he didn't appreciate it. I immediately rearranged my expression into one of serenity. "Cy, please tell me you didn't flood Kostya's lair."

"No, I didn't, but not because he didn't deserve it," she said, snapping off each word. "I wouldn't waste pre-cious water on that . . . beast! Do you know what he said to me?"

"Yes," I said, taking her arm and cutting off the rant I knew she so desperately wanted to make. "I think it would be better if we were to go back to town. Gabriel?"

He hesitated a moment, casting a glance toward the trees that screened the entrance to Kostya's newfound lair. "You go. I'll follow with Kostya."

I nodded and gave Cyrene a nudge. "Come on, twin of mine. Let's go back to town and get a drink. You look as if you could use one, and I certainly wouldn't mind a belt or two, myself. Gabriel will make sure your boy-friend is all right."

"He's not my boyfriend anymore. We're through. Do you hear me? Through! I'm done with him! Although I would like a drink. Do you think they have lemon Perrier? You know how I love that."

"I also know how drunk you get off it," I said, leading the way. I gave the lair a wide berth as I headed us back in the direction of the town. "Only a water elemental could find carbonated water literally intoxicating. But if you're a cheap date, at least you're an easily pleased one."

"You gonna leave your boss here?" Jim asked.

I released Cyrene's arm, turning to frown at where Magoth lolled on the ground. He stroked a hand sensuously down his filthy, leaf-bespecked chest.

"Much as I am tempted to do just that, I suppose the mortal world is safer with someone keeping an eye on him."

Magoth smiled. "You can deny it all you want, my sweet one—I have seen the truth in your dragon eyes. You want me. You need me. You crave that which only I can give you."

He was, I noted with dismay, showing signs of arousal again. I searched my mind desperately for something to distract him, not trusting the dragon shard to behave itself when he was at his randiest.

"Get your clothes on, and I'll treat you to a bottle of Bollinger's," I told him.

Magoth loved Bollies, but even that wasn't enough to drag his mind off his cursed penis. He got to his feet slowly, completely oblivious to the fact that he more resembled a muddy swamp monster than a seductive former silent-movie heartthrob. "Not even going to try to dispute the facts? Wise woman."

"I'm not going to argue the obvious with you, no," I said calmly, and gestured toward the direction we were headed. "Come along with us, or don't, but make up your mind. I'm not going to stand out here all afternoon and be eaten by mosquitoes."

"I would be happy to eat—" Magoth started to say.

"I think we can all imagine a suitably inappropriate and borderline sexually harassing comment, thank you," I interrupted.

He leered, but checked himself almost immediately, an angry look flashing in his eyes. "May the fires of Abaddon roast that bastard Bael," he spat out, his hands making aborted gestures of frustration. "I can't even enthrall you as is my due! He will pay for this, just as everyone will pay for the dishonors done to me!"

"You have nothing to complain about," Cyrene told him as he marched over to where we were waiting. "You haven't had your love and trust abused by the most hateful man ever!"

Magoth slid her a narrow-eyed look that, were we in Abaddon, probably would have rendered her as close to dead as an elemental being could be. She didn't notice, however, being fully immersed in righteous indignation.

"Your clothes?" I said as Magoth stormed past me, Cyrene hurrying after him as she continued to vent her spleen about Kostya.

"And then do you know what he said? He said he didn't have time for me anymore, that bringing together the sept would take all of his attention, and he wouldn't be able to deal with me, as well. Deal! Yes! He actually said the word 'deal' just as if I was a problem to be ... well, dealt with. Can you believe that? I'll feed his testicles to a shark—see if I don't!"

He ignored Cyrene, pausing just long enough to give me a haughty look. "I am Magoth, sixth principle spirit of Abaddon—"

"Former principle spirit of Abaddon," Jim said.

Magoth ignored the demon, too.

"—lord of thirty legions—"

"Now in the charge of Bael, or whoever he's found to replace you," Jim interrupted.

Cyrene whapped Magoth on his bare chest. "I am so not a problem person. I'm a naiad! We are the most pleasant of all the elemental beings! There's nothing about me with which he needs to deal, except my vengeance, which shall be as deep as the ocean and as dark as the ... er ... the ocean. In the bottom parts, that is, where it really is very dark."

"Marquis of the order of dominations!" Magoth bellowed, no doubt in order to be heard over the chorus of Jim and Cyrene, but the smidgen of power he still possessed gave his words an unexpected volume. His voice echoed for a few seconds, the harsh sound of birds screeching their objection to the noise slowly dying out.

We all looked at Magoth.

"I have no need of such things as clothes," he said, dismissing such mortal concerns with great dignity, turning on his heel to stalk back toward town.

"You wanna be the one to tell him he's got a big ole slug stuck to one of his butt cheeks?" Jim asked.

Magoth's shoulder twitched at the demon's question, but he didn't stop. He just kept walking.

# Chapter Five

"You could think the arrival of a naked, dirty, ex–demon lord would merit at least a few raised eyebrows," Savian said as I collapsed into a chair. "But no one seems to care."

"It's probably more they don't know what to think than they don't care," I said.

"That or they're just too horrified at the sight of a penis curse to take more than a quick peek." Savian glanced around the faux-medieval basement bar of the hotel at which we had taken rooms. At this hour of the day, it was empty of customers, a few morsels of gray light bullying their way in through thick, waved glass panes strapped with militant precision in what was no doubt supposed to be a design reminiscent of the court of Elizabeth I of England.

"Are you impugning my cock?" Magoth asked, his hands on his hips.

Savian looked startled for a moment. "I am not doing anything to your dick, let alone impugning it, although . . ." His gaze dropped to the member in question. "If the curse fits, wear it."

Magoth's eyes narrowed as he gestured proudly to his genitals. "This is a magnificent specimen of its kind! It is beyond magnificent—it is the epitome of cockhood. It can do things yours can only dream of! It is, in fact, a god amongst penises!"

"Oh, it wasn't *that* good," Cyrene snorted, rolling her eyes at Jim.

Jim clearly had many comments to make about that, but bound to silence, it could only raise its eyebrows and give Magoth's penis a long, considering look.

"Magoth, please, keep your voice down," I said.

"He," Magoth spat, pointing at Savian, "disparaged this most resplendent of cocks. I demand that you as my consort defend its honor. Change back into dragon form and roast him alive." He paused, a thought having occurred to him. "And then you can wrap your tail around me and—"

"No one is disparaging anything, least of all your genitals," I said quickly before he dwelled on the strange ways he got his jollies. "Calm down and take a seat before someone notices you."

He snorted, casting unimpressed glances around him. "I have to piss. I assume you will not let me hear the end of it if I do it here. I will take my commanding and august cock to the bathroom, where it will no longer offend your plebeian souls."

I exchanged a look with Cyrene as he marched off to the men's room.

"He really does love his penis," she said as if that explained things. "And don't get me wrong, it was fine and all, but magnificent? A god among penises? No. Maybe a duke, or a minor prince. But not a god."

"I really find it difficult to believe we're sitting here discussing Magoth's genitalia," I said, rubbing the smooth, cool wooden surface of the table. "It's just a bit surreal."

"Not nearly as surreal as this whole place is," Savian said from where he was examining pictures of boats on the walls. He nodded toward one. "Henley Regatta 1923. Not quite what you'd expect in Latvia."

I had to admit that the hotel wasn't at all what I expected. The question of why an obscure Latvian hotel in the small town of Livs would try so hard to re-create a half-timber English country house complete with wattle and daub was answered by a red-faced, balding man who bounded into the bar from a back room.

"'Ello, 'ello, I didn't realize we had customers so early. We don't do lunches here in the pub, just so you know. Those are done in the tearoom upstairs. All handmade pastries up there, nothing store-bought. My wife does the baking—she has a fair hand with pastries, too. You'll not be finding a better scone west of the Thames."

"We're not hungry, thanks," I said, leaning back so he could slap a paper coaster in front of me. "Drinks are fine."

"Right, then. You do look a sight. Been out hiking, have you? We get lots of Americans coming here for the hiking, now that the Russians aren't in charge anymore. Sisters, are you? You've the look of each other, that you do. Oh, but where are my brains today? I'm Ted Havelbury, ye olde host," he said with a chuckle. "Now, I know what you're thinking, I do indeed. You're thinking that old Ted is a bit out of his natural setting, and you wouldn't be far wrong there, but my wife's mum was from the old country, and when she died and left us this inn, we thought, why not? The children were grown and had families of their own, so off the missus and I went with nothing but a wish and a prayer, as they say. But now, you'll be wanting a few drinkies, won't ... er ..."

Ted, who had been chatting merrily to Cyrene and

me, nodded to Savian as he slid into the chair next to mine. Before he could finish his sentence, Magoth, in full snit, emerged from the bathroom, shoved aside Jim, and stomped over to stand in front of Savian. He glared down at the thief taker, who shot me a martyred look before heaving a sigh as he relinquished the seat.

"Er . . . ," Ted said again.

"Our friend had a little accident with a stream," I said, shaking out a paper napkin and placing it over Magoth's lap. "His clothes were too soaked to wear."

"Is that so?" Ted said slowly, his expression almost enough to make me laugh. "I don't suppose he'd like to get dressed before he has a drink?"

"Tell the slave that I wish a bottle of 1996 Bollinger, chilled to forty-five point nine degrees, with one glass," Magoth said in his most demanding voice.

"Slave?" Ted asked.

I leaned forward toward him, speaking in a low, confident voice I'd found worked well with mortals. "You'll have to excuse our friend. He's foreign."

Ted eyed the naked, dirty, arrogant Magoth with doubt. "He is?"

"South American," I said, mentally apologizing to everyone on that continent.

"Oh. Latin," Ted said, nodding. "That explains it. Impetuous people. Excellent dancers, but impetuous."

"I'd like a gin and tonic, my twin would like a bottle of lemon Perrier, if you have it, and Savian would like . . . ?"

"Brandy."

"Hmm, 1996 Bollinger's. I'll have to check the storeroom for that. I think we have some left over from the New Year's celebration. . . ." Ted took our orders with only one backwards look at Magoth before hurrying to the back room.

"You'd better pray no one else comes in here while

you're having your champagne," I told him. "Because as soon as you're done, you're putting some clothes on. Jim, stop wiping your nose on my hand. You can have some of Cy's Perrier, since she gets drunk if she drinks a whole bottle."

"I do not get drunk! I never get drunk!" Cyrene said, outraged at the slur against her character.

"May eighteenth, 1921. Long Island, New York," Magoth said, arching an eyebrow at her. "My house. Specifically, the garden. You, me, and three hundred of my closest friends."

Cyrene flushed and looked away. "That wasn't drunk. That was enthralled."

"It was an orgy," corrected Magoth. He thought for a moment, a smile erasing his pout. "A lovely, lovely orgy. Which resulted in the creation of the ever-adorable May, if I am not mistaken, and I never am about such things. Do you remember, sweet one? Do you remember being called into existence, and the exact moment when your life began, and your eyes first landed upon me?"

"Yes, I remember. I screamed."

"Music to my ears," he sighed dreamily. "I don't suppose—"

"No," I said hastily, and would have continued, but the sound of footsteps clattering down the bare wooden staircase to the basement arrested me.

A man paused at the bottom of the stairs, glancing quickly about the room, clearly about to turn around and go back upstairs. He caught sight of us, however, blinked twice, then turned and bellowed up the stairs, "Found her!"

"That doesn't sound good," I murmured as I watched a second man join the first. The pair of them walked toward us with unmistakable purpose—and scent.

"Demons," Cyrene said, wrinkling her nose as the smell of demon smoke hit us.

"Wrath, by the looks of them," Savian said, squinting at them.

Wrath demons, as anyone who's ever been to Abaddon knew, were not the sort of beings you welcomed into your company. They were like mini demon lords, with substantial powers, and minions of their own.

"What do they want?" Cy asked.

"No doubt that cur Bael has realized what a mistake he made in expulsing me, and is summoning me back to restore upon me the rightful estates and titles which your twin's carelessness so callously cost me," Magoth said, watching the two men approach with an anticipatory glint in his eye.

"May didn't do anything to get you kicked out of Abaddon," Cyrene said, much to my astonishment. Normally oblivious to slurs made against me, now and again she surprised me by jumping to my defense. "That was your own doing, and you know it."

"His Most Heinous and Imperious Majesty, the premiere prince Bael, has *not* sent us to deal with a has-been like you, Magoth," the nearest demon said, a sneer curling its lips. It stopped a few feet away from me and jerked its head in what I realized was acknowledgment of me.

"You will address me as Lord Magoth, you sniveling little scum," Magoth snapped, his words so chilling and filled with menace that Jim immediately backed up a few feet. I rubbed my arm nearest Magoth. Emotional outbursts caused him to leech the warmth from his environment, leaving me with the sensation of having brushed up against an iceberg. "And you will speak only when I give you permission to do so."

My eyebrows went up at his imperious tone. I'd heard him use it before, but only on his own minions, never another demon lord's followers, and certainly not the first-in-commands of the head honcho of all Abaddon.

The demons gave Magoth a scathing look and turned to me. "The Lord Bael desires your presence, dragon."

I bit back the retort that I wasn't, in fact, a dragon.

"What?" Magoth shrieked, leaping to his feet. "He wants to see my consort? About what?"

The demon nearest him raised its eyebrows as it studied Magoth's penis tattoo. The other one ignored the irate demon lord, its cold, flat eyes fixed on me.

"Why would Bael want to see me?" I asked it, since it obviously wasn't going to answer Magoth.

"I will ask the questions around here, slave," Magoth snarled, marching over to stand in between the wrath demon and me. He got right in the demon's face, shouting, "Answer me, you watery scum on the underbelly of a toad."

"I do not seek to question my lord's commands," the demon said, treating Magoth as if he were invisible. "I simply carry them out. He has commanded your presence, and we have been through three countries to find you. You hide your trail well, dragon. You will come with us now."

"Argh!" Magoth screamed, his hands waving wildly. "I will not be treated this way!"

I considered the two wrath demons, wondering how long Gabriel and Kostya would be getting the shard. "And if I choose not to?"

The penis-watching demon shrugged. "You will come with us. The Lord Bael commands."

"The Lord Bael commands, the Lord Bael commands," Magoth parroted in a snide voice. "Well, the Lord Magoth commands, too!"

"The difference being, of course, that you're no longer a reigning prince," Savian said.

Magoth spun around and sent him a look of pure poison. Savian flinched.

I had a feeling that if I didn't give in to Bael's demands, there would be trouble for everyone.

"All right," I said slowly as I got to my feet. I slid Cyrene a meaningful look. "Please tell Gabriel what's happened, and where I am. I will try to return as quickly as possible."

Cyrene's face looked pinched as she glanced between the demons and a now nearly hysterical Magoth, who was ranting about the good old days. "Are you sure you're going to be all right?" she asked in a whisper.

"I should be. Even Bael thinks twice about tangling with a wyvern's mate," I said with a lot more confidence than I felt. "Jim, you may come with me, although I want you to mind your tongue in Bael's presence."

Released from the command to be silent, Jim staggered a little with the strain of holding in its comments. It cocked an eyebrow at the wrath demons. "Hiyas. Long time no see, Sori. How they hangin', Tachan? Been forever since I've seen you guys. You still got a thing for rams?"

The penis watcher shot Jim an outraged look that nearly set the demon's coat smoking.

The sound of a man's singing grew louder as the barkeep evidently found Magoth's champagne.

"You guys stay here. I'll take care of whatever Bael wants and be back as quickly as I can. Don't forget to tell Gabriel I went willingly," I said hurriedly, one eye watching the storeroom door. "He doesn't need to come rescue me."

"That you know," Savian said, just adding that little extra dollop of worry that I needed to make my misery complete.

The demon named Sori grabbed my arm in preparation for yanking me through the fabric of being to Bael's presence, but before it could do more than slash an opening, Magoth screamed a battle cry and threw himself on me. Jim leaped up at the same time, intent on intercepting the attack, but was too late. Magoth hit me, sending me careening into Sori as it was pulling me through the opening, with the end result that all four of us went down in a tangle of arms, legs, and furry black tail.

"I assure you that such a dramatic entrance is not necessary," a cool, almost bored voice said as I tried to pull my limbs from the pile of others. Jim clunked its head on mine, making me see stars for a second.

I sat up, rubbing it, glaring at Jim for a second before Magoth used my head as a support to lever himself to his feet. "Well! You might have had your servants show a little more respect," he said, making a great show of brushing his naked self off. He made a brief bow to Bael. "Lord Bael."

Unlike Magoth, whose appearance never changed from his original, once-mortal form, Bael changed his at a whim. Today he was tall and thin, with a long Ben Affleck–type face, complete with stubble, and world-weary eyes. Those eyes turned on Magoth with extreme unction.

"Why did you bring *him*?" he snarled at his two wrath demons.

Both men bowed low, in a way that implied they were groveling without their actually doing so. "It was an accident, Your Greatness. He flung himself on the dragon as we were escorting her through."

"I did not fling myself on May. I have never flung myself on anyone in my life. I am a demon lord—if there is any flinging to be done, it will be of minions!" Magoth snapped.

Bael rolled his eyes for a moment before dismissing the demons, turning his attention to me. His gaze landed on Jim. He frowned. "Have not I seen you before, demon?"

I swear Jim curtsied. "That you have, your most infernal of all infernal beings. I'm Jim. Effrijim, really, but you being stuck with your alternate names of Beelzebub and Baalzuvuv know how it is—short and punchy is definitely the key to success."

Bael continued to frown, obviously not remembering who Jim was.

"I was here a few months ago with May. We kicked some wrathy ass, not that you probably want to hear that, but you know, if one sixth-class demon and a doppelganger can do that, you might want to up your standards a smidgen," it said with a helpful air.

I punched it in the shoulder.

"I'm just sayin'!"

"Well, stop it!" I said, waving my fist at it.

"If one of my wrath demons allowed you to get the better of it, then I can assure you it was not due to ineffectiveness," Bael said dryly as he moved around to sit behind a large, ebony desk.

"Yeah? Then why would ... shutting up," Jim said, having accurately read the look in Bael's eyes.

"And about time, too," Magoth said, grumpily shoving the demon aside to stand before his boss.

Bael, without looking up, waved a hand toward me. I took the chair he indicated. Magoth waited a moment, but no such nicety was extended to him. With audible grinding of his teeth, he hauled over a chair from against the wall to sit in front of the desk, plopping down into it with a rude noise caused by bare flesh on glossy leather.

Bael, in the process of opening a drawer, froze for a moment, but he pulled out a laptop and set it in the exact center of his desk without comment.

I glanced at Magoth. He had a testy look on his face, his legs mercifully crossed, his fingers drumming out an annoying tattoo on the chair's arm.

"You go ahead. Evidently my business is not nearly so important as that of my slave, my minion, my consort." His lips were tight as he answered the question in my eyes.

My curiosity prodded me to ask Bael, "I don't mean to harp on a subject you probably would like to forget, but are you saying your wrath demon held itself back when I was here a few months ago?"

I hesitated to bring up the reason why Jim and I had been in Abaddon, lest it rub a raw spot.

Bael flipped open the top of the laptop, and punched a couple of keys with laconic pokes of his long fingers. "That is correct."

"Why?" I asked, remembering the scene well. The wrath demon Jim and I had disarmed sure didn't seem to have been holding back anything.

"You are a dragon," Bael answered, his eyes on the laptop screen.

Magoth snorted and said something rude under his breath.

"And?"

Bael heaved a sigh, as if my questions were too tiresome to answer. "I find it best to adhere to a policy of noninvolvement with members of the weyr."

"And yet that doesn't stop you from holding a wyvern prisoner," I pointed out.

He waved a graceful hand toward me. "That was different. I did not seek to control the wyvern—she was sent to Abaddon, sent to my palace specifically. I merely provided her with . . . accommodations."

I forbore to point out the obvious.

"Until, that is, you released her." His eyes pinned me back, and I was very aware for a moment that he had enough power to squash me like a particularly ineffective bug. Then the dragon shard kicked in, filling me with dragon fire and a matching fierceness.

Bael's gaze dropped, and I was possessed with the sudden knowledge that what he said was true—he might hold Chuan Ren prisoner when she had been thrown into his lap, but he did not want to tangle with any of the dragons. It was the dragon shard he was wary of, not me, but that knowledge gave me a little kernel of reassurance.

"Without my knowledge or express consent, I hasten to point out," Magoth said quickly. "I did not, as you have claimed, order her to go against your wishes. I would *never* do that. I would *never* risk expulsion. It was all May's doing. If anyone should be expulsed, it is she."

"Oh, you did so tell me to do whatever I needed to do," I said, unable to keep from arguing with him. The dragon shard made me feel cocky, as if Magoth posed no threat to my borrowed strength. "You said, and I quote, 'I'm too busy to bother with your unimportant concerns. Feel free to do whatever you need to do, so long as it's without me.' And if that's not consent, I don't know what is."

Magoth bristled, the temperature of the room dropping by a couple of degrees. "How can you lie like that in front of Lord Bael!"

"I don't lie. You know that. And so does he."

"I never—"

Bael held up a hand, which thankfully shut up Magoth.

"This discussion bores me. You have been judged and sentenced, Magoth. Your punishment has been duly bound upon you."

"Not properly!" Magoth said, shooting me a couple of really nasty looks. I thought for a moment of setting his toes on fire, but managed to keep from doing so. He would probably consider it foreplay. "My rightful powers have not yet been restored."

"It is for that reason I've had you brought here," Bael said to me.

"Really? I assumed it was to chew me out for releasing Chuan Ren," I said calmly, embracing the dragon heart's strength. I felt particularly dragonish at that moment, allowing my fingers to change into curved, wickedly sharp claws as I tapped on the round-headed tacks pounded into the arms of the leather chair on which I sat. "It goes against my nature, but if you want me to beg you not to give Magoth back his powers, I am fully prepared to do so."

"May!" Magoth gasped.

Jim snickered softly to itself.

Bael's eyes lit with interest for a moment. "That might be . . . no. I suppose it would be best not to pursue that train of thought, tempting as it is. As you know, the Doctrine of Unending Conscious allows for a period of time before an expulsion is made permanent, a time during which the expulsed person may petition the princes for reinstatement."

Magoth lifted his chin. "Which I have done. You rejected my petition. Therefore, according to the laws set down in the Doctrine, you must restore to me all the honors due me, including my full powers."

I moved uneasily in the chair, the dragon shard filling my mind with all sorts of unlikely actions that were intended to keep Bael from doing just that.

Bael's gaze flickered to me for a few moments before returning to his laptop. "The law states that powers must be given to their rightful owner, yes."

"Fine, then," Magoth said, standing up, one hand on his naked hip. "I don't like it, but I will accept the expulsion. So long as I have my powers, I will simply turn my attention to ruling the mortal world. You can have my seat with my blessings."

"I don't need your—"

Bael's terse response was interrupted by a whirlwind that suddenly burst through the door.

"I'm so sorry I'm late! I got held up disciplining one of my legions. You wouldn't believe how insubordinate they were. I don't know what the last demon lord was thinking, but she totally messed up my minions. Do you know that all they want to do is write software? But that's a subject for another day. Did I miss it? Did I miss seeing you tell him? May, sugar! How lovely to see you again! And Magoth. Goodness! You're starkers!"

A giggling pink-frilled whirlwind, that is. One named Sally, who appeared to be accompanied by two nearly naked bodybuilders.

She stopped next to me, air-kissing the spaces about four inches from either side of my face. "You look simply scrumptious in that black leather waist cincher. It's amazing what that can do for your figure, isn't it? Magoth, my dear boy, is that your curse, or are you just happy to see me?" Having dealt with the niceties, Sally squealed her way over to Magoth and stroked a hand down his bare chest. "Still so yummy, even though a bath would probably be the best thing right now. Is that mouse droppings in your hair? Oooh. Kinky."

Magoth simpered at her. I kept my eye rolling to merely a desire, and greeted her politely. "Hello, Sally. I wondered what happened to you, since we haven't seen you in a few months. It looks like you've taken up coaching Chippendales dancers."

The nearest wrath demon flexed its zebra-striped thong at me.

"You mean Vincenzo and Gunter? Aren't they the most scrumptious things you've ever seen?" Sally blew them a kiss.

"Er . . . they're definitely something," I said, avoiding eye contact with them.

"Sugar, jealousy just doesn't look good on you. I'll send them away, since you know how much I value our friendship. Well, that and they're naughty little boys who don't like it when Mumsy pays attention to other men." She kissed Magoth's ear and made an elaborate gesture in the air. The two nearly naked demons disappeared.

"I wonder how I'd look in a thong," Jim said thoughtfully, squinting at the spot in which the two demons had been standing.

"Ridiculous," I told it before turning to Sally. "You look hale and hearty. I take it you're still apprenticing?"

"Gracious, no!" She looked crestfallen for a moment. "You didn't get the invitation for the ceremony? Hellfire! I knew I should have gone with Crane and Co. to do my announcements rather than having one of the minions handcraft paper from Yankee money. I'm sorry about that, May. It was a beautiful ceremony, truly moving when Bael sacrificed an entire legion to mark the occasion of my ascension to the throne. You would have loved it."

Somehow, I doubted that. Still, my eyes widened at the thought of Sally ruling Abaddon. "You took the throne?"

"You little backstabber," Magoth told her fondly, using the arm he had around her waist to give her a squeeze. "You used my banishment to forward your own cause. What a superbly self-serving thing to do."

She bit his chin. "I knew you'd approve."

"So long as it wasn't my seat, yes."

"To answer your question, May, I took over the seat left vacant by that demon lord who is now all dragonny," she said, giggling a little as Magoth goosed her. "You know her, don't you? I'd appreciate it if you could give her a piece of my mind. She's absolutely ruined all of my minions. You wouldn't believe the lax attitudes they have, not to mention a flat-out refusal to do anything truly evil. I mean, seriously, what's the use of having minions if they won't go forth and spread debauchery, depravity, and suffering in your name?"

"Shocking," Magoth murmured, both hands on her butt now.

I said simply, "What a disappointment that must be to you. I will be sure to pass along your complaint to Aisling."

"I'm sure she'll be heartbroken," Jim said, snickering just a little.

Sally, who had been whispering and giggling to Magoth, suddenly froze, her head snapping around to pierce Jim with a look that had the hairs on the back of my neck standing on end. "Who dares to speak to me without permission? What is your name, demon?"

"This is Jim," I said quickly as Jim backed up until it was pressed against my legs. "It's Aisling's demon, actually, although it's out on loan to me."

"It is impertinent," Sally said, and with a negligent hand drew a symbol in the air.

"Hey, all I said—" Jim disappeared, just flat-out disappeared.

Fury roared to life within me. "What did you do?" I almost yelled, stomping forward toward her.

She had the gall to look surprised. "Why, banished it to the Akasha, of course. I know you're not a demon lord, May, but really, your time here in Abaddon should have taught you that the only way to maintain control is to never allow impertinence in minions. It can only lead to worse things, like insubordination and outright mutiny."

"She's right," Magoth said, nodding. "I prefer torture, myself, since it entertains and is a good demonstration for other demons, but the idea is sound."

"Bring it back," I said, my voice a low growl that I didn't recognize.

"Don't be silly—it's just a sixth-class demon," Sally said, dismissing my concern to turn her head and nuzzle Magoth's filthy neck. She plucked a fern from behind his ear and proceeded to tickle his penis with it.

I slid a glance toward Bael. He was leaning back in his chair, watching me with an anticipatory light in his eyes.

"Bring. It. Back," I said again, my body elongating and shifting into that of a silver-covered dragon. I drew back my lips, sending fire through my clenched teeth.

Sally's eyes widened as I took a step toward her, sending fire to the very tips of her sparkly pink plastic shoes. "May! This is how you thank me?"

Magoth shoved Sally aside, his arms held wide as he welcomed me. "May! My own sweet, scaly May! You want to play? Right here? Right now? In front of Bael? I question your sense of timing, and yet, I am strangely excited by the thought. Let's go for it. Give me a piece of that sweet tail!"

The air cracked. A large *whump* followed as Magoth hit the far wall of the room, sliding down the wood paneling with a squeak of flesh against highly polished wood.

Sally watched him for a moment before turning back to me, her eyes thoughtful, her lips pursed. "I see."

"Do you?" I walked toward her, slowly, little compression tremors shaking the ground as I did so. "Do you, really?"

"Perhaps I was a little hasty in banishing your servant," she said quickly, backing up a couple of steps. "I don't want there to be bad feelings between us, sugar. What if I bring the demon back? Would that make you happy again?"

I let a slow smile curve my lips before I forced the dragon shard back into obedience, my body changing back to its normal shape. "That would make me very happy, indeed."

She spoke a few words, and gave me a very toothy smile when Jim reappeared, its eyes rather wild. She even went so far as to pat it a couple of times on the head before turning her perky smile on Bael. "I'm sorry, Lord Bael. I forgot you said . . . I forgot."

Bael gave her a long look before turning his head to consider the puddle of Magoth on the floor next to the wall. "He smudged my wall."

"He had a little accident in the woods and got a bit dirty," I explained.

Bael laced his fingers together and looked back to me. "It would appear he is also unconscious."

"He would have just kept pestering me until I knocked him out, so I figured I'd save everyone the trouble of listening to him rant and rave. Which, I assume, he'd do, since I suspect you have something to tell me he isn't going to like."

"Very astute, dragon," Bael said.

"Oh, goody, I haven't missed it," Sally said, beaming at me. "You're going to love this, May. Just love it. It's so—oh my gosh, so wonderful! I couldn't believe it when Lord Bael told me about it. 'May is just going to flip when she hears about this,' I told him, and so you are."

"Sally," Bael said, with a weary gesture.

"Oh. Sorry. Lips are zipped," she said, making a zipping action across her mouth. "Go right ahead and make May's day."

Bael leaned back in his chair, seemingly unaware of the wariness in my eyes, saying comfortably, "As I was saying before we were interrupted, there are rules that I must adhere to."

"I am tolerably familiar with the Doctrine of Unending Conscious," I said, mentally going over the set of rules that governed Abaddon for anything appropriate to the situation. Sally's reassurance of loving the surprise that Bael had for me confirmed my initial impression that I was about to be sent screaming in horror from the room.

"As your employer so abrasively stated, we must grant him his due now that the expulsion has been appealed, and the appeal denied. Therefore, I am doing just that," Bael said, flicking his fingers toward me.

I took a deep breath, holding tight to my anger and the need for the shard to dominate me. "Might I point out that Magoth running amok in the mortal world will have repercussions on Abaddon? You come and go into my world as frequently as you please—do you think you will be able to continue doing so once he rules it? Surely you must realize that he will hold a grudge, and will do everything possible to deny you access to the mortal world."

"No one can stop me from doing what I wish," he said with deceptive mildness. "That said, I have no intention of allowing Magoth to rule *any* world, let alone one in which I have an interest."

I frowned, confused, sliding Jim a glance. Its eyes looked like they were going to bug out of its head. I wanted badly to ask it what it saw that I didn't, but refrained. Bael would view such an act as a sign of weakness, and above all, I wanted him to continue thinking I was a badass dragon with whom it would be a very bad idea to tangle. "So you won't be giving him his powers back?"

"No."

"But the Doctrine . . . ?"

Sally giggled again. "This is so fabulous, May. I can't believe you haven't guessed!"

"Guess what?" I asked, but the second the words left my lips, a horrible idea came over me. I turned to

Bael with what must have been an appalled look on my face. "You don't mean . . . you can't . . . it's not possible, is it?"

"You are Magoth's consort," he answered with a little shrug. "As far as the Doctrine is concerned, you and he are of the same body. Therefore, it is to you his powers have been granted. I wish you joy of them, dragon."

# Chapter Six

My cell phone rang the same instant I walked in the front door.

"Gabriel?"

"Little bird! I got your voice mail. Where are you?"

"Home. In London, I mean. Bael summoned me to his English home, and pushed me out here rather than Latvia."

"What did he want of you? All your twin said is that two demons came to fetch you, but they did not want Magoth. And yet you took him with you?"

"I had no choice, either in seeing Bael or Magoth coming along." I gave him a brief recap of what had happened in Bael's house. "Gabriel, I can't tell you how upset Magoth is going to be when he finds out. The words 'going ballistic' wouldn't begin to cover the hissy fit he'll have. Not to mention the fact that I don't want to be a demon lord. I'm not Aisling. I'm not meant for this sort of thing."

"I doubt if Aisling feels she is, either, but that is nei-ther here nor there. Tell me again what Bael said—did he imply you were taking Magoth's place, or just receiving his powers?"

"Just getting his powers. *Agathos daimon*—you don't think he intends for me to take over Magoth's seat?"

"No. He would not want a dragon in power in Abaddon," he answered slowly.

Reassurance eased some of the worry that was leaving me feeling itchy and uncomfortable. "What am I going to do with his powers?"

"I wish I was more learned in the ways of Abaddon, but it's not something I've ever paid attention to. Aisling should be able to help you, however. Or rather, her mentor will, since I doubt if Drake will allow her to do more than speak to you."

"I planned on talking to both of them, but figured I'd check with you first to see if there was some way you knew of to unload these powers. Not to mention what on earth we're going to tell Magoth. And then how we're going to keep him from going on a rampage."

"I will see to it that he is taken care of."

I glanced out of the window, noting the taxi driver was struggling with a large object. "I don't think we have much time. Sooner or later he'll wake up, and notice he still doesn't have his powers. He might not guess that Bael would give them to me, but he will find out at some point."

"We could ask Aisling's mentor to banish him to the Akasha."

"I have no doubt Nora could do it, but it's really not such a good idea."

"Why not?"

I made a wry face at Magoth's body. "Because I'm bound to him, and he has just enough power left to summon me should he so choose. And I can guarantee you that if he was banished, he'd take me with him."

Gabriel uttered a word I decided it was best I not

acknowledge. "I will have Maata remove him from the house. That should give you a little breathing room."

I bit my lip, not sure if it was such a wise thing to have Magoth out of the way. "I suppose that's the sane thing to do. I'll start looking around for somewhere safe to keep him. And speaking of that, did you get the phylactery?"

He hesitated a second. My stomach tightened. "Yes and no."

"That sounds ominous. What is the no part? Oh, set him down over there on the couch, would you? Thank you so much. Let me just get my purse. . . . Here you go. Keep the rest."

The taxi man deposited the blanket-wrapped form of Magoth where I indicated, eyeing the large denomination of the bill I held out with an avaricious smile that remained on his face as he left the house.

"The yes refers to the Modana Phylactery—Kostya very grudgingly allowed me to see it to verify it is, in fact, the shard." There was a muffled sound like that of knuckles cracking.

"Uh-huh. You don't happen to have a black eye, do you?" I couldn't help but ask, suspecting there was a certain amount of physical persuasion that Gabriel had to apply.

"Mayling, you know full well I do not go out of my way to pick fights."

"Of course you don't. Now, answer the question."

He snorted into the phone. "No, I do not have a black eye."

I waited for a moment.

". . . now."

"I knew it. I hope that Kostya fared as well as you."

"Oh, yes." There was a distinct note of pleasure in his silken voice. "I'm told broken noses aren't particularly painful, but if they aren't set correctly, they can leave a permanent reminder. I find that thought very satisfying."

I ignored the grin in his voice. "So you got Kostya's shard. Then what's the problem?"

A heavy sigh sounded in my ear. "The problem concerns the Song Phylactery."

"Don't tell me Chuan Ren is going back on her promise?" I asked, keeping the irritation from my voice.

"Not entirely. The problem, I gather, stems from the fact that Fiat is technically in charge of the red sept."

Maata came into the room, having heard voices. Her eyebrows rose at the sight of the still-unconscious Magoth, but she said nothing other than, "Is that Gabriel on the phone?"

I nodded.

"I was just about to call. Tipene said he and Kaawa should be arriving early tomorrow morning."

I passed the message along before saying, "Chuan Ren has had, what, almost two months to take care of Fiat? I can't believe she hasn't ousted him from her sept since he took it over in a wholly heinous, and surely illegal, fashion."

"Heinousness and illegality have nothing to do with it," Gabriel said, his voice amused. "Chuan Ren would tear Fiat to little shreds and use them in a cat's litter box if she could find him. But he's gone to ground, and although he continues issuing commands to the red dragons—which, Jian assures me, no one is following—they can't find him to formally oust him. And until that's done—"

I sat down in the nearest chair, despair pooling in my gut. "Until that's done, she won't give up the shard."

"No."

"Well, ain't life just a bowl of cherries? What are we going to do?"

"I have offered Chuan Ren my help in locating Fiat before the *sárkány*, as has Kostya."

"Kostya volunteered to help someone?" I said, then immediately felt ashamed of myself for such a snarky comment.

"He wishes to be sure there will be no objections to the reinstatement of his sept into the weyr," Gabriel replied in a neutral tone that spoke volumes.

"He's standing right there, isn't he?"

"Yes. Your twin is on her way back to England. I take it that Jim and Magoth are with you?"

"One is. Jim had a message to go see Aisling for a bit. It seems she misses it, or something like that. But, Gabriel, the *sárkány* is tomorrow. Do you really think you can find Fiat in so short a time?"

"I have no idea, but it is vital we have that shard. I feel I must try."

"I understand. Where are you looking? I'll get on a plane and join the hunt," I said, grabbing my purse and pulling out my wallet for my credit card. "Maata can babysit Magoth."

"I don't want to babysit him!" Maata protested. "I'd rather throw myself into a lake!"

"Much as I would welcome your presence, there is work for you in London, little bird."

"Such as?" I sat down on the nearest chair, disappointment making me a bit tetchy. I assumed Gabriel would demand I be at his side as he hunted for Fiat. That he didn't do so stung my pride.

There was a pause for a moment; then Gabriel's voice dropped, pitched low and intimate. "I know what you're thinking, Mayling. It is not so. I desire you just as much today as I did yesterday, and all the days before it."

"One day I'm going to—"

"Read my mind, and then I'll be sorry. Yes, I know," he said, laughing.

I smiled at my hands, wishing I could see the dimples

I knew must be showing. "What do you want me to do here?"

"You must start training with my mother to learn how to control the shards."

"I control a shard already," I said, putting my wallet back into my purse.

Maata checked Magoth, grinned to see he was still out, and tiptoed out of the room.

"You control the shard bound to you. It is another thing entirely to control all the shards together. My mother has studied the diaries of Ysolde de Bouchier. She is the best resource available for understanding the process of re-forming the dragon heart. It is to her that you must look for training if you wish to be successful."

"I agree, but I still think I could be helpful in tracking down Fiat. There may be some trail I could follow in the shadow world."

"Leave the worry of Fiat to me, little bird. You have enough on your plate with the dragon shards. Protect my mother well."

"Do you think she's in any danger?" I asked, surprised by his demand.

His answer was slow in coming. "I sense there is a threat to her, yes, but that could be connected to the dragon shard you bear. I ask that you be very careful, May, with yourself and my mother. You are both very dear to me."

I warmed down to my toes with the love I heard in his voice. "I'm so glad you're not Drake."

"So am I. But . . . ?"

It was my turn to laugh. "Drake won't let Aisling so much as lift her arm without a spotter and three pillows to protect it."

"Her history might have something to do with that," he said, amusement back in his voice. "She has not always been so competent with her powers. But you are."

We hung up a few minutes later, after a few exchanges

of a more private nature. But something he said had me thinking, so after double-checking that Magoth was all right—he was snoring softly to himself, so I gathered no serious damage had been done to him—I went in search of Maata.

"Do I look any different to you?" I asked her when I found her.

She stopped putting clean clothes into her dresser and eyed me. "Should you look different?"

"That's not what I asked. Do I look any different? Or . . . feel any different to you?"

"I haven't felt you."

I made a face at her grin. "You're being deliberately dragon."

"I'm sorry," she laughed, closing the drawer and walking around me to examine me from all angles. "It's habit. Let's see. . . . No, you look pretty much the same as you did when you and Gabriel left. Why do you ask?"

It was on the tip of my tongue to tell her that I was now in possession of a demon lord's full powers, but I decided that was probably best kept to as few people as possible.

"Just a thought I had. I'm going to trot over to Aisling's house— What in the name of the spirits is that?"

Voices raised in anger could be heard from downstairs. The house had an elaborate security system, but due to the fact I was now bearing a priceless relic of dragonkin, Gabriel had added additional security in the form of extra patrols by silver dragons. The two dragons who watched the downstairs were yelling now, but it was a familiar, higher-pitched voice that had me racing down the hall to the stairs below.

"Sounds like your twin."

"It does indeed. And that man's voice is very familiar, as well. What on earth has she done to bring *him* down on our heads?"

The two dragons, Obi and Nathaniel, were doing their best to stop a very determined individual from entering the house, but Cyrene was getting in their way. Obi had his hands full with Cy, trying to pull her off the visitor, but it was difficult going, since she was determinedly fighting, kicking, making dire threats, and yanking the hair of her victim.

"How dare you!" she screamed at the top of her lungs. My eardrums rattled. I felt sorry for anyone closer to her than I was. "I am a daughter of Tethys! You will feel the true vengeance of a sister of the house of Hydriades!"

"Let go of me, you madwoman, or you will find out what vengeance really feels like!" the man yelled back.

"Is that— Hoo," Maata said, getting a good look at the man Nathaniel was all but wrestling.

"What in the name of the sun and moon is going on here?" I yelled, trying to be heard over the noise of so many people shouting. "Cyrene, let go of Dr. Kostich's hair."

"He called me a name!" she snarled, giving his hair a good yank. "He called me a tree hugger. *Me!*"

"You like trees. Let him go. And you can stop doing *that*, too."

Blood flowed from the punch Cyrene managed to get in to Kostich's nose.

"I may like trees, but I'm not a druid. I've never been so insulted in all my days!"

Druids and water beings, for some reason I've never been able to fathom, insisted on perpetuating a feud that went back at least a millennium. There was no insult worse in the water-elemental circles than to be thought in sympathy with druids.

Dr. Kostich bellowed an obscenity, trying desperately to fling Nathaniel, Maata (who was helping Nathaniel), and Cyrene off him. "Cease, you insane watery twit! I demand that you unhand me!"

"Watery twit? *Watery twit!* Oh! I'll show you who's a watery—"

"Stop it right now!" I yelled, grabbing Cyrene with both hands and pulling. The dragon shard wanted to help, but I didn't want to let it loose. I dug in my heels and pulled, finally ripping my twin off the head of the L'au-delà with a shriek that made my ears ring a second time.

"Just you wait," Cyrene panted, shaking her fist at him as both Obi and I dragged her over to a chair next to the wall. "Just you wait until there's no one around to save you, mage!"

"Cy, remember who you are speaking to," I warned, casting a worried eye over at Kostich.

"Oh, he can't do anything to me. The council of elementalists isn't afraid of the L'au-delà committee," she said, tossing her head. She straightened her clothing with dark mutters.

"I apologize for my twin's actions," I said, leaving her to see how Dr. Kostich fared. He slapped away Nathaniel's hands as the dragon tried to dust him off. His glare was world-class, almost as good as Magoth's—and almost as potent. It stopped me dead in my tracks for a few seconds, a horrible sensation of immobility gripping my entire body, including my heart and lungs, before I instinctively shadowed and slipped out of his control.

Dr. Kostich murmured something rude about doppelgangers under his breath as I dropped the shadow.

I handed him a couple of tissues, and said, "I'm going to pretend I didn't hear that, mostly because I feel bad that you and Cyrene got into a fight, but also because I suspect the dragons wouldn't take kindly to you insulting their wyvern's mate. I take it you came here to see me, and not Gabriel?"

"... never been treated in such a manner. What?" He stopped muttering as he dabbed at his bloody nose.

"Yes, of course I came here for you. You and that turn-coat thief taker who has been shielding you."

"Savian Bartholomew?" I shook my head. Gabriel and I had discussed the fact that sooner or later Dr. Kostich was going to find out where I was, and I was confident that I could placate him by some means or other. "He's not here. In fact, he's out of the country."

Dr. Kostich wadded up the bloody tissue and flung it onto a nearby table. "Then I will simply track him down as I have tracked you down. You are under arrest, May Northcott, and wyvern's mate or not, you will accept the punishment meted out to you by the council!"

"No," I said, shaking my head a second time.

Dr. Kostich stared in surprise at me for a moment.

"You go, girl. Don't let that arcane bully push you around. You're *my* twin! He can just stick that in his—"

"That's enough from the peanut gallery, thank you," I said hastily, giving Cyrene a quelling look that she completely ignored. "Dr. Kostich, I recognize the fact that you feel it's necessary for me to pay for alleged crimes, but I am— Oh, what now?"

Through the partially opaque bulletproof glass that lined either side of the front doors I could see the shapes of two men as they pounded the knocker. A sudden familiar sense struck me just as Nathaniel went to answer the door, an awareness that I recognized came from the dragon shard, not me.

"No, don't—" I started to say, but at that moment Nathaniel reached the door. It was flung open with a violence that sent the dragon flying backwards into Maata, who had rushed forward to stop him.

A man stood in the doorway, dark-haired, dark-eyed, large, and imposing, his long dark chocolate hair pulled back from a widow's peak.

"Baltic," I said, my breath caught suddenly in my throat.

His ebony eyes lit on me, amusement filling them. "Mate. I thought I would find you here."

"I am not your mate. You would think after I've told you that so many times you'd begin to understand that. Would it help if I wrote it out on flash cards?"

"I understand more than you can possibly conceive," he answered with typical dragon arrogance.

"Who is this?" Dr. Kostich demanded to know, his eyes narrowed on the newcomer. "Who are you, sir, that you would interrupt official L'au-delà business?"

It was clearly up to me to make the introductions. "This is Baltic, Dr. Kostich. Sometimes referred to as the dread wyvern Baltic, although I believe that title was granted him in the past, back when he was leader of the black dragon sept."

"Baltic." Dr. Kostich frowned as he tried the word a couple of times. "Baltic. I believe I remember something about a dragon with that name."

I smiled to myself at the irritated look that flashed for a moment in Baltic's eyes. It was interesting to see that even the cool, collected Baltic had an ego that could be prodded.

"Wasn't there some business concerning you that ended with the death of a wyvern? A female, one who fought against you. Had a French name."

"Ysolde?" I asked, trying to think of anyone who could fit that description. My knowledge of dragon history wasn't that great, but I had read what I could find about the silver dragons. "She was a wyvern's *mate*, not a wyvern. Although she did have a French name: Ysolde de Bouchier."

"That's it," Kostich said, giving a curt nod before considering Baltic again. "You destroyed a wyvern's mate."

Baltic's face grew dark. He stalked over to Dr. Kostich, whom I had to admire for not even flinching in the face of a furious dragon. "I did not destroy Ysolde. Constantine Norka did that!"

I felt my jaw sag a little as I slid a glance toward Maata. "Ysolde was killed by the silver wyvern?" I asked her in a whisper.

Her face was impassive as she watched Baltic. "That was before my time."

Typical dragon nonanswer.

"I thought you died," Dr. Kostich asked, flicking a piece of lint from his arm with studied nonchalance. I might be a master at presenting a calm appearance in a highly charged situation—or rather, I might have been before the dragon shard embedded itself in me—but I had to give Dr. Kostich kudos; his indifferent, placid expression made me look like an amateur. "I am sure they told me you were killed by one of your own sept members."

Baltic's jaw tightened as he gave Dr. Kostich an assessing once-over. "You have the smell of alchemy about you, mage. I assume you received your quintessence back again?"

"Again?" I asked, curiosity overriding my better sense. "No, I think that's far enough, Baltic. Gabriel won't be happy to hear that you forced yourself into his house; he'll be furious if you insist on coming any farther than the front hall."

"You want us to throw them out, May?" Maata asked softly, her body language relaxed, but she stood on the balls of her feet, ready to pounce.

"No, I don't think that will be necessary. Whatever you have to say to me, Baltic, can be said here. And your little buddy can stay outside."

The man who stood silently behind Baltic, as dark and menacing as his leader, stiffened at the insult. All three silver dragons stiffened with him, just as if they were panthers about to spring. Baltic lifted his hand and his man backed down, taking a few steps backwards until he was on the front steps leading up to the house.

"If you don't mind, what exactly do you mean by *again*? Was the quintessence stolen recently?" I asked.

Unexpectedly, a little smile quirked the corners of Baltic's mouth. "You should know; the word is that you stole it."

"And returned it promptly the next day just as soon as was humanely possible," I said quickly, glancing at Dr. Kostich.

To my extraordinary relief, he was still focused on Baltic. "I *know* they said you were dead."

The muscle in Baltic's jaw jumped again.

"The word 'again' implies it was stolen before. You wouldn't happen to be interested in alchemy, too, would you?" I asked Baltic.

He shot me an irritated look. "I am no glorified chemist playing with potions."

"But the quintessence—"

"May be the focus of an alchemist's interest, but I have no use for transforming matter at all. He can keep his precious quintessence," he interrupted with a particularly wolfish smile. "I have come for my shard, mate."

Dr. Kostich sucked in a breath, his fingers twitching. Mages frequently drew elaborate runes in order to access their power. Although he stood in a relaxed position, with his hands apparently calmly at his side, I could see that his fingers twitched and jerked in what I realized was a subtle pattern. He was drawing a rune.

Of the two evils, Kostich was definitely the lesser. The L'au-delà was governed by rules and laws; Baltic clearly made his own as he went along. Therefore, it would behoove me to throw my lot in with Kostich, no matter if it was only temporarily.

I lifted my chin and gave Baltic a long, calm look. "We've had this out before, Baltic. I'm not going to let you kill me just so you can get the shard."

Kostich's pupils flared for a few seconds as he glanced at me.

"I was referring to the shard you stole from my lair earlier today, although now that you speak of it, I agree that it would be more convenient to take both now than be forced to return for the second one later."

I tipped my head to the side as I looked him over, the dragon shard gleefully throwing caution to the wind. "I did not steal any shard. Well, not in the last couple of months. The Modana Phylactery was taken by its rightful owner, Kostya, not me. As for the other—the phrase 'over my dead body' has always seemed overly dramatic to me, but at this moment, it seems particularly apropos."

"You will find there are several bodies you will have to overcome in order to harm May," Maata said, taking a step forward. The other two dragons did likewise, their faces wearing identical expressions of intent as they moved into flanking positions.

Dr. Kostich's fingers continued to weave a rune of power against the fabric of his pants leg.

"You are threatening me?" Baltic asked, genuinely amused. I glanced toward the door where his cohort stood, half-afraid he'd come charging in, but he merely leaned against the doorframe, looking not at all worried.

That fact made me more uneasy than anything else.

"We will do whatever is necessary to protect May," Maata said, inclining her head.

"Then you will die with her," Baltic said with a shrug. "You will all die if you try to stop me from retrieving what belongs to me."

"I'm a naiad," Cyrene suddenly said. She jumped up and hurried over to stand next to me in a show of support. "I'm immortal. I can't die."

Baltic slid her a quick look. "Would you like to place a wager on that assumption?"

Cyrene showed rare circumspection by saying nothing other than a whispered, "Kostya was right—whoever this dragon is, he's a pain in the butt. Show him what you're made of, May."

"Kostya?" Baltic lifted his head as if he was scenting the air, his gaze narrowed on Cyrene. "You are his . . ."

"Mate," she said quickly.

Baltic's eyebrows rose.

"Oh, all right, all right! I wish everyone would stop doing that when I tell them I'm Kostya's mate. It's annoying! I'm mate lite, OK? Not quite a full-fledged mate, but close enough to count. Not that I want him anymore, the heartless, unfeeling bastard. But if I did, I'd be his mate. Sort of."

We all stared at Cyrene as she had her verbal hissy fit.

"Are you done now?" I asked politely.

"Yes." She crossed her arms over her chest, stuck out her lower lip in a truly world-class pout, and spread a glare among us all.

"Good." I turned back to Baltic. "I'm a little busy being arrested, so if you want to spew threats and enigmatic comments, you'll have to do so later. Good-bye."

Baltic smiled. It was not a pleasant smile, despite his handsome face, and it did, in fact, light up his eyes, but it was a light that boded ill for anyone who stood in his way.

"Your false sense of bravery is laudable. Useless and misguided, but laudable. I admire your courage."

"Thank you. Now bugger off," I said, using a British phrase I'd heard in the street.

He gave an abrupt shake of his head. "Not without the shard."

"The shard doesn't leave me," I answered.

"You insist on doing this the hard way. . . . Very well." His fingers danced in the air for a moment, but before he could do anything, Dr. Kostich finished drawing his runes. The air in the room suddenly collected at one point, then punched outward toward Baltic with the force of a luxury liner. Baltic's startled yell as he was sent flying through the open door, stopped only by his dragon friend, was almost as loud as the compression blast made by the explosion.

"My ears!" Cyrene screamed, clapping both hands over her head.

"That was not nice, mage!" Baltic charged forward with a snarl, a ball of light bursting into being in front of him, stretching itself into a long, glittering blue-white shape. It was the light blade I'd seen him wield before, a weapon that no dragon should be able to use.

Dr. Kostich gawked at it for a moment, stammering, "That is a . . . you cannot have that. . . . Who *are* you?"

"Would it be a cliché to say your worst nightmare?" I asked.

"Yes," Maata, Cyrene, Nathaniel, and Obi answered.

Dr. Kostich was too busy staring at the sword Baltic swung toward me.

I didn't wait for any more bons mots to occur to me; I took one look at Baltic, and let the dragon shard have free rein.

It shifted me immediately, and I took advantage of the momentary surprise in Baltic's black eyes to tail-slap him backwards, out the door again.

Maata and Nathaniel shifted, as well, their silvery scales reflecting the light from the overhead chandelier as they flanked me. Obi remained in human form, clearly torn between joining us and protecting Cyrene and Dr. Kostich.

"You're outnumbered," I called out to Baltic, sauntering with dragon ease to the door. "You might have the light blade, but are you strong enough to take on four dragons?"

"Four dragons and one really pissed-off naiad,"

Cyrene said, pushing her way between Maata and me to stand with her hands on her hips.

"That's it?" Baltic sneered. "That's all you have to oppose me? Do you have any concept of just what powers I have learned? Can you even guess as to what I could do to you and your friends with the merest flick of my fingers?"

I was ready for the attack even before he started forward. With one hand I shoved Cyrene backwards, a little harder than I would have liked, but she was vulnerable, and I would not put it past Baltic to strike at her in an attempt to weaken me.

His sword flashed as it swung toward me. I spun around, my tail sounding a whipcrack as it slammed into him, but I wasn't quite fast enough—the light blade bit deep into my leg, burning me with an icy fire the likes of which I'd never before felt. I slammed shut the door in the face of Baltic's companion, roaring my fury as Maata and Nathaniel rushed forward into the fray. Baltic didn't shift to a dragon form; he simply parried all the attacks with his sword, looking almost bored, the bastard.

"Enough!" Dr. Kostich bellowed, his hands drawing the last of another set of runes. "This will end now!"

Another explosion of air and light rocked the house, sending all of us flying backwards—all but Baltic.

Kostich stared at him with mingled horror and confusion for a moment before the dragon shard, tired of my feeble attempts to direct my foreign dragon body around, took charge of the situation. In a flash, I was on top of Baltic, having knocked him to the ground, his blade skittering away on the marble floor, great arcs of light flying from it as it spun. I snarled and bit at Baltic as he flung me off him, leaping to his feet in order to run after his sword.

"Oh, no, you don't," I growled, lunging forward onto him, dragging my claws down his back, cutting deep through material into his flesh.

He screamed with pain and spun around, trying to dislodge my hold on him. "We will finish this now," I yelled, biting hard on his shoulder. I tasted blood, spitting it out as he threw himself onto the floor in a rolling move meant to loosen my hold on him.

It worked. I slid across the floor, scrabbling desperately with my claws for a hold. Maata and Nathaniel raced toward him, but Baltic was too fast in human form—he snatched up the blade, leaping over Maata as he headed toward me.

Kostich's blast of light must have lit up the block. It wasn't the same sort of compression blast of air as he'd used before—this one was a golden halo of light that suddenly burst through me, burst through the entire block, bedazzling and blinding and bringing everything and everyone to a complete halt for a few seconds.

As the light dissipated, I shook the dazzle from my brain, and looked around for Baltic.

He was gone. The front door stood open, but when I rushed to the street, shifting back to human form as I did so, it was bare of dragons. The few people that stood outside had odd expressions on their faces, as if they were bemused.

"They will not remember what happened," a voice spoke behind me. "Mortals seldom do."

I turned to search the face of the man beside me. "You saved us."

"No." Kostich shook his head, his expression grim. "You did that. All I did was give you a little time."

"Whatever it was, it worked."

"No," he repeated. "If it had worked, he would be incapacitated at best. But while everyone else was stunned by the light, he escaped. He should not have been able to do that."

"What exactly was the light? It left me feeling stunned."

"It was an arcane concussion blast, a minimized version. A full concussion would have blown out the walls of this house. As it is, it merely served as a brief distraction." Kostich looked worried as we returned to the house. "The dragon should have been affected by it as we were, but he was not. And there is the blade—he should not have that light blade. It belonged to a famous archimage."

Slowly, I closed the door and leaned against it while I considered Dr. Kostich. "I'm not going to allow you to send me to the Akasha, you know. I have too many things to do here. Baltic is one of those things."

He hesitated for a moment, glancing from Cyrene to the dragons and back to me. "I believe we might be able to come to an accord regarding that."

"What sort of an accord?" Cyrene asked, coming forward. She stopped at a look from me. "Sorry, May. I thought you might need a little bit of help, but . . . never mind."

"What sort of an accord?" I asked Kostich.

"One which we will each find satisfactory. You wish to be pardoned, and I wish to have the von Endres blade. Do you think we can help each other?"

I stared at him for a moment. "You want Baltic's sword?"

"Yes. It disappeared when the archimage von Endres died. I had thought it lost to us, but to see it now being wielded by a dragon . . ." He shook his head, his expression puzzled. "I do not understand how it can be. No dragon can use arcane magic."

"Perhaps one who was resurrected can," I said slowly.

Kostich's look was piercing. "He was resurrected? You are certain?"

"Fairly. There's no other way he could be alive now otherwise."

"I begin to see the light," Kostich said slowly, his gaze directed inward. "That could be why my quintessence was stolen. If so . . . very well. This will take some doing. I will not be unprepared next time I meet him. A triumvirate, I think, will answer. My apprentices are ripe for such a challenge, and with your aid, I believe we will be successful. You agree to my terms?"

"I don't even know what they are," I said cautiously.

*"Tch."* He made an impatient gesture. "You will assist me in acquiring the von Endres blade, and I will grant you a full pardon for those crimes of which you are charged."

"Do you think it's possible to take the sword away from Baltic? If it's something important, he's not likely to let it go without a serious fight. And while I'm up to kicking him out of my house, I don't know that it will be possible to get the sword from him without killing him."

Dr. Kostich evidently came to some sort of a decision, for he nodded his head twice and murmured, "Yes, it will be a good test for Jack. Tully is weaker, but such an experience will be invaluable to her." He raised his voice and added, "Does it matter if the dragon is dead? Given your reputation, I would have thought you would relish an official sanction to destroy him."

"I am not a hit man, if that's what you're implying," I said rather huffily, straightening my shoulders and trying to look down my nose at him. "I'm a thief, and even then, there are extenuating circumstances. I do not go around murdering dragons, even those that threaten me."

He made a careless gesture. "Whether he lives or dies is not a concern. The blade is. Do we have an agreement?"

I bit my lip and looked at the others in the room. Cyrene nodded her head and gave me a thumbs-up. Na-

thaniel and Obi watched me carefully, but I sensed their
approval. Maata alone looked concerned, her silver eyes
dark with worry.

"Yes," I said, coming to a decision. In for a penny, in
for a pound . . . "Yes, we have an agreement."

# Chapter Seven

Dr. Kostich hadn't been kidding when he commented that a full arcane concussion blast could blow out the walls of Gabriel's house.

"He underestimated it, however," I said to Cyrene as we sat huddled in a police car some eleven hours later. "It blew out the walls of the houses on either side, too. I hope they find the two cats belonging to the old lady who lives next door."

"And her fish," Cyrene said, hugging the blanket that was the only thing between her bare skin and everyone else. "I feel so bad about the fish. What was Baltic thinking trying to blow us up like that? He knew we wouldn't be killed."

"No, but we're vulnerable now," I said in a hushed voice as yet another policeman bustled past, talking into her radio and carrying a clipboard. "We don't have a stronghold to keep him at bay, and he knows it. We'll have to set up camp at a hotel or find another house. But even that—it wouldn't be safe against Baltic. Not until we've had some time to put in security systems."

"I know a house that's safe from Baltic," Cy said, yawning.

"Really? Where?"

"That yummy Drake. I bet he'd take us in if you asked nicely."

I opened my mouth to protest, but nothing came out. And really, why should I protest? As I thought the idea over, I realized just how sound it was. Drake's house was sure to be protected from unauthorized entrance. Not only that, we'd have the power of the green dragons to help in case Baltic might, somehow, make it into the house. There really was no downside to the idea.

"Congratulations, Cy," I said, pulling out my cell phone to call Gabriel again. "You've had your first good idea. I'm so proud of you, I've got tears in my eyes."

"That's what you said the last time I had a good idea," she said smugly.

"Way back in 1922. You may want to pace yourself just in case you overload your brain," I said with a deadpan face.

Regardless of my joking, it *was* a good idea, and although Gabriel approved of the plan, he did sound somewhat worried. "Drake will not allow harm to come to you, but I don't like you being under his roof for any length of time."

"Worried I'll succumb to his charms?" I teased.

"Not in the least. Aisling would turn you into a slug or something equally unappealing if you so much as laid a finger on him. I'm more concerned about what reaction the shard will have after a prolonged exposure to him. They are not your sept, but the shard might not recognize that fact, and may force you to act in a way that is ... er ..."

"Illicit?"

"Inappropriate," he said. "As for your first question,

no, we have not found Fiat, although I believe his trail is fresh. I hope to have him by the morning."

"I miss you," I told him, glancing around to make sure I wouldn't be overheard. "I miss you a lot."

"And I you, little bird. But now I must go. We are taking portals to our destination in order to conserve time, and you know how they discompose me."

"Bon voyage," I said, smiling at the memory of how rumpled portals made Gabriel and the other dragons feel. "Wish me luck with the police. So far, they believe the story of an unexplained bombing, but that has much to do with Cyrene hysterically recounting a tale of a militant extremist boyfriend."

"I should have been an actress," Cyrene said with a smug look on her face. "I really am good."

It took another two and a half hours before the police, firemen, and emergency services people were willing to release us. As I surveyed the wreckage of Gabriel's rented house, I didn't blame the police for wondering how we'd all survived unscathed. The other silver dragons who had been present when Baltic made his midnight second assault had left on my advice—I felt we had a better chance at glossing over any trouble points the mortal police might raise with only a couple of us to be explained.

"Jim, you can talk, but if you bitch at me one more time, I will do something extremely unpleasant to you," I told the demon as we slumped into the back of a sleek black BMW, Nathaniel behind the wheel.

"Like being hit on the head by a chair as it flew out the window?" it quipped. "How about losing the hair on half of my head? Or making all my whiskers drop out? Oh, I have it—how about pointing out the fact that I was almost blown to smithereens a couple hours after I returned to you?"

I lifted a finger. "Anything more?"

"No, sheesh. It's not worth getting banished over. My magnificent coat will grow back, even if I look like a leper until then. I wonder if they make prosthetic whiskers?"

"I'm sorry about your hair and whiskers. You don't look like a leper," I said, averting my eyes from the singed side of its head. "And I told you I'd take you to be groomed as soon as possible. I owe you something after you found those two cats for the lady next door. Although you didn't have to drool on them quite so much."

"Eh. It was no biggie. Those cats were too bony, anyway. They wouldn't have made a proper meal."

"You made Mrs. Patterson deliriously happy by finding them; that is counting heavily in your favor," I said, patting it on the furry side of its head. "But don't push it. It's been a long day for all of us."

"Yeah." Jim slumped for a moment, then perked up. "I can't wait to see the look on Drake's face when we all come trooping in and tell him Baltic blew up your house. He's going to be torqued."

"I just wish we'd been able to find Magoth," I answered, more worried over the missing demon lord than about Drake. "I wonder where he got to? He couldn't have been hurt, could he? He's not technically a demon lord anymore. He's not really anything."

"Just immortal," Jim agreed. "If you didn't find his severed head, oozing and smoking and covered in guck, then he's alive somewhere. Probably got the hell out of Dodge while the getting was good."

"I wish I'd thought of doing that," Cyrene grumbled, pulling the blanket tighter over her chest when Jim ogled her mostly visible breasts.

I don't know how most people would react to a small army of dragons showing up on their doorstep, but Drake was completely unconcerned ... until Aisling hauled herself downstairs to find out what was going on.

"Judging by the fact that Jim's coat—what remains of it—is smoking, Cyrene appears to be naked under a blanket, Maata is walking crooked, and May is wearing nothing but one of what I assume is Gabriel's shirts, I gather something happened over at Chez Silver Dragons."

"Baltic bombed us," I said, trying to look as calm as Drake. When faced with us on his doorstep, he had simply ushered us into the house, not even a simple "What happened?" passing his lips. "We could go to a hotel if there's not room for us."

"Don't be silly," Aisling said as she started down the stairs. "There's plenty of room. Let's see. I'll put you in the ... no, Catalina commandeered that room. How about the ... oh, wait. René is there. I know! You can have the yellow room; it has a view of the river. And Cyrene can have ... hmm."

"I like rivers," Cyrene said, yawning. "The yellow room will be fine for me."

"No, wait—hang on," I said, holding my twin back when she was about to go up the stairs. Guilt dug at me with spiky little fingers. "I appreciate you putting us up—I really can't think of anywhere safer we could stay—but if space is short, then Cy can go back to her flat. She has one in town."

"So do you!" she countered.

"Not anymore. I gave it up a few weeks ago."

"You can't expect me to go back to my flat alone! All by myself?" she squeaked. "I'm emotionally distraught! I'm a wreck! I shouldn't be alone at a time like this— everyone knows that!"

"You broke up with a boyfriend, something you've done several hundred times over the last thousand years, so I think you can handle one more," I pointed out.

She glared at me. "You have no heart, Mayling."

"I have a heart. I also have an idea of how many people Aisling has crammed under her roof right now, and I'm sure the house is about at capacity."

Cyrene gave Aisling a pathetic look, allowing her lower lip to quiver just a smidgen. "Aisling?"

"It is a bit tight now," Aisling said.

Cyrene sniffled, and did her utmost to look pathetic and frail. "Fine. I'll just go back to my cold, dark, lonely, empty flat, and think cold, dark, lonely thoughts."

"You forgot empty," Jim said helpfully.

She stepped on its toes.

"Ow! You're not allowed to abuse me! Only Aisling can do that! Or I suppose May could if she wanted to, but May is obviously not the evil twin, and would never do anything so cruel and heinous as stepping on my toes."

I pinched its ear.

"I'm going to be black-and-blue all over by the time Aisling pops that baby," Jim grumbled, huffing its way over to sit next to Aisling.

"There is the attic," Aisling said slowly, tapping her fingers on her belly as she thought. "Those rooms are habitable, aren't they, Drake?"

"Yes, but they have not been decorated since the First World War," he answered.

"Anything is fine, truly," Cyrene said, making large puppy-dog eyes at her. "I just don't want to be alone."

Aisling smiled. "I'm sure we'll fit you in. There are four attic rooms, so that should take care of Cyrene, Maata, and the two other bodyguards."

"You know, I should really have the yellow room," Cyrene said as we trooped down the hallway. "It has a river view, and as a naiad, I'm the best choice for the room. Don't you think?"

I didn't buy that line of reasoning, and told her so, much to her irritation. Despite that, it wasn't long before we were all settled into our respective rooms. Drake refused to allow Aisling to do more than bring me a new toothbrush, a couple of towels, and a bar of soap. As green and silver dragons bustled back and forth, getting bed linens and other necessities, I pulled Aisling aside into the small room in the back of the house given over to me.

"You're limping. Were you hurt in the explosion?"

"No, that's a souvenir from Baltic's earlier attack. Maata did the best she could with the wound, but it is still a little tender."

"I could get a green dragon healer—" Aisling gestured toward a phone.

I waved aside her offer. "It's not necessary. I'll be fine."

"All right, but if you change your mind, let us know. I'm sorry that you and Cyrene will have to share a bathroom with Nora and René," Aisling apologized as I sat on the edge of the bed. She eased herself into an old gold and rose damask-covered armchair. "I'd dearly love to boot Catalina out so you can have the room that you and Gabriel normally have when you stay with us, but I think it would take an atomic bomb to get rid of her," Aisling said with a heavy sigh. "I'm so glad you have a nice mother-in-law. I'd offer to trade you, but I wouldn't wish Catalina on anyone."

"I didn't think she was that bad," I said with a little smile. "A bit forceful, and refused to believe me when I said I wasn't deranged, but some people are like that. And stop apologizing for the accommodations—we're nothing but grateful that you are willing to put us up."

"I want to hear all about what happened with you and Baltic," she said, casting a glance toward the open door. "But Drake will be coming back as soon as he gets your bodyguards settled, so it'll have to wait until morning."

"Actually, I had something else I wanted to talk to you about. Rather, talk to you and Nora about." I gave her a concise recounting of the events with Bael.

"Holy moly," she said when I finished. Her eyes were wide as she looked me over. "A demon lord's powers, but not a demon lord. You're not proscribed, so I assume you haven't used the dark power?"

"I don't know what that is, so I guess not."

"You'd know it if you used it. Have you tried using any of the power?"

"No, nor do I intend to. The dragon shard possessing me is quite enough, thank you."

"That must be why you're able to keep it from messing with you the way it did me," she mused, her hands rubbing her big belly. "It just about drove me nuts, but you've got that piece of dragon in you, and everyone knows dragons aren't easily controlled by anything. In a way, it's lucky you have the shard."

I let that comment go. "What I want to know is what I can do about the situation. I was hoping you and Nora would be able to advise me."

"Absolutely," Aisling said quickly. "She'll be happy to help, as will I. Jim, what the devil do you have on now?"

Jim paraded past the opened door, tangled long black strands of hair straggling from its head. "Wig. Found it in the attic. Needs a bit of trimming, but I think it'll do until the rest of my coat grows back."

"Oh, for heaven's sake . . ."

"Would you like me to banish it for you?" I asked Aisling.

"May!" Jim said, one eyeball glowering at me through the mass of black wig. "Ixnay on the anishbay, would ya?"

"It's tempting, but not just yet," Aisling said, looking thoughtful. "If it gets overly snarky, though, feel free to command it to spend time with Catalina."

"I'd rather be banished," the demon grumbled.

"I'll see you later in the morning to talk about your problem, OK? Sleep well. Jim . . ." She gave Jim a helpless look, shook her head, and left the room mumbling something about there being no words to describe her thoughts.

"Hey," Jim said, swinging its head so the long strands of hair wafted in the breeze. "How long do dreads take? You think Gabe would set me up with some?"

I slumped a little, emotionally drained by the events of the last day. "Go to bed, Jim. And please don't bother anyone, especially Aisling."

"I think it would be a good look for me," Jim said as it continued to swing its head. "It works for Gabriel; it could work for—"

I closed the door in its face and crawled into bed, exhausted, worried, and missing Gabriel. We hadn't been parted much since my return from Abaddon, and I was somewhat bemused with just how easily our lives had meshed. I felt comfortable around him; more than comfortable, I felt right. It was as if I were shadow walking when he wasn't with me, life taking on a bleak, insubstantial cast. Things seemed to click into place only when he was around, a fact that worried me to no end.

"What do you look so pensive about?"

I jumped, startled by the voice. "Cy, you almost scared me to death."

"You can't die," my twin said, closing the door with a mildly disgruntled flash in her eyes. "And don't give me that look—I knocked, but you didn't answer. I just peeked in to see if you'd gone to sleep with the lights on. Are you all right? You have the strangest expression on your face. How much of the river can you see? Oh. Not much of a view. Ah, well."

Indecision warred within me, yet another emotion that was unfamiliar to me. I was normally a very decisive person, making plans and following them through. Now I was flooded by strange emotions, and they were starting to take their toll on me.

"Mayling, it's just me. You can tell me whatever's bothering you," Cy said, plopping down on the end of the bed, giving my feet a little pat. "Go on. I can see you want to talk."

I opened my mouth to tell her I was just fine, that nothing was bothering me, but that's not what came out. "It's Gabriel. I'm worried."

"About Chuan Ren hurting him?"

"No, I know he can take care of himself well enough. It's what Gabriel means to me," I said, miserable enough that I was willing to share my concerns with my less-than-sensible twin.

"You love him."

"Yes, I do. And he loves me. The loving part isn't the issue."

"Then what is? Oh!" Her eyes, so much like mine, opened wide with understanding. "You don't like the fact that you love him."

"What a ridiculous thing to say," I said scornfully. "Why would I not want to love the man who loves me?"

"Because it means you're not on your own anymore. Because now you're tied to him, bound to him, and nothing will ever be the same. Let's see, you've been living with him for almost two months. . . . Yup. That's about right. The bloom is off the honeymoon, and now you've realized what the relationship is really about."

I stared at her with surprise. "How on earth do you know these things? You've never had a relationship that lasted more than a few weeks."

"I've been with Kostya almost as long as you have been with Gabriel," she pointed out. "Longer if you count the time we spent together while you were trapped in Abaddon."

"Do I have to remind you that you officially de-boy-friended Kostya today?"

The look she shot me was venomous. "No, you don't.

Up to the moment when he dumped me, cruelly and heartlessly, and wholly without cause, just so he could go off and be Mr. Important Wyvern, up to that time we were a very successful couple. So don't tell me I don't know about relationships, because I do. I've had enough of them to learn a thing or two."

I digested this strange new awareness in Cyrene, and admitted that she had come close to pinpointing my concerns. "I don't regret loving Gabriel. I welcome it, welcome him into my life. What worries me is the fact that *he's* become my life."

"Dominating, you mean? He didn't strike me like that. Drake, now, he's dominating."

"No, not dominating." I thought for a moment, trying to put the feelings into words. "He's everything to me, Cy. Not just the romantic stuff like the moon and stars and all that—I mean that when he's not with me, life seems to be not right, not quite real."

"And that worries you?" She smiled. "That sounds like true love to me."

"I told you that the love we share is not the issue. I'm confident in that."

"So you're worried that because life doesn't have a sparkle when he's not there to share it with you, that you're ... what? Too dependent on him?"

"No. I know he needs me just as I need him. The problem is ..." I stopped, not wanting to speak the words aloud.

"What?"

I bit my lower lip.

"Mayling, you're my twin. I love you. I want to help you if I can, and we both know I never get the chance to help you because you're always too busy helping me, instead. But I know men, and I know relationships, and by Neptune's grace, you're going to be helped! Now, tell me what the problem is so I can reassure you that it's not as bad as you think it is, and then I can go take a nice long soak in the tub."

I laughed at her determined face. "I'm not trying to deny you a moment in the sun, I assure you. It's just that it will sound silly."

"I'm all over silly," she said with perfect seriousness. "Spill."

I looked down at my hands, my fingers their normal strong, capable-looking selves. But I knew differently. I knew how easily they could change into digits tipped with curved, wickedly sharp crimson claws. "What if it's the dragon shard making me feel like this?"

"You think it is?" she asked, giving the thought serious consideration.

"I don't know. But if it is, then it follows that it's the shard that Gabriel is reacting to. He told me once that he had never become involved physically with anything but female dragons. I was his first human. When we make love, he likes me in dragon form, Cy. It's more than like. . . . I think he *prefers* me in dragon form."

"Well . . . he is a dragon," she pointed out.

"I know, but . . ." I hesitated, wishing I'd never spoken, but unable to keep from pouring out all my worries. "What if it's the shard he loves? Oh, that sounds so silly—I knew I shouldn't say it. I know he loves me. He loved me before the shard. I *know* that. But . . . oh, never mind. It's too idiotic for words." I covered my face with my hands to keep myself from shadowing. I just wanted to crawl into a hole and let the world go by without me for a while.

Cyrene surprised me yet again by not making light of my concern. "I think I know what you mean," she said after a few moments of chewing it over. "You're worried that he loves you more now because of the shard. But does he really love you more?"

"Yes," I said without having to think about it. I uncovered my face, driven by some urge to make her understand. "When I first met Gabriel, we were . . . well, it was an instant attraction. Part of it was the biological fact that I was his mate, but there was also something that transcended that, a fitting together, if you will. And sexually . . ." I gave her a wry smile.

"I know. You don't burn down a hotel if things aren't good in the sex department," she said with an answering grin, and then patted my foot again. "I will admit that I was worried about you at first, Mayling. You'd never been with a man, and I worried that you lacked the experience of sharing your life with someone."

"I share it with you," I pointed out.

"But we're not lovers, and Gabriel was. Oh, don't puff up and tell me you were on top of it—so to speak—because I could see well enough that you guys were getting on just fine."

"We were. We did. We still do. But there's a difference—we've settled into a life together. I really know what it's like to have him be a part of me. I know what he's like in the morning, when he's just woken up, and is kind of grumpy until I kiss him. I know what makes him laugh, know what he values, know what makes him angry."

"That sounds perfectly normal to me," she said.

"It is. And yet . . . I didn't have this insight into him before the phylactery exploded. Hence my concern about what will happen between us when the shard is decanted into a nonliving phylactery."

She nodded her understanding.

I gave her a long look. "Not going to tell me I'm being foolish and imagining that Gabriel loves me more now because of the shard, and once the shard is gone, we'll be just fine?"

"No, I'm not." Her gaze met mine with unflinching honesty. "I'm not because I think it's very possible that what you say is true."

My heart crumbled.

"Gabriel is a dragon. You bear a piece of a dragon heart inside you. Of course he's going to react to that. It would be impossible for him not to. It would be like me turning my back on a pool of calm water."

"You could if you had to," I grumbled, feeling hurt and dejected by the realization that she spoke the truth.

"No, I couldn't." She took my hand, squeezing my fingers until I looked up. "Mayling, this is hard for you to understand because you're not a water elemental. But water isn't just an interest—it's my life. It rules me; it drives me; the focus of my being is completely on it. When I'm near a stream, I have to see it, have to touch it, have to glory in its beauty and purity. I *am* the stream, May. Do you understand that? It's as much a part of me as my arms and legs and brain are—I'm an extension of it, that's all. Just an extension. And I imagine that's how Gabriel feels about the dragon shard—it's part of the heart that beats in all dragons. It's an integral part of him, just as water is to me. And now, to him, you're part of that equation."

"So long as I bear the shard," I said dully.

She looked at me for a moment, then slid off the bed. "I know you've been worried that you're losing yourself to the dragon shard, but has it ever occurred to you that the reverse might be true?"

"Huh?"

She padded over to the door, picking up the towel she'd set on the dresser. "I think the shard is changing you, May. But maybe you're changing it, too. Maybe when it's gone, you won't be who you used to be. Maybe you'll be who you were meant to be. And maybe you'll change the dragon shard to be something more than just a piece of the heart."

# Chapter Eight

I puzzled over Cyrene's bizarre suggestion for some time, until the sky started to flush with rosy light. Cyrene didn't reassure me that Gabriel would love me as much when the shard was gone as he did now, but I realized I valued her honest reply more than any platitudes. I rubbed the small scar on my chest where the shard had entered my body, and stared out at the streaks of red and gold as they lit the horizon, wondering what Gabriel was doing, content, at least, to know he missed me as much as I missed him.

I went downstairs a few hours later, tired from lack of sleep and too much introspection. I thought I was seeing things when Jim ambled toward me from the dining room.

"Heya, Mayling. You look like you were pulled through Abaddon backwards on a porcupine."

"Jim ... didn't you lose part of your fur?" I touched the side of its head that had been singed, then slid my fingers lower, to its chest, rubbing a large white spot. "And where did this come from? Is it paint? Dye?"

"Naw, I had Ash send me to Abaddon for a couple of minutes so I could get a new form, one with all the fur on it. You like?" The demon twisted around to examine itself. "The tail's not quite as fluffy, but this form has the white spot, which everyone knows is a babe magnet. Oh, and look! Three white toes! Kinda racy, huh?"

"Very handsome," I agreed. "I'm ... er ... sorry. I didn't realize the lack of fur was bothering you so much. I hope you didn't pester Aisling."

"Jealous?" it asked with a waggle of its eyebrows.

"Certainly not."

"Uh-huh. I can tell you're peeved I didn't have you send me to Abaddon, but you can rest easy, sweet cheeks—I had Aisling do it because she was up and trying to avoid the crazy lady, and besides, I wasn't sure you knew how to do it."

"Crazy lady? Oh, Drake's mother?"

Jim gave a shudder and looked over its shoulder. "She's in there now with Aisling. Drake is refereeing. I'm off for walkies with Suzanne. You wanna come? I'm prairie doggin' a bit, but I promise not to pinch a loaf right in front of you, if you do want to come."

"How very considerate. I think I'll pass just now, if you don't mind."

Suzanne, István's girlfriend, who acted as cook to Aisling and Drake's household, emerged from a back room with a leash and a handful of plastic bags.

"Walkings time," she said in a heavily accented voice. "You will come with us, May?"

"Not this morning, thanks. Jim, I'm sure Aisling already told you this, but in case she didn't—behave."

Jim rolled its eyes as it marched to the front door, Suzanne in tow. "Why does everyone think they have to tell me that? It's not like I ever *mis*behave. . . ."

Thankfully the door shut on the demon's complaining, although it opened again about two seconds later.

I took one look at the woman walking in, and felt a strange sense of relief. "Kaawa!"

"Wintiki!" Gabriel's mother, a tall, elegant figure in silver and black linen tunic and pants, rushed forward to hug me. She had skin the color of rich milk chocolate, shoulder-length hair that was pulled back into a bun, and a smile that warmed me to my toes. I felt enveloped in comfort, wrapped in a cocoon that whispered to me of the wind and the sky and the creatures that danced in and out of the Dreaming. Kaawa was a shaman, of the earth, but transcending mere mortality to become something more, something wholly unique.

"I'm so happy to see you," I said, hugging her for all I was worth, grateful that Gabriel had such a wonderful mother.

"You are well, little night bird?" she asked, holding me at arm's length, her gaze stripping away layers of my being to peer straight into my soul. "My Gabriel is making you happy?"

"Deliriously so," I said, pushing down the worry that seemed to be ever present.

She said nothing for a moment, simply cupping the side of my face with one hand while she continued to pierce through to my very core. "You are happy, yes, but there is a shadow on your heart. All is not well?"

"All is fine," I reassured her. "I'm just a bit stressed about the dragon shard."

She nodded, letting her hand drop. "It distresses you. Gabriel said you were worried it was taking over. We will see that it does not."

"Thank you. Have you met Aisling?"

Her eyes lit with interest as we turned toward the sitting room, her arm around my waist. "No, but I have heard much about her from Gabriel. At one time I thought . . . but that is unimportant."

I gritted my teeth for a moment at her train of

thought, then laughed out loud. She paused to cast me a questioning look.

"Jealousy is never pretty, but it can be funny sometimes," I said, then continued when she raised her eyebrows. "I know that at one time Gabriel thought seriously about challenging Drake for Aisling. I'm OK with that. Well, not OK, but I understand it."

"Because you know he would never have been happy with her?" she asked, her head tipped to the side as she watched me.

My smile grew. "More because I know Drake would never have let Gabriel have Aisling. And she would have made his life a living hell if Drake slipped up and let her go."

She laughed, squeezing my waist as I opened the door. "You are a wise wintiki."

If I had worried what the volatile Catalina would make of Gabriel's much more down-to-earth mother, I didn't after seeing the two women together. Catalina might treat Aisling with rudeness, more or less ignoring her, but she settled down comfortably enough with Kaawa to discuss common dragon acquaintances.

"Nora had a little issue she had to deal with— something about a kobold outbreak in Islington. But as soon as she's done cleaning that up, we'll put our heads together about your problem," Aisling said.

"I don't want to put you to any trouble," I said, glancing at her large stomach. "You probably don't feel like moving around much. Is there any word on when the baby might come?"

She sighed and patted her belly. "Bean—my midwife—said she could try inducing labor, but she didn't recommend it. Evidently, it's not unheard of for a baby of mixed parents to take a bit longer than normal. So I'm going to tough it out a few days more before we decide if it's time to force the latest green dragon to hatch."

"Hatch?" I looked at her in horror. "You don't mean—"

"No, no, no eggs!" she said, laughing. "Dragons are born in human form. And stop worrying about asking for help; I don't mind doing it at all. In fact—" She cast a swift glance across the room to where Kaawa and Catalina sat deep in conversation. "In fact, I'd be grateful for an excuse to do things other than listen to my mother-in-law tell me how inadequate I am, so your problem will be a welcome distraction."

"What problem is that?" Drake asked as he strolled over to hand his wife a bottle of water.

I sat silent, feeling guilty about involving Aisling when she must be focused on the approaching birth.

Drake looked from me to Aisling, his emerald eyes narrowing. "What problem?" he repeated, a bit more forcefully this time.

"It's nothing, sweetie, just a little . . . issue . . . May has run into. Nothing to get your knickers in a twist over."

Drake's gaze went wary. "You are not doing anything even remotely dangerous, *kincsem*."

"I wouldn't consider any such thing," she replied, smiling up at him. "Not so close to baby time, anyway. May simply has a little point regarding demon lords she'd like cleared up, and I know if Nora and I put our heads together, we can give her an answer."

The wary gaze slid to me, assessing me for potential hazards to his mate. I smiled at him, as well. "I just want a little information, and won't require Aisling to do anything at all other than think."

"See that you don't." He rejoined his mother and Kaawa after giving us both a warning look.

"Bossy," Aisling muttered fondly as he left. "Oh,

good, there's Nora now. We have a little issue for you to work on," she told the woman who entered the sitting room, Jim following her. Nora was, I knew, technically Aisling's mentor, but I suspected their relationship was more on par with partners than a teacher and student. Nora was in her early forties, black, with warm, dancing eyes behind red-rimmed glasses.

"What sort of an issue? Good morning, May. I understand you've come to visit Aisling for a bit."

"Just a few days until we can find a new house. Ours was demolished by a very angry dragon."

Jim snorted. "Understatement of the year, babe."

"Don't you have something to do?" I asked the demon.

"Did it, and I won't go into specifics because Ash'll tell me I'm disgusting," Jim said with a little Muttley snicker.

"You've been watching cartoons again, haven't you?" Aisling asked it.

It did the wheezing snicker again.

I gave Nora a brief recap of the events of the last few days, including my visit to Bael.

Her eyes grew wider and wider as I explained.

"He gave you Magoth's powers?" she asked in disbelief.

I nodded. "I don't want them, so the question is, what can I do to get him to take them back?"

She looked at Aisling. Aisling gave me a half smile. "You know Bael as well as I do, May. Probably better. Can you imagine making him do anything, much less take back something he forced on you against your will?"

"No." My shoulders slumped. "You're right, of course, but I was hoping one of you might have some sort of trick up your sleeve that I could use. I can't keep them. Not with the dragon shard—it's just too dangerous."

"Absolutely," Nora agreed.

"The only thing I can think of is to pass them on to someone else, someone you trust not to use them," Aisling said.

"The people I trust I wouldn't burden with the powers, and the ones I don't trust I'd never consider, so I'm kind of at a loss—"

The door slammed open, startling everyone in the room.

"Thought you could hide from me, eh?" Magoth shouted, hauling a green dragon in behind him. "Thought you could simply leave me to sizzle away in the basement while you ... while you ..." He came to a stop, and not because the dragon who answered the door to him finally managed to halt him. He stared at me. He squinted. He stood, hands on hips, his mouth hanging slightly open as he examined me as if he hadn't seen me before.

"I'm sorry," the green dragon apologized, casting a nervous glance at Drake. "He got past me before I could tell him that I'd ask the silver mate if she would see him."

"You've got dark powers," Magoth said finally, just a split second before realization struck him.

"Oh, god, no," I murmured, wanting to slip into the shadow world. I contented myself with slumping over and dropping my forehead to my hands.

"Hoo, boy, now it's gonna hit the fan," Jim said, sauntering over to me. "Man, Ash, I said 'it,' not the other word. Stop looking at me like that!"

"You have *my* powers!" Magoth bellowed, his fingers flexing as he stalked stiff-legged toward me. The dragon shard, riled up already, tried to push me toward him. "You treacherous little bitch! You thieving, conniving, despicable little two-timing backstabber." The words evidently struck him, for he paused for a moment be-

fore suddenly throwing himself at my feet, prying one of
my hands off my head and clutching it in order to press
chilled, wet kisses to it. "Fire and brimstone! You are the
most perfect woman I've ever met!"

"Oh, god," I said again, head still in my remaining
hand, squelching down hard on the shard. I would not
give in to it. I had fought it and won, and I would continue to fight it.

Jim smirked. "Oh yeah. Nothing turns on a demon
lord more than a touch of maleficence. Nicely done,
May."

"Oh god, oh god, oh god," I moaned into my hand.

"I knew one day you would admit that you wanted
me," Magoth said, still pressing slobbery kisses onto my
knuckles. "You've made me the happiest demon lord
on earth. Take me, my adorably evil one. Take me like a
two-bit gigolo! Ride me like a rented mule! Bitch slap
me as you've never bitch slapped before! Only with your
tail, because you know how much I love that."

"I believe that will be enough," Drake said, taking
charge of the situation.

Magoth glared over his shoulder at the wyvern. "Who
are you?"

"Drake Vireo, wyvern of the green dragons, and the
owner of this house. I am also a friend to Gabriel, and I
can assure you he would not appreciate you wiping your
lips all over his mate's hands."

Magoth got to his feet, still holding my hand, tossing
his head and leveling Drake a look that had intimidated
many a minion over the centuries. "She is *my* consort.
I have the right to put my lips wherever I like on her,
dragon."

"No, you don't," I said, finally managing to get my
hand free from his grip. I shoved him none too gently
aside. "You divorced me several weeks ago."

He donned a sultry pout. "I didn't mean it. I was

angry. Besides, it takes more to divorce a consort than simply saying you want to divorce her."

"Such as?" I asked.

"Death," Nora said.

Aisling nodded. "Banishment works, too, although that's trickier to pull off, since technically the banishee is still alive."

"There is also a repudiation ceremony," Nora continued as she eyed Magoth. He gave her a quick leer, then snatched up my hand again, rubbing my knuckles in a way that made my teeth grind. "But as that requires the sacrifices of fifteen virgin souls, it's not often done."

"Aisling did it with chickens one time," Jim piped up.

I stared at her in surprise.

"Bael didn't specify who the souls had to belong to," Aisling said with a nonchalant gesture. "I thought roast chickens were ideal because they were an answer to his demands, and dinner, all in one."

"It's a dessert topping! It's a floor wax!" Jim said. "It's the answer to all your demon lord problems!"

"No more *Saturday Night Live* reruns for you," Aisling told it firmly.

"So what you're saying is that I'm stuck with him?" I asked Nora.

"What is going on over here? Who is this dark and compelling man who wears the tight breeches?" Catalina demanded to know as she and Kaawa came over to join the fun. She eyed Magoth as if he were a piece of candy being offered to her.

He didn't so much as throw a glance her way.

"This is Magoth, my ... er ... for lack of a better word, boss," I said, introducing her. "Magoth, this lady is Drake's mother, doña Catalina de Elférez."

"I have no interest in other women now that you have shown your true colors to me, my dark and deadly one," Magoth murmured as he sucked my knuckles.

I tried to wrench my hand free. He just dug his fingers in harder, sending me a smoldering look.

"He smells like the demons," Catalina said, strolling around behind him to get a look at the rear view. "He has magnificent buttocks, though."

Magoth stopped sucking my knuckle to turn and look at her.

She ogled his pants for a moment. "*Very* tight breeches. I like tight breeches."

"Mother," Drake said, with a look on his face that spoke volumes.

"Do not mind him," Catalina said, her eyes half-shut as she gave Magoth a come-hither look. "He does not like to think of his mama having lovers. But I am different. You remind me a bit of my husband. Drake, does he not look like your accursed father?"

"No," Drake said adamantly at the same time Magoth pounced on a word I knew he would enjoy.

"Accursed?" he asked, giving Catalina a return ogle. "You have the unmistakable aura of one who truly understands the needs and desires that all demon lords feel. Tell me, my Spanish beauty, how do you feel about restraints with regards to lovemaking?"

"They are most necessary," she said with a little shrug. "How would you be able to torment your partner if he could stop you?"

Magoth dropped my hand and all but shimmied over to her, pressing his lips to her palm. "I like how you think, my exotic little olive. And nipple clamps? Your opinion on them?"

"Again, necessary," Catalina said. "Although I prefer piercings to clamps. Much more reliable when used for leashing purposes."

A little shudder of ecstasy shook Magoth as his tongue swept out over her palm. "You are a woman who knows her pleasures."

"Stop licking my mother!" Drake demanded, and looked like he was going to use bodily force to stop Magoth.

"Words I never thought I'd hear," Jim snickered.

"On the other hand, whips are overrated," Catalina volunteered. "A cat, however . . ."

Magoth trembled, his eyes closing for a moment. "One with hundreds of tiny little barbs?"

"Excellent for ensuring that you have your partner's full attention," she agreed.

"Dear heaven, what hath we wrought?" Aisling asked, gesturing to Drake, who assisted her to her feet. "Potty break. Be back in a minute. Or maybe longer if they're going to go into any more specifics. Jim, heel."

"What? Hey! I wanna watch and see if Magoth is gonna pork Drake's mom—"

The door closed on the demon's objections.

Kaawa, who had been standing watching the scene with a slight smile, met my gaze. "Perhaps now would be a good time for us to discuss what you will need to do to re-form the dragon heart."

"Absolutely," I said, with heartfelt appreciation at the suggestion. Anything that got me out of Magoth's way was going to have my full approval. "Drake, I hate to disturb you when you're busy scowling at Magoth, but is there a room we can use?"

"Mother!" Drake said a bit more forcefully, his green eyes glittering at Magoth, who, I'm sure it need not be said, totally ignored him. "You will remember your agreement—you may stay here so long as you do not upset Aisling."

"She's not even in the room," Catalina cooed, biting Magoth's ear.

"You know what I mean."

I tugged on Drake's sleeve until I had his attention, saying softly, "He can't hurt your mother, can he? I mean that since she's a wyvern's mate, she's immortal, correct?"

"Immortal, yes. Possessing good taste?" He turned back to glare at Magoth. "Clearly she's failed in this regard."

"Then if you don't mind, I'd appreciate it if you let them ... er ... for lack of a more circumspect phrase, go at it."

Drake looked at me in surprise. Kaawa hid a little chirrup of laughter behind her hand as she pretended to cough.

"It will keep him off my back while I learn what I need to do with the shards," I explained.

He didn't like it, but in the end, Aisling helped me persuade him that they couldn't do any harm to each other.

"Things are starting to get a bit tight around the seams, but I think we can squeeze you in," Aisling said to Kaawa as we slowly made our way upstairs. "There's one last room free, although it's not normally one I'd put a guest in, especially such a distinguished guest as Gabriel's mom."

*"Psht,"* Kaawa said, waving away the apology. "I spend most of my days out in the bush, so a soft bed and a roof over my head will be a luxury."

"There's the problem of Magoth, though," Aisling said, her forehead wrinkling. "I'm afraid we're fresh out of rooms. I suppose he could sleep on the sofa or something."

"He will not sleep here," Drake said decisively from behind her, giving her a little boost to make it up the last few steps. "I will not have a demon lord in the same house as you while you are in such a delicate state."

She spun around so quickly she whomped him with her belly. "I'm hardly delicate, Drake. I'm as big as a leviathan, and twice as ungainly."

"Three times, actually," Jim said, eyeing her. "You know, it's actually a wonder you can fit through a door with that thing. I wonder if you'll just keep growing until one day you explode."

"May I?" I asked Aisling as she stopped in front of a door.

"Please do."

"Do what?" Jim asked, its eyes suspicious. "Ow! Ow, ow, ow! Someone call the demon-abuse hotline! I'm being abducted by a sadistic doppelganger!"

I grabbed Jim by one fuzzy black ear and hauled it upstairs with me to my room. There I lectured it again about inappropriate comments to Aisling.

"No one around here can take a joke anymore," it grumbled when I was done. "I didn't mean she was really going to explode."

"Perhaps not, but she's more worried than she lets on about the baby taking its time, so you just lighten up with the explosive comments," I said, patting it on the head. Jim was fond of Aisling, I knew, and wouldn't really want to hurt her, but obviously had not been as observant as it might have been. "Go watch some movies or something, but watch the cracks to Aisling about the baby."

"Aw, do I have to? I want to hear how to re-form the dragon heart," it said as I ushered Kaawa into a small upstairs sitting room that Drake had told us we could use. It was dark and slightly musty-smelling, as if it hadn't been occupied much.

"Why on earth would you want to do that?" I asked, opening the curtains.

Jim shrugged. "You never know when something like that might come in handy."

I glanced at Kaawa.

"I don't mind if the demon stays," she said, watching Jim closely. "It appears to be one of the rare sixth-class demons, and thus should not pose a hazard to you."

"It's not me I'm worried about," I said, wondering what sorts of powers a demon in possession of the dragon heart would be able to wield. The thought left me a bit sick to my stomach, so I moved on.

The following two hours were spent learning the steps of the ceremony to decant the shard, most of which was rote memorization of a couple of incantations. The language the incantations were spoken in was Zilant, a Slavic language that all dragons learned early on, and that, until recent centuries, had been the common language between the septs. I've never been much of a linguist, and it took me several tries, aided by copious notes, before I felt comfortable conducting the invocation that would separate the shard from my body, and allow it to re-form the dragon heart.

"Where did you learn all this?" I asked as I closed the notebook in which I'd been making notes. "Gabriel said you were very learned in dragon lore, but I'm surprised you know so much about something so outside of your normal interests."

She smiled, and continued to rub Jim's belly as she had been doing for the last half hour. The demon was on its back, legs kicking gently in the air, soft little half moans, half snores of pleasure coming from its furry black lips as it slept. "You know of Ysolde de Bouchier."

I nodded. "You've mentioned her before. She left some notebooks behind about her experiences with the shard after she became a phylactery, right?"

"That is correct."

"That's reassuring. If the invocation worked for Ysolde, it's a sure thing to work for me. Despite the interesting experience of turning into a dragon, there's nothing I want more than to get rid of the shard."

Her eyes widened slightly. "I did not mean to imply that the invocation was foolproof, wintiki. There is still a very large element of the unknown to the process of re-forming the heart. Much of what I've told you is speculation."

"But you had Ysolde's notebooks," I said, suddenly worried. I had assumed all along that I would be able to get rid of the shard. But what if I couldn't? What if I was stuck with it? Forever?

My stomach dropped at the thought.

"Yes, but they did not provide a detailed step-by-step guide to ridding oneself of a dragon shard. They merely gave information about what Ysolde herself did, and what sorts of things could happen should one try to re-form the heart, or use the shards by themselves."

My heart sank to join my stomach. "So you don't have any idea if the ceremony is going to work?"

She shook her head, sympathy rich in her eyes and face. "I wish there was a foolproof method, but we are talking about the dragon heart. It is not controlled, never controlled. If it wishes you to, it will allow you to use it, but never against its wishes."

"You speak of it as if it's alive," I said, gently touching the mark on my chest where the shard had entered my body.

She smiled. "It has powers, little night bird. It may not be alive in the sense that you are alive, but it is sentient. It will not allow you to use it if it does not approve of you, or the use to which you wish to put it."

"Well, great. Here I am trying to get rid of this shard, and it'll probably go tell the rest of them what a horrible person I am, and they'll all refuse to re-form."

She laughed and patted my hand as she stood up, much to Jim's unhappiness. "It is not *that* you have to worry about."

"Oh really?" I caught something in her tone that made me uneasy. "Is there something else I should be worrying about?"

She hesitated a second before saying no.

"Kaawa," I said, rising as she reached for the door.

She stopped, her shoulders slumping for a moment

before she turned back to face me with a perfectly innocent expression. "Yes, wintiki?"

"I appreciate you trying to protect me, but I assure you I can take care of myself. Gabriel knows that. That's why he's not fussing around while I take care of this. So if there's a danger involved—other than the obvious one of being vulnerable while the decanting and re-forming processes are going on—I'd really appreciate you telling me what it is, so I can be ready for it."

Her hesitation and concern were almost palpable, making me worry anew.

"I would not for the world insult you, May, and I would never hide something that you could use to protect yourself."

"But?" I asked, waiting for her to finish.

"But you possess many qualities of humans, and not so many of dragons." She looked away, obviously not wanting to meet my gaze.

I went over everything she had told me about the shards, everything that Ysolde de Bouchier had done ... and enlightenment dawned.

"Kaawa?"

She held on to the door as if she wanted to escape. "Yes, child?"

"Did Ysolde disappear immediately after she re-formed the dragon heart, or did she vanish when Baltic died?"

Her dark eyes, rich as mahogany, and filled now with sadness, studied mine. "We don't know. It's ... it was a confusing time, you must understand. Three things apparently happened at the same time: the black dragon heir killed his wyvern, Ysolde re-formed the heart and sharded it into their phylacteries, and the silver dragon wyvern disappeared."

A few seconds of digging around in my memory pulled up a name. "Constantine Norka? Wasn't he also supposed to be mated to Ysolde?"

She was silent a few moments, her fingers absently rubbing on the edge of the door. "No one knows for certain what happened. Until now, it was thought all were dead, but with Baltic having returned, perhaps he could clear it up and tell us what exactly did transpire."

I almost snorted at the thought of Baltic doing anything but spouting mysterious, ambiguous comments. "I'm not going to hold my breath waiting for him to explain. So basically, the theory is that she was either Baltic's mate or Constantine's, and when they died, she died, too? Or was it the dragon heart that did her in?"

"We don't know," she said, looking even sadder. "Her diaries don't say."

I swallowed back my fear. "You're a shaman, Kaawa. You see things that most people can't even imagine exist. You can look into the shadows, look past time and space. What do *you* think happened?"

Her fingers tightened on the door. "That is not a wise question to ask, wintiki."

"Unwise because you don't wish to answer it, or because I won't like what you have to say?"

"Perhaps both."

I looked at my hands for a moment, absorbing what she hadn't said. "You think the dragon heart killed Ysolde."

"No."

I glanced up.

"I think it used her up," she said. "I think—I have no proof, mind you; this is all simply speculation—but I think that Constantine Norka tried to save her, and was destroyed along with her."

"Would the dragon heart do that to dragons?" I asked, sick at the thought of risking Gabriel. I knew without the slightest doubt in my soul that he would sacrifice himself to save me.

"It has the power to destroy the entire weyr," she said wearily. "Perhaps even the mortal world."

*"Agathos daimon,"* I swore under my breath. I had always assumed that the dragon heart was a benign thing, a relic of the first dragon that represented everything dragonkin were and would be, something that encompassed the best parts of all the dragons. But what if it was a harbinger of the power dragons tapped into rather than a celebration of their abilities? What if it was, in fact, a curse, not a boon?

Now I understood why Kaawa had warned me repeatedly of its power.

"Do not look so grim, child. Ysolde de Bouchier's path is not yours," Kaawa said quietly.

"I don't know what's going to stop me from ending up like her," I said, giving in to a moment of despair.

She came back into the room and kissed the top of my head before returning to the door. "Ysolde did not have what you have."

"You?" I asked, grateful for her wisdom and insight, even if it did give me moments of terror.

"My son." Her eyes glittered with humor for a moment. "His father trained him to be a warrior, a strong wyvern and protector of all silver dragons, but he learned much from me, too. Gabriel will not allow anything to happen to his miracle."

I smiled at the word, a warm, comfortable feeling washing over me at her words. Perhaps she was right. Perhaps Gabriel and I together could get the better of the dragon heart. Ysolde had been alone, torn between two warring wyverns, but I had Gabriel's strength to see me through anything.

I was about to say just that when Kaawa suddenly held up her hand, her expression abstracted. "Listen. Do you hear it?"

I stilled for a moment, then sighed. "It's my twin. But I have no idea why she's yelling, unless . . . oh, merciful spirits, tell me he didn't show up, too."

# Chapter Nine

Kaawa stepped aside with nimble awareness as I dashed past her and down the stairs. I stopped just short of plowing into Kostya as he stood, legs braced apart, arms crossed over his chest, his face tight with anger as Cyrene harangued him.

"... and I don't care if he is your brother—I was here first, and that means you have to find somewhere else to stay."

I stepped aside to admire her form for a moment. Her eyes were lit with fury, her hands waving wildly as she threw accusations at Kostya.

"You followed me here! Admit it—you followed me here so you could be with me without apologizing."

Kostya's voice came out a growl. "I didn't follow you here. I came to my brother's house—my *brother's* house—because I had no choice, you insane naiad, not because I was following you!"

"Well, you can just think twice about that, Konstantin Fekete," Cyrene said, clearly on a roll and not about to stop for anything like a breath or conversational give-

and-take, "because I said I was through with you, and so I am! It's over, got that? Over!"

"I'm not here because I want to see you again!" Kostya's grip on his temper, never very strong, snapped. He leaned forward and bellowed into Cyrene's face, "In fact, if I never saw you again, I'd die a happy dragon!"

"You can't die, you odious, fire-breathing beast," Cyrene yelled back. "More's the pity! If I had my way, I'd drown you in a—"

"I think that's about enough, Cy," I interrupted, taking her arm and pulling her back a few feet. "Whatever your relationship issues are, Kostya is right in that this is Drake's house."

"But—but—" she sputtered.

"And Drake has very kindly allowed us all to stay here, a fact I'd appreciate you to remember."

She sputtered a bit more, but contented herself with looking daggers at Kostya when I asked, "What did you mean you didn't have a choice? I thought you had a house in London?"

"He does," Cyrene said, looking down her nose at him. "It's not very nice, though."

"Cy," I said, giving her a warning look.

She sniffed and feigned interest in a picture on the wall.

"My house, my *perfectly nice house* with an expensive security system that was installed after my lair was repeatedly burgled—" Kostya shot me a meaningful look, pausing with dramatic grace for a few seconds. "My charming and well-furnished house was destroyed sometime during the night. When I returned to it from the airport, I found nothing but the scorched remains of what was once a desirable residence, miles of crime-scene tape, and several extremely thorough arson investigators who interviewed me extensively for the last five hours. That, my annoying little water sprite, is why I am here rather than where I would much rather be."

Cyrene stiffened at the water sprite comment, but a warning pressure on her arm reminded her of her party manners and she harrumphed her way over to a chair in the corner, all the while giving her ex-boyfriend a look that would probably have killed a mortal.

"Your house burned down? What—oh, I'm sorry. Kostya, do you know Kaawa, Gabriel's mother?"

Kostya stiffened for a moment, then swung around to flash an overly bright smile at Kaawa. He bowed, saying, "I have not had that pleasure, although I have met her mate on more than one occasion."

Kaawa had been standing at the stairs watching the scene, joined by Jim, who evidently had been woken by the noise. She came into the room now, acknowledging Kostya's bow, her eyes bright on him for a few moments before she said, "Yes, I remember. You almost killed him twice."

"Awkward," Jim said, snuffling Kostya's shoes before plopping its big butt down on my left foot. "Heya, Kostya. You have fun in Paris?"

"He wasn't in Paris, nosy demon," I said, shoving Jim off my foot. My toes had gone to sleep. "He was in Latvia with us, remember?"

"Yuh-huh. But you can't tell me that he hasn't been in Paris in the last twelve hours, because there's no place other than the City of Lights that leaves such a pungent scent on shoes."

Kaawa and I both looked at Kostya, who was suddenly intently interested in picking a piece of fluff from his sleeve.

"Did you take a flight that went through Paris?" I asked, not sure why it mattered.

"You don't get it, May," Jim said before Kostya could

answer. "He's been in Paris. In the *city*, not in the airport. Out walkin' in the . . ." He snuffled Kostya's nearest shoe again. "Smells like the Fourteenth Arrondissement."

"I don't believe there's a law against going into Paris," Kostya said dryly.

"No, of course not," I agreed. "Although you gave the impression that you'd returned to England straight from Latvia. Speaking of which, how is your lair?"

His eyes narrowed on me. "Why do you ask?"

"If your house burned, I expect your lair was endangered. Unless it was deep underground, and heavily protected from everything short of planetwide destruction, like Gabriel's is."

His nostrils flared. "Gabriel has a lair in London? I thought that was in New Zealand."

Dammit. Maybe I wasn't supposed to let it be known that Gabriel had a new lair. Still, there was nothing Kostya could do about it; the lair was well protected, even with the remains of a destroyed house on top of it. "He had a new one built to house the shards while we were assembling them."

"Interesting," he said, turning away as Drake emerged from belowstairs.

"You didn't answer my question," I pointed out.

"I'm aware of that." He strolled over to greet his brother, dismissing us.

"Just as if we were unimportant gnats," Cyrene called from her corner exile, her eyes shooting evil looks at his back. "How in the name of Neptune am I supposed to stay in the same house with *him*?"

"What's so important about Paris?" I mused aloud, wondering if Kostya avoided my question about the state of his lair simply because dragons hated to answer questions asked of them, or if he had an ulterior motive to not address the issue. "Cy, does Kostya have a house there?"

"I wouldn't know," she said, sniffing irritatedly as she continued to glare at Kostya. Her voice rose noticeably. "I have washed out of my brain any and all facts about such a detestable, loathsome, two-faced, hypocritical, self-serving, traitorous—"

"I think you made your point," I said.

"You forgot slimy, disreputable, and untrustworthy," Jim told Cyrene.

"—slimy, disreputable, and untrustworthy dragon!" she finished in a yell.

Kostya's back stiffened.

"I'm going swimming!" she added, stomping on the floor as she leaped to her feet and stormed toward the stairs to the basement.

"Don't drown," Kostya said in a voice so sweet it could choke a moose.

She stopped long enough to blast him with a glare. "Oh, blow it out your . . . your . . . your fire hole, dragon!"

"Gotta give her five out of five for style," Jim said, watching as she raced downstairs.

"She's very interesting, your twin," Kaawa said in a somewhat thoughtful voice. "Not at all like you."

"She gave up her common sense to create me. That explains a lot about her. And she's really a very lovely person once you get to know her," I said, driven by loyalty to defend my sometimes annoying twin. "She's just a bit emotional right now, but once she settles down again, you'll see that we're not too horribly dissimilar."

Kaawa didn't reply to that statement. She simply murmured something about calling some acquaintances, and disappeared up the stairs toward her room.

"Jim, does Kostya have a house in Paris?" I asked, figuring perhaps the demon would know.

"Not that I've ever heard of," Jim said, snuffling the floor where Kostya had stood. "He stays at Drake's house when he's there."

"So then what did Kostya find so irresistible in Paris that he's had to hide his visit there?" I was really thinking out loud, not expecting an answer, but to my surprise, Jim gave me one. Of a sort.

"You're not asking the right question," it said.

I glanced over to where Drake and Kostya stood in quiet conversation. Drake nodded at something his brother said; then the two of them parted, Drake going downstairs while Kostya headed upstairs. I waited until they were out of sight before I turned back to the demon. "You don't strike me as the sort of demon who sticks too tightly to the rules."

Jim shrugged, an amused glint in its eyes. "I'm sixth-class, remember?"

"Fallen angel, I know. You weren't born to Abaddon, and thus, you are the weakest of all the demonic beings."

"We prefer 'benign' rather than 'weak,'" it said with a sniff.

"Sorry, benign. All right, then, since you want to stick to the rules that say a demon can't offer information unless directly asked, let's play a game of twenty questions."

It waggled its eyebrows. "How about the strip version? If you ask the wrong question, you have to take off a piece of clothing."

My knife slid out of the ankle holster with the faintest of honed-steel whispers.

"Regular version is fine with me," it said quickly, backing away.

I smiled and tucked the knife away. "Let's start with, what dragons live in Paris?"

"You're kidding, right? 'Cause there has to be at least a hundred of them."

"All right, let's narrow it down." I thought a moment. "What dragons do you know who live in Paris?"

"Who do I know personally?" it asked, scrunching up its face.

"Who you know who have a home in Paris."

"Well, there's Drake."

"Other than Drake."

Jim looked thoughtful. "Green dragons or other septs?"

"Any dragons."

"Full-blooded dragons, or halvesies, too?"

I closed my eyes for a moment, gripping my patience. "Any dragon."

"That's a lot of dragons," it pointed out.

"All right. Let's go with dragons who Kostya would know."

"Hmm." Jim looked thoughtful. "Living or dead?"

"Jim!" I growled, the dragon shard begging to take control.

"I'm just trying to pinpoint what it is you want to know," it said with an injured sniff.

I took several deep breaths. "I want to know what dragons live in Paris who Kostya might know. Living dragons, of any sept, any heritage, who are not Drake."

"You know, you're turning kinda red. Maybe you should have your blood pressure checked—"

Its words were choked off when I let loose the shard, shifted into dragon form, and wrapped my tail around the demon's middle, hoisting it high.

"Fiat lives there!" The words tumbled out of the demon's mouth. "He has a house there."

"Where?"

"How am I supposed—"

I hung it upside down.

"Left Bank, Left Bank! Ack! All the blood is rushing to my head! I'm gonna black out!"

"Where exactly on the Left Bank?"

"Rue Delambre, near the Rosebud Bar, where Orson

Welles used to hang out. Can you let me down now? I'm seeing spots."

"Which arrondissement?"

"Fourteen! Everything is going black...."

I shifted out of dragon form, which meant I had no tail to hold Jim. The demon fell a few feet to the marble floor with a loud *whump*.

It lifted its head up and glared at me. "You could have put me down first!"

I smiled and dusted it off as it got to its feet. "And you could have answered my question five minutes ago. So Kostya was visiting Fiat, hmm?"

"Not necessarily." Jim sat and licked a few spots of fur that had been rumpled. "I just said Fiat had a house there."

"You think Bastian has taken it over?"

It shrugged. "Dunno. I think I bit my tongue when you dropped me. Is it bleeding?" It stuck its tongue out at me.

"No," I said, still trying to figure out why Kostya would want to keep a visit to Fiat secret. "I wonder if it has anything to do with the *sárkány* tomorrow?"

"You got me, sister," Jim said.

"Stop calling me that. I am *not* your sister." I glanced at the clock.

"If I didn't know better, I'd say you were miffed about something," Jim said, its head tipped to the side as it watched me. "You've got that pissy look that Aisling gets sometimes, and fabulous as I am, I know it can't have anything to do with me. What's up?"

"Gabriel," I said absently. The demon started to leer, but I quelled it with a slight twitch of my fingers toward my knife. "And you can just refrain from making the obscene comment I know you were about to make. I was referring to the fact that Gabriel is uppermost on my mind at the moment. He should have called by now."

"You jealous?" Jim asked, still watching me closely. "You think he's gettin' it on with some other dragon? You think he and Tipene are out cruisin' for babes while you're stuck here learning how to make an attractive and nutritional meat loaf out of a bit of hamburger and a couple of dragon shards?"

"Of course I'm not jealous," I said quickly, hoping the demon would take warning from my frown. "I trust Gabriel implicitly."

The corner of Jim's furry mouth twitched upward.

"There is nothing to be jealous of," I insisted. "He trusts me just as I trust him. There's no way he would go out cruising for anyone other than Fiat. And no, I don't mean he's bisexual."

Jim, who had been about to comment, snapped its teeth shut with a grumble.

"Gabriel is an honorable man," I pointed out. "He would never betray me in that fashion."

"He probably can't help it. Babe magnets like him usually have to beat the chicks off them with big sticks. I know—I've seen it with Drake. Aisling is always scorching the hair of some woman or other who goggles a bit too much at Drake."

"Oh, stop it. Gabriel is handsome, but women don't fling themselves at him. And I am not Aisling."

It shrugged. "Denial is a river in Egypt."

"And just what's that supposed to mean?" I asked, my fingers twitching slightly.

Jim whistled a tuneless little whistle for a few seconds. "Just that I've seen the way mortal women look at him—Gabe's definitely a babe magnet. If he was *my* dragon, I'd sure as shooting never let him go off on his own where he could be swarmed by great big herds of lust-crazed women."

"Great big herds of women," I snorted, seeing through the demon's feeble attempts to rile me. That is, I saw through them until the dragon shard reminded me of just how handsome Gabriel was. No, handsome wasn't the word—his mercurial eyes set against the warm, latte-colored skin were enough to make my breath catch in my throat. Add in dimples that could melt knees at fifty paces, an infectious laugh, and a body that positively screamed controlled power and grace. But even that wasn't what bound me to him—it was his essence, his sense of self, that indescribable dragon being that lit up his gorgeous body, and ensnared my heart. If it could do that to me, what chance did mortal women have against it?

*My* mate, the dragon shard snarled, and for a moment, I seriously contemplated flying out to Gabriel in order to set fire to every woman who was near him.

"May? You OK? Your eyes just went all funny, like Drake's when he gets what Aisling calls dragonny."

At the sound of Jim's voice, sanity managed to bully its way through the intense jealousy. I blinked a couple of times and realized the pain in my palms was due to scarlet claws digging into the tender flesh. I de-dragoned my hands, and rubbed the red marks. "I'm fine. Just . . . thinking. You haven't actually seen any women throw themselves at Gabriel, have you?"

"Oh, no, you're not jealous at all," it answered, grinning.

"You have?" Fury roared through me. "Who?"

"Who what?" Cyrene asked as she came up the stairs.

"Nothing." I glared at the demon for a moment before turning to her. "I thought you were going swimming."

"I was, but Aisling wanted to use the pool. The midwife is here, and thought that if she were to float around in the water a bit, it might help things along." She sighed. "And that beast is down there with her and Drake. Who were you talking about?"

"No one," I said quickly, but not quickly enough.

"She's got her panties in a bunch because Gabe is out on his own."

"I am not in the least bit bunched," I told it grimly. "I just got done telling you that I trust Gabriel."

"Yes, but it's not him you have to worry about," Cyrene said, to my gut-wrenching dismay.

"I am *not* jealous," I repeated.

"I'm not saying you are, or even that you should be. Gabriel is devoted to you. Anyone can see that."

"I'm glad you agree," I said, glad the matter was closed. I told the dragon shard to go back to sleep, intent on regaining control over my errant emotions. I had a list of things I wanted to do before Gabriel returned, and now was as good a time as any to get started on them.

"Mind you, I'm not saying that other women are going to respect that," she continued thoughtfully. "He's a handsome man, a very handsome man. With those eyes and those dimples and that lovely, lovely chest—"

"I will thank you to stop ogling my mate's chest," I said, grinding my teeth just a smidgen.

"Well, you can stop me from doing that, but you can't stop the rest of the world, Mayling. And trust me, other women have noticed his chest, too."

My mouth dropped open a tiny bit. "Do you guys have some sort of an arrangement to suddenly try to drive me into an insane fit of jealousy over Gabriel?"

"Of course not. Don't be silly." Cyrene made a dismissive gesture. "I'm just trying to point out that although you may trust him not to willingly betray you, the mortal women of the world may not give him that option." She thought for a moment. "And some of the immortal women, too."

"On the contrary, I will be most faithful to my sweet May once she gives herself to me," Magoth said, strolling out of the sitting room. He paused for a few seconds before admitting, "Perhaps 'faithful' isn't the best word. Shall we say 'devoted,' instead, given all the mortal and immortal world that the delectable Cyrene so wisely realizes finds me completely irresistible?"

"We weren't talking about you," Cy said with a bit of a frown that Magoth completely missed because he was too busy glaring at Jim.

"Why do you always have that demon with you?" he asked me. "You are a demon lord's consort, not a lord itself. It is unfitting that you should be attended by a sixth-class demon. If you wish to have a companion, you may have one of my wrath demons."

"Oh, yeah, like Drake's going to allow a wrathy in his house," Jim drawled.

"I'm taking care of Jim while its master is busy, which you very well know, since I explained it to you earlier. Really, Magoth, is it too much trouble for you to pay attention to me when I talk to you?"

"Yes," he said blithely, giving Jim one last glare before turning to me. "I prefer actions to words. Let us go have sex and I assure you I will hang on to your every gesture."

"That's it. I have no more patience left," I said simply, and grabbed my purse. "I'm going home—what remains of it—per the request of the police and fire investigators. Hopefully, some of our things will have survived the blast."

"I'll come with you," Cyrene said quickly, snatching up her coat.

"I think it would probably be better if I did this alone."

"Yeah," Jim told her. "You'll just see the puddles left by the firemen and want to splash around in them."

"You're not coming, either," I told the demon.

"Why not?" It opened its eyes really wide. "I'll be good! Promise!"

"You don't know the meaning of the word 'good,'" I said acidly.

It stuck out its lower lip. "No, but I can pretend."

"Come on, it'll be fun. Just the three of us," Cy said persuasively. She took my hesitation for another denial, and added a plaintive, "I really don't want to have to be here by myself with that rat bastard."

"Surely you can come up with some better insults for me than 'rat bastard'?" Magoth asked, idly sorting through a stack of mail that sat on a small hall table. He held one up to the light. "You used to be quite inventive."

"Not every conversation revolves around you," Cyrene said, making indignant little noises. "I was referring to my boyfriend. Ex-boyfriend. One I really don't want to be alone with."

Magoth opened a letter and scanned the contents. I debated chastising him for that, but figured any truly important mail would have been given to Drake or Aisling already.

"The house is about ready to explode with people," I told Cyrene, feeling guilty nonetheless. "You're hardly alone."

"You know what I mean. Please, Mayling."

"Me love you long time. You take me. Please with dog hair on top," Jim begged.

"Squalid little matters." Magoth tossed the letter onto the table and looked over to where I stood, hesitating. "Where are we going?"

"*We* are going nowhere. I am going to see the police. I suppose if you two wish to come, you can, but, Jim, you have to be silent around mortals," I told Jim as I opened the door and stepped out into a gloomy drizzle. "Cyrene, you will please remember that you are a guest of Drake, and not refer to his brother as a bastard."

She harrumphed.

"Let me think. . . . There is a new cockfighting arena that I have been asked to open, but that is not until this evening," Magoth said with a glance at his watch. "And my appointment to get a Brazilian wax is early afternoon. There is a collection of circus-freak memorabilia up for private auction that I wish to peruse—so many good memories there—but I can put that off, since the owner, a deliciously wicked poltergeist, wishes me to show her how to design a truly effective iron maiden. Yes, I will be able to accompany you now, wife, although if you wish to participate in sex afterward, we will have to hurry. I refuse to be rushed when it comes to pleasures of the flesh."

I stared at Magoth. "You're just one long, unending pain in the butt, aren't you?"

A leer touched his lips. "I would be happy to do so, although I had no idea your taste ran to that."

I closed my eyes for a second, battling both irritation and the dragon shard, which had been trying to force me into contact with Magoth. I had no idea why the shard was suddenly seeking power from whatever source it could find, but determination filled me. I would not yield to it. "I'm leaving now. And stop calling me wife."

I marched down the stairs, not caring who followed and who stayed.

"I thought cockfights were illegal?" Cyrene's voice drifted to my ears as I stopped at a corner for a traffic light.

"Mortals are so uptight about things like that," Magoth answered her. I was aware he stopped directly behind me, since the air near my spine cooled a good ten degrees. "But since they have outlawed human battles to the death, one must take one's pleasures where one can."

"I take it back what I said about you when you couldn't hear me," Jim said softly, brushing my hand as it cast a glance backwards toward Magoth. "You're not nearly as bad as a real demon lord."

The ride to the Metropolitan Police station was long and filled with my warning all three members of my little troupe to behave themselves.

"No talking in front of anyone mortal," I told Jim, one eye on the taxi driver. He had a small portable radio blaring out Middle Eastern music, so I doubted he'd hear.

Jim sighed and adopted a martyred look. "Just once I'd like to go somewhere without someone telling me to shut my yap."

"That day will never come. And you ..." I pushed Magoth's hand off my thigh and fixed him with a stern, unyielding look. "... you remember what Gabriel said he'd do if you tried to touch me again."

I wanted badly to lay down the law to Magoth, but knew it would do no good. He was still technically my employer, and although I might have his powers, he was more than aware that I'd never use them.

He gave me a coy look, lolling back on the seat of the taxi, taking up far more than his fair share of the seat. "And what will you do if I am good, sweet one? Will you reward me?"

"Reward you how?" I asked cautiously.

His eyelids dropped to half-mast. The look he gave me would have melted a lesser woman, and as it was, I had a hard time struggling with the shard to keep my hands in my lap. "I think some playtime will be in order. Say tonight? Ten o'clock? Your room? Bring your dragon scales."

"Ew," Jim said, shuddering. "That's just so wrong. A demon lord and a dragon."

"Don't worry, it's not going to happen," I told it. "Magoth will behave himself."

He examined a fingernail and said in a deceptively bland voice, "You have no way of ensuring I do so. I understand the mortal police take very seriously accusations of arson."

"You wouldn't dare," I said, fury shoving aside the irritation that was my normal response to him.

"No?" He raised his eyebrows and gave a long cool look. "Perhaps not. But perhaps you should reconsider my invitation for tonight. Acceptance of such is likely to satisfy me for a while."

I ground my teeth, annoyed at having to deal with him, but there was no way short of locking him up somewhere that I could stop him. "Fine, you want to come to my room tonight at ten so I can tail smack you around? You got it. Just bring a jumbo bottle of aspirin, because I plan on knocking you out cold for hours."

He shivered in delight, suddenly lunging forward to grab me, his fingers digging into my arms as he kissed me. The dragon shard roared to life, making me part my lips under the onslaught of his mouth and tongue, but even as it delighted in the contact, my heart shuddered and shrank away. The mouth moving on mine wasn't warm and spicy. The tongue moving in a sinuous dance didn't stir me. And the black eyes that burned down into mine held no heat. I gathered up my strength and heaved, shoving Magoth backwards.

"Gabriel will kill you for that," I said, wiping my mouth.

Magoth smiled a long, slow smile. "He can try."

# Chapter Ten

Gabriel called while I sat in the office of the arson-investigation unit.

"I can't really talk right now," I said, smiling brightly across the desk at a middle-aged, balding man as he shuffled through some paperwork. "Detective Inspector Flores is explaining to Magoth and me the results of their investigation thus far."

Gabriel swore. "What is *he* doing there?"

I pulled my hand back from where Magoth had been caressing it. "Oh, you know Magoth. Whither does he wander, and all that."

"My wife must be speaking with her lover," Magoth told the police inspector, who shot me a startled look.

"Erm . . . is she?" he said.

I smiled again, trying not to strangle Magoth on the spot. "Ignore him," I told the inspector. "He found a few mushrooms in the park this morning and ate them. We're hoping his hallucinations fade soon."

Gabriel muttered a few choice words under his breath

that I wholeheartedly agreed with. "Can you not get rid of him? Is he making things difficult for you?"

"No, and of course, but I'm coping. Magoth was most interested to hear, as was I, that it was a faulty gas line that blew up the house, and wasn't arson at all, as we thought."

"Most interested," Magoth said, grabbing my chair and hauling it closer to him so he could drape an arm over my shoulders. "My darling one, sit closer to me. I cherish the nearness of your lush, ripe body."

The inspector pursed his lips and looked from Magoth to me, speculation rife in his eyes.

"Ah, so it was a faulty gas line?" Gabriel asked, his voice amused for a moment. Clearly he hadn't heard Magoth in the background. "I am relieved to hear it was that, and not something more worrisome, such as a murderous dragon bent on our destruction."

"Yes, I thought you'd be happy to hear that."

"Our relationship is complicated," Magoth told the inspector in a confidential tone, his fingers trailing down the back of my neck. I gritted my teeth against the touch, not wanting to protest lest Gabriel hear. "She has one lover; I have thousands. But we share a love of the same things: violent foreplay, the torture of minions, threatening to disembowel those who cross us—and it's that sort of bond that truly makes a relationship last, isn't it?"

"Sign there? Certainly." Hastily, I scribbled out a signature on a release that would relieve the Metropolitan Police from any responsibility for our welfare should we insist on examining the remains of the house. At that point, I would do anything to escape from the inspector's office.

"Are the mortal police giving you much trouble?" Gabriel asked.

"Not much. I should be through here in a few minutes."

"That's not to say that my sweet May and I obtain sexual fulfillment from the same sorts of things. Not at all. Nor would I want us to—similar sexual proclivities are not something you should seek in a sexual partner," Magoth continued to enlighten the by-now-wild-eyed policeman. "How are you going to truly enjoy tying down your partner to a Catherine wheel and tormenting her if you know she secretly enjoys it? You may take my word that such a thing takes all the fun out of the experience."

"How are things going for you? Have you found what you were looking for?" I asked Gabriel, hoping he wouldn't hear the desperate note in my voice as I glared at Magoth.

"Not exactly."

The police inspector stared openmouthed at Magoth. "You're a wack job, you know that?"

"I am a connoisseur of sex," Magoth said simply with a nonchalant little shrug. "It is more or less the same thing."

I smiled another tooth-laden smile at the policeman, and swiveled slightly in my chair as he gave Magoth one last long look before entering some information into his computer. "How do you mean? You didn't find him?"

"Is Kostya there, too?"

I frowned at the question. Although Gabriel sometimes exhibited the dragon trait of answering a question with a question, he was normally forthcoming with information when I asked. "Not with us, if that's what you mean, but yes, he's back from Latvia. He ... er ... had a little accident with his house, too."

To my surprise Gabriel wasn't the slightest bit interested in that. "Stay away from him, little bird."

"That's going to be a bit on the difficult side, since he's staying in the same house as us," I said cautiously.

"Kostya is at Drake's house?" Gabriel's voice was sharp with irritation. "Why is he there?"

I covered my cell phone's mouthpiece for a moment, speaking to the detective. "I'm sorry. My ma—um—partner is having a little family issue. I really need to take this call. I won't be long."

"No doubt they wish to indulge in phone sex," Magoth said, picking up a file from the inspector's desk and flipping through it. "They are always having sex."

The inspector snatched the file away from Magoth, saying, as I got to my feet, "We will need a statement from Mr. Tauhou, as well."

I nodded and wound my way through a dozen or so other desks to the hallway.

"My love to the beast master," Magoth called after me.

I growled to myself as I hurried out of the office and down a hallway to a distant stairwell. Luckily, it was empty. "Sorry, Gabriel. I was in too public a place to talk. What in the name of midnight is going on? What do you mean, you didn't exactly find Fiat? And why should we stay away from Kostya? Does this have something to do with his trip to Paris?"

Gabriel's voice, when he finally spoke, was guarded and tense. "Did he tell you he went to Paris?"

"No. As a matter of fact, he wouldn't answer me when I asked him that, but Jim said he'd been there. What's happened?"

"We missed Fiat by what must have been minutes, but a calling card was left for us."

Fear poked irrationally at my gut. The silver dragons had no bone to pick with Fiat, and yet I had a premonition that boded ill. I cleared my throat a couple of times before I could ask, "What sort of calling card?"

Silence answered me for the count of eight. "There are sixty-eight dead blue dragons in France."

*"Agathos daimon,"* I whispered, horror creeping up my flesh. "He killed his own sept members?"

"No. The dragons killed were those who followed Bastian, not Fiat."

"He's insane," I said, my mind not able to get past the idea of such a horrible slaughter.

"There is no one who will disagree with that." His voice sounded weary, and my heart went out to him. Gabriel was a wyvern, strong and arrogant, but he was also a healer, and I knew he took that role very seriously. Facing such a wholesale slaughter of innocent people would wound him grievously on a deeply personal level. "It will take me another day before I can return home to you, but until that time, I must know that you are safe."

"I don't understand what Fiat going on a murderous rampage has to do with Kostya. How are the two connected?"

Again, silence answered my question for a few moments. "Fiat could not have acted alone. There are too many deaths for the small band of ouroboros dragons who follow him," he said slowly, and I could feel the regret that surrounded him. "I suspect he left the actual killing to his accomplice."

"Who is that? You don't mean Kostya, do you? That doesn't make sense, Gabriel. He's keeping his nose clean right now because of the *sárkány*."

"There will be no *sárkány* today. Chuan Ren and I must see to things here before we can return to England for the meeting."

"I understand that, but you haven't explained why you think Kostya is involved. Gabriel . . ." I hesitated for a moment, unsure of how to say what I wanted. "There have been grave problems between you and him, but even so, I don't see him eliminating half of Bastian's sept for Fiat. He might be a little out of line where it concerns the silver dragons, but he's not outright insane. He would know that if he supported Fiat, the weyr would not recognize his sept, or his right to lead it, and he wants that above all else. He wouldn't endanger that."

A muffled voice sounded over his sigh. "I will be right there. Mayling, I must go. I'm being called to tend a survivor. I know it goes against your grain to do something without a reason, but please trust me on this—stay away from Kostya at all costs."

"He wouldn't—" I started to say, but Gabriel cut me off with a sharp word.

"Kostya was seen leaving the scene in Paris. Do you understand? He was there, May. He was seen. Get my mother and Maata and the others, and get out of Drake's house. I must go. I will call later, when I can."

The phone clicked off as I stared with unseeing eyes at an official police notice pinned to the stair door.

"Ms. Northcott?"

It took a few minutes for me to realize that the detective inspector was saying my name. I dragged my mind from the abyss of confusion that had claimed it, and rallied my scattered wits. "I'm sorry?"

"I asked if you were unwell. You look distressed."

"Just a little family issue, I'm afraid. Did you have more forms for me to sign?"

"No. I would, however, request that you take your husband home. He is perilously close to being charged with assault."

I hurried back into the office to retrieve Magoth, who sat perched on a female police officer's desk, openly leering down her blouse.

"You promised to behave," I said as I grabbed his arm and pulled him away from the poor woman.

"Have I mentioned I love it when you get dominant?" he purred, following me out to the lobby. "And I am behaving. I didn't once mock the mortals as I wished. I didn't tell them who you really were, or what your scaly boyfriend was. I didn't even correct their mistaken impression that our house was blown up by a gas line."

"It's Gabriel's house, and our deal is off. Where's Cyrene and Jim?"

I looked around the busy lobby, but my twin and the large demon weren't anywhere to be found.

"I am a prince of Abaddon," Magoth said, straightening his sleeve. "I am not a diviner."

"You're a pain in . . ." I stopped before I got caught up in another argument. "Stay here while I look for them. Maybe she went to the ladies' room."

I don't know why I expected Magoth to actually do something I asked. He didn't let me down, following me into the restroom, much to the chagrin of the women in there. Unfortunately, Cyrene wasn't one of them.

"She probably saw something shiny, and the magpie in her demanded she go see it," I said, tight-lipped with annoyance as I emerged from the building to see the street lined with fashionable shops. "Great. It'll take at least an hour to ferret her out."

"She always was easily distracted," Magoth commented, following as I headed for the nearest shop. "I have no idea how you put up with someone who is so easily—oooh, leather!"

"I'm going to check out this side of the street. You can do the other," I told him. I'd just reached the shop door when I heard my name being called. I spun around, catching sight of a furry black tail disappearing into a small pub. I dodged pedestrians to cross the road, pausing for a moment as I entered the bar to let my eyes adjust. "Jim?" I said, squinting a little bit.

There were only a couple of people in the bar, none of whom was Cyrene. There was also no sign of Jim.

"I'm sorry to disturb you, but have you seen a large black dog?" I asked a couple who were sitting at a table.

They sat stiffly, as if uncomfortable. "He came in just a minute ago."

"Jim is in the back, along with your twin," a smooth voice said behind me. I froze as the Italian accent filtered through my brain. The couple at the table rose to face me, and I noticed immediately that they weren't humans—they were dragons.

Blue dragons.

I turned slowly. Fiat held a businesslike black gun, unfortunately pointed at my forehead. "I'm sure they will both be delighted to see you."

"You do know I'm a doppelganger, yes?" I asked. "Not only am I immortal; I can slip into the shadow world, where you and your bullets can't harm me."

"But they can harm your twin, can they not?" he asked smoothly.

"She's a naiad. All shooting her would do is make her very angry, and you can take my word for it that you don't want to be in a confined space when she's angry. She tends to get a bit elemental, if you get my drift."

Before he could answer, Magoth strolled into the bar, clad in a black leather vest and matching skintight pants . . . ones without the seat.

"Assless chaps, Magoth?" I asked, distracted enough that I just had to ask him.

He posed so I could see the muscles of his behind flex. "They are made of the softest bull-scrotum leather."

"Yes, but . . . *assless* chaps?"

He flexed a couple more times. "The mortals in the leather shop liked them. They offered to tattoo my arse, as well, but I showed them the curse on my cock and they said they couldn't match that, so I just took the clothes and left. What are you doing here?" He sniffed a couple of times. "Bah. More dragons. Who is he, another of your lovers? Why is he holding a firearm on you? Are you having potentially lethal foreplay without me?"

The questions were asked of me, but directed to Fiat, who, I was amused to note, looked somewhat disconcerted when Magoth marched over and put his arm around me. Normally I wouldn't have tolerated such an embrace, but I figured there were times when the devil you knew was better than the dragon you didn't.

"Who are *you*?" Fiat countered.

Magoth gave him one of his superior looks, the kind he reserved for wrath demons belonging to other demon lords. "I am Magoth, prince of Abaddon, and this is my consort. I ask again—why are you pointing a firearm at her? If you are planning on using that to have sex with her, you'll have to include me, as well."

Fiat dragged his bemused gaze to me. "You are consort to a bisexual demon lord?"

"I'm not bisexual. I'm all-sexual," Magoth said, buffing his nails and preening a little. "I'm an equal-opportunity demon lord."

Fiat considered this for a moment before asking me, "Is it now mandatory that all wyverns' mates have some tie to Abaddon?"

"Could be Aisling and I are starting a new trend," I said agreeably, elbowing Magoth when his fingers tried to slip down into my shirt. "I don't suppose you'd like to explain why you've apparently kidnapped my twin and a demon?"

"No," Fiat said simply, and gestured toward the back of the bar. "Go."

I toyed with the idea of refusing and shadowing, but both Fiat and I knew that although he couldn't kill Cyrene with his gun, he could damage her mind enough that she would not recover her faculties. It was a threat that all immortals lived with—a body that lived on while a mind was destroyed—and we tended to take such threats seriously.

"Alas, I cannot accompany you," Magoth said, eyeing

the reflection of his bared behind in a mirror next to the door. "I have appointments that must not be missed. I assume you will deal with this dragon and be at your bed at the appointed time?"

"I wouldn't count on her being in her bed any more than I would count"—Fiat gestured toward two men who sat near the door; they rose and took up positions in front of it—"on you making your appointments."

"Perhaps a tattoo of myself during my film days on the left cheek," Magoth murmured before Fiat's words sank in. He stopped admiring himself and turned a chilly glare on Fiat.

I stilled, noting that although Magoth was almost powerless, he still had a little corona of blackness around him that, when he was riled, snapped out at the unwary.

"You dare to defy me, dragon?" he asked, his voice as slick as ice.

I knew that voice. I knew that look in his eyes. What I didn't know was whether Fiat would respond to the threat that suddenly soaked the very air around us.

Fiat leaned forward and smiled at Magoth. "Gossip flies quickly in the Otherworld. I have had word of you, and know that you have been expelled from Abaddon without your powers."

Magoth's gaze shifted to me for a moment, and I froze solid, terrified he would do or say something that would bring attention to the fact that I now had his powers. "My consort has initiated an appeal. My reinstatement should be forthcoming soon, a fact you would be wise to remember lest I seek payment for the insult you do me."

Magoth was lying through his teeth about the appeal, but no one but he and I knew it, and I certainly wasn't going to correct him. He would never go to Gabriel of his own accord and tell him I was in trouble, but when it became known that Cyrene, Jim, and I were missing,

ME AND MY SHADOW

Gabriel would hunt down Magoth and get the truth out of him.

Fiat made a mock sigh. "Everyone fights me. No one sees the sense in just doing as I ask. Renaldo?"

One of the two blond dragons behind Magoth took a step forward, then whipped his arm around from where he'd been holding it behind his back. Before I could call out a warning, he walloped Magoth on the head with a weighted leather blackjack.

Magoth's expression turned to one of ecstasy for a moment; then his eyes rolled back and his body slumped to the ground.

"Now he's going to want you to do that every night," I told the dragon named Renaldo as he and the other man picked up Magoth.

Fiat poked me in the side with the gun. "You will come with me now."

"Looks like I have no choice," I said calmly, and went down the passage he indicated, Magoth hauled behind us.

# Chapter Eleven

The only thing that surprised me about the house was that it was so remarkably normal-looking.

"Normal if you're used to gorgeous Tudor redbrick mansions, that is," I murmured to myself as we drove through the security gates and up a mile-long drive. The house sat on the crest of a gentle hill, framed by a semi-circle of stately willow and lime trees along the sides and back of the house, beyond which I could see the glint of water—probably a large pond or a small lake.

"What are you talking about?" Cyrene asked.

"Nothing. What did you ask me to do?"

"Uh-oh. You're not hearing voices, are you? Ash started doing that, and it turned out really bad," Jim said, covertly wiping its mouth on Fiat's shoes.

Cyrene shot a glance toward Fiat, moodily looking out the window, before she leaned in close to whisper into my ear, "Don't leave me alone with him."

I let my gaze feast on the house. It truly was superb: a lovely example of Tudor architecture at its finest, all stone quoins, parapets, and a solid, sturdy square center that rose three stories. I'd seen some lovely houses during the last few months with the dragons, but this one made my mouth water. The parkland rolled away from it like green velvet pouring down toward us, the right side ending in what looked to be a yew maze, while the left was a formal garden, right now abloom in a riot of bronze and orange and pink flowers. I fell madly in love with the garden, the grounds, and the house at that very moment. "It's so perfect. So exquisite. I wonder if Gabriel would like it. It's very earthy, don't you think? He likes earthy. I'm willing to bet he likes velvety green lawns, and lovely flowers, and hedges and trees, as well."

I caught a glimpse of the look Cyrene was giving me just as Jim said, "Great. May's mind has snapped. Gotta be the voices."

Fiat continued to ignore us, so I addressed Cyrene and Jim as I gazed with wonder out of the window as we approached the house. "My mind is perfectly sound, thank you. Merciful deities, is that a folly in the distance? Could this property be any more perfect?"

"Mayling!" Cyrene nudged me hard in the ribs. I dragged my gaze off the white iron filigreed structure in the distance, beyond the flower gardens.

"What?"

She glanced significantly toward Fiat. I looked at him. He stared out of the window as if we bored him to death. My gaze slid past him to the sight of a silvery stream that curled around the yew hedges and disappeared around the back of it. "A stream. Of course. Not too deep, but deep enough to splash around in on a long, hot summer afternoon. Just before you stroll behind the yew maze and take a refreshing dip in the lake."

"Stream? Lake?" Cyrene was momentarily distracted enough by the thought of freshwater sources to shove me backwards so she could peer out of the window. "It does look like a very pure stream. It probably feeds into

the lake. I bet the water isn't too cold to swim in. . . ."
She paused and gave me a dirty look. "You did that deliberately. Stop trying to divert me."

I sighed and made sure Fiat was still ignoring us before I answered in a low voice, "I told you that it's me
Fiat wants to use as a bargaining chip. I'm sure he has
some evil plan under way that requires the use of me
as hostage to get Gabriel to do whatever it is he wants
done. OK? Happy now? Good. Are those mullioned
windows? Oh, my, they really are outstanding. Fiat's
taste certainly has improved from that house in Italy. I
wonder if he'd consider selling?"

"He wants to steal me for his mate," Cyrene whispered as we pulled up outside the front doors. I whimpered softly to myself at the sight of the fluted white
columns and cut-glass panels on either side of the doors.
I wanted this house with an overwhelming need that was
almost alien to me, and yet was so familiar I wondered
why I'd never felt it before with anything but Gabriel.

Fiat's two blond bodyguards leaped out of the front
to open the car door.

"May!"

The worry in her voice filtered through the house lust
that held me in its grip. I shook images of myself strolling through the house from my head, and focused on my
distressed twin. "Cy, we've been over this several times
already—you're not a wyvern's mate."

"I am mate lite. I told you that! And besides, if I wasn't,
why would Fiat want to steal me away from Kostya?"

"Gotta pee. Back in a mo. Don't go completely wacko
until I'm back to see it," Jim said, leaping out of the car
and heading for a shrubbery.

Fiat exited the car. Magoth, still unconscious, rolled
off the seat and onto the limo floor, his head thumping
like a ripe melon on the floor.

"I can just about guarantee you that Fiat isn't going

to try to steal you for his mate," I said, patting her on the arm. She was truly worried about such a possibility, I knew, which didn't ease my exasperation with her, but it did let me temper my voice so it wasn't quite so obvious.

"That's what you say," she said with a dark look at me. "But you haven't seen the way he watches me! He *wants* me!"

"Of course he does. You're very pretty—a lot of men want you."

"Not that way," she said, watching him narrowly through the opened car door as he spoke to his bodyguards. "He wants me for his mate so he can take over the dragons."

I wasn't quite sure how her reasoning went from stealing another wyvern's mate to control of the weyr, but I didn't have time to indulge my curiosity. Instead I simply said, "Stop worrying. I won't let him take you."

"Come," Fiat said, turning toward us and holding out a hand. Impatience was evident in his voice, so evident I half expected him to snap his fingers at us. It was on the tip of my tongue to say something that I was sure I would regret, but I remembered in time that the house was his, and if I wanted any chance at all of calling it mine, politeness would be the order of the day.

I pushed aside the question of why I was suddenly possessed with the desire to own the house. No, "desire" wasn't the right word—I had a deep, buried need to have the house. "It had once been a home, and it will be one again," I said on a breath.

Cyrene gave me another odd look, but it was nothing to the confusion I felt over my statement. What on earth had I meant?

"Come!" Fiat said more forcefully, and this time he did snap his fingers.

Cyrene bristled at the gesture, but I grabbed her arm

and hauled her out of the car after me, determined to be polite and persuasive. "This is an absolutely stunning house," I told Fiat, allowing him to assist me out of the car, my eyes drinking in the glorious sight of the front of the house. The afternoon sun caressed the warm red stone, slid along the freshly painted white trim, and settled itself to glitter on the numerous leaded windows, winking little flashes that mesmerized me.

Fiat looked over the house with a critical eye and shrugged. "It is tolerable."

Tolerable? My mind shrieked at the word, so profane was it when applied to the house.

"I prefer something more modern, but I suppose it is in a pleasant setting. Please remember that your twin will be at my mercy should you try anything." A smile lit his eyes, but it wasn't at all friendly. "And mercy is a quality that I particularly lack."

We entered through the doors, and passed through a reception hall. I breathed deeply the heady scent of furniture polish and lemons, closing my eyes for a moment to enjoy it before feasting on what I knew would be an outstanding interior.

The staircase was a work of art, all dark wood with Corinthian newel posts, an elaborate balustrade, and matching dark paneling on the walls. Tapestries covered much of the walls, some vibrant, but most faded with the passing of time. I stopped before one that looked vaguely familiar, gawking when I recognized a name. "Is that . . . that isn't William the Conqueror, is it?"

"It is," Fiat answered.

I squinted closer at the tapestry. It was protected by a wall-mounted conservation case, the kind with special lighting that would not fade the treasure within. "It looks just like something out of the Bayeux Tapestry."

"It is the Bayeux Tapestry."

I spun around both at the words and the voice. It

wasn't Fiat who had answered me, as I had thought—the man who stood next to him with his arms crossed had dark brown hair, not blond, with a pronounced widow's peak, and ebony eyes that glittered like the windows. "Hello again, Baltic. What are you doing with the Bayeux Tapestry?"

He strolled past me to admire it. "It's only part of the tapestry: William's coronation. It pleases me to display it, since it reminds me of a happy time."

"You were there?" I asked.

"Not at the coronation, no, but I did help the mortals fight many times."

"I was there. It was nothing exciting," Cyrene said, giving Fiat a hostile glare. He frowned at her in response. "London was very dirty then, and the people were very rude, always throwing rotten vegetables. I much preferred Paris."

"Why would you want to help the mortals fight?" I asked Baltic, momentarily distracted by the idea of a dragon interfering with human issues.

He smiled. "Have you never beheld the sight of a battlefield, a sword gripped tightly in one hand, your shield in the other, a blood-enraged destrier between your legs? Have you not breathed deeply of the scent of blood and bowels and earth as mortals slaughtered each other? Have you never felt the battle lust grip your being, your heart pounding so loud it almost drowns out the screams of men, your arm burning with the strain of hacking and hewing, slashing first to the left to take down a pikeman, then to the right to cut the legs out from under an attacking infantryman?"

"No," I said, feeling faintly sick at the picture that rose in my mind.

He shrugged. "Then you would not understand. Fiat, you may leave."

The penny dropped then. "This is *your* house?" I

asked, feeling slightly sick at the thought of such a magnificent structure in his possession. It should be mine, a little voice in my head demanded.

"Yes." He flicked a glance my way. "I had it built as a gift for my mate."

"Ysolde?" The thought that the house was Ysolde's made me feel a smidgen better, although I couldn't quite decide why. For all I knew, she could have been just as destructive as Baltic, although I suspected not.

His gaze shifted from me to the paneled wall, but I doubted he was really seeing it. For a moment, for a tiny little moment in time, Baltic's expression softened, his eyes going from a hard, glittering obsidian to something with shadows, like a shaft of sunlight piercing a deep pond. His voice changed, as well, losing some of its clipped cadence, the words striking a richer tone, more Slavic in flavor. "She helped me design the house, but she would have no other hand working on the gardens, so she laid them out herself. She loved flowers, wanted them blooming year-round. I told her this wasn't the climate for that, but she had been born here, and would not hear of living anywhere else."

"What I saw of them looked exquisite," I said, meaning every word. I was filled with a strange sense of kinship, of sharing a great love with this man, but that was insane. It didn't make sense. I shook my head, trying to disperse the odd feeling.

"She wanted to have the acceptance ceremony in the garden, surrounded by honeysuckle and lime trees," he said, still looking inward at the memories. "She said it was fitting that she should formally become my mate here, in the house I built for her."

"You did an outstanding job with the house. It's almost beyond description; it's so perfect. I don't know why, but it seems almost to speak to me. It's as if . . . I don't know. It's hard to put into words. It's just . . . perfect."

"Yes, it is." He turned back to me with a half smile on his lips, and suddenly, I was in his arms, caught up in the memories he had shared, in the emotions that the house stirred within me.

"You loved her," I said, my breath on his lips.

"More than life itself," he answered, his mouth brushing mine.

"Whoa! I didn't see that one coming!" I heard Jim say just as Baltic's arms tightened around me. The sense of kinship grew, accompanied by a rightness that filled me with vague shadow memories, images that danced on the edge of my awareness.

"May? Goodness—May?" Cyrene's voice drifted through a red haze of fierce need in me, but I could no more attend to it than I could stop the rush of emotion inside me.

Until Baltic kissed me.

The second his lips possessed mine, a cold wave of dislike squelched the fires the dragon shard wanted so desperately to fan.

"Ysolde," he murmured against my mouth.

I put both hands on his chest and shoved him back hard, catching the fleeting expression of surprise in his eyes before it turned to calculating anger.

"I am not Ysolde," I said simply.

"May, what are you doing?" Cyrene tugged at my arm, giving Baltic a wary look. "I know you are jealous of all the women who are no doubt trying to seduce Gabriel, but this is not the answer! You must trust me on this—I have much more experience with men than you do, and I can assure you that trying to make a man jealous by toying with another one is not the way to go. It just ends up very poorly, usually with one man dead."

"It was the shard," I said, still feeling it thrum inside me, and shaken to my very core by what had happened. When the shard reacted to Magoth, I knew it for what it was—an attempt to seek power. But this was different—this was tied up to the faintest shadows of Ysolde. She had loved Baltic, I realized at that moment. She had loved him desperately, absolutely, beyond all reason. And he had built a house for her, just to please her, because he, too, loved with an all-consuming passion. I could only guess at the depth of the pain he felt at losing her ... but it did not excuse his actions. I lifted my chin and gave him a long, level look. "The shard is what's making me react to the house ... to you."

Baltic looked bored. "You bear the shard my mate once possessed. I have no doubt she imprinted something of herself upon it. All the more reason for me to have it." He turned to leave and saw Fiat. He frowned. "What are you still doing here? I told you that I had no further need of you. You may leave."

A parade of emotions passed over Fiat's too-handsome face; disbelief was quickly followed by anger, which settled into a deep fury. I'll say this for him—he kept his emotions in check, the only hint of his feelings visible in the glint to his eyes.

"Take them below," Baltic said, waving toward Cyrene and me as he turned to leave the room.

Two dragons emerged from the shadows, one of whom was the man who'd accompanied him to Gabriel's house.

"Below where?" Jim asked somewhat nervously, pressing into me. "Below as in a comfortable suite with digital TV and a hot tub?"

Baltic paused at the door and smiled again. It wasn't a nice smile. "It pains me to be clichéd, but I believe in keeping a dungeon traditional in its accoutrements. You might not find the torture devices as entertaining as digital television, but I certainly will."

"No," I said simply.

Baltic gave me a disbelieving look. "You will not defy me, mate."

"I think I just did," I said calmly, hoping my usual placid expression was hiding the fact that my heart was beating wildly, my palms suddenly sweaty. "I will not move one foot from this spot until you tell us why you've had Fiat kidnap us."

"I don't have to explain anything to you," he said, his brows lowering. He took a menacing step toward me. I raised my chin a smidgen and gave him my blandest look.

"It can't be the dragon shard. You wouldn't kidnap Cyrene and Jim to get that—you'd just lop off my head and take the shard. Therefore, you must want us all for a specific purpose, and the only one I can think of is that it's a trap of some sort, and we're the bait."

"Clever little witch," he said, moving close enough to me that I could feel his breath on me. I felt something else, too, something familiar, some sense of déjà vu that I couldn't pinpoint. "Too clever for your own good, as the saying goes."

"Gabriel isn't stupid," I told him, clamping down on the sense of familiarity. I didn't want to be familiar with Baltic. I didn't want a repeat of that kiss or, more important, of the sense of kinship that I had felt with him when he talked about the house and Ysolde. I didn't want her memories of him; I wanted him at arm's length, back to the status of an evil, despised foe, not of a man who loved a woman so much he was willing to give her everything he had. "He's not going to walk blindly into any trap you set, no matter if you use me as bait or not."

Baltic looked at me long and hard, as if he could see my thoughts. At length he merely asked, "What makes you think I want Gabriel?"

I stared at him in incomprehension. If he didn't want to trap Gabriel, why kidnap me?

Fiat's bodyguards staggered into the house with Magoth. Baltic, once again on his way out of the room, hesitated as he looked at the demon lord, then spun around to give me a questioning look.

"Surely you know by now that I never travel anywhere without my little posse," I said, nodding toward Magoth.

He didn't appreciate my joke, which was fine, as I didn't appreciate his kidnapping us.

"Let us see if you are still laughing tomorrow," was all he said before leaving the room.

"Tomorrow? You never answered me about what you have planned for us. Baltic! Damn him." I called after him, moving toward the door to follow him. His men blocked my way, both of them large enough that it gave me pause. I eyed them for a second, trying to decide if I could take them both on in dragon form, and what repercussions such an act might have, when Fiat exploded.

*"Che cazzo stai dicendo?"* he snarled, making me glad for a moment I didn't speak the language. He pushed past me to fling open the side door that Baltic had just used to leave, and screamed after the other dragon, *"Nessuno me lo ficca in culo!"*

Jim looked shocked.

"On a profanity scale of one to ten, how bad was what Fiat just said?" I asked the demon softly.

"Fifteen."

"Ouch." I grabbed Cyrene and pulled her out of the way when Fiat spun around, his face black with anger as he stormed past us. Only he didn't pass us—he veered off and grabbed me by the arm, instead.

"I will not tolerate this! You are *my* prize, not his! If he thinks he can treat me as a minion, he will soon see just what a force I am," he growled as he half dragged me across the room.

"Ack!" Cyrene yelled, ducking behind me despite

the fact that Fiat wasn't even touching her. "It's started! He's trying to steal me! He thinks you are me!"

*"Fanculo,"* Fiat spat at her, backhanding her at the same time, sending her reeling backwards into the wall.

The dragon shard would have burst into action, but my own temper won out. Before Cyrene even hit the wall, I had my dagger out and was pressing the tip of it into his throat, right where his jugular vein pulsed. "No one," I said in a voice hoarse with anger, *"no one* hurts my twin."

Fiat shifted, the flesh beneath my blade going from beige to blue in an instant. He swung a heavy scaled arm at my head, but I ducked, instinctively shadowing. The room was well lit, but not so bright that I was entirely obvious when shadowed. "Jim, protect Cy," I ordered, flattening myself on the floor for a few seconds when Fiat spun around searching for me, his tail whipping over my head by the barest of inches.

With identical shouts of anger, Fiat's two bodyguards dropped Magoth's unconscious body and shifted into dragon form, as well. I scurried out of their way, trying to stick to the less-lit areas of the room, but that idea went to hell in a handbasket when Baltic's two attendants, who had been ordered to take us downstairs, also shifted. I made a mental note that they were black in color, not white like Baltic.

"It's a dragonpalooza," Jim said, standing guard over Cyrene as she pushed herself up into a sitting position, shaking her head.

"Mayling?" she called, searching for me, squeaking in horror when one of the black dragon guards lunged toward her. He was heading for Fiat's men, however, leaping on the back of the one named Renaldo. The two of them went down in a flurry of scales, claws, dragon fire, and screams that echoed down the length of the long hall. The second black dragon tackled the other blue bodyguard when he went to save his buddy, the former yelling something in what I assumed was Zilant.

The dragon shard demanded I shift and confront Fiat, who was standing in the center of the room, peering around for me. I pressed myself deeper into the shadow cast by a huge sideboard, knowing that he would see me if he spent any time examining the area.

"Come out here, *cara*," he called, his voice almost normal—almost. "I told you what would happen if you were to hide from me."

The lights in the room suddenly dimmed. Cyrene stood at a panel near the entrance, punching off a row of lights as fast as she could. Jim was at one of the huge windows, hauling closed heavy dark blue draperies. Bless them, they were trying to give me an even playing ground.

"And let you take out on me the fact that you're pissed at your boss?" I called to Fiat as he spun around, starting toward Cyrene. I had to get his attention back on myself. "I'm not that stupid, Fiat."

He turned back toward me, lashing out with his tail as Renaldo and one of the black dragons rolled past him, blood staining the floor with smeared, inky streaks. I used the opportunity provided by the distraction to race across to the other side of the room, deep in the shadows now, thanks to Jim.

"He is not my boss," Fiat snarled, his head sweeping back and forth as he searched for me. "Open those drapes so I can see her," he snapped at his men, but they were too involved to do as he commanded.

"No? You sure take orders from him as if he was. Just what is your connection with him, Fiat? Do you think he'll help you retake control of the blue dragons?" I inched my way down the long room, away from Cyrene.

"I have no need for another sept," Fiat answered,

taking the bait. His eyes burned with blue intensity as he searched the shadows for me, slowly following. "I am wyvern of the red dragons."

"I think you'll find Chuan Ren will disagree with that. She's back, you know. Oh, but you must know—Gabriel said you were hiding from her." I said the last with deliberation, knowing Fiat would not take such a blow to his ego without revenge.

He snarled and leaped forward, suddenly not more than a foot away from me, his fingers digging deep into my throat. I gasped and grabbed his hand with both of mine, trying to ease the intense pressure on my throat.

"If Baltic did not want you alive, I would kill you right here for that insult," he growled, his tail sliding around my legs to hold them in a vise. I couldn't reach my dagger, couldn't get enough of a purchase on the floor to fight him, couldn't even draw a breath. Spots danced lazily in front of my eyes as I stared silently into his.

*Shift!* the dragon shard demanded, and with no other choice, I did so. I tried to shove him off me, tearing desperately at the fingers so deep in the flesh of my neck they must surely be touching, but despite my being in dragon form, his strength was just too much for me.

"Then again, the pleasure it would give me to kill you would far outweigh Baltic's displeasure at the act," Fiat hissed, his face shoved into mine. There was madness in his eyes, madness and a bloodlust that scared me to death. His face was beginning to go gray, to lose focus, and I realized with a shock that he was killing me, cutting off blood and oxygen to my brain, and that I would never see Gabriel again.

"Love sport without me? This will never do. I must insist on having the premiere role in it, although if you beg nicely, perhaps we'll allow you to join in, as well."

The voice that spoke beyond Fiat was cool, but a

bit ragged about the edges. It had the desired effect, however—Fiat jerked his head to see who was behind him, but he wasn't fast enough. Magoth swung a huge andiron shaped like a peacock in full display at Fiat's head, connecting with a horrible smashed-melon sound.

Fiat stared at him in surprise for a moment before he crumpled to the ground, blood spraying in a fine arc on the wood tiles beneath him.

The last thing my brain registered before the blackness enveloped me was Magoth's smile.

# Chapter Twelve

"The shadow world is not really so much a whole different world as it is simply an extension of what we know as reality. It goes by many names, and can be accessed by a number of methods—fae folk are particularly comfortable there, although they refer to it as the beyond, which, now that I think about it, is a pretty good description of what it is. It is beyond. Nothing more, nothing less."

"Why are you telling me this?"

The voice that spoke was male, deep, smooth as silk on water, and just hearing it made me smile. It took a few minutes before the meaning of what the voice said filtered through the bemusement that held me so tightly. Slowly, inch by inch, my body ceased floating on an infinitely soft bed of oblivion, and returned to the domain of my mind. I realized with an odd start that the first voice that had spoken was mine.

My eyes popped open to behold a face leaning over me, watching me with a mixture of amusement, desire, and relief. "Gabriel?"

"Your wits have returned. I was concerned that you had suffered some trauma."

There was a certain translucent quality to the face that had my spirits dropping. "We're in the shadow world, aren't we?"

The amusement left his eyes. "Yes. You were unconscious. What happened?"

Images flashed in my mind, of a house so perfect, so astoundingly desirable, it left me salivating. "The house. I want the house. *Agathos daimon*, how I want the house. You'd like it, too, Gabriel. There is a lawn so smooth it could be made of satin, and trees and flowers and what looked like it was a maze where we could run and hide and make love out in the open. We wouldn't have to swim in the lake if you didn't want to. But you would like the maze."

"Yes," he agreed solemnly. "I would like a maze. I would like to make love to you outside, with the sun shining down on your lovely flesh. I would allow you to make love to me under the stars, with the cool night air caressing your delicious little breasts as you arched above me, riding me, your hips moving in that way that drives me insane, and when you shadowed with your climax, I would know that you really were my little night bird, my wintiki."

"I want to make love to you right now," I said, my fingers twitching impotently, desperately wanting to touch him, to pull him down onto me. I needed to feel his mouth on mine, to catch his breath as I touched him, to taste him as he entered my body. The need for the house was tangled up somehow with my need for him, but he was only a projection into the shadow world, not really here. "I want to touch you, Gabriel. I want to slide myself across your chest, tasting you, stroking your lovely warm flesh. I want to have foreplay. I want to take you in my mouth like we've talked about, but never seem to be able to do because you drive me totally and completely witless the second you touch me. I want you buried so deep inside me, I can feel your heart beat."

Gabriel groaned and closed his eyes for a moment, his hands fists as he knelt next to me. "Do you have any idea what you're doing to me? I'm not near you, May. I'm not even in the same country as you, and yet I'm hard and burning for your heat."

I was silent for a moment as the last shreds of my wits that had been scattered by Fiat's attempt to kill me gathered up and coalesced into my normal reason. "Where are you?"

"France. I will be home soon. I will be in your arms sooner. What happened to you?" He reached for me, as if he were going to stroke the hair from my cheek, his hand fisting again as he dropped his arm to his side.

"Fiat tried to kill me."

He was so still that for a moment I thought he hadn't heard me.

"Then he will die for that folly."

I smiled, warmed to the tips of my toes by the cold, icy threat in his voice. "He didn't succeed."

"So I gathered. Fiat? You are sure, Mayling?"

"Quite."

He swore. "How did he slip past us? We were watching all means of transportation, monitoring all the portaling companies."

"I have no idea, but he's definitely here, and Kostya wasn't with him."

"What happened?"

I gave him a brief rundown of the events that led up to us meeting Fiat in the bar. "Fiat more or less went off, and picked me as a likely recipient of his spleen venting. And much as it distresses me to admit it, he might have succeeded if I hadn't been rescued."

Gabriel watched me for a few seconds, emotion running so high in him I could swear I felt it even over the distance I knew separated us. "Who rescued you?"

"I never believed I'd ever actually have cause to say these words, but Magoth saved me. He coshed Fiat over the head with an eighteenth-century andiron in the shape of a peacock, which I have to admit is somewhat fitting. Gabriel, it's not Kostya Fiat is working with—it's Baltic. He's here. This is actually his house. How or why he got Fiat to kidnap us is beyond me."

Gabriel stiffened. "Where is this house?"

"About two hours outside of London." I described the route we'd taken out of London. "Baltic said he and Ysolde designed the house. He said she was going to have an acceptance ceremony here."

"I am less interested in history than I am in why Baltic has taken you," Gabriel said grimly. He glanced over his shoulder. "Do not move. I will return in a minute or two."

I laughed as I looked around me. During the conversation with Gabriel, I'd taken in the surroundings. Even though I was in the shadow world, it retained enough similarity to the real world that I knew exactly where I was—in the bowels of the house, deep down in a dimly lit, earth-walled room that served as a dungeon.

I slid off the table upon which I'd been sitting, and examined the prison. There was one small door set at the far wall, no windows, and only the faintest flicker and buzz from a bare electric light overhead. Although sometimes the shadow-world version of an environment could look significantly different from what we knew as real, there was none of that feel about this room. The angles were all true, not slightly off, as was frequent in the shadow world. There were a table and three chairs, all broken and lying in a heap in the corner. The room was musty and earthy smelling, but there was an acid note to the air that had my nose wrinkling. I couldn't figure out quite what it was, though, and took a few tentative sniffs to see if I could pinpoint the origins.

"It is fear, little bird," Gabriel said behind me.

I spun around. He looked tired and depressed, the light in his normally shining eyes dimmed somewhat. "What's fear?"

"The scent you smell. I recognize it."

"Ugh. What's wrong?" I asked, wanting to soothe away the distress I could see in his handsome face.

The look he gave me spoke volumes. "My mate has been taken by another wyvern, my house destroyed, more than sixty dragons are dead by the hand of a wyvern I should have stopped long ago, and Chuan Ren is being unusually difficult."

"Sorry. That was a stupid question. Don't worry about me—I will get us out of here just as soon as I make sure everyone is unharmed. As for Fiat—he's not your responsibility, Gabriel. He's a big boy, and knows what he's doing. Don't take upon yourself any blame that should lie solely on his head."

Gabriel was silent for a moment, his hand raised to touch my cheek. I felt nothing but the faintest of breezes, however. "If I said it was my job to rescue you, what would you say?"

I kissed the air where his palm was. "I'd tell you to stop being silly, and hurry up and come home so we can re-form the heart and get rid of the shard once and for all."

"I have alerted the others to the fact that Fiat has slipped through our fingers," he answered. "Do not do anything rash, mate."

I smiled at the rough note his voice had taken. "I love you, too."

Cautiously, I slipped out of the shadow world, but I really had no need of covertness.

"Mayling!" Cyrene said as I stepped away from the wall, out of the deepest shadows I had instinctively sought. Relief dripped from her voice. "There you are. Have you found a way out?"

I stepped over a prone form, then a second one. "What on earth happened here?" I asked, ignoring Cyrene's question.

"Your twin told Fiat that it was Magoth who slugged him," Jim said from where it sat on Fiat's chest. "So the F-man started duking it out with Magoth, screaming he was going to have revenge, only Mags is a bit lacking in the power department, so when Fiat went all dragon on him, Cy and I decided we'd better even things up."

I looked from the two men sprawled unconscious on the floor to Cyrene. "So you hit them both over their respective heads?"

"No, of course not," Cyrene said, pulling herself up with an indignant snort. "What do you take me for? I am a naiad! I am devoted body and soul to the worthy and altruistic cause of benefiting the planet! My being, my very reason for existence, is to better the world for mortalkind. For you to even suggest that I would do something so heinous, so evil, as bash someone over the head just because he was annoying and would not shut up no matter how much I threatened him is the purest slander. *Purest slander!*"

I waited for a minute. "Are you finished?"

"Not quite." She took a deep breath. "I would never do anything to harm anyone. Ever!"

I let the silence say it all.

"I am good," she said with much dignity. "I am not in the least bit bad."

"Yeah, 'cause holding someone down while a demon

lord beats the snot out of him isn't bad at all," Jim said, snickering.

"Holding someone's arms is not the same as holding them down," Cyrene said with a glare at the demon.

"Yuh-huh. I see now why you and Magoth hooked up."

"Oh!" Cyrene said, outraged.

"Enough bickering, you two."

"I didn't hold Fiat down," Cyrene reassured me. "I just helped Magoth get a tiny little edge."

"Whatever. Can we move on?" I asked.

"That's why you were dancing around yelling, 'Smash the tar out of him, Mags!' the whole time?" Jim asked.

Cyrene gasped. "Lies! Scandalous lies! You take that back!"

Jim made a motion that on a human would be a shrug. "OK, OK, don't get your panties in a wad. I take it back. Magoth didn't beat the snot out of Fiat. There was enough left in him to brain Magoth a few times on the rack over there before Cyrene bopped him upside the head with a cat."

Cyrene, to my extreme surprise, was holding a rust-stained cat-o'-nine-tails, swinging it gently from side to side. "That was purely self-defense, and thus doesn't fall under the heading of bad," she said, giving the cat a little twirl. "I knew if Fiat had me alone, he'd try to claim me."

I let the claiming comment go and eyed my twin for a few seconds. "Why the sudden emphasis on being good? Oh, Cy. You're not in trouble again, are you?"

"No," she said quickly, but her gaze dropped. "Not really. It's just that Neptune is still a bit annoyed about that whole thing with letting my spring get tainted while I was taking care of Kostya, and when he gave it back to me last month, he made me swear that I wouldn't do anything that could be considered detrimental to either the Otherworld or the mortal world for a year, or he'll take away the spring permanently. And you know I couldn't let him do that."

"No, of course not," I said, mentally giving kudos to Neptune. Perhaps he could control my wild twin where I could not.

"He really is the most unreasonable of persons, you know. He's all blond and surfer boy, and has those lovely white teeth, and really impressive biceps, but he's not at all as scatterbrained as he looks. And I swear he has it in for me. He's always picking on me."

I let that comment go, too, and focused on what was important. "We need to get out of here. Door?"

"Bolted from the other side," Jim said, getting up off Fiat and shambling over to me, nuzzling my hand for a moment before cocking a canine eyebrow. "Any other bright ideas?"

I glanced around the room. "Not really. Cy, is there anything you can do?"

"Flood the room?" she asked, also looking around.

"That would do nothing but drown us."

She stilled for a moment, her eyes closed as she opened herself up to the earth. "The pond is too shallow, and the stream is at its lowest peak. Neither source would be effective against the foundation of the house. Other than those two, there are no sources of water nearby that I could use."

"Damn." I eyed Jim. "I know demon lords can move through space the way demons can, but I don't know how to do it. Do you have any pointers?"

"Yeah. Don't do it."

"Why not?" I asked the demon.

It shook its head. "Aisling tried it and got proscribed. I don't think you want to end up that way, because it would give Bael some sort of control over you, what with you being bound to Magoth and all."

"Good point," I said, reluctantly releasing the idea of

using the dark power. "What we need is for a demon to rip open the fabric of space for us so we could leave."

"We have a demon," Cyrene said, pointing to Jim.

"No can do," it answered, shaking its head. "I'd like to, but I can't. Gotta have a direct order from my demon lord. My *real* demon lord, not someone with the temporary ability to command me."

"Damn," I said again, thinking furiously. "We could wait for Gabriel to save us, but that could take longer than we have."

"There's Magoth," Cyrene said, poking him with the toe of her sandal. He moaned gently.

"I am not giving him his powers while he's in the mortal world," I said hastily.

"No, not all of them—just the ability to travel through rips and such."

I thought about that for a minute, then looked at Jim. "Is that possible?"

"Maybe for someone who was familiar with the power, and had a firm grip on it, but you?" It made a little face. "Nope. Not doable."

"What about Jim?" Cyrene asked brightly.

"I just told you I can't do that without a direct order—"

"No, no," she interrupted, turning to me with a sunny smile. "What if you give Jim Magoth's powers? Then it can open up a rip for us and we can escape."

"Leaving Jim in full possession of a demon lord's powers," I pointed out.

"I am so behind that idea," Jim said.

"Well, I'm not. Cy—it's a demon. As in . . . *demon*."

"Why do people always talk about me like I'm not here?" Jim asked no one in particular.

"It's a good demon," she pointed out.

She had a point. Not a big one, but it was a point. I eyed Jim for a few moments, amused despite myself by the big puppy dog eyes it was giving me. "No," I said, deciding it was just too big of a risk. "I can't do it."

"Oh, for heaven's sake, then give the powers to me," she said, disgusted.

"You? Miss 'I am the purest thing that ever walked on two legs'? The one who pledged an oath to not do anything wrong for the next year? I bet Neptune would take a dim view of a proscribed naiad."

She whomped me on the arm. "I'm an elemental being, silly. We can't be proscribed."

"You can't?" I'd never heard that before. "Since when?"

"Since always. Why do you think I survived Magoth enthralling me? A thrall kills most beings, but not us. Elemental beings are particularly resistant to dark powers. Everyone knows that."

"I didn't know," I said slowly, wishing for a second that doppelgangers were considered elemental beings.

"Well, now you do. And don't pull Neptune on me again—using the power to get us out of here is a good act, not bad. He can't say a thing about it."

"Yes, but who's to say that you won't inadvertently use the powers in some other way?"

She straightened up, giving me a look that was almost intimidating. "I am over a thousand years old, Mayling. I think I can handle a little demonic power."

I wasn't convinced, but after another twenty minutes of arguing the point, I conceded that there really was no other option, and proceeded to—reluctantly, and with many dire warnings regarding the misuse thereof—transfer the power to her.

"This is going to be so handy," Cyrene said, her voice filled with excitement as Jim guided her to the proper procedure for tearing open the fabric of space. "I can't believe I never thought of doing this before. No more flying, Mayling! No more long lines at a portal station.

No more trains and cars and ships! Just a rip and a tear, and a shove through the fabric, and voilà! Instant transportation."

She swung her hands around as she spoke, tearing off little strips of reality.

"Don't forget to focus on where you're going," Jim warned, ducking as one of her swings went a bit wild. "You have to keep that focus or you'll end up in Timbuktu. Man alive! You almost took off my ear!"

"Sorry. Focusing." Her face scrunched up as she held an image in her mind. "Now tear?"

"Yeah." Jim retreated back to where I stood, well out of her reach. "You do know that there's going to be a price to pay for this, right?"

"What do you mean, a price?" she asked, her eyes still screwed tight as she reached out blindly to select just the right possibility, the threads of location that would take us where she wanted.

"Dark power isn't free. You use it, you pay a price."

"I'm elemental—"

"Yeah, yeah, you can't be proscribed, but you still pay a price."

One of her eyes popped open as I asked, "What sort of a price? It's nothing dangerous, is it?"

Worry gathered in my belly. Had I just done something extremely stupid?

The demon shrugged. "Won't know until you use it."

"I'm an elemental being," Cyrene said with a shake of her head as she reached back out to find the threads she wanted. "There's nothing dark power can do to me."

"Famous last words, eh?" Jim said five minutes later as it released Magoth's feet. I heaved the upper part of him onto my bed in Aisling's yellow bedroom, and let him drop with an audible grunt.

"And I thought Fiat was heavy," I grumbled, rubbing my back as I straightened up. Fiat was sprawled, still unconscious, on the armchair next to the bed. I made sure both men were still out before I turned to look at my twin, flinching just a little as the light hit her full on.

Cyrene stared in horror at her reflection in the small mirror next to the door. One hand rose slowly to touch her hair. "It's ... white. I'm ..."

"Black," Jim said, giving her a visual once-over.

She turned to look at me, her expression frozen. "My eyes ..."

"Orange," I said, trying to absorb the new look to my twin. "I think you've done a flip colorwise, Cy. All the colors are reversed. Your skin is now very dark brown, your hair is white, and your once-blue eyes are orange. It's an interesting look."

"That's one way of putting it," Jim said, its head tipped as it considered her. "It's like you're a negative image of yourself. Fun."

She blinked at me with those eerie eyes and then opened the door, her face still frozen in shock. "I need water. Lots of water. I'll be in Drake's pool."

"I just hope Aisling isn't down there giving birth," I said as she tottered off.

Jim cocked its head. "No screaming. Besides, she was going to do that in the big tub before she changed her mind and decided on some sort of big chair with a hole in the seat."

"Birthing chairs are very common, I believe. I suppose I'd better go tell Drake he has a guest."

"Yeah, I'd better check on Ash and let her know we're back. She worries about that sort of thing, and that's probably not too good for her right now."

I ruffled the demon's head as I followed it into the hall. "Just when I get thinking you're nothing but a pain in the butt, you go and show you're just a big softy."

"Love ya, too, babe," it said, rubbing its head on me as we headed down the hallway.

# Chapter Thirteen

I knew the second Gabriel entered Drake's house. The air thickened, and seemed to vibrate with energy. I froze, the words I had been speaking drying up on my lips.

"May? Are you all right?" Aisling asked. She was tucked into bed, with Drake lounging beside her, both of them with attentive expressions on their faces as I told them about our adventures with Fiat and Baltic.

I leaped to my feet, every nerve in my body suddenly tingling as I raced out of the room and down the stairs. Behind me, I could hear Aisling asking Drake what was going on.

"Her mate is here." His voice drifted out after me, but I paid little mind to my bad manners, intent on only one thing.

Gabriel met me halfway up the stairs, a frantic, desperate look in his beautiful eyes. I flung myself off the top of the stairs onto him, knocking him backwards into the wall, my arms and legs wrapping around him as I kissed every inch of him my mouth could reach.

"Mate," he growled, his normally lovely voice rough

with need, dragon fire running high within him. His mouth burned mine, literally burned it, when I dug my fingers into the familiar soft dreadlocks and sucked his tongue as it did an enticing little dance in my mouth.

"Good evening, May," a male voice said gently.

It was an effort, but I managed to stop kissing Gabriel's face long enough to greet his second bodyguard. "Evening, Tipene. Maata's in the attic. Nice to have you back."

He bowed, struggling to keep his face straight as I returned to kissing Gabriel, the scent and feel of him filling my mind to the exclusion of everything else.

"Fiat's here," I said in between kisses, squirming against his body when his hands stroked down over my behind. "Aisling hasn't had her baby. Cy has Magoth's demon lord powers. I need you. *Right now!*"

"I need you, too, mate," he growled, his eyes scorching me as I gave myself up to another one of his breath-defying kisses, the dragon shard humming to itself as it made suggestions, trying to force me to shift.

I groaned when Gabriel bit my ear, his ragged breath the sweetest music I'd ever heard. His body was tense and hard, and I knew he was just as aroused as I was. Dragons, I remembered, had an overwhelming need to claim their mates when they had been separated, a policy I wholeheartedly embraced. I tried to peel myself off Gabriel so we could at least go to my room, but his scent, that woodsy, earthy, primal scent that made my soul sing, set me alight. I reared back, my legs still wrapped around his waist, and ripped the black raw-silk shirt right off his body.

"I missed you so much," I almost sobbed, kissing a hot line across his chest. He moaned, his fingers digging into my behind as I took one adorably pert little nipple in my mouth, and breathed fire on it.

The dragon shard demanded I give in to it, to do

things to him that would be impossible in human form, but I was determined to be in control.

"Mate, you must stop or I'll take you right here on the stairs," Gabriel managed to say, his voice almost hoarse with desire. His body was urgent against mine, a thousand little touches speaking wordlessly of his emotions, of his needs.

I unlocked my legs and slid down his body, panting with the effort, allowing my eyes to feast on him. He was so beautiful, so uniquely wonderful, it made me want to weep with joy. He was mine, all of him, every last little bit of him, everything from those glittering argent eyes to mobile lips that were the sweetest on earth, right on down his body, every single part of him made to satisfy me.

"I must have you now," he said roughly, picking me up and leaping up the stairs. "I can't wait, little bird. You were taken from me—I can't wait. Which room are we in?"

"Third floor," I started to say, then remembered that although Drake had removed Fiat to a secured room downstairs, he had left Magoth lying across my bed. "Dammit! Magoth is there."

Gabriel paused at the head of the stairs, turning first one way, then another. "There must be a room we can use. Sitting room?"

"Too public. Jim tends to wander at night."

"Drake's study."

"Drake is often up at all hours fetching something for Aisling."

His fingers tightened on me. "Kitchen."

"István and his girlfriend sleep right off the kitchen. They'd hear anything we did there—"

He growled, actually growled. "There has to be somewhere!"

"There's the pool, but I think Cyrene is going to be there for a very long time."

"Gah!"

I slid out of his arms, the emotions and images pouring out from the dragon shard finally too much for me. I took a step back from him, my fingers curling into fists, the sharp claws biting into my palms as I looked away for a moment, trying to gather the strength I would need.

"I will ask Aisling," Gabriel started to say, but as he walked past me, I slid a hand down his back. He froze, half-turning toward me, his eyes so bright they warmed my soul.

I leaned toward him as if I was going to kiss him, pursing my lips to blow a breath on his mouth, instead.

His eyes widened as he realized what I was doing. "Mate?"

I turned my back on him, walking to the stairs, the dragon shard cheering within me.

"Mate," he said again, his voice an octave lower, the word so full of sexual intent I almost climaxed right there.

Halfway down the stairs I threw a look over my shoulder. He was still standing in the same spot as if rooted there, his body taut, his eyes aglow, a small ring of fire around his feet. I smiled.

He sucked in his breath.

"I love you," I told him just before I spun around and leaped down the last of the stairs.

A challenging roar echoed through the house as I raced down the darkened hallway, driven by the urges of the dragon shard, but for a change fully in control of it. It wanted me to play with Gabriel, to treat him as if I were a dragon, to initiate love play, and so I would—but on *my* terms. Dragon play, I had learned over the last few months, involved chases. Females fled; males pursued. It was all very chauvinistic, my modern mind thought as I dashed through the hall into a pitch-black kitchen, searching frantically for an exit—but it was the way of the dragons, and Gabriel loved it. He loved hunting me, and I loved being found. Usually the dragon shard overwhelmed me, forcing me into dragon form for the chase, but this time, I had it firmly in control.

"You cannot hide from me, little bird," I heard Gabriel call. He was close, too close. I caught a brief hint of his scent, and raced through the door that led to the outside of the house, pausing for a moment to consider the layout of the area.

"You wish to toy with me? To drive me insane with desire for you? You do not have that far to go, Mayling, which you will realize once I find you." His voice was rich with both promise and passion. I shivered in response.

I had to find a spot for us, somewhere with privacy, somewhere we both could give vent to the emotions running so hotly through us.

"Park," I said softly to myself, remembering that there was a large park just a few blocks away, one with a small lake, a boathouse, and several beautiful garden areas. Most important, it would be closed at night, providing a silver-eyed dragon and his mate room to play.

I leaped over the trash cans and ran around the side of the house toward the street, where late-night traffic droned softly in the background, Gabriel's voice calling out over it. "Do you think to lose me in traffic, mate? Do you think you will get away from me?"

I smiled to myself as I ran as fast as I could, dodging the pedestrians and cars, ignoring both the odd looks and occasional blasts of horns as I dashed across the streets, heading for the bulky black outlines of trees that I could glimpse between buildings.

"You have never been able to get away from me before. I have always found you, and I will do so this time, as well."

As if I wanted to get away from him. Happiness sang in my ears, mingled with a healthy dose of my libido as I raced toward my goal.

"There will be retribution for this act, you know. Grave retribution." Laughter was in his voice now, laughter and a tension that bespoke his enjoyment of the play. I just hoped I'd be able to last long enough to see the chase through to the end, rather than flinging myself upon him as I wanted.

I found one of the gates to the park at last. The locked gate gave me no trouble, not just because I didn't stop to unlock it. I simply swarmed up the wrought iron fence, leaping off the top to land on my feet on the other side, taking a moment to get my bearings before I set off toward what I remembered was a traditional English garden located in the southeast corner.

"Wise little bird. A park. Very fitting. There will be no witnesses to see what it is I will do when I catch you."

A little ripple of pleasure went up my back at the velvet edge of his voice. Behind me, I heard the sound of metal on metal, just as if someone else was climbing the gate. I smiled again, and dashed past the boathouse, suddenly spinning 180 degrees to run alongside the boathouse, wading into the water as quietly as I could. It was cold against my now-fevered flesh, and momentarily took my breath away. I held it for a moment, not wanting Gabriel, with his heightened hearing, catching the sound of me gasping, but after what seemed like an interminable amount of time, I grew accustomed to the cold. I swam out under the dock connected to the boathouse, clutching a pillar as I peered around it to see what Gabriel would do.

I had to wait only a few seconds to see. The moon was not full, but gave enough light for me to see the silhouette of a man as he raced past the boathouse. I held my breath again, not wanting him to hear even the slightest hint of sound.

He paused, obviously scenting the air for me. "Where are you, little bird?" he asked, slowly turning around toward the direction he came. "You are near, I know. I can feel my fire in you. The breeze whispers your name, so you must have just passed by here. Show yourself to me, and I will take mercy upon you."

I grinned. I knew his idea of mercy would involve endless rapture for me, but I also knew just how much he enjoyed anticipating that time. Silently, I dived under the water and swam close to the shore. He had moved a few yards away, taking hesitant steps away from me, but he obviously realized it was the wrong direction.

"Mayling," he said again, his voice deep and rich and filled with all sorts of promises. "I appreciate your desire to play with me, but you were taken from me. Our separation was not of our doing, and thus I must reclaim you."

I shadowed and quietly hauled myself out of the water, onto the bank behind him, stealthily picking my way down the path until I was about twenty yards behind him.

"You have to catch me before you can claim me," I said, deshadowing as I spun around to run for a line of trees.

He whirled even as he shifted into dragon form, hot on my heels. I ran as I'd never run, relishing the mad beating of my heart, my lungs sucking in the cool night air, a burning warmth behind me that I knew was Gabriel. He was gaining on me, and I couldn't help myself—I laughed with the sheer joy of it all. Moonlight and dim bluish white lights from nearby streetlamps dappled the ground as I wove through the trees, calling over my shoulder, "You're losing your touch, Gabriel. The last few times we did this, you had me in under three minutes."

"You will pay for such insolence," he answered, laughing, as well. The line of trees was ending, but I caught sight of a small rock garden to the right. I made a dash for it, but never stood a chance. Silver flashed in my peripheral vision, and then he was on me, flinging me to the ground, his body twisting in midair, curling around me protectively so it was him, not me, that hit the hard earth. He grunted as I landed on him, his body shifting back to that of a human, his hands hard on me, a low growl coming from his lips just before they claimed my mouth. "You hid from me in the water. That was not fair."

"All's fair in love and dragon chases," I said, sliding my hands up the hard, warm planes of his chest, nipping his tongue.

"You wish to do this as humans?" he asked, his hands busily removing my wet clothing. I shivered a little, both at the cool night air on my flesh and at the look in his eyes.

"Yes. Love me, Gabriel. It's been so long."

"Two days," he agreed, losing any finesse he had and simply shredding the rest of my clothes off my body. "An eternity."

"Should we even try for foreplay?" I asked, moaning when his fingers found sensitive flesh. I tugged at his belt buckle until it came undone, quickly releasing him from his jeans.

"The chase was foreplay," he answered and, before I could respond, lifted me up over him before plunging me down. I was ready for him, more than ready, and moaned again when he slid into my body, the feel of him so hard and intrusive, and yet at the same time so very much a part of me. He bucked beneath me, his hands sliding up to my breasts, gently palming my highly sensitive nipples until I thought I would come undone. My back arched against the sensation even as my muscles tightened around his intrusion.

"May, I'm sorry. . . . I must . . . I know you want to do

this as humans. . . ." Pain laced his voice as his hips pistoned upward into me.

I leaned down to kiss him. "Fire. Give me your fire, Gabriel."

He shifted then, his body elongating and stretching, the lovely warm skin shimmering into flowing silver scales. He lifted me off him, twisting as he did so until I was on my knees, with him behind me. I clutched his arm as he parted my legs and came into me again, the hard invasion of him enough to push me over the edge. I cried out his name as he bent me down, his belly on my back, his body making hard, deep thrusts into mine until he tipped his head back and bellowed out my name.

It took me a long time before I was able to rally my wits. I lifted my head and looked over my shoulder at the man whose body was draped protectively over mine. "I'm not complaining—there's absolutely nothing in your technique that I could find fault with even if I wanted to, and I don't—but just once I think I'd like to try traditional foreplay."

One silver eye opened to consider me. Gabriel's chest was still heaving against my back, testament to the fact that he was as exhausted by our lovemaking as I was. "That sounds very much like dissatisfaction."

I rolled onto my side so I could face him, my hands unable to keep from touching his chest. "On the contrary. It's just that . . . well, let's take your chest, for instance."

"I'd rather take yours," he said with a leer, his hands warm on my breasts.

I tried to summon up a stern look. "Stop distracting me."

He sighed and rolled over onto his back, his arms open wide. "You've become a demanding little bird these last few months. You wish to work your feminine wiles upon my human form?"

"Oh yes." I got to my knees, sitting back on my heels as I looked over the vast panoply of man lying before me. "Every time I look at your chest, I want foreplay."

"My chest?" He lifted his head and looked down at himself, touching the middle of it with a hand. "Why?"

"It's just so . . ." I bit my lower lip, then slid my hand down the lovely curves of his torso. Instantly, interest lit his eyes. "No," I told his eyes.

"'No' is not the word I want to hear," he answered.

"No, as in no, you're not going to distract me by making love to me. You told me months ago we could do foreplay."

"And you told me you didn't need it."

"I've changed my mind." My hand moved lower, down to his belly button. He sucked in his breath. "Besides, even your mother thinks we should make time for foreplay."

He grinned at me. Any other man would be shocked or appalled that his mother and lover were discussing his sexual technique, but Gabriel was not any other man. "My mother has excellent advice, although I seem to recall you being horrified when you found out I had talked to her about my lack of control with you."

"That was just because we were newly mated. We're old hands at this now," I said, swirling my fingers around his belly button. "Kaawa says that she raised you to be considerate of a lover, and that the fact that you can't seem to control yourself around me speaks volumes about you."

He made a little face. "Perhaps, but she knows the way of dragonkin. She, as a mate, is aware that there are times when a dragon must have his mate in the most elemental of ways."

"Yes, but we seem to have an awful lot of elemental experiences. What I'd like is the chance to experience what other people do."

"You mean mortals."

"And immortals. Nondragon immortals. Your chest is lovely, Gabriel. I like looking at it. I like touching it. I want to taste it."

Fire lit deep in his eyes and body.

"I want to taste you. All of you. I've heard that oral sex can be most gratifying. I'd like to try that."

He stopped breathing.

I smiled a secret little smile and bent down to flick my tongue over his nipple. "It all starts with your chest, you see, because it's so very wonderful. It doesn't have a huge amount of hair, but it's not bare as a plucked chicken, either."

"I'm glad you think so," he said, his voice sounding like he was gargling cement. "I haven't spent much time thinking about it."

"That's all right, because I have." I paused, struck by a thought. "Did you choose this form, the way a demon chooses its? Or did you one day shift to human form, and this is what happened?"

"Human form is always a matter of chance, just as it is for mortals," he answered, suddenly stilling, his eyes going wary. "You are troubled by the fact that I appear ethnically different from you?"

"Mortals make much out of differences in outward appearance," I said, kissing the sudden doubt right out of him. "We are not them. We both look beyond a mere form to the person within."

He relaxed, his hands reaching for me again.

"Hands flat on the ground, please," I instructed, waiting until he complied before I rewarded him with another kiss, one to each dimple. "Where was I? Oh, yes, this trail of hair, now," I said, stroking the silky line of hair that gathered in the center of his torso, and headed to regions south. "This trail makes me go all weak in my knees."

He groaned, his eyes shut as I let my fingers wander around his hips and belly, avoiding his rapidly growing erection.

I kissed my way down his chest, savoring the salty tang of it, taking a tentative little nibble on his ribs.

"This is going to kill me, May."

"No, it isn't. You're a strong man. You can do this."

"I'm not a man. I'm a dragon, and dragons take their mates when they insist on touching and tormenting and tasting. Dear god. Do that again."

I chuckled as I dipped my head down to his flank, licking the lovely indentation around his hip joint with long, sweeping strokes of my tongue, a line of fire following my mouth. "You see? I knew you would enjoy this."

His body twitched as I kissed a path over to his belly, pausing to bite it gently, blowing fire on it, too.

"I'm sorry, May. I know you want to do this, but—"

His hands closed on my shoulders, obviously ready to pull me over him again, but I held him back with a hand on his far-too-delectable chest. "I can see I'm going to have to take your mother's advice after all."

His eyebrows rose. "Which advice?"

"She told me that if you couldn't control yourself, I would have to do it for you."

I could feel his confusion as I moved away from him a few yards, digging through the wet pockets of the jeans that looked as if they'd been through a shredder. Luckily, the objects I brought out survived Gabriel's method of removing clothing.

"You intend to restrain me?" he asked as he saw the thin strips of rope I held.

"Mother knows best," I said with a smile as I tied one of the ropes around his wrist. I looked around for something to anchor the rope. "Ah, that'll do nicely."

We were close enough to a tree that I could loop the

rope around its narrow trunk, then back to Gabriel, where I tied it around his free hand, shortening the rope so that his hands were pulled up to his ears.

He frowned. "May, I am a wyvern."

"I know you are."

I checked the knots on his first wrist. They looked solid.

"Wyverns are naturally dominant. We do not like being restrained."

"Mmhmm. Is the rope too tight?"

He considered his hands, wiggling his fingers. "No. I think we should discuss the fact that, about this, my mother may be wrong."

"You think so?" I sat back and admired my handiwork. "I have to admit, Gabriel, there is something strangely exciting about seeing you spread out before me, every glorious inch of you just lying there waiting for me to touch you, and there's not a thing you can do about it. You can't distract me, you can't touch me, you can't stop me. Oh, yes. Kaawa is a genius."

His frown faded as he gave me a jaded look. "It would take more than a bit of rope to keep me from touching you, little bird."

"Oh, we both know you could snap that rope like it was a piece of thread," I agreed. "But that's not its real purpose. You're well aware that the only reason I tied your hands is because it's important to me to be able to touch you the way I want to."

His eyes glittered with the cold light of the moon. "You did not tell me that you were troubled by the method of our lovemaking, mate. I have allowed myself to indulge in dragon ways because you bear the shard, and thought you understood and shared those pleasures, but I realize they are foreign to you. I will adapt to your desires in the future."

I kissed him quickly, his breath hot on my lips as I

said, "Don't you dare—I told you I had no complaints, and I meant it. The way you do things is just fine with me, Gabriel, as if you weren't aware that you make me mindless with pleasure. I just want to try this, too."

He glanced over at one of his bound hands, then sighed. "Very well," he said, letting his head fall back to the ground. "Proceed. Although I should warn you that I am uncomfortable with the idea of being bound, and thus am likely to not respond the way I would should you release me and allow events to proceed in a manner befitting drag—glargern!"

The gibberish word spilled out of him just as I bent down and took him into my mouth. Despite being bound to the sexiest dragon in the history of the planet, I had never managed to fulfill my wish to pleasure him with my mouth. Unfortunately, once I had him in that position, I wasn't too sure of how to continue.

"Gabriel?" I asked after a moment of more or less rolling him around my tongue.

"Hrn?"

"I'm not quite sure what I should be doing. Maybe you could give me a little direction?"

"Neff."

I looked down at him. His penis was now slick with saliva, waving gently in the breeze as his groin muscles twitched, his legs taut, his belly rigid. He was gripping the rope in either hand, the veins in his arms standing out starkly, giving hint to the strain of holding himself still for me.

Love filled me at such self-sacrifice. I made a mental vow to reward such devotion, and bent to my task, deciding that I'd just try out a few things and see if I got any response.

I swirled my tongue around him, gently cupping his

testicles, causing him to moan nonstop, his hips bucking upward.

"Now, isn't this fun?" I asked, an audible pop sounding as I pulled my mouth off him. "I'm enjoying this. You taste so wonderful, Gabriel. All woodsy and earthy and dragonny. Not at all like a urinal cake, like Cyrene said men taste, although how on earth she knows what a urinal cake tastes like is beyond me. You are enjoying this, aren't you?"

He gurgled at me.

"Good. Cy swears by something called Pink Mango Massage Oil. I thought we could try that next. I have a little sample of it in my pocket. I think if I dribbled it around your penis and slicked you up—"

I moved over to my jeans, reaching for the tiny plastic container, when I was yanked backwards, the ground suddenly beneath me, and Gabriel above, shredded bits of rope trailing from his wrists. "My turn!"

"I don't need to be restrained," I said as he wrapped a bit of rope around first one wrist, then the other. "Gabriel! That's *my* Pink Mango Massage Oil."

"Not anymore, my little tormentor," he said, snatching the packet from my hand. He bit off the soft plastic top, spitting it out before dribbling oil in a serpentine pattern down my chest, to my groin. He grinned, his dimples flashing at me, causing heat to flush upward from my belly. "Now let us see how you like being the recipient of the attention of a wyvern."

My toes curled at the look he gave me. He spread the massage oil across my breasts, kneading them with strokes that had me writhing on the ground.

"Shall I tell you what I'm going to do with this oil? I will start with it at your breasts, those two delectable mounds that fit so perfectly in my hands and mouth. I shall blow gently on your delicious chocolaty nipples, savoring the taste of them and you as I whip you into a frenzy. I will rub my whiskers on them, making you moan and beg me to end the torment. I will take them into my mouth and bite them gently, causing you to writhe uncontrollably."

My breath caught in my throat and didn't seem to move as his words filled my head.

"Then I will spread the oil around your belly, using it to caress all of those lovely curves, over to your hips, the sweet line of which makes me want to fall to my knees. Just when you think you can bear it no more, I will rub it lower, into your sex, caressing it into you, after which I will lick it all off. I will bring you to my mouth, and show you that two can play at oral sex. And then, when I have wrung at least three more orgasms out of you, I will push myself into your Pink Mango–flavored self, deep into your fiery depths, and give you fulfillment like you've never had."

I almost forgot how to breathe—so exciting were the images he brought to my mind. My body strained against his touch, wanting to feel all of it, all of it right now. But then he put his mouth down to my now-hard nipples, and I stopped thinking altogether. "*Agathos daimon!* That's ... that's ... oh, my, yes! More mouth! More fire!"

His mouth was on my stomach, swirling little curlicues of fire around it as he licked up the massage oil, and everything was just fine until I slid my leg up alongside his, rubbing my foot down the long, muscled lines of his calf.

He reared back as if he'd been shot, stared at me with eyes of purest mercury, then was between my legs, lifting my hips to meet his thrust, the burning brand of him deep in my body the most exquisite of sensations. It took even less time than our previous bout, his climax coming almost immediately, with mine following as the last echoes of his roar of completion faded away into the night.

I didn't recover for at least ten minutes, but when I did, I couldn't help but laugh.

"I don't even have the strength to open my eyes to see what it is you find so funny. You have worn me out, mate, and that is not something that happens frequently to a dragon," he said, and then defied his words by opening both eyes and rolling over onto his side, pulling me close against his body. "What is it you find amusing?"

I kissed his nose, tugging gently on one dreadlock until he gave me his fire. "I was thinking that the people in this neighborhood are going to report us if we keep it up. I love you, Gabriel."

"And I love you, my adorable little dominatrix. I failed at foreplay again, didn't I?"

"Yes, but I'm not complaining."

He smiled, and it was a smug smile, a purely male smile, a gesture that acknowledged his awareness that he had pleasured me to the tips of my toes.

I bit his shoulder and snuggled up against his chest, all worries temporarily driven away by the dragon who lay curled protectively around me.

# Chapter Fourteen

The sanctuary we had found in the park ended with the sound of a police siren passing by. Gabriel stretched and gently pried me off him so he could get up. "I suppose we should return to Drake's house. I wish to see Fiat."

I groaned as I sat up, muscles worn and well used in the vigorous lovemaking that was so common with Gabriel. "He was conscious when I went to bed. Mad as hell, but conscious. I think Drake was going to wait until you arrived to talk to him."

"Drake knows it is my right to kill him," he said matter-of-factly as he pulled on his pants and shoes.

I looked with dismay at the remains of my clothing. "You're not going to kill him. Crap. I ripped your shirt off you, didn't I? How am I going to get back to Drake's house?"

"Why shouldn't I?" He ignored my last question to address my statement, offering me his hand. I took it and let him pull me to my feet.

"Because you're not a vindictive person," I said, looking around for anything I might use as a covering. He picked me up in his arms.

"Shadow. I will carry you home."

"That's going to look a little odd," I pointed out as he started off to the gate.

"It can't be helped."

He was silent as he strode through the streets, keeping out of the streetlights as much as possible. He did, in fact, garner a few odd looks from passersby as he carried an apparently invisible burden, but the street was dark enough that I doubted if anyone saw my naked form.

István opened the door to Drake's house. Gabriel had set me down, standing in front of me as the light spilled out of the house onto the front steps.

"May we borrow your shirt?" Gabriel asked István.

The green dragon blinked a few times, but obediently peeled off his shirt and handed it over to Gabriel, who shoved it behind his back. I took it, pulling it on over my head, shivering with the cold now that I didn't have Gabriel to warm me.

István said nothing as Gabriel stepped aside and I entered the house clad in only the shirt.

"It's a long story," I told István.

He just grinned, closing the door behind us.

"Is Magoth still unconscious?" I asked as we headed for the stairs.

"No." He made a face. "He is with Catalina."

Gabriel raised his eyebrows.

"You don't want to know," I told him. "Neither, for that matter, do I. I'm going to bed."

Gabriel didn't join me for an hour, and then he had only just fallen asleep before it was time to wake him up for the *sárkány*.

"I hate to do it," I told Kaawa as we walked slowly up the stairs from the breakfast room. "He only got to sleep an hour and a half ago, since he insisted on dragging Fiat from his bed."

"Is that what all that yelling was about?" Kaawa asked as we rounded the landing and started on the second flight. "I wondered about that when I heard his voice raised in anger, but since there was no general outcry, I assumed it was some dragon business."

"He evidently went in to scare the crap out of Fiat, but you know how hotheaded Fiat is. He threatened to dismember me, or something along those lines, and Gabriel snapped. I was going to stay out of it, since the sight of me seems to enrage Fiat, but when I heard Gabriel bellow, I decided a calmer mind might be needed. I got there just as Gabriel tried to decapitate Fiat, but luckily, Drake was there ahead of me, and he and his men, and Tipene and Maata, managed to pull Gabriel off Fiat before he could do anything more than slice him up a bit."

"I can't think of the last time Gabriel truly lost his temper," Kaawa said as we reached the top of the stairs. We paused outside the door to my room. "How very unusual of him."

I said nothing for a moment, remembering how Gabriel wielded a shadow sword against Baltic. "He really needs his sleep, but I guess there's nothing for it but to wake him up."

I had my hand on the door when Pál emerged at the far end of the hall. "There you are," he said, coming up to us. "Drake wishes to see you."

"Now?" I glanced at Kaawa's watch. "I have to get Gabriel up for the *sárkány*. How's Fiat, speaking of that?"

He made a face. "He healed."

"Figures."

"Drake said it was most urgent," Pál urged.

I followed him down a flight of stairs to Aisling's bedroom.

"—the most unreasonable, arrogant, stubborn dragon in the whole entire history of dragons—oh, May, thank god. A voice of sanity. Will you please tell this deranged wyvern I've married that it's perfectly safe for me to ride in a car?"

Pál melted away, closing the door quietly after having delivered me to the room. I looked from an obviously distraught Aisling to Drake, standing stoic and silent in the middle of the room, his arms crossed, and over to Jim, who lay on a large dog bed set against the window, evidently playing with a handheld game device.

"Didn't I tell you to stay out of Aisling's way?" I asked it.

"Yeah, but she said I could stay in here so we could play our PSPs together. Ah, damn. You made me crash into Darth Vader. Now I have to start this level over again."

A look in Drake's eyes warned against the flip comment I was going to make about dragons being overprotective. Perhaps there was a reason he wanted Aisling at home other than general stubbornness. "I assume you're peeved because he's insisted you can't go to the *sárkány*?"

"Bingo," Jim said, looking up from its game console. "Give the girl a cigar."

"I'm his damned mate," she said, glaring at Drake, her hands on her hips. "He's made sure I am dragged off to every other dragon event, but now he is being totally and completely unreasonable!"

"Bean said the baby had turned. You could go into labor at any moment," Drake said, his eyes somewhat wary.

I bit back a smile. "Bean the midwife?"

Aisling nodded. "She's a lovely person, really, but she's admitted herself that she's never dealt with a human having a dragon baby, and that the timeline is a bit off because of that. So there is no reason whatsoever I should not go to the *sárkány*."

"You are not leaving the house," Drake said firmly. She took a deep breath, obviously about ready to yell. He held up a hand to stop her, adding quickly, "Since it means so much to you to be there, and more importantly, since I am unwilling to leave you at this time, we will bring the *sárkány* to us."

Aisling blinked at him a couple of times, her mouth ajar slightly. "You're having it here?" she asked, clearly astounded.

I knew how she felt. A *sárkány*, so Gabriel had told me, was a formal meeting of wyverns, used to address issues of the gravest importance. They were sometimes volatile meetings, ones that could have deadly repercussions, such as the one that had been held when Baltic stormed in, his guns literally blazing.

"I thought it would please you," Drake said smoothly.

"Oh. Well . . . it does please me." She gave him a blinding smile. Jim clicked its tongue and went back to playing its game machine. "I knew you could be reasonable if you tried. I should probably go check with Suzanne to make sure we have some snacks and beverages. Jim! Heel."

"But I'm about to go after Vader," it complained, shambling after her. "You're just pissed because you can't make it past the Yoda level."

I waited until the two of them were down the hall and out of earshot before I turned back to Drake. "I assume Gabriel told you about what he and the others found?"

His expression turned dark. "It was not Kostya."

I studied his face for a minute. Drake was a hard man, I suppose technically handsome, with bright green eyes, dark hair, and an obstinate jaw, but he wasn't what I thought of as particularly flexible. He was, I suspected, very loyal.

It was for that reason I picked my words with care. "I find it difficult to believe that Kostya would do something so heinous, but Gabriel insists that Kostya was seen. Have you spoken to him?"

"Kostya?"

I nodded.

Drake's expression grew blacker. "Briefly. I told him the *sárkány* was moved to this house, and asked if all was in readiness on his end. He assured me it was. I do not fear for the safety of Aisling with him around, if that is what you are so carefully hinting. He is my brother. I know him. He has been tortured and tormented for many decades, and he has much darkness inside him, but he would not act in the way Gabriel suggests."

There wasn't much I could say about that. I happened to agree with him, but I was very cognizant of the fact that I was expected to show nothing but support for Gabriel's decisions. Although I felt a certain amount of leniency toward that archaic rule could be shown while I was around Drake and Aisling, I didn't want them thinking I wouldn't back up Gabriel no matter what choices he made.

The fact that I'd simply persuade him away from doing anything stupid was beside the point.

"I just hope you have a lot of green dragons who can keep everyone civil," I said. "If Kostya is planning on bringing his full delegation, and the other wyverns bring their members, the house is going to be very, very full."

"We will open up the downstairs rooms," Drake agreed. "It was once a ballroom—it will suffice."

And so it was that slightly over three hours later I stood next to Gabriel at one end of the long room that ran the length of the house. It had been divided up into three smaller rooms, making up the large sitting room, a small morning room, and the dining room, but now the screens normally covering the folding walls were pulled aside, most of the furniture had been removed, and the long heavy dining table was pulled into a central position with five heavy wooden chairs set around it.

I brushed Gabriel's hand, needing the comfort of his touch, but not wanting to do anything that could be considered inappropriate in front of the other dragons.

He took my hand without looking at me, his fingers rubbing across my knuckles. "Do not fear, little bird. I will not allow Fiat to disturb the *sárkány*."

I said nothing, just straightened my shoulders, sliding a quick glance to my left at Maata. Behind us stood Obi, Nathaniel, and Tipene. Like the other silver dragons, they wore what I thought of as the formal dragon wear: knee-length tunics of a black material that seemed impossibly dark, heavily embroidered with silver to the point where the fabric beneath was almost impossible to see. The embroidery consisted of abstract shapes and swirls, a detailed, intricate pattern that seemed to shift and move in the light. Gabriel's tunic was heavy with silver, real silver, I knew from examining it earlier, glittering as bright as his eyes, patterned into several fantastical shapes of dragons leaping and cavorting. He had presented me with a tunic, as well, one bearing only one dragon, but I loved it the most—it was clearly based on Gabriel's dragon form, and the head of it lay directly over my heart.

Gabriel also wore a belt slung low over his hips, a familiar sword hanging from it. It was the shadow sword I'd taken from Bael's wrath demon, a powerful weapon that I prayed he would not need to use.

"Showtime," I said under my breath, straightening my shoulders and trying to look calm and collected as Kostya strode through the doorway. He was followed by two women and one man, all three of his attendants dark-haired and dark-eyed.

"Is that his entourage?" I asked Gabriel quietly.

"His guard, yes. Drake mentioned he had at last formalized them."

Kostya stopped in the middle of the room, and made a formal bow first to his brother, then to Gabriel. The latter tensed, but did nothing other than return the formal greeting. A *sárkány*, I had learned, was a very rigid affair, and followed innumerable rules, evidently put into place to keep the volatile dragons from killing one another should tempers run high.

"The others have not arrived yet?" Kostya asked Drake.

"Fiat is here," Drake answered with the briefest of glances toward us. "Chuan Ren will no doubt be here. Bastian called a short while ago and said his flight was delayed, but he would be here immediately upon landing. I expect him momentarily."

While Drake talked with his brother, I studied Kostya and his little group, noticing as I did so that Gabriel, normally a very sociable person, made no effort to join their discussion. I knew Fiat's involvement with Baltic had thrown him a bit, for which I was frankly grateful. I had no desire to get on Drake's bad side should Gabriel pursue the idea that Kostya was behind the murders of all those innocent dragons.

"Those two women don't look like they could take down a curtain, let alone a dragon intent on attacking Kostya," I murmured to Gabriel.

Maata, on my left, heard me and snorted under her breath.

"Knowing Kostya as I do," Gabriel said, his dimples flaring briefly to life, "I suspect they are there more for effect than actual use."

I had to agree. The women were of average height and slender builds, looking more like expensive models than bodyguards. They were dressed in black, matching leather bustiers trimmed with straps and chains, and tight black pants that looked like they'd been painted on. One wore shiny leather stiletto boots that probably could have put someone's eye out; the other had open-toed sandals with laces that crisscrossed up the calves of her pants. The man was just as somber as his companions, his long hair pulled back in a short ponytail, his goatee nowhere near as charming as Gabriel's.

"He would have to bring them here. I can't begin to tell you what sort of hell there will be to pay if Cyrene sees Kostya with his little harem," I said softly.

Gabriel shot me a questioning glance. "I thought she broke up with Kostya?"

"Cy's method of breaking up isn't final until the man dies or moves to another continent," I said wearily. "She'll keep moping over him for at least six months. If we're lucky, she'll find someone new who will drive all thoughts of the faithless Kostya from her mind."

"May." Kostya approached, giving me yet another bow. "It is a pleasure to see you again."

Mindful of my manners and dragon etiquette, I smiled, and did not ask him if he cold-bloodedly murdered sixty-eight dragons in the last few days. "Thank you." I searched through available topics of conversation that would not address any touchy subjects. "I imagine you're happy the *sárkány* is finally being called. It must have been a difficult two months for you."

There was a questioning look in his eye as if he sensed I might be insulting him, but he simply inclined his head in agreement. "I am indeed. As, no doubt, you have been waiting for this."

He waved a hand and the male black dragon stepped forward, pulling from his inside coat pocket a long ebony case. Kostya took it, his gaze shifting to Gabriel. "I will not insult you by asking if you intend to honor your agreement."

"I have yet to be accused of violating a vow," Gabriel

said calmly, although his placid expression hid a veritable inferno of emotions.

Kostya studied him for another few seconds, then handed him the long wooden box, turning away and returning to his brother's side without another word.

The two supermodel guards eyed first Gabriel, then me, their expressions as blank as a wall. They followed Kostya, silent and stalwart, although I noticed one of them, the smaller of the two, was giving Gabriel a look that bespoke a personal interest.

The damned hussy. Eyeing him right in front of me.

Gabriel slid aside a metal lock and opened the wooden case for a moment. Lying on a bed of dark navy velvet was a long glass tube wrapped in intricate gold filigree. Inside the tube, a glittering crystal was suspended in some form of viscous liquid. I thought at first it was a clear crystal, somewhat quartzlike in appearance, but as Gabriel examined the phylactery, I realized that the shard wasn't clear—it held innumerable colors, each of which flashed as light caught a plane of the shard. It was incredibly beautiful and just as incredibly impressive, positively reeking of power.

"So that's the Modana Phylactery," I said as Gabriel closed the case and handed it to Tipene. "It's really lovely."

"May, I can't believe you would do this to me—so it's true!"

"Oh, no," I said, my heart sinking as Cyrene stood posed in the doorway, glaring dramatically at Kostya.

"You are having a *sárkány* now! You deliberately tried to exclude me! And who are those ... those ... *hussies* standing around that pig of a dragon?"

# Chapter Fifteen

"Dammit, Jim," I said in a low tone to the demon who straggled in behind my twin. "You were supposed to keep her shopping."

"Hey, there's only so much a demon can do in the face of a rampaging naiad! The second Cyrene heard the *sárkány* was for this afternoon instead of being put off until tomorrow, like some perfidious doppelganger told her, she dropped everything and came roaring home."

"And just how did she hear that?" I snapped, pinching its ear.

"No pinching! Ow! It might have slipped out, that's all. Man, I'm going back to Aisling. She might lose one or two of my toes, but she doesn't pinch me all the time!"

Jim backed out of the door as Kostya strode forward a few feet.

"You have no place here, naiad," he said scornfully, looking down his nose at Cyrene, his two models posing on either side of him. "You are not a member of any sept, nor are you a dragon, and you sure as hell aren't a mate."

"Oh, no," I moaned softly. "He didn't say that."

"You would think he would have learned by now what a red flag that is to her," Gabriel agreed, momentarily diverted by the scene to relax a smidgen.

"Oh!" Cyrene bellowed, stomping forward with surprising noise considering how petite she was. She stopped directly in front of Kostya, less than a foot away, turning her glare first on one hussy, then the second before finally settling it on the focus of her ire. "You take that back! You know full well I was your mate until you let greed and avarice take hold of you."

"I have allowed nothing to take hold of me but good sense. You are not a wyvern's mate," Kostya ground out, his hands fisted. I watched him warily, ready to spring forward if he should lose his temper and try to get violent with Cyrene. I didn't dispute that she was enough to try anyone's patience, but I would not allow him to hurt her.

"I'm not talking about being a *wyvern's* mate," Cyrene shouted, taking me by surprise. Judging by the looks on the faces of the others around us, they were suffering from a similar emotion.

"Then what are you blathering about?" Kostya asked, and the two models took a step toward Cyrene, their attitudes menacing.

"How bad a breach of etiquette is it to punch another wyvern's bodyguards in the face?" I asked Gabriel.

The dimple nearest me quivered for a moment. "Bad. Please do not indulge yourself."

I sighed. "All right, but I want brownie points for restraint."

"I'm talking about the person meant for you, you idiot!" Cyrene yelled, punching him in the chest. He rubbed it absently, frowning down at her, as she continued. "Not a dragon's mate, just *your* mate. You know, the person you love and adore and want to spend a couple of centuries with. You told me you loved me! You said you couldn't live without me!"

Kostya, to my great amusement, looked embarrassed, his gaze flickering around the room at us as we all watched with interest while Cyrene lambasted him.

"That was spoken in a private moment," he said in a low voice, sending her a furious look.

"Screw private!" she snapped, poking him in the chest again. "You told me you loved me. You said we were meant to be together. Then you let that stupid lair ruin everything. You're just a pig, Kostya! No, you're a pig-dog! A pig-dog dragon, and I loathe the very sight of you! I never want to see you again. Do you hear me? Never want to see you again!"

Cyrene was panting with emotion, her eyes blazing as she shoved him in the chest a third time.

Kostya stared down at her with a black expression for about half a second; then with a growled profanity, he grabbed her, pulling her up against his chest as he kissed the living daylights out of her. That lasted for about five seconds before Kostya yelped, lifting his head with surprise. There was blood on his lip.

"Pig-dog!" Cyrene snarled at him.

"Insane watery tart," he spat back.

They stared at each other for another few seconds; then this time, Cyrene flung herself at his head and locked her mouth over his.

"Well," I said, clearing my throat, but couldn't think of anything to say.

The two models looked at each other in stunned surprise for a moment. Then both narrowed their eyes and glared at the back of Cyrene's head. Kostya hoisted her up, his hands on her behind, as he continued to kiss her, Cyrene making happy little moaning noises as she wrapped her legs around his hips.

"I'm so glad Jim isn't here to see this," I said to Gabriel.

He chuckled before his expression turned serious again as Chuan Ren entered the room, followed by two red dragons. One I recognized as her handsome son, Jian; the other was a man I hadn't seen before.

Chuan Ren was not my favorite dragon. Outwardly she resembled a tall, elegant Chinese doll, all porcelain skin and long silky black hair, but she was meaner than Magoth, and twice as deadly. She looked around the room with dark brown eyes with deep red lights, her gaze pausing for a moment on the sight of Kostya and Cyrene locked in a kiss.

"Where is Fiat?" she asked after giving them a look filled with scorn and disgust.

"He will be here when the *sárkány* is called to order," Drake said placidly.

"You will hand him over to me now," Chuan Ren demanded in her officious manner. "You agreed I could punish him for the attempt to take over my sept."

"Chuan Ren. You have met my mate, May, I believe?" Gabriel interrupted her, pulling me forward as he approached her.

She spared me only a harsh glance before turning her attention on him. "I have acknowledged her as such, yes."

Gabriel waited a moment.

She made an annoyed sound and gestured sharply to her two companions. "I present to the silver mate my mate, Li, and son, Jian."

"It's a pleasure to meet you," I told the man who was her mate. He smiled, and bowed, as did Jian.

"I am glad to see you in good health," the latter said, taking my hand to press a kiss to the back of it. "We owe you much in returning Chuan Ren to us."

"Ever the diplomat," she said in a contemptuous tone to her son.

I wasn't surprised. Chuan Ren seemed to feel force was the only way to achieve a goal.

"You are in command of the red dragons again?" Gabriel asked her.

"Did you doubt I would take control the second I was released from Abaddon?"

He smiled. "I knew you would not tolerate another ruling the red sept, but you said you had not found him to challenge him. He returned to England while we were hunting for him in Europe. How, then, did you challenge him for control?"

Her eyes narrowed on him. "I do not need the stupidity of a challenge to take control of what is mine," she said in a low, mean voice. "The red dragons belong to me and no other."

"What did I miss? I heard yelling," Aisling said as she rushed into the room, Jim at her heels. She came to an abrupt halt at the sight of Kostya and Cyrene, still engaged in a kiss. "Good god."

"Fires of Abaddon," Jim said, goggling. "He's gonna boink her right there!"

"Quiet, demon," Aisling ordered absently, blinking at the sight of the two lovers.

Drake was immediately at her side, gently pulling her over to a chair. "*Kincsem*, I said I would fetch you when it was time. You are early. You will tire yourself."

"Stop fussing," she said, but there was love in her eyes as she kissed his cheek when he bent over her. "I'm fine. What's happened other than Cyrene and Kostya checking each other's fillings?"

"It would appear that Chuan Ren hasn't formally taken over control of her sept yet," I said, watching the red wyvern.

Her lip curled at me. "Gabriel, tell your mate I will not repeat myself to her. I am the red wyvern. Nothing that puling little turd Fiat can do will change that, as you will see if you will have him brought to me so I may torture him as he deserves."

"Excellent! I thought we might be late, but we're just in time for the torture," Magoth said, flinging open the door. He was dressed in his usual pair of black leather pants, with a black shirt open to his navel, his favorite bullwhip wrapped around his waist. Next to him was the sultry-eyed Catalina, listing somewhat to the side as if she couldn't stand up straight.

"Mother?" Drake took a few steps forward, frowning first at his mother, then at Magoth. "What has happened to you?"

Magoth leered. "We had a very interesting night. Your mother is most . . . inventive . . . in her ideas of pleasure."

Catalina's hair was mussed, her clothing wrinkled, her mouth red and swollen, and her eyes looked a bit vague, as if she'd been through a particularly strenuous orgy. "Inventive," Catalina agreed, her expression dazed.

Drake swore under his breath as he tidied her blouse to cover a breast that was almost exposed. "I expected better of you, Mother. You look like a loose woman."

"Loose." She weaved at him, looking like she might fall over.

Magoth grabbed her quickly and propped her up against the doorframe, rubbing his hands as he entered the room. "What sort of torture are you having at this dragon gathering, hmm? I'm happy to act as consultant as to what is the best for large-group participation."

"No one will be tortured at the *sárkány*," Drake said, gesturing toward his mother. Immediately Pál and István, who had been standing at the other end of the room, moved to her side and started to take her out.

The word "torture" seemed to bring her around.

"Release me," she said, shaking her head as if to clear it. "I can walk." She gave both dragons a haughty look before straightening her shoulders, lifting her chin, and sailing into the room with a pale imitation of her normal aplomb.

She was fine until she spotted the twosome. The sight of them seemed to give her new energy.

"What is this?" she demanded, stalking into the room to stand next to the Cyrene/Kostya entity. "Who is this besom sucking the face of my firstborn, my delicious Kostya? Drake, what are you thinking allowing this?"

"Kostya is old enough to deal with his women as he likes," Drake said smoothly, although he shot his brother a look as he said it. "I would, however, appreciate it if he managed to refrain from outright sexual intercourse during the *sárkány*."

"You know how to take the fun out of any get-together," Jim said.

"I insist that he stop!" Catalina said, hands on her hips. She nodded to the two models. "Remove that naiad from the person of my dear son."

The two models hesitated, eyeing Cyrene. "I dare not contradict the wyvern," one of them finally said.

"You will do as I say," she said, gaining control of herself with every passing moment. "Remove her!"

"We cannot," the second model said, casting an appealing glance toward the male bodyguard.

"We answer only to the wyvern," he explained, somewhat lamely to my ears.

Catalina didn't like that.

"Drake!" she demanded. "Do something! She will smother him."

"Mother, I told you that your presence, no matter how charming, was not required at the *sárkány*," Drake said, moving toward his mother, pausing only to glare at Magoth as he tried to look down Aisling's top.

She drew a ward in the air that had the demon lord leaping back with a yelp.

"You obviously are not yourself right now. You will return to your room and rest," Drake continued, taking his mother by the arm and propelling her toward the door.

"You will not order me around like that! I did not rip you screaming from my body only to have you order me around now! *Madre de dios*, she will kill him! She will suck the life out of his body! Drake! You will cease pushing me out the door." She lurched to the side of the door, clutching the doorframe.

"Only dragons in septs recognized by the weyr may attend the *sárkány*," Drake answered, prying her fingers off the frame. "You are a black dragon, and the black dragons have not yet been recognized. I will tell you later all that happens."

"I will not have this!" Catalina yelled as Pál and István, each taking an arm, hauled her toward the stairs.

"Inventive, but alas, a bit on the shouty side," Magoth said, taking my hand and pressing a wet kiss to the back. "It is better she is taken off. You look delicious as ever, wife. I see your twin will be hosting an orgy. Dare I hope that will take place during the torture?"

I yanked my hand from his, but I really needn't have bothered.

Gabriel lifted Magoth up by the neck, and started to squeeze.

"May, do something," Magoth squeaked, his face turning red.

"You know better than to bait Gabriel," I told him, but mindful of the scene my twin was already creating, I decided that circumspection was the best course. I touched Gabriel on the arm and gestured toward the floor.

He hesitated a moment; then he, too, realized that strangling Magoth on the spot wouldn't be in the best interests of the *sárkány*. He released him with a warning of, "Touch her again, and I will remove your curse."

"You can't remove it," Magoth said blithely, then froze as the meaning sank into his lust-fogged brain. His hands moved protectively over his groin as he glared at Gabriel. "Wife, one of these days your lover will go too far."

"Stop calling me that," I said as Drake marched over.

"Your presence is not required, either," he said, gesturing toward the door. "Leave."

"I think not," Magoth said, sitting down in a chair set at the wall.

"You are not a dragon. This is a *sárkány*, a meeting of the weyr. You cannot be allowed to stay," Drake insisted.

"Ah, but my consort is here, and where she goes, so goes me. I. Me. Whichever. Those are the rules, and since you are such a stickler for such, I'm sure you will have no difficulty agreeing I should follow them."

Drake shot me a questioning look.

"Unfortunately," I said, my shoulder slumping a little as I leaned into Gabriel, "he's correct. The rules say he can demand to be in my presence at any time."

Drake said something that wasn't very complimentary to anyone, but let it go, turning when the door opened again to admit a very handsome blond man, followed by two other men, both with light brown hair and bright blue eyes. "A thousand apologies for our lateness. The flight was delayed."

"Bastian," Aisling called from her chair. "How nice to see you. Did you have much trouble getting into Fiat's lair?"

"None at all, dear lady. You look radiant as ever. Will you be having that child soon?" he asked, bowing over her hand.

Drake growled and elbowed him aside.

Aisling laughed. "Very soon, I hope. Forgive Drake— he's overdosed on expectant-father genes."

"Ah, but it is understandable." Bastian greeted Chuan Ren, who nodded coldly to him. He turned to us with a warm smile. "The blue dragons offer greetings to Gabriel and his charming mate. May, I present to you Duarte and Godhino, my guards. And is that your twin who Kostya is kissing?"

"I'd say the reverse was technically the truth, but by now, it's a moot point. Yes, that's Cyrene. Please ignore them. They appear to be trying to break a world record," I said, smiling at the blue dragon bodyguards as they grinned back at me before moving on to chat with Tipene and Maata.

"And this is . . . er . . ." Bastian didn't quite know how to take Magoth, I could see. "This is . . . ?"

"I am Magoth, sixth principle spirit of Abaddon, lord of thirty legions, marquis of the order of dominations," he said with an odd expression of concentration as he scanned Bastian's face. "Don't I know you?"

Bastian looked startled. "No. I've never met a demon lord before. Other than Aisling, of course, but she doesn't really count because she is not evil."

"Yes, I do. I know you," Magoth said, continuing his scrutiny. "It was Milan in the last century. I was there for an opening of one of my films, and you were in the villa next to mine. You tried to seduce me. I would not let you because I was, at that time, busy enthralling a certain naiad who apparently has the ability to hold her breath for an inordinately long amount of time, but it was you—of that I'm sure. Well, well, well. And now you're a wyvern?"

Bastian looked a bit wild around the eyes. "I've never seen you before. I've never had a villa in Milan! My villa is in Santa Christina!"

"I *know* it was you," Magoth insisted.

"It could have been Fiat," I said thoughtfully. "You

look almost identical, although it's odd that Fiat didn't remember you."

Magoth grunted his agreement. "I am unforgettable as a lover."

That was probably the understatement of the century. "I didn't know that Fiat was of that persuasion, but I suppose anything is possible."

Magoth shrugged and looked away, bored. "He had his cock buried in the wife of the local mayor at the time he propositioned me, so he probably does as I do—whatever pleases him at the moment." He glanced back at Bastian, about to ask an obvious question.

"No," Bastian said quickly, much to his bodyguards' amusement. "I am not interested."

"Your loss, as my sweet May can tell you," Magoth said, blowing me a kiss.

Gabriel moved so fast I didn't even see him. Magoth did, though. Or rather, he felt the result of Gabriel's fist smashing into his nose. Magoth's head snapped back, slamming into the wall.

"My apologies," Gabriel said to the room at large, returning to my side. Maata snickered. Tipene grinned broadly. I sighed. "I had a muscle spasm, and my hand must have hit Magoth."

"Muscle spasm," I said, giving him a look.

His dimples flared to life, and I considered for a moment duplicating my twin's action, and leaping on the man I loved.

"Later, little bird," he said, the dratted man reading my mind again. He took my hand and tucked it into his arm. "Then you may have your way with me again."

"Enough!" Chuan Ren said in a demanding tone. "Let us begin the *sárkány* so that I might seek my revenge against that worm Fiat."

I eyed Gabriel, thinking all sorts of thoughts that

weren't at all appropriate to a *sárkány*, as the dragons gathered around the table.

"Kostya," Drake said, standing next to his brother.

Neither Kostya nor Cyrene stopped their epic kiss.

"Konstantin Fekete," Drake said in a louder voice, invoking Kostya's full name to get his attention. When Kostya still didn't respond, he gave him a hard shove, saying in a lower tone, "For god's sake, Kostya, we've seen enough. Pull yourself together. The *sárkány* is ready to start."

Kostya managed to pull back from Cyrene, a dazed look on his face. *"Sárkány?"* he asked, clearly not registering the word.

"Oh, Kostykins," Cyrene cooed, sliding down his body until her feet were under her again. "I knew you cared. I just knew it. You admit it, don't you? You love me more than some silly treasure."

Kostya's expression hardened as intelligence returned to his eyes. A faint dusky flush rode his cheeks as he glanced around the room. "Erm . . . I was momentarily distracted. I apologize for such behavior."

"Oh no, you're not getting away from me before you admit it," Cyrene said, latching onto the front of his black tunic. "You have to say it before witnesses. I'm not going to repeat what I've gone through these last couple of days. You say it."

"Now is not the time, woman," Kostya said, prying Cyrene's hands off his shirt.

"Of course it is. Say it!"

"The *sárkány* is about to begin. We will deal with our personal issues later," Kostya insisted, taking Cy by the wrist and pulling her over to a chair next to the wall. He shoved her down into it before striding over to the table.

"Like hell we will! Say it!" She was there in front of

him again. "Say it or so help me, I'll smite you as you've never been smited!"

"'Smitten,' I think, is the word. Is it not?" Bastian asked Duarte. "Which tense is that? English has always confused me."

"You can't smite me," Kostya said with a smug quirk to his lips. "Naiads don't smite."

"Oh, no," I said, suddenly realizing where the conversation was going to go. I glanced at Magoth, my fingers tightening around Gabriel's hand. "Cyrene, I hate to agree with Kostya, but really, another time would probably be better for this."

Gabriel wasn't slow on the uptake. He glanced down at my hand for a moment; then his brow cleared. "I agree with my mate. Another time, Cyrene."

"You think you know everything, don't you?" Cyrene said, glowering at Kostya. "Well, you don't!"

I dropped Gabriel's hand and hurried over to my twin. Magoth, blast his hide, must have caught one of my glances toward him, because he stood up, watching me with close attention. "Cy, really, this isn't a good time. You can yell at Kostya later, after everyone's gone, OK?"

She completely missed the emphasis I put on the word "everyone."

"Stop yanking me," she snapped, jerking her arm out of the grip I had on her. "And stop siding with that pig-dog!"

"You will cease calling me that," Kostya spat, a truly world-class glare pointed at her. "It is unfitting, and you are out of control."

Cyrene cast her arms wide, and black sparks snapped off her fingers, sending the two cover-model dragons squealing as they scrambled backwards. "I'll show you who's out of control!"

"May!" The roar of anger almost shook the house.

I closed my eyes for a moment, then opened them and met Gabriel's sympathetic gaze. "Too late," I told him.

He smiled. "You can always shift and knock him unconscious?"

"That is my power!" Magoth bellowed, I mean, really bellowed. The kind of bellow that makes windows rattle. Drake stood protectively in front of his wife, looking daggers at Magoth. "She has my powers! That . . . that . . ."

Cyrene turned on Magoth with a look that would have scared a lesser demon lord. Streaks of black lightning edged with gold crackled between her hands, a manifestation of the dark power. "That *what*?"

"That is *my* power," he snarled, striding toward her, little tendrils of black crackling off him, floating to the ground as a fine ebony powder. "You stole it! By the dominions over which I rule, you will return it to me, or I will grind you into the earth you so fervently worship!"

"Get Nora," Aisling said, tugging on Drake's shirt. He said nothing, just nodded at Pál, who had returned with István. Pál disappeared out the door.

"I didn't steal anything," Cyrene squeaked, suddenly looking afraid despite the fact that she was in possession of more power than she knew how to use. Her eyes widened as he continued toward her, the black glow between her hands fading to nothing as she pointed. "May gave it to me!"

Magoth whirled around and pinned me back with a look that chilled me to my toenails. "You I will deal with later, slave."

"This isn't good," I muttered to Gabriel. He wrapped an arm around me, narrowing his eyes at Magoth until the latter turned back to my twin.

"Return it, and I will let you live," Magoth said, gliding toward her.

Cyrene's gaze flickered from me to him. "I . . . I . . . May wouldn't like that."

"No, I wouldn't, any more than I like Magoth threatening you. If you have a bone to pick with anyone, it's me, so stop trying to intimidate Cyrene. She has no idea how to give your power away, and she wouldn't do so even if she did."

Magoth turned slowly to face me as I spoke, his eyes black pools that promised retribution.

Instantly, Gabriel was in front of me, the wrath demon's sword held easily in his hand, his legs braced in an obvious battle stance.

Nora and Pál appeared in the doorway just as Magoth said, "You think you can stop me with a pathetic blade, dragon?"

Gabriel raised the sword. "Try me."

I think Magoth would have—I truly think that even though he knew he didn't have enough power to confront Gabriel and win, he was enraged enough that he would try to get through Gabriel to reach me. Luckily, Nora took the situation in almost immediately, and slapped a binding ward on him.

He snarled and spat out curses while she quickly drew an even-stronger confinement circle around him.

"I'm sorry, Drake, but I will need Aisling's help. I've never done this before," she said a few minutes later.

Drake started to object, but Aisling grabbed his arm and used it to haul herself to her feet. "On it, Nora. Drake, stop glaring—your face will freeze like that. You can hold me, if you like, while we do this."

Magoth realized at that exact moment what they intended, and turned his ire onto me.

"Wife!" he bellowed. "I will take you with me! By all

that is unholy, this I swear to you—you will pay for the treachery you have performed this day!"

I leaned into Gabriel, drawing strength from him. "This isn't going to be pretty, you know."

He turned me to face him, his mouth warm on mine as he spoke. "I can stop it."

"No. It really is the only way. I just hope Nora is fast, because Magoth knows that he will have very little time to inflict a punishment on me before I'm summoned back."

"Is there no other way?" he asked, licking my lips with dragon fire.

"No. Just tell her to be quick, OK?"

Magoth screamed, a horrible sound that was punctuated by several explosions of glass objects in the rooms.

"I'm so glad we had the window glass demon-proofed," I heard Aisling say as Magoth's scream rose higher and higher, piercing my brain.

I wrapped my arms around Gabriel's head, clutching him tight to me as I kissed him, taking in his dragon fire, letting it wrap around me, wrap around us, bonding us together in a fiery melding of love, regret, and passion.

"Shadow, little bird," was the last thing I heard before Magoth, banished by Aisling and Nora to the Akashic Plain, summoned me to his side.

I hit the ground running, shadowing instinctively as Magoth gathered what remained of his power and whipped it around me, yanking me back to him.

"Did you think you would escape this?" he snarled, his eyes burning with black revenge.

At best guess, Nora would take about three minutes to complete the summoning, which meant I had to stay alive long enough for there to be anything left of me to summon. There was only one answer for that—I shifted into dragon form and slammed my tail upside Magoth.

An interesting note about the Akasha: because it

is outside the realm of reality, what applies beyond it does not necessarily apply within. Although Magoth had been stripped of most of his powers, in the Akasha, what he had was amplified, enlarged, and strengthened. He didn't have the ability to get himself out, but he was overall *more* than he was in our reality.

I threw everything I had into the slam against him, and fully expected him to go flying. He didn't. He grabbed my tail as I hit him, and used the momentum to throw me a good fifty feet, striking a spiked outcropping of rock with enough force to knock me out for a few seconds.

When I came to, I was in human form again, and Magoth was crouched over me, my dagger in his hands, both of which were raised over my chest.

"First I will dig out your heart and slowly crush it beneath my heel. Then I will hack off all your limbs, slowly, so you can feel each stroke of your blade; then I will sever the veins in your neck one at a time, so that you can feel each exquisite moment as your brain is starved of blood. The last thing you see will be me, licking your blood off the dagger. The last thought you have will be that I destroyed you even as I helped make you."

"You always were such a ham," I said, every atom of my being aching. "Overacting every scene, just as you are now."

*"Cunnus,"* he snarled, plunging the dagger into my heart.

# Chapter Sixteen

". . . What mortals sometimes think of as limbo, a place where beings are sent to be punished."

"I know what it is. I may be an elemental being, but I am familiar with things beyond my domain, like the Akasha. What I don't know is how you expected to get Mayling *out* of there."

"It's tricky, but not impossible. It helps that Nora had summoned her from Abaddon before. There's some sort of a sympathetic link between the two of them now that eases the more difficult summoning from the Akasha, which is why it only took Nora three tries to get May. Oh good, it looks like Gabriel has brought her around."

I opened my eyes to find those of the purest silver peering down at me with concern.

"I'm not dismembered?" I asked the eyes.

Tiny little laugh lines appeared around them as Gabriel smiled. "No."

"I still have my heart?"

"Yes. It was pierced, but it's healed now."

"The dragon shard?" I touched my chest, worried.

"Is still in you. For now."

"Magoth?"

"Successfully banished."

I relaxed. "And my silver-eyed wyvern?"

"Still madly in love with you. How do you feel?"

"All right. A bit woozy." I let him help me up into a sitting position on the dining table that had served, I gathered, as a makeshift operating table. I glanced down at the ruined tunic, gently fingering the gaping hole on the front where the embroidered dragon's head had been. "He ruined my dragon."

"*That* dragon can be replaced," Gabriel said with pointed emphasis as I got to my feet. He had an arm around my waist, holding on to me while I waited to see if my legs were going to cooperate. "You lost quite a bit of blood, but we got the dagger out and the wound sealed as quickly as possible."

I swayed into him, and whispered very quietly, "I know I was taken from you, but if you had plans to sweep me off my feet and take me up to the bedroom—"

He stopped me with a quick, hot kiss, his eyes twinkling and his dimples blaring as he said just as softly, "The standard rules do not apply when the mate in question has been injured. At least, not for an hour or two."

"Deal," I said, warming up nicely by the look in his eyes.

"May, I cannot believe that you didn't tell Magoth I had his powers," Cyrene said, her hands on her hips as Gabriel escorted me over to a chair.

Aisling murmured something about juice and cookies, but thankfully, the glass Gabriel handed me was filled with the spicy red dragon's-blood wine that I knew would do more to restore me than juice ever could.

"I didn't tell him because I knew he would have exactly the same reaction as he did, and I wanted to avoid being forced to banish him to the Akasha," I said when I could speak again. I eyed the glass of wine. It had coursed through me with the subtlety of a bulldozer, filling me with fire. I waited until the scorched feeling in my esophagus faded before adding, "Luckily, he can only do so once every half-year. Besides, I thought you'd have enough sense to keep from mentioning it in front of him."

"Sense," Kostya said, snorting. "She has no sense."

Cyrene turned on him. "I'm not done with you! You still have to say it!"

"Sit down," Kostya growled, and his two models closed in on Cy. She spun around and gave them such a warning look they backed off a couple of steps.

"Are they still at it?" I asked Gabriel, rubbing my face on his tunic for a moment as I breathed in the wonderfully woodsy scent of him.

His hand was warm on the back of my neck. "They haven't stopped."

"We did so," Cyrene said, interrupting herself to snap at Gabriel. "We stopped while Nora summoned May, and then while you pulled the dagger out of her chest. But we have unfinished business, and I insist that it be taken care of before the meeting is started."

"Our business has nothing to do with the weyr," Kostya growled.

"It does, and you know it. You're just in denial, but I'm done humoring you. I know you were tormented and tortured and held prisoner for decades, but you're free now, and it's time to move on, emotionally speaking. It's time to admit your feelings." Cyrene looked mean enough to arm-wrestle a grizzly. "If you don't say it now, I'll . . . I'll . . ."

"You'll what?" he asked, nose to nose with her now, and honestly, I didn't know what to think. "You'll smite me?"

Cyrene straightened up, her back as stiff as a broom handle. "I will leave you."

Kostya began to turn away, obviously dismissing her threat.

"Really leave you. *Forever.*"

He froze, and I knew then that it wasn't what she said that stopped him, but the way she said it. The pain in her voice came from her heart. I was a bit surprised— Cyrene had fallen in and out of love with regularity over the century I'd known her, but her heart had never really been touched. Until now, it seemed . . . and with Kostya of all people.

Kostya's expression grew blacker and blacker until I thought he was going to burst. And then he did. "Fine! You want me to admit it? You want me to bare my soul to you? I love you, you deranged water twit! I accept you as my mate! Are you happy now?"

The echoes of Kostya's declaration faded softly away as we all stared in disbelief at the two people standing in the center of the room.

"Can he do that?" I whispered to Gabriel. "Accept her as a mate if she's not one?"

"Yes," he said, taking me by surprise again. "She is not a dragon's mate, but he has accepted her as a substitute. It is binding. I am curious that he has chosen to do so in front of so many witnesses, however. That gives your twin status in the eyes of the weyr."

"That's not really the action of a man who is so intent on destroying the sept or weyr," I pointed out, eyeing Cyrene as she flung herself on Kostya and started kissing him all over his face.

"On the contrary," he said, gesturing to Tipene, who pulled a chair next to his at the table. He helped me back up to my feet—a gesture I found oddly touching—and took my hand to lead me to the table. "It could be a very clever strategy, given the power she bears."

"Cy would no more use the dark power against anyone than I would," I said gently, rubbing his hand against my cheek for a moment. Although the memory of my few minutes spent in the Akasha was fading, a few tendrils of despair still remained, making me infinitely thankful for Gabriel. "Less, really, since she doesn't have a dragon shard trying to make her do all sorts of inciting things."

He said nothing to that, but I knew he wasn't convinced, nor was he entirely easy with the idea of Cyrene now being given formal status.

As for Kostya, he suffered Cyrene's enthusiastic embrace for a few seconds, then said something in her ear that had her standing at his side in a reasonable facsimile of a person in control of her wild emotions.

The room was cleared of nondragons, with the exception of mates, mate substitutes, and demons in shaggy-dog form. Aisling evidently felt sorry for silencing Jim.

"You can speak, so long as you don't interrupt proceedings," she told it before she ordered it over to a spot near the wall.

It rolled its eyes as it stomped over to the appointed spot. "You've been taking mean lessons from May, haven't you? Boss, boss, boss, that's all the two of you ever do. Does it occur to either of you to just ask me to do something? Nooo, it's all about pushing innocent little demons around."

"Did you *want* to see Cecile this weekend?" Aisling asked sweetly.

Jim glared mutely at her, obviously getting the point.

"Who's Cecile?" I asked Gabriel.

His eyes were solemn as he watched Kostya take his seat, get thumped on the back of the shoulder by Cyrene, and leap up to get a chair to place next to his. "An elderly Welsh corgi. She is owned by Aisling's friend in Paris. I do not like it, May."

"I can take or leave corgis myself, but—"

"No, I mean that I do not like the air of contentment Kostya is wearing. You might not believe he is part of the heinous crimes committed yesterday, but he is up to something."

"The *sárkány* will begin," Chuan Ren said loudly, slamming her hand down on the table.

"Ugh. Don't tell me it's her turn to chair?" I asked Maata in a whisper.

She nodded, her face inscrutable. Both she and Tipene stood behind Gabriel. I thought it was interesting that despite there being three—four if you counted Kostya—wyverns with mates, only five chairs had been set around the table—one for each recognized wyvern, and the fifth for Kostya, who assumably would be recognized at this meeting. Each wyvern had to bring an extra chair to the table for his or her mate—the symbolism did not escape me.

"Bring Fiat!" Chuan Ren, never one to expend energy on extra words when a few sharp commands would do, almost yelled the order to Drake.

He merely raised his eyebrows. Aisling narrowed her eyes, and I could see her fingers twitching, as if she was dying to draw a ward.

"I believe the agenda lists the petition by Kostya for recognition," Drake said calmly.

Chuan Ren gripped the edge of the table until her fingers were white, but she didn't come unglued as I half expected. She merely gave Kostya a piercing look. "Konstantin Fekete, the weyr acknowledges your petition for recognition and reinstatement of the sept of the black dragons. You are familiar with the laws which govern members of the weyr—do you now agree to abide by and uphold those laws?"

Kostya rose, looking at everyone for a long, long moment. "The black dragons have been valued members of the weyr since its inception, and our inclusion within it is long overdue. Although we have had a somewhat troubled history—"

Gabriel stiffened as Kostya shot him a quick glance.

"—we have resolved our differences and are willing to let the ghosts of the past rest easily."

I wondered if he really would, whether he had realized what a folly it was to try to battle the silver dragons, or whether it was all a horrible deception meant to lull us into a false sense of security. On the whole, I believed he was sincere. He wanted to be back in the weyr just too much to endanger it by pursuing the idiotic idea of reclaiming the silver dragons.

"As wyvern by right of tanistry, heir to the former wyvern Baltic—" He choked just a smidgen on that name, but he recovered nicely. "As heir, I swear upon my life that the black dragon sept will abide by and uphold the laws of the weyr."

Chuan Ren looked bored and impatient. Barely had Kostya finished his little speech and sat down before she was on her feet, demanding to know, "You have heard the petition for recognition. How say the wyverns?"

"Aye," Drake said clearly. "The green dragons will welcome the reinstatement of the black dragons to the weyr."

Aisling smiled at Cyrene, who was positively bouncing in her chair next to Kostya. I frowned at her, but she just grinned back at me, and blew me a kiss.

Chuan Ren's nostrils flared, but she said nothing, just looked pointedly at Bastian.

He cleared his throat and stood, bowing to the table in general before saying, "As the rightful wyvern of the blue dragons, I, too, say aye. We will be delighted to see Kostya and his dragons in the weyr once again."

"I like him," Cyrene said to Kostya. I think she meant it to be a whisper, but she was so excited, everyone heard. "He's so much nicer than his nephew."

Bastian flashed her a quick smile before sitting down.

Chuan Ren took a deep breath, her fingers still tense on the table, as she glanced to Gabriel.

Gabriel watched Kostya closely for a moment, his expression benign, but his eyes blazed. "There is a fact about which the weyr is ignorant that I believe should be taken into consideration."

"Fact? What fact?" Kostya shot Gabriel an irritated look.

"You were seen in Paris," Gabriel answered. "Shortly before it was discovered that sixty-eight dragons living in France had been brutally slaughtered."

Kostya's eyes narrowed. "And you think I had something to do with that?"

"I think it's possible that your relationship with Baltic was not destroyed when he was," Gabriel said evenly. "I think you conceal your true intentions from us. I think you are capable of killing innocent dragons in the pursuit of whatever goal you feel worthy."

The look on Kostya's face was telling. Disbelief mingled with anger, followed by a furious look that told me more than mere words that he was outraged by Gabriel's statement. Kostya was innocent of the deaths; of that I was sure. "I had believed the silver dragons still possessed some honor. I see now I was wrong."

Gabriel stiffened and rose slowly. Maata made a checked movement, as if she was holding herself back.

Drake sighed and shook his head.

"You speak of our honor?" Gabriel asked, his lovely voice hard and brittle.

"I do." Kostya lifted his chin. "I was in Paris, and thus

I must be responsible. That is the way of your thinking, is it not?"

"Do you deny you were in Paris at the time?"

"No."

The room was silent for a moment as everyone digested that.

"If you were not involved in Fiat's destruction of the blue dragons, what were you doing there?"

A muscle in Kostya's jaw tightened. "You have no right to ask me that. I am not obligated by any law in the weyr to make you privy to my movements, or the reasons behind any action I take."

The silence grew thick with suspicion and animosity.

"Kostya—" Drake started to say wearily, but his brother cut him off with a gesture.

"Regardless, I will explain my presence in Paris, because I wish to further goodwill between the black and silver septs."

Maata snorted. I had to admit I didn't quite buy his altruism.

"My men had been watching a house in Paris that we believed Baltic was using. I was alerted that there had been unusual activity, and went to see for myself if it was anything while on my way back from Riga."

Gabriel waited, his posture relaxed, but I knew better. I could feel the tension thrumming through him.

"There was activity, as my man had reported, but it was Fiat, not Baltic. I had no idea of what Fiat was up to, or I would have stopped him." His gaze moved to touch on everyone in the room. "I returned to England shortly after verifying that Baltic was not present. I did not hear about the massacres until later."

I watched Gabriel, feeling the depth of emotion in him, but not sure what he was thinking. Would he believe Kostya? I did. Truth rang out in his voice. He might not be forthcoming with everything, but I did not believe he had participated in the wholesale murder of all those innocent people.

Kostya must have felt Gabriel's unwillingness to accept his explanation, because he made a quick, frustrated gesture and added in a voice rife with irritation, "For Christ's sake, Gabriel—have I harmed anyone since I was released from the aerie? Have I attacked any of the silver dragons? Have I harmed your sept in any way? Whatever else you may think of me, I've never given you grounds to claim I'm a psychopath!"

Gabriel was still silent, obviously weighing Kostya's words.

"Gabriel?" Chuan Ren prodded him with an impatient word. "How say you about the black sept?"

All eyes were on us.

"I accept your explanation," Gabriel said finally. "And I retract my statement of your guilt in that matter."

Kostya inclined his head in acknowledgment of the apology. Cyrene beamed at us and hugged his arm.

"Our history with the black dragons is known to all here," Gabriel said slowly, his voice once again rich and smooth. "It cannot be denied that we have long sought autonomy from them, and yet, they were once our friends, our family. They were a part of us. And while we do not pursue either justice or revenge against them for acts done in the past, we are not so quick to lay our ghosts."

Kostya stiffened in his chair, his brows lowering.

"Too many lives have been lost to the black dragons." Gabriel was silent for a moment, anguish deep within him. "Too many families were destroyed for us to simply forget those who sacrificed, or were sacrificed. We honor their memories now as we always will."

I held my breath. I knew that under normal circumstances Gabriel was too honorable to go back on his word to Kostya. But what if he felt he was justified? What would the weyr do if the black and the silver dragons were once again battling with each other? There had been war recently in the weyr, one that had been forced to an end, much to Chuan Ren's disgust. Would another one be the result of the day's actions?

"Nor can we forget the price that those of us who survived have paid. It was only by a miracle of the most profound nature that I have found a mate, the other half of my being, but the other silver dragons must bear the punishment a black dragon placed upon them."

Kostya shifted in his chair, but said nothing. Cyrene's smile had faded during Gabriel's speech until she looked lost, her gaze moving between Kostya, Gabriel, and me. I felt Gabriel's sorrow even as I was warmed by his declaration, but it drove home the fact that even if the black dragons rejoined the weyr, they could not remove the curse.

Only Baltic could do that.

Gabriel's silky voice rang out strong and clear in the silence of the room. "But even as we have acknowledged that pain, we have sought this moment, the day when old wounds could at last heal. The silver dragons welcome our long-lost brothers to the weyr with open hearts."

Tears burned briefly at the backs of my eyes as Gabriel sat down beside me, taking my hand in his. I rubbed my thumb against his, trying to tell him without words how proud I was of him, how much I loved him.

"Well-done, Gabriel," Aisling said softly.

Cyrene gave a moist sniffle and dug through her purse for a tissue. There was an echo of a sniffle from the side of the room, where Jim sat. I glanced at it, but it was licking its front leg.

Kostya stared at Gabriel for a long, long time, then nodded his head again, and turned expectantly to Chuan Ren.

"I am in agreement with the other wyverns," she said crisply. "The sept of the black dragons is herewith recognized as a member of the weyr, as Konstantin Fekete is recognized as wyvern. The *sárkány* has thus been fulfilled and is at an end. Fetch Fiat!"

# Chapter Seventeen

"So, are there going to be snacks for the dragon-heart thing? Because I missed lunch, being Cyrene's decoy, and that gyro she bought me isn't going to last until dinner. Hey, Fiat, long time no kidnap. Massacre anyone lately?"

"Jim, so help me god, one more word out of you, and you're going to be visiting Magoth," Aisling snapped.

I hurried over to where the demon sat, watching Drake's two men bring Fiat into the room, filled with contrition. "I'm sorry, Aisling. I should have been watching it. Jim—"

"There's no need for *you* to yell at me, too," it said with an injured sniff as it plopped itself down in front of the fireplace. "Ash already chewed my ass off. Man. Grumpy much?"

"I've just had it with you," Aisling said, moving uncomfortably in her chair. I was about to rejoin Gabriel, but I stopped next to her.

"Are you all right? Did the *sárkány* tire you out?" I asked.

"Yes, I'm fine."

I examined her face. She looked tired, black smudges under her eyes.

She waved a hand toward her belly. "It's just the baby. I wish she would make up her mind to come. Drake actually told the midwife she has to move in with us tonight. He wants her to do a C-section, but she doesn't think there's a need for that yet."

I patted her on her shoulder. "I'm sorry that I've been so distracted I haven't been watching Jim like I should."

A smile lit her tired eyes. "Don't worry about it. To be honest, I missed the big galoot when it was at your house. It's just that things are a bit tense with all the wyverns being prickly with one another, although, thank god, the issues with Kostya are now over. That stress, at least, is gone."

"I know Drake will probably have a fit at the idea, but would you like Gabriel to make sure everything is OK with you? Maybe the baby is moving or something."

"Oh, she's moved. She's always moving, usually kicking me right in the bladder," Aisling answered, shifting again. She heaved a sigh that seemed to come all the way up from her toes. "I just hope she decides to come soon, because I'm awfully tired of feeling like a fully loaded Goodyear blimp."

I glared at Jim as it opened its mouth. "Don't you dare!"

"Sheesh!" was all it said, looking away.

Aisling laughed, drawing Drake's attention from Fiat, who was loudly demanding to be released. He hurried over to us just as Kaawa entered the room along with Nora.

"Are you in pain, *kincsem*?" Drake asked.

"No. Just need to use the expectant Goodyear blimp's room. Help me up?"

He lifted her up, watching with worried eyes as she toddled out the door.

"Gabriel would be happy to check her over if you're worried," I told Drake, feeling a slight pang of betrayal toward Aisling, since I knew she hated to be fussed over.

He actually thought about it for a moment before shaking his head. "Our midwife will be here in a few hours. If Aisling goes into labor before then, we will have Kaawa attend to her."

I'd forgotten that Gabriel's mom was a midwife, as well. "I'm sure she'll be happy to be of help. I'm afraid I'm utterly useless when it comes to this sort of thing, but I want you and Aisling to know that if I can do anything to make her more comfortable, I'll be delighted to do it."

Drake thanked me, and moved toward the door, ostensibly to greet Fiat, but clearly waiting for Aisling to return. I wandered over to where Kaawa and Nora were chatting.

"Do you mind if I watch the shard being re-formed?" Nora interrupted herself to ask me, her eyes bright with interest behind the red rims of her glasses. "From what Kaawa tells me, it's truly a remarkable occasion, and I would dearly like to witness it, if I may."

"Of course. I don't know that there's going to be any fireworks, but you're welcome to stay and watch. I just hope I don't bungle the ceremony." I hoped no one saw quite how nervous I was about the upcoming event. My stomach felt like it was filled with jumping beans, and I had an uncomfortable presentiment that something was going to go horribly wrong.

"You'll be fine, I'm sure," Nora said, flashing a smile at me. "I have no doubt Kaawa prepared you well for it."

"My daughter could do no less," Kaawa said with simple majesty, making me feel simultaneously unworthy of such trust and filled to overflowing with a determination to do both Gabriel and her proud.

A persistent worry soon took care of any warm, fuzzy feeling I might have had at Kaawa's praise.

"Are you sure now is a good time to do this?" I asked Gabriel, pulling him aside for a moment. "Kostya is here, and Baltic is still out there doing god knows what, and now Fiat is here and is pissed as hell. Maybe we should do this later, when no other dragons are around."

He wrapped an arm around me and pulled me to him, speaking into my temple. "Do not fear, little bird. I won't let anything happen to you or the dragon heart."

"I know you won't, but . . ." I stopped, unable to put into words the heavy feeling that hung over my heart. The dragon shard had been oddly quiet inside me, much to my surprise. I had been grateful that it hadn't tried to get me to throw myself on any of the other wyverns present, but now that I had a chance to think about it, it hadn't been prompting me to do anything particularly dragonish. It was as if it was holding its breath in anticipation.

That thought made me more nervous than anything else.

"No, I will not sit down! I have had enough of this treatment! You will release me now or pay the consequences!" Fiat yelled, jerking his arm out of István's hold.

Everyone stopped talking to eye him.

"I have been unfairly detained by Drake and Gabriel," Fiat yelled. "You are all witnesses to this fact! I demand that a *sárkány* be called to punish them!"

Chuan Ren's eyes narrowed on him. When Fiat had entered the room, both her son and her husband had been blocking her, obviously intending to prevent her from killing him dead on the spot. "You have no status in the weyr," she said now, pushing aside her son to stride forward.

I saw the glint of metal in her hand before I could speak, but she wasn't fast enough.

Drake had just unlocked the handcuffs that held Fiat, which was a lucky thing considering Fiat caught Chuan Ren's wrist just as she was about to plunge the dagger into his heart.

"Oh, please," he said, scorn dripping from his voice as he twisted her wrist. "Do you think I have been wyvern as long as I have without anticipating assassination attempts?"

She snarled something that was most likely obscene, but yielded when both Drake and Jian grabbed her arms. With an immense amount of control, she shook off both men and stood watching Fiat with hooded eyes. "I repeat: you are no longer recognized by any sept within the weyr."

"You are mistaken," Fiat said just as calmly, rubbing his wrist where the handcuffs had bound him. "I am the wyvern of the red dragons."

"You lie," Chuan Ren spat. "You have never challenged me for my sept. You were too cowardly to even face me when I was released from Abaddon."

"I don't have need to challenge you," he said, shaking his head as if saddened by her ignorance. "I challenged, and defeated, the previous wyvern, the one who took over when you were banished. Thus, by the laws that govern the weyr, I am the recognized wyvern, not you."

Chuan Ren seethed, positively seethed with fury.

"I'm surprised she's not exploding all over him," I murmured in Gabriel's ear.

"She has been wyvern for more than a millennium," he answered in an equally low tone. "You do not remain in power that long without having the ability to control your emotions."

"Drake will tell you that I am right," Fiat said, nodding toward the green wyvern. His eyes flickered around the room, pausing for a moment on his uncle Bastian before moving on to us. "As will Gabriel. Tell her. Tell her that I am the wyvern."

Drake and Gabriel and Bastian all exchanged glances that were silent, but filled with meaning.

"I do not have to challenge you. Bao was never wyvern, so you defeating her did nothing other than eliminate a troublesome sept member."

"And yet your own son acknowledged her as wyvern," Fiat said smoothly.

Everyone looked at Jian, who avoided meeting his mother's eye.

"Is this so?" she demanded.

He hesitated a moment, then nodded.

"You see? Everyone knew you were in Abaddon and would not be released anytime soon." Fiat shot me an acid look before continuing. "Thus my challenge and victory over Bao was perfectly valid, and it is you, my dear, who is ouroboros, not me. I have been gracious in allowing you to live despite your attempts to usurp me, but should you continue to try my patience, I may regret such generosity."

Chuan Ren turned to stone, or at least that was what it looked like to me. She froze for about forty seconds, her body so tightly strung I was sure even her vaunted control would snap, but she was made of sterner stuff than I had imagined.

Slowly, inch by inch, her muscles relaxed. Her husband and son watched her warily, though, as if she might go off at any second. "Your words are meaningless, as usual. It matters not whether my son recognized Bao—he is not my heir."

Jian shot her a startled look.

"Perhaps not, but the rest of your sept accepted her, as well, as did the weyr," Fiat said.

"I think the time is right, mate, for you to tell just what

you saw two months ago," Gabriel interrupted, causing everyone to look in surprise at him, including me.

We had agreed not to mention those events, since it would leave me open to a challenge by Fiat, but evidently Gabriel had changed his mind. Or perhaps given the current situation, he felt there was little to fear.

"Approximately seven weeks ago my twin, Gabriel's guard Maata, and I made a covert call on Fiat's house in Italy."

Fiat spun around and focused his sapphire gaze on me, making me feel stripped and powerless. Gabriel's hand brushed mine, restoring my balance.

"We entered through a subterranean passage several meters beneath the surface of the lake. There we were witness to a scene between Fiat, Bao, and Baltic."

"This is news to me," Bastian said, frowning as he turned to Drake. "Were you privy to this information?"

"Yes."

Bastian didn't like that, but was wise enough to hold his tongue.

"It was clear to all of us that Fiat and Baltic had some plan under way, although what that was we didn't know. When Baltic left, Fiat was left alone with Bao. The two of them were also working together, a relationship that ended when Fiat snatched up a sword and beheaded her when she was off her guard."

Silence held the room in its grip for a few seconds, long enough for the sound of a door closing in the back of the house to reach us.

"There was no challenge," I said, meeting Fiat's furious gaze. "He simply grabbed a sword off the wall and hacked off her head, then told his men to clean up the mess—meaning, we supposed, her guards."

"Why did you not come forward with this information earlier?" Bastian demanded to know just as Chuan Ren spat out some extremely rude words toward me.

Instantly Gabriel moved between her and me. "May was silent at my request. Drake and I discussed the issue, and decided that it would be better to keep Fiat in a position where he would be visible, and thus monitored."

"And look what a fine job you did of that," Chuan Ren snarled, turning her back on us all. "How many dragons did you let be murdered by him?"

Bastian's face was pale, his expression anguished at Chuan Ren's words, but that was nothing that came close to touching the pain I felt within Gabriel.

"We did not anticipate Fiat going on a killing spree," Drake said quickly when Gabriel faltered. "The blame lies on both of us for that. I should have guessed that Fiat would retaliate for Chuan Ren returning."

"This isn't going to end easily," I whispered to Gabriel.

"No, it is not."

"He's going to fight no matter what the outcome."

"I know. Drake will not be happy with Aisling present."

"I can take care of that."

Gabriel slid me a questioning glance. I leaned into his side and said almost silently, "Aisling gave me a Taser this morning, in case something like this happened."

A slight frown marred his brow. "I do not like it, little bird."

"I know. But it's better than someone getting hurt."

"All this is unimportant except for one thing," Chuan Ren said, interrupting Drake as he continued to explain why no one had thought to watch innocent dragons. She spun around, her long black hair whipping out behind her, and stalked forward until she was a few feet away from Fiat, her eyes snapping with pure, undiluted hatred. "As rightful wyvern of the red dragons, I demand that Fiat be turned over to us for punishment for his attempted challenge to my control of the sept."

"No!" Bastian took a deep, shaky breath, then stepped forward to stand next to Chuan Ren. "Fiat was my problem, my responsibility. He escaped from us, and it was blue dragons he so brutally slaughtered. He must face the penalties for the crimes he has committed against my sept."

Fiat shot his uncle a poisonous look. "You don't even have the ability to keep your precious dragons safe. How do you expect to punish me, old man?"

"He is ours, not yours," Chuan Ren snapped at Bastian.

"I beg to disagree with you. The most heinous of crimes were against blue dragons, not red," he argued.

"This is ridiculous. I will not stand for this," Fiat said, and started to shift into dragon form.

I was ready for him this time. Before he got so much as a toenail transformed, I shadowed, slipped behind him, and had the Taser planted at the back of his neck.

"Not again," he managed to get out before he fell to the floor, twitching and spasming as the electric charge coursed through his still-human body.

"Consider it poetic justice," I told him before turning off the device.

"Brava," Bastian breathed, giving me a profound look of appreciation. That look died when Chuan Ren gestured her menfolk forward.

"Take him."

"No! He is mine!" Bastian straddled his nephew's body.

"I do not acknowledge your claim," Chuan Ren said stubbornly.

Bastian hesitated a second, then turned to Drake. "I will let the weyr decide who shall receive Fiat if Chuan Ren swears to abide by the decision."

She looked like murder for a moment; then her face became as implacable as ever. "Very well. The weyr shall decide."

"Kostya?"

Kostya and Cyrene had been silent during the entire scene with Fiat, a fact I found interesting given suspicions about Kostya's involvement with the rogue blue wyvern.

His black eyes moved from Fiat to his brother. "The black dragons feel that Bastian's claim is stronger than Chuan Ren's."

She didn't like that, but turned her gaze to Drake.

He was silent for a few moments before saying slowly, "About this, I am in agreement with Kostya. Bastian's claim is stronger."

"You pathetic little mewling bastard," Chuan Ren said. "Ever afraid to go against popular opinion. What about you?" Her eyes went to Gabriel. "Think well before you vote, for I will not release the Song Phylactery should your vote cause me to lose confidence in you."

My jaw sagged for a moment at the audacity in her threat.

"We had an agreement," Gabriel said, his voice a little rough around the edges. Tension built inside him, but like Chuan Ren, he had masterful control over his emotions. "You were released from Abaddon as part of that agreement. You must honor that, or run afoul of the weyr."

Muscles in her jaw worked for a second. "The weyr does not control me!"

"My vote is also for Bastian to have Fiat," Gabriel said in defiance of her fury. "It is his dragons who have suffered the most by Fiat's actions, and the survivors must determine how justice will be meted out. The red dragons suffered little in comparison."

"You have just damned your mate to bear the shard forever," Chuan Ren snorted, tossing her head.

"No, he hasn't."

The voice that spoke was low and soft, but firm in its

intent. Chuan Ren looked first in shock, then unmasked rage as Jian walked over to Gabriel, bowed, and presented him with a golden box. "I made the agreement on behalf of my mother. I will honor it even if she is temporarily of another mind."

Gabriel didn't wait for Chuan Ren to respond. He simply took the box, handing it to Maata before thanking Jian. "It will be returned shortly."

"I know," Jian said simply, turning to face his mother's wrath.

"We are done here," she snarled, her hands fists as she shoved him out of the way, pausing at Gabriel. "I expect the phylactery to be in my hands by the time the sun sets tonight, or I will destroy you and your little mate."

Gabriel said nothing, just arched a brow at her. She muttered under her breath as she charged out of the room, Li scattering muttered apologies as he followed in her wake.

Jian inclined his head to everyone and left, as well.

"I wouldn't want to be in his shoes," I said softly.

Gabriel smiled a slow smile. "I think he will make a very fine wyvern one day."

"Wyvern? I didn't think it was possible for the child of a wyvern to be one, as well. Don't you have to have a human parent?"

"Yes." Gabriel leaned close and whispered in my ear, "I thought at first that he was her actual son, but have since learned that my first suspicion was correct—her children are all dead. The term 'son' in this instance implies an heir rather than a blood relationship."

"But she just said he wasn't her heir, and he acknowledged Bao as wyvern."

"She was warning him that she would disinherit him should he go against her wishes. As for Bao—I am not privy to what went on within the red sept, but I suspect he was following the wisest course."

"Thank you," Bastian said, watching as his guards hefted the now-comatose Fiat onto their shoulders and hauled him out of the room. He reached into his pocket and pulled out a slim leather envelope, handing it to Gabriel. "The Marcella Phylactery. I know you will guard it well."

"Indeed we will," Gabriel said, accepting it. A sense of relief filled me—we had all the shards now, all the pieces needed to re-form the dragon heart.

Bastian hesitated. "I would like to see the heart re-formed, but I will understand if you are not comfortable with the thought of me being here."

"The decision is not mine to make," Gabriel said, turning to me. "May must perform the ceremony. If she wishes privacy to do so, I cannot gainsay her."

I glanced at Gabriel, trying to judge whether he had a preference, before I answered. "It won't bother me to have you present, Bastian, although I don't promise there will be much to see."

He smiled. "I will just make sure that Fiat is taken care of, then. I will return as quickly as possible."

"That was very exciting," Nora said, her eyes alight with interest. "I had no idea you could be so deadly, May. When you vanished from sight, and then reappeared behind Fiat, I gasped. I truly gasped. It was magnificent."

"We mates have to do what we can to take care of our wyverns," Cyrene piped up, putting her arm through Kostya's and giving him an adoring look.

My lips twitched a little at the martyred expression on his face.

"Are you sure you know what you're doing?" I couldn't help but ask him.

"No," he said, then smiled when Cyrene bit his arm. "But it seems I have little choice. Your twin insists I can't live without her, and unfortunately, she's correct. Maddening, but correct."

I laughed at the look of outrage on Cy's face as she poked him in the chest, and would have warned Kostya of what he could expect living with her, but at that moment, two things happened.

Aisling appeared. "Drake, that thief taker is at the door. Pál won't let him in until you give him the OK."

Drake started to leave, but she stopped him by putting a hand on his arm. "There's one other thing."

He frowned down at her.

"My water broke while I was in the bathroom. I think the baby's annoyed, because she gave me a hell of a contraction, and I have a nasty, suspicious feeling that another one is—"

Her face screwed up in pain as she gasped and doubled over.

Drake roared and scooped her up, carrying her up the stairs as he called over his shoulder, "Get the midwife!"

# Chapter Eighteen

"That's probably the midwife," I said, leaping down the last couple of stairs to run to the front door. "I'll get it, István. You go back and keep Drake from murdering Gabriel, will you? Savian tried, but got knocked out cold for his efforts."

István rolled his eyes but, at the sound of Drake yelling, bolted up the stairs.

"Ouch," Jim said from where it sat on a settee, calmly reading the paper. A crash reverberated through the house. "Did that sound to you like the noise a wyvern's head makes when he's slammed up against the wall? 'Cause that's what it sounded like to me."

"I told Gabriel to stay out of the way and let his mom deal with Aisling, but he insisted that he's had more experience with dragons than she has. I just hope Drake calms down and realizes he's trying to help." I glanced at one of the security systems that scanned visitors at the front door, saw the green light that indicated the person was not armed, and punched in the code to unlock the door, flinging it open with a relieved, "Thank heavens you're here. Aisling isn't fully dilated, but Drake is going berserk—oh."

The person standing on the steps wasn't the midwife, wasn't even a dragon for that matter.

"My interest is not with Aisling Grey today, fully dilated or not," Dr. Kostich said, brushing past me into the house, followed by a man and a woman. "I told you that I would return just as soon as my apprentices could be summoned. This is Jack and Tully. We are here to make plans regarding the dragon you refer to as Baltic."

"I'm sorry, but things are a little hectic right now. Perhaps you could come back later? Aisling has gone into labor, and everyone is running around making sure she's comfortable."

"I just told you my business was not with her," Dr. Kostich answered, stripping off leather gloves and removing his heavy overcoat. "We will meet with the green and silver wyverns to discuss matters. I have exactly two hours I can give this subject."

"Yes, but—"

He pinned me back with a look that had me wanting to shadow. "This is not a courtesy visit, Mei Ling, nor is your participation optional."

I was aware of a subtle pressure to do as he bade, a pressure that would probably have sent a mortal running to do as he wanted without thinking twice about it. But I was not a mortal, nor was I about to let him run roughshod over everyone.

"Ooh, a demon. Can I pet it?" the man named Jack asked as he examined Jim.

"If you give me five bucks, I'll let you rub my belly," Jim said, rolling over onto its back.

Jack laughed and obliged.

I turned back to Dr. Kostich. "I'm sorry, but things are too disturbed right now to have this meeting. Aisling is in labor."

"And, according to you, will probably be so for hours," snapped Kostich, shouldering me aside and heading for the sitting room. "We could have this business done before she has need of her wyvern."

I hesitated a second, wondering if we could deal with Kostich and get rid of him before Aisling gave birth. From what I knew of birthings, they weren't fast or immediate.

He took my hesitation as acknowledgment, gesturing toward me as he went into the sitting room. "Let us be done with this business quickly."

As he disappeared, I stared after him, wanting to give him the rough side of my tongue, but knowing it wouldn't be a wise course.

"Arrogant, pushy mage," I said under my breath.

The man named Jack evidently heard me.

"Archimage, actually. That's the difference, you know," he said, looking up from where he was squatting next to a gently moaning Jim, scratching the demon's belly. "We lowly mages don't get to push anyone around, but the second you become an archimage? Blammo! You're da man."

"Sorry. I didn't mean to be rude," I muttered.

He stopped scratching Jim (over the demon's protests) and strolled over to me, a friendly smile on his face. "No offense taken. I've never seen a real doppelganger before. You're not what I expected."

He was slightly taller than me, with short, bright red hair, and a heavy splattering of freckles.

"I have to admit that I'm having a bit of trouble with you, as well," I said with a smile. "You are a *mage*, yes?"

"Would my apprentices be anything but mages?" Dr. Kostich asked from the doorway. He looked annoyed. "Is this a delay tactic?"

"No. I'll get the others, although I make no guarantee that Drake will be willing to leave Aisling. Or Gabriel, for that matter."

He grunted and returned to the room.

Jack's smile changed to an outright grin. "He may seem a bit brusque, but he's actually really concerned about this dragon mage."

"I have no doubt he is." I took his coat, and the one handed to me by the silent woman.

"Jack!" Kostich yelled from the room. "Bring me the satchel!"

Jack grabbed a leather case and waggled his eyebrows at me as he hurried off to do his master's bidding.

"Hiya. I'm Jim," the demon said, strolling over to sniff the woman. It looked puzzled for a moment. "You're not a mage."

"Yes, I am. Well, I'm an apprentice," she said, giving Jim's head a quick pat before turning to me. "Dr. Kostich said you were a dragon's mate?"

"That's right. I'm May. Gabriel, the silver wyvern, is my mate."

She examined me curiously for a few seconds before excusing herself with a slight smile. "I'm sorry. I'm being intolerably rude, aren't I? It's just that I've never seen a wyvern's mate. I expected you to be . . . bigger."

"Unlike Jack, you look just how I expect a mage to look," I said with a little smile of my own.

"How's that?" she asked, her eyebrows rising slightly. She was a tall woman, tall and willowy, with long, straight ash blond hair, eyes so dark they were almost black, and a narrow, delicate-boned face. There was something comfortable about her, a sense of ease and warmth that reminded me of the pleasure found in returning home after a long trip.

"Well . . . I hope this doesn't sound rude, but it's been my experience that mages are always very reserved, keeping to their own. They're very controlled, as well. And extremely mysterious, like they are holding tight to any number of secrets, and that pleases them."

Her smile grew a few degrees warmer. "That is a very apt description of mages, but I'm afraid that I am a much duller creature than that. I am not a very successful apprentice, you see. Dr. Kostich hopes that the experience to be gained by helping with this mysterious dragon will go far to further my education."

"I'm sure it will." I nodded toward the sitting room. "If you want to go in there, I'll go see if I can get the others, although honestly, this would be better done another time."

"According to Dr. Kostich, there is no time left," Tully said, gliding toward the door. I watched her for a moment, startled by the word as it popped into my mind. She didn't just walk; she glided, her movements so graceful they were almost dreamlike.

"May," Jim said, nudging my hand with its wet nose.

"Why do I have a feeling that's a truer statement than I'd like?" I asked myself as I made a beeline for the stairs.

"Because it is true," Jim said, following me.

I glanced down at it. "What do you mean?"

"That Tully person isn't a mage."

"She said she was."

"Yeah, well, she lied. Or no . . ." The demon's face twisted into an abstracted expression. "Not lied. Just wasn't speaking the truth."

"What's the difference?" I asked as we headed down the hall toward Aisling's room. I froze for a moment when I saw who was stretched out on the floor, Tipene hovering over him, before I bolted the last few steps. "István! I asked you to stop Drake from killing Gabriel. How badly is he hurt?"

"Not seriously," the love of my life answered, his lip split, and his right eye swollen shut. "Drake was a little upset when Aisling had a particularly hard contraction. Savian tried to intervene."

"I think I'm dead," Savian moaned from where he lay on the floor of the bathroom next to Catalina's room.

"I'd hate to see what Drake would do when he's really upset," I said, gently touching Gabriel's face. "You would insist on being in there."

"My head is killing me." Savian hauled himself up to a sitting position, his hand gingerly feeling his face. He touched a tender spot, wobbled for a moment, then fell backwards onto the bath mat. "Ow."

Gabriel grimaced as Tipene applied a bit of salve to his lip and eye. "I have delivered more dragons than my mother. Her experience is mostly with mortals, but Drake did not feel that mattered. He preferred her to me."

"Seriously, I think I'm dead. Could one of you nice healers come and heal my broken head?"

"I think, my love, that in this you should have heeded your mother," I said, gently kissing his nose when Tipene had finished with him.

He gave me a lopsided smile. "I'm willing to concede that point. Is the midwife here?"

"I'm a ghost, aren't I? I died and now you all can't hear me, and I'm going to spend the rest of my life haunting this bathroom with a headache that would drop an elephant. Hello," Savian said as Jim wandered over and peered down into the thief taker's face. "Are you an angel?"

"Ex-sprite, now a demon. Ash isn't going to like you bleeding all over her bathroom. You gonna clean all your brains and gunk up? Someone could slip on them and hurt himself."

"My brains," Savian whimpered, and I took pity on him.

"No midwife as yet, although she's expected momentarily. Tipene, would you?" I asked, nodding toward the prostrate Savian.

Savian greeted him with soft little coos of relief.

"I'm sure your mother will do just fine with Aisling," I told Gabriel as I helped him to his feet. "Unfortunately, the person at the door was Dr. Kostich."

Gabriel's smile slipped. "Don't tell me he's here to discuss the situation with Baltic?"

"Yes. Do you think Drake will be willing to leave Aisling?"

He opened his mouth to speak, but before he could do so, a tremendous blast shook the house, the force of it so great I could feel the entire structure shake.

I shadowed out of sheer instinct, following Gabriel as he spun around and raced down the stairs. Behind me I could hear Drake's bellowed question, but I paid that little mind as I leaped down the last couple of steps into the entrance hall.

Another percussion blast shook the house, the shock wave of which caused painful pressure on my ears. "*Agathos daimon!* What is it?" I asked as I deshadowed.

The three people standing staring at the front door slowly turned to face us. Tipene and Maata skidded to a stop behind us.

"We're too late," Dr. Kostich said, his face utterly blank. "He's here."

A third blast hit the house. I covered my ears, biting back a cry of pain.

Drake and his bodyguards jumped over the balustrade from the floor above, landing as light on their feet as cats. "Damn him," Drake snarled, punching a few buttons on the security-system panel. "He would pick now to do this. István, put out the call to the others that we will need them. Pál, ready the lair. I'll take Aisling down to it. He can bring the house down around our ears, but she'll be safe in there. Kostich, what are you doing here?"

"Trying to prevent disaster, but I fear I am too late."

He eyed us all for a moment, then spoke quickly. "We will do what we can to aid you. Jack, see to the seals on the ground floor. Tully, you take the upstairs rooms. Do not forget to set traps at any entrance point, no matter how insignificant it might seem."

Jack hurried off to do as he was bidden. Tully hesitated a second. "I don't know that my traps and seals are strong enough to stop a dragon, master."

"They don't have to stop them. They just have to alert us to any breach. Go now. I, myself, will see to strengthening the front door, since that appears to be where the focus of his attack is being made."

Kostich suited action to word, his hands flying in intricate patterns as he wove a net made of arcane magic across the front door.

Drake watched him for a moment before deciding it was adequate. He turned to us. "Gabriel?"

"This is my fight as much as yours," Gabriel answered, pulling out the shadow sword. "More so, since it concerns my mate. We will form the frontline defense."

"Oh man, it's Baltic?" Jim had managed to make it down the stairs without being heard, something not common for the hefty dog. "He's got a hell of a sense of timing."

I left them planning their defense to hurry over to Jim.

"What are you doing here? Go back and protect Aisling," I ordered it.

"She wanted to know what was going on. And she threatened to castrate me because I'm male, and that somehow makes me to blame for the pain."

"Well, go back and help Kaawa get her ready to move," I said, shooing it.

"I'm a dog," it said in an exasperated voice. "No opposable thumbs, remember?"

"You're right." I narrowed my eyes at it for a moment, pushed past my limit on patience. "Effrijim, by the power granted to me by your demon lord, I command you to take human form. *Clothed* human form."

"Oh, man . . . ," it said, its voice a whine that trailed off as its body shifted form into that of a black-haired, black-eyed man of bulky build in jeans and a T-shirt. It looked down at itself. "How'm I ever going to tell Cecile about *this*?"

"You can go back to your normal form just as soon as we take care of this situation," I said quickly, shoving it toward the stairs. "Go help Kaawa and Aisling. And don't scare her."

"Like she's not gonna freak when she sees me come marching in without my fabulous form?" Jim trudged up the stairs, loosening the belt of its pants as it climbed. "I just bet you—aw, damn! I was right! This form totally sucks in the package department!"

"GO!" I yelled, pointing at the top of the stairs.

A fourth blast rocked the house, this time accompanied by the sound of glass tinkling in one of the back rooms.

Nora appeared at the top of the stairs, her eyes wide as she stared behind her. "I'm not quite sure. . . . Was that Jim?"

"Yes. Is Aisling all right?" I asked as Drake came over to us.

"She's fine, just concerned about what's going on."

"I'm taking her to the lair," Drake said, moving past us at a speed that was most definitely not human. "Nora, you and René will stay with her?"

"Of course. René is with her now, trying to distract her. Let me get some things to make her more comfortable. . . ."

Nora ran after Drake, the two of them heading upstairs, as Tipene and Maata scattered, assumably to check the windows.

Kostya suddenly emerged from the basement, tucking his shirt into his pants, his hair slicked back and wet. Cyrene was on his heels, her hair likewise wet, her clothing just as disarranged.

"What's going on?" Kostya asked. "We heard an explosion."

"We thought at first it was just really fabulous sex, but then we noticed the towels were coming off the shelf next to the sauna, and we realized something else was going on," Cyrene said, hurriedly buttoning her blouse. "It's Fiat, isn't it? He's come to steal me now that he knows I'm really and truly Kostya's mate! I just knew he would."

Kostya froze for a moment. "It's not Fiat. It's Baltic," he said, his voice filled with anger.

"Oh, him," Cyrene said, frowning. "He doesn't seem to want to steal me. What does he want now?"

Everyone looked at me.

I sighed. "Me, I'm afraid. Or, rather, the shard."

"Not just one shard," Gabriel corrected. "All of them. He waited until all the shards were brought together before attacking."

"He wants the dragon heart," Kostya said softly, and there was so much blackness in his voice, I shivered and moved closer to Gabriel.

Instantly, his arm was warm around me, offering both comfort and protection. "I will not let him harm you, little bird."

"I know," I said, smiling up at him. "I have every confidence that we'll be able to repel him as we've done before, but, Gabriel, this has to stop."

"It will stop. It will stop *now*," Kostya said, striding out of the hall to Drake's study. He returned a moment later with a couple of long swords in his hands, sending Cyrene a querying glance. "I assume you don't know how to use this?"

"You assume wrong," she said, obviously taking him by surprise, as she held out her hand for the sword. "All the sisters of Hydriades are versed in swordplay. We had a retreat seven or so hundred years ago, after some crusaders got a little frisky with our members, and we all learned how to use long swords, short swords, flails, and halberds. I did the optional course on throwing axes and culverins, but I much prefer a nice Glock to the latter."

Kostya stared at her for a moment before shaking his head and taking up a stance at the front door, the barrage from outside having momentarily stopped. "Stay in the back, Cyrene, and protect yourself. You will not be battling mortal crusaders this time."

"You will cease speaking of me as if I am a hindrance," she said, straightening up to her full height, indignation causing her back to stiffen. "I have protected myself for centuries before you were born, dragon. Besides, I have demon lord powers now. I can use those, too."

Kostya rolled his eyes and turned his attention back on the front door.

"You know, Drake would probably be happy for an extra hand to protect Aisling," I said thoughtfully, wanting to get her out of the immediate battle area. Despite the truth in her statement, I worried over the thought of her trying out newfound powers without supervision. "She and Nora would be able to give you advice about Magoth's powers, too."

Cyrene thought about that for a moment, obviously cherishing a mental vision of herself as a female Saint George ready to slay a dragon. "But then I wouldn't be able to help Kostie."

"Kostie will have us to help him," I said, fighting a smile. "This is not a moment for thoughts of glory, Cyrene. Aisling is in a very vulnerable state and Drake's dragons will be stretched rather thin."

She nodded. "You're right. Poor Aisling. I will go

and defend her and her baby. No one will get past me. Maybe Nora can tell me how to summon up all of Magoth's legions? I bet I could order them to help protect her, too."

I had a horrible moment where I envisioned the house full of demons running amok under Cy's command, but realized that there was no way Nora would ever let Cyrene summon anything. "Thanks, Cy. We'll hold down the fort here."

"*Viva la* black dragons," she called out, blowing Kostya a kiss before heading for the kitchen and the stairs down into the underground lair.

Savian staggered down the stairs, listing to starboard and weaving somewhat, but relatively hale and hearty as he joined us.

"You don't think she'll really summon demons, do you?" Kostya asked me, looking momentarily unsure.

"Oh, she'll want to, but no one will tell her how, and Cy doesn't have a clue about how to do it on her own. I'm beginning to think she's the ideal person for Magoth's powers. She'll never use them."

He nodded and turned back to the door.

"Where are your supermodels?" I asked, suddenly realizing what was missing.

"My what?"

"Your female guards."

He looked nonplussed. "They ... er ... Cyrene thought they would be better suited to duty elsewhere."

"Ah." I bit my lower lip to keep from laughing. I had no doubt that one of the first things Cy would do was to get rid of his harem.

But before I could say anything, before Kostya could turn back to the door, before so much as a second passed, the entire front entryway of the house exploded, sending us flying backwards in a barrage of glass, wood, plaster, and metal.

# Chapter Nineteen

I was stunned for a few seconds, shadowing without knowing it, hearing only the ringing in my ears from the explosion. When my head cleared, I realized the noise I heard was not an echo—the clang of metal on metal sounded loud and sharp.

"This day is never going to end, is it?" a familiar male voice said in deep resignation next to me. "The world is not going to be content until it bashes in my poor head once and for all. Ow. Oh, ow."

I yanked a brocade chair off the once-again-prone form of Savian, yelling as I got to my feet, "Gabriel!"

"I like that. I'm right here, with my ribs crushed in, and my spleen ventilated, and bits of my brains hanging out, and she is worried about her immortal boyfriend. Did I say 'ow'? Because seriously, ow."

"If you can complain, you're fine," I told Savian as I peered through the cloud of dust for a familiar form.

"Stay back, May," Gabriel called, leaping upward several feet as a dragon swung low at his legs with a huge sword.

"The mate is here," another yelled, and pointed at me. I counted quickly as a familiar figure strode through the twisted, smoking, gaping hole that had been the front door. There were only three dragons, the redheaded woman, and Baltic—hardly a huge force. We more than outnumbered them.

"Take her, then locate the other shards," Baltic called out, surveying the destroyed entryway. His eyes lit on Gabriel with amusement. "I told you I would be back."

"And I told you that you would never have my mate," Gabriel snarled, and shifted into dragon form, handily decapitating the dragon who was about to skewer him. "Shadow, May!"

I didn't argue; I shadowed, coughing on the dust generated by the explosion.

"Find the mate," Baltic demanded, then leaped aside and screamed as Gabriel lunged toward him. One of his guards hit Gabriel full in the chest, and the two of them went down.

A growl behind me had me crouching in defense, but the man who shoved aside the chair next to me was no danger to me. "Oh, she didn't come. Tell me she didn't come," Savian said, his eyes alight as he focused on the redhead, standing as still as a statue next to Baltic. "The world could not be so good to me."

A slow smile spread across his lips as he ignored his bloody hands to crack his knuckles.

"I take it you're suddenly feeling better?" I asked.

He didn't take his eyes off her. "Oh, yes. It's payback time. I can't tell you how much I've been looking forward to this." He hefted a bit of broken furniture, weighed it in his hand for a moment or two, then tipped his head back and howled before charging at the woman.

All hell broke loose. Dragons fought dragons. Savian, with the advantage of surprise, threw himself on the redhead, and was on the floor rolling around with her,

his piece of wood flailing madly, while Dr. Kostich ...
*Agathos daimon!* The explosion! Dr. Kostich had been
near the door, still working on it when Baltic had blown
it up.

I avoided being seen by Baltic's henchman who rushed
toward where I had been standing, skirting the edges of
the room until I came to the remains of the front door.
A long piece of the metal had twisted off it, embedding
itself in the floor. As I started to move around it, I saw
movement. Kostya was underneath the door, pinned to
the floor by the long spearlike strip of metal.

"Don't move," I whispered, making sure none of
the dragons was near me as I braced myself against the
wall, using my full strength to yank the impaling metal
from his body. It took three tries, but I got it out at last. I
dropped to my knees, crouching when a dragon, alerted
by the noise of the metal falling, came over to investi-
gate. "How bad are you?"

Kostya waited until the dragon had moved off before
answering. "Well enough to do what needs to be done."

"Good. I have to find Dr. Kostich."

I pulled his sword over to his hand, then moved off
as he clawed his way to his feet, listing heavily against
the wall, leaving a long smear of blood on the gold and
green wallpaper as he finally pushed himself upright.

The expression on Baltic's face as he caught sight of
Kostya was one of sheer delight. He roared something
in Zilant, kicking aside a bit of debris as he ran for him,
his body changing into the form of a white dragon.

Kostya yelled, leaping to the side and shifting into
dragon form, as well, his sword dancing in his hand as
Baltic descended.

Gabriel had killed a second of Baltic's men, and was
now battling the third, who had ceased searching for me
when Gabriel descended upon him, eyes blazing, sword
flashing. I averted my eyes from the sight of the corpse,

knowing they would have destroyed us without a single thought, and searched through the rubble for any signs of Kostich.

I found him as Gabriel and Kostya battled furiously.

"Dr. Kostich, can you hear me?"

"Yes."

He lifted his head as I pulled a piece of wall off him, his face battered and bloody, pain dulling his eyes. "Can you move, or are you badly injured?"

"Not badly. I shielded myself with a cushion, but I believe my arm is broken." He winced when I pulled a piece of twisted metal and wood off his left side.

I grimaced. "It looks like it."

"Wrap it for me," he said, gritting his teeth.

I looked again at the bloody, torn mass of his arm. "I do not have the healing abilities of the silver dragons—"

"I know that. Just bind the damned thing so I can move."

I will do my utmost to forget the five minutes that followed. I certainly hope Dr. Kostich does, as well, although he didn't say a single word as I ripped off the bottom half of my embroidered tunic, using it and some of the wood to fashion a crude splint.

He was pale and shaking, sweat beading his brow despite the cold air pouring in around us, by the time I was done. I didn't feel much better, but I managed to get him to his feet, the battle still raging around us as I propped him up against the stairs, well out of the way of the battle. "My apprentices," he croaked, his body shaking with shock. "I need them to channel for me."

"Master, we are here," Jack said from behind us. He emerged from the shadows, half-dragging, half-carrying Tully out of the passage leading to the kitchen. There was blood on her hair and face, and she looked dazed and confused, as if she was only partially conscious.

"You are injured," Kostich said, momentarily closing his eyes.

"Tully hurt her head, and I am cut up by flying glass, but I am able to serve you."

"Get her to safety, then return to me," Kostich ordered, his voice a pale imitation of its normal self.

"Go below, to the basement," I told Jack. "The lair is down there. Take her there and Kaawa will tend to her."

Tully roused herself enough to protest. "Take her to the kitchen, then," I said, pointing. "She can recover there."

Another crash shook the room, but this time it was from the impact of a heavy dragon body being slammed into the wall.

Baltic screamed for his man to get me, and headed toward our spot on the stairs. Gabriel, fighting to keep the dragon as far from me as possible, likewise screamed. "May! Go to the Dreaming!"

I stared at Gabriel for a minute, then nodded and shadowed.

Baltic stopped his charge, laughing as he faded from sight. He'd gone into the shadow world, fully believing he'd find me there.

Clever, clever Gabriel.

Dr. Kostich got to his feet with Jack's help. "Did he just . . . ?" He gestured to the spot where Baltic had disappeared.

"Yes," Jack said grimly, one arm around the archimage's waist. "Can you walk, sir?"

"This is unprecedented," Kostich muttered as I hurried, unseen and silent, up the stairs. With everyone down in the lair, attention was drawn away from the upper floors, just as Gabriel had known it would be. His ploy to get Baltic out of the way for a few minutes was just what I needed to escape without anyone noticing where I went.

"I just hope I can do this," I murmured to myself as I fled down the hallway of the third floor to the room that had been given over to me. I pulled out the strongbox that Gabriel had told me would be under the bed, and persuaded the lock to open.

The phylacteries lay within. I spread them out on the bed, pulling out another box, this one unlocked, bearing the five gold-bound crystal amulets we'd chosen to house the shards. Each unfilled phylactery was chased with gold, bearing the emblem of a sept. Gabriel and I had worked hard on the designs, and I touched them now, pleased with the results.

A roar from below alerted me to the fact that Baltic had discovered I wasn't in the shadow world with him.

"Do it, May. Gabriel's going to run out of ways to keep Baltic distracted," I scolded myself, my hands cold and shaking as I knelt by the bed, trying desperately to calm my mind and heart. Kaawa had stressed the fact that the dragon heart must agree with my wishes for the re-formation to be successful, and it wouldn't appreciate my full-fledged case of the nerves. I spread my fingers over the four shards that lay before me, aware of a dull heat inside me where the shard resided. It hummed with energy, and I knew it recognized both my intent and the nearness of the other shards.

I cleared my mind and, with a prayer that went out to any deities that might wish to answer it, began the incantation. The words, spoken in Zilant, were themselves meaningless to me, but Kaawa had explained what I was saying. "In my thoughts I have seen the heart that is within all dragons, echoing with essence of the First. I am humbled before thee, before it, before all dragonkin. I beseech thee to show me the brilliance of the First again, in order that I might ensure its safety and purity for all ages. Heed me, heart of the dragon, and lend thyself to my hand that I might preserve thee."

The words hung heavy and awkward in the air, as sounds of battle drew nearer. I put away from me the worry that Gabriel would not keep Baltic from me, that I'd re-form the heart just in time for him to steal it and destroy everything, put away even the distress that I wasn't downstairs fighting with him. I focused on the shard, double-checked my memory, and spoke the words again. "Heed me, heart of the dragon, and lend thyself to my hand that I might preserve thee."

Nothing happened. The sounds of fighting had reached the floor below me. I ran desperately over the ceremony that Kaawa had described, my own heart wailing that I had failed.

"In my thoughts I have seen the heart that is within all dragons—" I started to say a third time, then stopped. It was wrong. I could feel the shard reacting to what I was saying, and it was unmoved by it. The formal words weren't what it wanted from me. Kaawa was going by the description Ysolde gave when she re-formed the heart—perhaps the words had to be unique for each person?

I blocked out the noise of fighting dragons (growing ever closer), and thought about the ceremony, thought about what it was I wanted to tell the shard.

"I'm not going to miss you trying to get me into dragon form all the time," I said hesitantly, feeling silly talking to it, but not knowing what else to do, "but I do appreciate you giving me an understanding of what it is to be a dragon. I will forever hold that in my heart, just as I hold Gabriel there. I resented you at first because I felt you were trying to take me over and make me into a dragon."

I could hear Gabriel's voice now, hear Kostya's battle cry, hear Kostich chant as he cast arcane spells intended to slow down or destroy the dragons. They were close, almost to this floor. I ordered my brain to come up with some nice things to say to the shard. "I will miss having the experience of shape-shifting. I will miss the scarlet claws. I will miss the dragon chases that Gabriel and I had, and I will definitely miss knocking Magoth out cold with one swipe of my tail."

The shard was paying attention—I could feel that— but still, it wasn't enough. It didn't want honeyed words. It wanted what was in my heart.

"I didn't want to be a dragon. I wanted to be myself. But now I know that I am a dragon—if not in physical being, then in heart. I am May Northcott, wyvern's mate and doppelganger, a dragon of the silver sept, and I thank you for making me such."

Beneath my fingers, the phylacteries grew hot, the shard inside me suddenly burning with a searing heat that I knew was the first dragon's fire. It burst out of me in a blaze of fire that glowed so bright it momentarily blinded me.

I stared openmouthed in wonder as the shards gathered together before my face, hanging in midair, slowly twisting themselves into an intricately spun circle of fire. Behind it, the air gathered, and a vision coalesced, that of a dragon's head, slowly turning to regard me with eyes that reflected the ages. It was a white dragon, but not white—it held all the colors of the spectrum, light shimmering along its skin like a million fireflies. The dragon head shifted, changed into that of a man, and for a moment, for the infinitesimally small time between heartbeats, I was judged by the first dragon.

The heart, the spinning fire that made up the heart, suddenly burst into a glorious nova of light that made my soul sing with joy. It was a thousand times stronger than the feeling the quintessence gave me, a trillion times stronger, and in the time it took to burst, I felt the heart of every dragon in the world suddenly lighten and sing with mine.

I was judged and found worthy. The heart re-formed, then exploded with a song that sang to the heavens. I sank back onto my heels as the light from the now-shattered heart faded; I was moved so profoundly I couldn't begin to sort through the emotions.

The shard was gone. It lay before me glowing softly in its crystal case, alongside four other cases. I smiled when I saw it, touching the newly filled phylactery with reverent fingers. Gabriel and I had argued over what to put on the phylactery for my shard. He claimed that it now belonged to the silver dragons, since I possessed it, but I insisted that it be left unmarked, thinking we would work out later to whom it really belonged.

"Smart shard," I said, smiling as my fingers stroked over the gold symbol of the silver dragons that now bound the phylactery. "We will see that you are well taken care of."

The door behind me flung open. Gabriel threw himself across the doorway, once again in human form, turning his back to me as he fought like a madman to keep Baltic out of the room.

Baltic grabbed him by the neck and yanked him forward, spinning to fling him down the hall. He turned back to me, panting heavily, blood streaming from several wounds on his arms and torso, his eyes lit with an unholy light.

"Mate," he snarled.

"True enough, but I will never be yours," I answered, scooping up the phylacteries and dumping them back into the strongbox.

"I felt something. What have you done?"

"Nothing you can change."

He snarled at me. "You think not?"

I shoved the strongbox behind me, and pulled out

my dagger as he reached for me. "What you felt was the dragon heart being re-formed and resharded. I saw the first dragon, Baltic. I saw him, and I know."

He froze, confusion in his eyes. "You . . . know?"

"I saw him. You won't have the dragon heart now. It's been sharded again."

Gabriel reached him just as he threw back his head and roared his anger. Eyes as bright as the full moon, Gabriel jumped onto Baltic, twisting his body as he did so, using the momentum to pull Baltic from the room, back out into the hallway, yelling over his shoulder, "Fly, little bird!"

I fled into the shadow world, taking the box of phylacteries with me, slipping past where he and Kostya battled Baltic, once again in dragon form. Baltic must have sensed me passing him, for he suddenly spun around and charged toward me. Gabriel yelled and threw himself on the dragon's back, shifting as he did so. He brought Baltic to the ground, their sleek dragon bodies twisted together as they fell. I paused at the top of the stairs, not wanting to leave Gabriel, but knowing I should get the phylacteries to safety.

Kostya shifted to human form, yelling at Gabriel, "He is mine!"

Savian staggered up the stairs, one arm hanging limp, his usable hand still clutching his piece of wood. "Took care of that redheaded she-wolf. Just the one dragon left? Good," he said, then keeled over on the floor.

"Must I do this again?" Kostya bellowed, raising his sword over his head. "How many times must I kill you before you stay dead?"

"Gabriel!" I yelled, coming out of the shadow world.

"May, go!" Gabriel shifted at the last second and leaped out of the way of Kostya's downswing. The sword flashed in the air as it passed through the spot that a nanosecond before was occupied by Baltic, and embedded itself deeply into the floor.

# Chapter Twenty

"Where's Baltic?" Aisling asked, her face red and shiny with sweat. "What's happen—oh, god, not another one!"

I waited until her contraction was over before handing the lockbox containing the phylacteries to Drake, who rose when I entered the small inner room that was part of his lair. I tried to keep from looking around, knowing how touchy dragons were about having their treasures regarded by other dragons, but I couldn't help but raise my eyebrows at a couple of familiar-looking paintings hanging on the wall. I wondered if the appropriate museums knew they had forgeries as I eyed the gold items, chalices and aquamaniles, as well as numerous other treasures, all glinting warmly, making my skin feel sensitive and hot.

"Would you like a Cajun crisp?" René said, offering her a package of potato chips. "Or I have a chocolate orange if you'd like something sweet."

"No ... orange ... just ... Baltic ...," Aisling panted as she worked through the contraction. At last it was over and she waved a feeble hand at me. "Someone tell me what's happening."

I obliged her. "Baltic is gone. He disappeared into the shadow world again. For someone who bears the title dread wyvern, he sure runs away fast enough when a battle doesn't go his way."

"We felt the heart re-forming," Aisling said, still panting a little, taking a sip of water from a glass Nora held for her. "You got it sharded all right?"

"Yes." I glanced at Drake as he held the strongbox clamped under one arm. "They're all there, all five. Gabriel would like you to keep them safe until they can be distributed to their proper owners."

Drake released Aisling's hand, nodded, and put the strongbox onto a shelf. I did look around then, amazed at the objets d'art that Drake had gathered over the centuries. "This is an impressive collection. But not so much gold as I expected to see."

Aisling laughed, twitching at the sheet that covered her. She was lying on some sort of a raised platform, a mattress from a bed having been laid on top of it. "You haven't seen what I'm giving birth on, have you? René, would you?"

I was a bit surprised to find René in the inner room with Aisling while she labored, but evidently Aisling was comfortable with him there. He grinned and pulled up the corner bottom of the mattress so I could see what was underneath.

It wasn't a table, like I'd thought. It was a long wooden case with a glass top, lit from within with soft lights that caressed the surfaces of the gold coins that filled it almost to the rim.

"I just hope that Gabriel doesn't make you give birth on top of his hoard of gold," Aisling said with another laugh that trailed away into a shriek of pain.

Kaawa bustled over as Drake helped Aisling into a sitting position, allowing her to press back against him as she strained.

"This is looking good," Kaawa said from her position between Aisling's legs. "Another couple of good pushes, and I think the head will crown."

"Time for me to leave," I murmured, averting my eyes from the sight. There were some things I was quite happy to leave as a mystery until such time as I needed to know. "Good luck, Aisling. We're all outside thinking of you."

Her eyes screwed up as she continued to scream, but she managed to wave a hand at me to let me know she'd heard.

I left the inner room, passing through to the outer one, where István stood guard at the lair entrance. He opened the door for me, asking how it was going.

"Head's about to crown, so it probably won't be much longer. Drake looks exhausted."

István smiled as Gabriel, outside the lair waiting for me, stood up. "I hope it is fast. Drake told me he was never going to go through this again."

I laughed and allowed Gabriel to gather me into his arms, breathing deeply of the scent of him. Kostya sat on a bench leaning against the wall as Tipene tended to the damage on his torso, Cyrene clinging to his hand as she wept over him.

"Did you tell Drake that I would be happy to offer my assistance with Aisling? Did you tell him that I have more experience with dragon births than my mother?" Gabriel asked, nuzzling my ear in a way that sent shivers down my arms and back.

"Yes," I lied.

He nipped my earlobe. "You do not lie well, little bird. How do you feel?"

I looked up at him in surprise.

"You no longer bear the shard. Do you miss it, or is it a relief to have it gone?"

I remembered the sensation of seeing the first dragon, of having him see me, acknowledge me, judge my heart and soul, and find them not wanting. I remembered the wisdom in those eyes, the history that they had seen, and continued to see, and I smiled. "I am a dragon now. The dragon heart is a part of me just as it is a part of you, so no, I don't miss the shard. It will remain with us forever."

"I give that about a three point two on the profound-o-meter," a male voice said.

I stopped nuzzling Gabriel's neck to look behind me. Jim stood there, its hands on its hips, an extremely disgruntled look on its face.

"Can I have my magnificent form back now? Or is there something else you'd like me to do? Tote a barge? Haul a bale? Or just stand around and be a laughing-stock to amuse everyone?"

"Oh, Jim, I'm sorry. I didn't mean to forget about you. But you're not a laughingstock, I'm sure. You're actually a very handsome man in that form. Isn't he handsome, Gabriel?"

"Eh."

I poked him in the ribs.

"I suppose as human forms go, it's not outright repulsive," Gabriel allowed, his dimples dimpling.

"Ignore him. You're very handsome. I particularly like the cleft chin."

"He lacks a certain *something*," Savian said from where he was flaked out inside the sauna, recovering, he said, from the various traumas his body had gone through in the last few hours. "He looks like the sort of man who would drool on another man when he was lying in a pool of his own brains and blood."

Jim narrowed its eyes at the towel-clad Savian. "Drake's going to be all pissy if he knows you've been keeping the door to the sauna open while you have it running."

Savian pursed his lips for a moment, and considered whether he wanted Drake pissed.

"Don't listen to Savian—he's feeling challenged because he doesn't have the corner anymore on the unattached-handsome-man market," I told him.

Gabriel pinched my behind. "You think *I'm* handsome!"

I grabbed two handfuls of his hair and pulled him down for a quick kiss. "More than any other man on the planet, but I did, in fact, say *unattached* handsome man."

"Yeah, yeah, handsome, riiight," Jim answered, making a rude face. "That's why Aisling almost had a heart attack when I went up to help her, like you ordered me to do."

"You probably just took her by surprise," I said, licking Gabriel's lower lip.

He growled at me, his eyes bright with interest, then gave me what I wanted and kissed me with all his fire, all his passion, and all his love.

"Kaawa yelled at me because Aisling was laughing so hard when she saw me that she totally blew off pushing during a contraction. That ain't handsome, sister."

Gabriel lifted his head. "Don't call her that."

I laughed when Jim made another disgusted face. "Go ahead and change back to your preferred form. I'm sure Aisling will thank you later for all the help you gave her and Drake."

The demon's form shimmered and condensed down to a large black shaggy dog. It sighed with relief. "Oh, man, that's so much better." It lifted a leg and checked, then plopped its butt down and cocked an eyebrow at me.

"Whew. Package is A-OK. All right, get on with the nitty-gritty. What happened with Baltic? How come there's not a big ole dragon corpse rotting away upstairs? Why did Savian insist Drake lock that redheaded chick in the storage room? And why is Dr. Kostich so pissed?"

Before I could answer, the door to the lair opened and Nora popped out, flustered but excited. "Well! It's happened! It's a boy! Drake is thrilled. Aisling is furious. She insists that Kaawa has made a mistake, because she knows she is supposed to have a girl, but I looked, and there's no mistake. It's a boy."

I leaned into Gabriel, pushing him into the wall as he was about to move toward the lair. "Give Aisling and Drake our congratulations, please."

"Mayling, please let me go. My mother is not as experienced as I am with dragon—"

I clapped a hand over his mouth and smiled at Nora as she laughed and went back into the lair.

"Your mom is doing just fine," I told him as he gently bit my hand. "You, however, would just cause Drake to go ballistic. You will stay here and explain to Dr. Kostich what happened to Baltic, because if he yells at me once more, I'm going to go steal something else from him, and this time I won't give it back."

Gabriel laughed, squeezing me tightly. "All right. Let us go upstairs and deal with the archimage. Tipene probably has his arm healed by now."

We made it two steps before Nora appeared at the door again, this time looking harried and flushed. "It's . . . it's a girl!"

We all stopped and stared at her. "I thought you said it was a boy?" Cyrene asked. "You said you checked. Didn't she say she checked?" she asked Kostya, who nodded.

"I have a niece, not a nephew?" he asked.

"I did say I checked, and I did. Check, that is. But no, you're not understanding me—it's a girl, *too*. Aisling has had twins. Er . . . real twins, not like you two," she said, glancing between Cyrene and me.

"Twins. Double congratulations, then," I said, and wondered aloud what Aisling and Drake would do about names. "How is Aisling holding up?"

"A lot better than Drake," Nora giggled. "And as for names, I couldn't say for certain, but I do know the names Aisling had picked out were Iarlaith if it was a boy, and Ilona if it was a girl, so I assume they will use those. I had better get back. There was a bit of blood and fluids and suchlike before the first baby came out, and René fainted at the sight of it. Men are so silly, really. I should go revive him. This is such an exciting day!"

Nora disappeared into the lair again.

Jim made hacking noises. "Baby guck! May, can you please take me to Paris so I can stay with Cecile until Aisling gets over gushing out babies and ooky stuff?"

"I'm sure we'll find a way for you to go visit your girl-friend while Aisling is recovering," I said, shooing the dog upstairs. We followed, pausing once we got to the hallway.

Drake's call for reinforcements had brought a number of green dragons to his house, most of whom were now devoting themselves to clearing up the mess, and beginning the repairs. Pál was overseeing both, asking us for news as we trooped into the sitting room, which luckily remained more or less intact.

"Twins, boy and girl. Aisling's fine, Drake is a mess, and René fainted."

Pál laughed. "He was boasting to Aisling about his seven children, and how useful he was to his wife in the delivery room. That's why she asked him to stay with her. That, and to distract Drake."

"Sounds like he wasn't horribly successful on either front."

"I'm exhausted," Cyrene said, tugging on Kostya's arm. "I think I'm going to go take a nap. I'll see Aisling and the babies later, once they're cleaned up. Kostya's tired, too. All that being stabbed and fighting wore him out."

Kostya looked surprised for a moment, then caught the glint in her eye and agreed. "Perhaps a nap would be a good idea," he said, and gave her a wolfish grin that had her giggling and running up the stairs.

I shook my head as they left, and said softly to Gabriel, "I don't know that I'm ever going to get used to that."

"You and me both," he said with a wolfish grin of his own, and I thought seriously for a few minutes about demanding a nap.

"There is still much we must do," he said, accurately reading my mind. "But later, once it is done, then I will do all those things you are thinking about. Particularly the one where you are on your hands and knees and I take you from behind—"

I stopped his words with a quick kiss, then straightened my shoulders and entered the sitting room.

Dr. Kostich was there, but he wasn't alone.

"Sally?" My brain, somewhat fried by this point, sluggishly tried to figure out what on earth the newest demon lord in Abaddon was doing in Aisling's sitting room, chatting happily with Dr. Kostich.

"—Mama always said that there's a place for everything and everything in its place, and I always believed that was true, but you know, my time spent in Abaddon has been quite the eye-opening experience. I see now that my dear mama just wasn't right, no, she wasn't. Because honestly, how do you explain portals? If your arcane magic was as strong as you say, why, then, you could just seal portals to Abaddon and no creepy-crawlies would ever get through, would they? But they do. Therefore, dark magic has to be the stronger. May! You look horrible, sugar, just horrible. Are you using that salt scrub I recommended?"

Sally ceased patting Dr. Kostich's hand, which was a good thing, since he was staring at her with unadulterated disbelief.

"What are you doing here? How did you get in?" I asked, looking around the room to see if any other demons were in attendance. I knew Drake had some sort of a demon alarm, but it must have been disabled with the attack and subsequent rebuilding.

"Oh, some very nice workmen let me in when I said I was a friend of yours." She smiled her sharky smile at me.

Dr. Kostich transferred his horrified gaze from her to me. "This . . . woman . . . is your friend?"

"Well . . ." Sally's eyebrows rose.

I cleared my throat, not wanting to cause trouble. "Sally is a demon lord, and she served as Magoth's apprentice for a few weeks. I know her from when I was trapped in Abaddon."

"I see." His brows lowered.

"Yes, we did meet there, and we had ever such a lovely time, didn't we, May? We had lots of fun talking about all sorts of girl things, like interesting ways to accessorize spikes, and how to get bloodstains out of leather harnesses, and just exactly what Magoth's penis curse says. But silly chatterbox me, here I'm keeping you standing there when you clearly need to get some rest. I'll get right to the point: I'm here because of Magoth."

"*Agathos daimon*—he's out?" I asked, trying to figure out how he could have gotten out of the Akasha.

She bent a stern look upon me. "No, and that was very naughty of you to have him banished without telling Lord Bael. He was most displeased when he heard what you'd done."

"Why would Bael care what happened to Magoth?" Gabriel asked.

"Why? Because May is bound to Magoth," Sally said just as if that explained everything. "And Magoth was a subservient prince to Lord Bael."

"The key word there being *was*," I pointed out.

"Exactly." She smiled and patted me on the cheek.

I sagged against Gabriel. "Sally, I don't have the energy to play clever word games. Just spit out what it is you want to say."

"Well, I will, but I have to say I don't much appreciate your attitude," she said crossly. "You were bound to the demon lord Magoth, yes?"

"Yes," I said, an uneasy feeling springing to life in my stomach. I leaned a little harder against Gabriel, relishing the feeling of his arm around my waist.

"But Magoth is in the Akasha, and you can't be a demon lord if you're banished to limbo, can you?"

"I guess," I said warily, the bad feeling growing.

"Magoth is no longer a demon lord, and thus your existence is negated."

I blinked at her in confusion. "What on earth does that mean?"

"It means, sugar, that you owe servitude to a demon lord, and since Magoth is banished to the Akasha and technically no longer a demon lord, then you must be bound to some other lord. Lord Bael considered this problem for a very long time, and decided that you should be bound to me. So I'm here to take your oath of fealty, after which we can discuss your schedule and duties."

My confusion turned to outright horror.

"That is out of the question," Gabriel said firmly. "I have never heard of such a thing, and I will not have it."

"I assure you there's provision made for this situation in the Doctrine of Unending Conscious, and since May was bound to Magoth, and he was governed by those laws, then they apply to her now."

I looked up at Gabriel, a horribly hopeless feeling gripping me. I didn't want to be bound to Sally. I didn't want to be bound to anyone anymore other than Gabriel.

Gabriel's lovely eyes narrowed. "What would happen if Magoth were returned to the mortal world? Would May still be considered bound to him?"

"Yes," Sally answered, picking at a fingernail. "But Lord Bael would not be happy about that. He truly would not. And you know, May and I would have fun together. I would greatly enjoy having her by my side as I made my mark here."

I shuddered. "Here? Here as in the mortal world?"

"Why, yes, sugar!" Her smile widened until I could see every last one of her teeth. "Didn't I tell you? Lord Bael feels I'm just the person to reinstall the concept of hell on earth to the mortals. He is such a doll, isn't he? Imagine me as the supreme overlord of all mortals? It's enough to give a girl goose pimples!"

I looked at Gabriel. Gabriel looked at me. Dr. Kostich swore.

"I'll have him brought back," I said wearily.

Gabriel nodded, looked thoughtful for a moment; then slowly a smile curled his adorable yet manly lips. "Yeees, I think that will work quite well."

"What will work?" I asked, watching him closely. "What brilliant plan have you concocted?"

His gaze touched on Sally for a moment, speculation replacing amusement.

"Magoth has no way to contact the world beyond the Akasha, isn't that so?" he asked me.

"No way whatsoever."

"Then you will have to go back there, little bird. You will present him with an offer—he will be returned to the mortal world, but only after he pays a price."

Enlightenment burst into glorious being.

"Oh, you don't want to do that," Sally said, finishing with her cuticle examination. "Lord Bael would not like that, and you don't want to cross him. He's not happy with you as is, and if he was really annoyed? Noooo, not good at all."

I began to chuckle. "Bael's happiness is not my concern anymore. Especially if I'm no longer bound to Magoth."

"But how—" She frowned until she, too, realized what Gabriel had first hit upon.

Dr. Kostich looked thoughtful. "Clever. Very clever. But no concern of mine. I must go find my apprentices so that we can return to lay charges against this dragon."

He left the room as I kissed Gabriel very gently. "Sexy as sin, dimples to die for, eyes that could melt ice, and a brain. You, sir, are one fabulous dragon."

He laughed and pulled me to his chest, kissing me until I stopped listening to Sally protest behind us. When we finally came up for air, Sally was leaving the room.

"Who are you?" Gabriel called to her as she went through the door.

She froze and looked back at him, her face a mirror of confusion. "I beg your pardon?"

"Who are you?"

Sally smiled as she tipped her head toward me. "Perhaps he's not *quite* as bright as you think, sugar."

It occurred to me then what Gabriel was asking, and why. "You're not really a demon lord, are you?"

"I assure you I am," she said smoothly. "Lord Bael himself appointed me."

"No, I mean that you're not really demon lord mate-

rial. You're a bit wicked, and I think you're enjoying all
this greatly, but you're not . . ." My hands fluttered for a
moment. ". . . not evil."

She looked insulted.

"You haven't really done anything truly reprehen-
sible," I pointed out. "Oh, you talk the talk, but your actions speak louder than that."

"Name one good thing I've done," she said, straightening her shoulders with a belligerent glare at me. "Just
one!"

"I can name three." I ticked them off my fingers. "You
saved me from the thief taker in Paris."

"I told you then—they were the good guys. I don't do
good guys," she said huffily.

"Uh-huh. Then you pointed out to Magoth that, with
me as a consort, he could leave Abaddon and enter the
mortal world."

"I hardly see how unleashing a demon lord on the
mortal world is a good thing," she said with an acerbic
sting in her voice.

"One who is effectively stripped of his powers? On
the contrary, that was very clever," Gabriel said. "And it
allowed May to return to me."

I nodded. "I have absolutely no doubt whatsoever
that you were the one pushing Bael to expel Magoth
for good, which ended up with him permanently out of
commission, powerless and ineffective."

She looked away, but I could have sworn I saw the
tiniest hint of a smile. "That was just an unfortunate con-
sequence of a really excellent plan to stab you both in
the back."

"And now here you are, warning us that unless we do
something, Bael will claim my bondage to Magoth, with
the end result that we see a way clear to freeing me from
him forever. An evil person wouldn't do that."

"You think not?" She made a little face. "You'll have Magoth hanging around your neck for the rest of your lives. If that's not evil, I don't know what is."

"Annoying, but not evil. I can live with Magoth whining at me so long as I'm no longer bound to him," I said quietly.

"So who are you?" Gabriel asked, taking a step closer to her. "You can't be from the Court of Divine Blood. Bael would recognize that taint to you. You aren't a Guardian. You aren't even immortal—or you weren't until you became a demon lord. Who, then, does that leave?"

Silence fell for a few seconds while she looked at him, really looked at him. Her gaze was sharp as a whip, but amused. She said nothing, just smiled, then went through the door.

"What do you think?" I asked Gabriel when we heard the front door close. "Could it be a glamour to confuse us?"

"No." He rubbed my back absently while he thought. "I don't know who she is, but I do know this—she has been a true friend to us, and I will not forget that."

"I'll go see if Nora is up to sending me to the Akasha," I said, heading for the door. "I think I'm really going to enjoy *this* visit."

It took almost five hours to accomplish our goals of sending me to the Akasha and negotiating my freedom from Magoth. Aisling, Gabriel told me later, had wanted to be there to watch Nora conduct the banishing and resummons, but Drake refused to let her out of bed, and I doubt if she argued that point too much.

Gabriel was waiting for me when Nora resummoned me. I fell straight into his arms, clinging to him while I tried to forget the miasma of despair that filled the Akasha.

"Little bird," he murmured into my hair, his hands

busily checking to make sure all my pertinent parts were where he had last seen them. "You are shaking?"

"Just with happiness," I said, letting him fill me with dragon fire.

He stiffened, and I felt a cold whoosh behind me.

"It's about time," Magoth snapped, glaring at the three of us. "Where is this foul document I must sign?"

Gabriel gestured toward the table. Magoth swore a colorful variety of oaths as he read over the emancipation papers. He gritted his teeth, but he signed them, snatching the knife Gabriel held out, and making a small cut on his thumb. He pressed a bloody mark next to his name, and threw it at me. "There. I am free of your ingratitude at last."

"Not quite yet," Gabriel said, and slid another paper toward him. "There is this you must sign, as well."

I craned my neck to see what Magoth was supposed to sign. "A divorce decree?"

Gabriel winked at me. "May will be my wife, and no other's."

Magoth rolled his eyes, but signed the document with only a few testy words.

"You don't have to do that, you know," I murmured to the love of my life. "I'm not a mortal who holds with such conventions as marriage."

"I know. I just don't like him referring to you as his wife," Gabriel said. "Besides, my mother wishes us to be married in front of her people, and this will make everything easier."

"Done," Magoth snapped, slamming down the pen and knife. "Now you owe me one thing."

"We just gave you your freedom. What could we possibly owe you now?" I asked.

He growled. "You will tell me where that betrayer Sally is. She will pay for her perfidy—of that I swear.

Tell me her whereabouts that I may exact my lengthy and incredibly unpleasant revenge upon her."

"I think she said something about going to Los Angeles," I said without once blinking my eyes. I looked at Gabriel. "Didn't she say Los Angeles?"

"Yes," he lied, also without the slightest hesitation. "That is what she said."

"Then that is where I will go," Magoth declared, his face tight with intensity. "Los Angeles! The City of Angels will weep by the time I am through tearing it apart to find her! Good-bye, former wife. I will return to deal with you once I have meted out justice to Sally."

He was gone with a dramatic flourish that would have done a Shakespearean actor proud.

Nora had been silent during the entire conversation, but she looked thoughtfully at the door now, and said, "I'm afraid to ask, but why is he so angry at the demon lord Sally?"

"Probably because I told him Sally was behind everything, including convincing us to banish him."

She regarded me from behind her red-framed glasses, her eyes unreadable. "But that is not the truth."

"No, but it gives him a focus for his wrath."

She looked slightly puzzled. "You said that you consider Sally your friend."

"We do."

"And yet you would set Magoth on her?"

"Not really, no. We told him she was in LA. She's not. She said something earlier about going to Germany."

"But won't he simply realize she's not there and turn elsewhere to find her?"

"I highly doubt if he'll even think about her once he hits LA. He really is the biggest ham at heart. He'll get out there, be smitten all over again with all the Hollywood glitz and glamour, and will fling himself back into the world of acting. He really did love his years there, you know. I have every expectation that in a few years we'll see him back on the silver screen."

It took her a moment, but at last she smiled. "That was very smart of you. Congratulations on both your freedom and your upcoming nuptials. If you have no further need for me, I believe I will go see if Aisling needs anything. She's a bit lonely now that Jim is in Paris with Cecile for a few days, and I must reassure her that it was quite happy when I delivered it there."

"Life," I told Gabriel after she left, kissing his nose to emphasize my point, "could not be better."

# Chapter Twenty-one

"Did you see the little ones?" René asked several hours later when I entered the now-tidy sitting room. "I aided Aisling to birth them, and I can tell you that, with the exception of my own, they are the two most perfect *bébés* in the world."

"I haven't seen them yet. My appointment is for"—I glanced at the card that István had given me—"half an hour from now. Don't you think it's a little odd that Drake made up an appointment schedule to see the babies? Is that normal?"

"Eh." René shrugged. "He is a new papa and very protective. To him, it makes sense."

"But to go so far as to don surgical garb when visiting them? My card says I have to be outside Aisling's room five minutes early so I can pick up sterile clothing."

"He is a little overprotective."

"And then there's the baby-holding training class he made us take after lunch. I thought that instructor was rather rude implying that just because Cyrene and

Kostya and Gabriel and Nora and I didn't have children, we wouldn't know how to hold a newborn."

René couldn't really argue with that, especially since Drake had made him, the father of seven, attend the class, as well. "He is *very* overprotective," René finally said.

"And the blood tests and retinal scans to verify our identities?"

"He is doing blood tests?" René asked, interested. "I did not have a blood test."

"You will. Pál is wandering around the house jabbing everyone like some sort of bizarre dragon-vampire hybrid."

"But what is the test for?"

"No idea, but honestly, retina scans? Does Drake seriously believe someone is going to go to the trouble of trying to pretend they're any of us just to go in and see his children?"

René sighed, and gave a short little laugh. "He will learn, I think. Aisling will not allow her children to grow up coddled in the wool of cotton. You must give Drake a little time. And you, how do you fare now that you have found yourself?"

"I wasn't aware that I had been lost," I said carefully.

"Ah. Then I am mistaken."

Silence fell for about a minute. René softly hummed to himself and looked out the window at the workmen who were busily rebuilding the front entryway.

"You're talking about the dragon heart, aren't you?" I asked, unable to keep quiet any longer.

He smiled. Just smiled.

"You fates can be very annoying sometimes," I said, softening the insult with a smile of my own. "As it happens, yes, I found myself."

"Did you tell your Gabriel?"

"Yes." I thought for a moment. "But he didn't believe me. Or, rather, didn't understand."

"That is the way with dragons," René said sagely. "But you will show him, *hein*?"

I lifted my hand and watched as the fingers curved and elongated into scarlet claws, the skin shimmering into silver scales that swept up my arm. I smiled. "Yes, when the time's right, I'll show him."

"He will be happy. But will you?"

"Yes, I think I will be. I realize now why the dragon shard chose me," I said, letting the scales slide back into human flesh. I flexed my fingers. "It wanted me to stop being a shadow of someone else, and start being myself."

"And that can only be a good thing." René glanced at the clock and *tsk*ed. "But I am making you late for your baby visit. I will be quiet now, and let you go see the adorable little ones. I must pick my wife up from the train station in a short while. She has come to see the *bébés*, as well."

I said nothing more as he bustled out of the room, and followed more slowly as I savored the feeling of relief. I was free from Magoth at last. Nothing would ever take me from Gabriel again, and I was happy with who I was—not strictly a doppelganger, not strictly a dragon, but something in between, something unique.

Gabriel emerged from Drake's study, giving Maata approval on the house she found for us to rent. "Tell them we will take a lease for a year, but only upon May's approval," he said before catching sight of me. He gave me a rueful smile as I moved automatically to his side, his fingers immediately seeking mine. "Are you ready for the foolishness?"

"Not really, but I do want to see Aisling and the babies. Did you have the blood test?"

He sighed, our fingers entwined as we mounted the stairs. "I would say Drake had lost all his reason, but it is common for male dragons to be very protective of their spawn. Drake is most likely overreacting because of all the people in the house."

"No doubt. We've been so busy with Magoth, it's totally slipped my mind, but what will happen with Thala?"

He shot me a curious look. "I do not know, little bird. Kostya has claimed her as a prisoner of war, but whether Drake will release her to him is in question. She must answer many questions to the weyr."

"Baltic will be back for her."

"Possibly. But I do not think he will find it so easy to free her," Gabriel said dryly as we arrived at the room that had been given over to racks of sterile surgical wear. We quickly changed our clothing, and presented ourselves and our appointment cards to István, who stood guard outside Drake's bedroom.

"We haven't seen the last of him, you know," I said in a whisper when István went in to check if Drake would clear us for the visit.

"No. The weyr will meet to discuss the issue he presents. We cannot let him continue destroying dragons. He will have to be stopped."

"Do you think he'll seek revenge for us keeping the dragon heart out of his reach?"

"It is possible, but you know I will always keep you safe. Do not fear, Mayling—you are my mate, and my heart. Nothing and no one can change that," Gabriel said, kissing me as the door opened up and István bowed us into the room.

Drake hurried over to us as we entered. He gave Gabriel a suspicious look before eyeing us quickly to make sure we met with his standards. "Do not mention the appointment cards or the security measures," he said quickly in a low voice. "I will not have Aisling upset by trivialities."

I bit my lip to keep from laughing, noting that Gabriel's dimples were fighting to come out.

"May! Gabriel! I thought you'd never come to see my babies. What on earth are you wearing? Drake! I told you to stop making people dress in those silly outfits." Aisling was propped up on a huge bed, her color high, her face a bit drawn, but radiating pride and happiness. Two beautifully carved wooden cradles stood next to her, draped in pristine lace.

"Until we know the children's immunities are strong, I will not allow germs near them," Drake said sternly.

Aisling rolled her eyes. "No one is going to endanger them. May, would you like to hold Ilona? Gabriel, what do you think of them? Aren't they the most beautiful babies you've ever seen? I know all mothers say that, but you have to admit, these two really are outstandingly gorgeous."

I looked down at the blotchy-skinned, red-faced, pointy-headed babies, and said with absolute conviction, "They are completely and utterly adorable, Aisling. I'm sure they're going to grow up to be just as beautiful as you and Drake."

Gabriel duly admired the babies, then gave Drake a long look before grinning and punching him in the shoulder. "You have fine children, my friend. They will grow up strong and wise."

Drake returned the compliment by socking Gabriel in the arm; then the two men embraced.

"They are beyond fine. They are extraordinary," Drake said, looking with obvious pride at his babies. "But I expected nothing less from Aisling."

"That's not what you said when I threatened to pull your scrotum over your head so you could share the experience of natural childbirth with me," she said with a grin.

He cleared his throat, adjusted a blanket infinitesimally, then waved us to chairs. "You were in pain. Much can be forgiven when a woman is in the throes of childbirth."

We sat with them for a half hour before Aisling began looking tired, and left her with a promise to return the next day.

Drake tucked her in, checked the babies, then accompanied us out of the room. "The mortals have a custom to celebrate with whisky and cigars. You will join me?" he asked.

"Of course. May?"

"I'll pass on the cigars, but a little shot of whisky would go a long way right now," I said.

Dr. Kostich was waiting for us when we reached Drake's study. He glowered at us for a moment before saying to Gabriel, "One of my apprentices, Tully, is unwell."

"I will see to her, naturally. And you? Tipene has tended to your arm?"

"He has. The silver dragons well deserve their reputation for healing abilities," Kostich said stiffly.

Gabriel smiled at the grudging compliment, and went off to the sitting room to check on the apprentice.

"I wish to speak with you," Dr. Kostich told me.

Drake murmured something about being in his study when I was free, and retreated to that room.

Dr. Kostich considered me for a moment before saying, "I begin to regret my leniency with regards to you."

"I have done everything you asked of me," I pointed out.

"You misled me."

"Misled you how?"

"You withheld information from me about the dragon lord Baltic, information that was vital for our success. And because you saw fit to withhold it, I have neither the light blade of Antonia von Endres nor the dragon himself, who I assure you will answer to the acts of violence he has perpetrated upon my person, and those of my apprentices."

"There's also a little matter of more than sixty blue dragons who were brutally slaughtered, but I guess you don't care about that," I said, annoyed that he could make so light of that atrocity.

Dr. Kostich's expression did not change. "Crimes against dragonkin are beyond the authority of the L'au-delà."

I acknowledged that it was so. "I merely wish to point out that although we have all suffered at the hands of Baltic, there are those who have suffered far more."

"You did not tell me that the dragon in question could access the beyond," Dr. Kostich accused, his gaze once again pinning me down.

"No, I didn't. I didn't think it was pertinent, and to be honest, I'm not sure why you think it is."

He almost sighed, but caught himself in time. "Dragonkin cannot enter the beyond. It is a well-known fact that only by extraordinary means can one do so, and yet this one appeared to enter it with ease, and without any assistance from one who has routine access. This dragon is clearly something . . . unusual."

"But you knew that. You knew he had the ability to cast arcane spells, and to use the light sword."

"Yes, but I did not know he could also enter the beyond. A dragon who understands and harnesses arcane power is extraordinary, but it might possibly be explained. But one who can enter the beyond—that is truly miraculous, and I do not like miracles." He bit off the last few words as if they left a nasty taste in his mouth.

"I'm sorry. I didn't know. He's sought refuge in the beyond so many times, I didn't think about just how unusual it was. What difference it could have made to today's events is, pun aside, beyond me."

"He has escaped us!" Dr. Kostich said, his voice icy. "Had I know he could use the beyond as a way to avoid capture, I would have put precautions into place to ensure he could not simply vanish just as we were about to take him."

I wondered how he could arrange for that, but figured mages must have abilities in the shadow world that were far greater than mine. "I'm sorry, but I just didn't think to tell you. But if you are worried that we have seen the last of Baltic, you can rest your mind. He isn't the sort of dragon to let a little thing like defeat stop him for long. I have every expectation that he'll be back raising hell soon. We might have stopped him from getting the dragon heart or shards, but I have no doubt he'll continue to be a thorn in our side, and sooner or later, the weyr will have to do something about him."

"What the weyr does is none of my concern," he said darkly. "I will have that sword. Where did you put the prisoner you took?"

"Thala? Drake has her in a storage room, I believe."

"I will question her. Perhaps she can be of some use to us," he said, turning on his heel and striding toward the back of the house.

I followed him a few steps, debating whether I wanted to go with him, let Drake ply me with whisky, or see how the apprentice was doing. A strong, overwhelming need to be with Gabriel won out, sending me to the long sitting room. I found Gabriel kneeling next to the apprentice Tully, who sat hunched over in an armchair in the corner of the room. Savian was flaked out on the couch, covered with a blanket.

I sat on my heels next to Gabriel as he asked Tully to continue.

"I'm ... it's difficult," she said slowly, her voice thick with some strong emotion. Pain? Loss? It was something she felt deeply. "There was something—something indescribable. It filled me with happiness and dread at the same time, as if I was being torn from paradise and flung into Abaddon. A light shone through me, a brilliant golden light, so pure it made me want to weep with joy, but then it was gone, and blackness filled its void."

"She is describing the re-forming of the heart," Gabriel said softly, his hands on her knees. "She felt the dragon heart re-form and be shattered."

"I thought only dragons could feel that?" I asked.

He nodded. "All dragonkin felt the re-forming of the heart. It connects all of us. But this mage ..." His gaze didn't waver off her for a second.

Tully, clearly uncomfortable with his regard, covered her face with her hands and sobbed.

"What is wrong with her?" Savian asked from where he lay on the couch.

I looked at Gabriel. "Dragons can't be mages."

His gaze moved from Tully to me, his eyes troubled. "One has managed to do so."

"But ... surely there is no connection?"

"I have never done a better day's work, and I have guided well over a hundred new souls into this world." Kaawa entered the room, stretched, and looked around her with pleasure. "I am glad to see you returned from your visit to the Akasha, wintiki. Your journey was successful?"

"Yes, it was. I'm officially free from Magoth." I stood up to greet Kaawa, moving slightly away from Tully to do so. At the sound of another voice, Tully stopped sobbing into her hands, fumbling in her pocket for a tissue to wipe her eyes.

Kaawa started toward us, caught sight of the woman on the chair, and faltered, her face suddenly frozen with shock. She lifted a hand and pointed at Tully, her mouth moving, but no sound coming out.

"What's wrong?" I asked as Gabriel went forward to her side.

"Mother? Are you unwell?"

"She," Kaawa said, still staring in absolute astonishment at Tully. Her finger wavered a little as she pointed. "It's her."

"The mage apprentice?" I asked, glancing at Tully. She looked up in complete befuddlement at Gabriel's mother, clearly not understanding why the other woman was so stunned to see her.

"No." Kaawa shook her head, then said the last thing in the world I expected her to say. "That is no apprentice. That is no mage."

Gabriel and I exchanged confused glances before looking back at his mother.

She stared at Tully with an intensity that raised the hairs on the backs of my arms.

Savian propped himself up on the couch, watching with interest as Tully rose from the chair, one hand at her throat. "I'm sorry. I don't . . . do I know you?"

"That is a not a mage. That is a black dragon," Kaawa announced, her voice ringing pure and clear in the silence of the room. "That is a wyvern's mate."

Goose bumps crawled up my spine as I looked at Tully.

"That is *his* mate. That is Ysolde de Bouchier. She is alive. Baltic's mate is alive."

Read on for an exclusive peek at

# LOVE IN THE TIME OF DRAGONS

*The first novel of the Light Dragons*

By Katie MacAlister
Coming from Hodder in 2010

I stood in the kitchen doorway and watched as a group of four men rode into the bailey, all armed for battle.

"Ysolde! What are you doing here? Why aren't you up in the solar tending to Lady Susan? Mother was looking for you!" Margaret, my older sister, emerged from the depths of the kitchen to scold me.

"Did they get her out of the privy, then?" I asked with all innocence. Or what I hoped passed for it.

"Aye." Her eyes narrowed on me. "It was odd, the door being stuck shut that way. Almost as if someone had done something to it."

I made my eyes as round as they would go, and threw in a few blinks for good measure. "Poor, poor Lady Susan. Trapped in the privy with her bowels running amok. Think you she's been cursed?"

"Aye, and I know by what. Or, rather, whom." She was clearly about to shift into a lecture when movement in the bailey caught her eye. She glanced outside the doorway and pulled me backwards, into the dimness of the kitchen. "You know better than to stand about when Father has visitors."

"Who are they?" I asked, looking around her as she peered out at them.

"An important mage," she answered, holding a plucked goose to her chest as she watched the men. "That must be him, in the black."

All of the men were armed, their swords and mail glinting brightly in the sun, but only one did not wear a helm. He dismounted, lifting his hand in greeting as my father hurried down the steps of the keep.

"He doesn't look like any mage I've ever seen," I told her, taking in the man's easy movements under what must be at least fifty pounds of armor. "He looks more like a warlord. Look, he's got braids in his hair, just like that Scot who came to see Father a few years ago. What do you think he wants?"

"Who knows? Father is renowned for his powers; no doubt this mage wants to consult him on arcane matters."

"Hrmph. Arcane matters," I said, aware I sounded grumpy.

Her mouth quirked on one side. "I thought you weren't going to let it bother you anymore?"

"I'm not. It doesn't," I said defensively, watching as my father and the warlord greeted each other. "I don't care in the least that I didn't inherit any of Father's abilities. You can have them all."

"Whereas you, little changeling, would rather muck about in the garden than learn how to summon a ball of blue fire," Margaret laughed, pulling a bit of grass from where it had been caught in the laces on my sleeve.

"I'm not a changeling. Mother says I was a gift from God, and that's why my hair is blond when you and she and Papa are redheads. Why would a mage ride with three men?"

Margaret pulled back from the door, nudging me aside. "Why shouldn't he have guards?"

"If he's as powerful a mage as Father, he shouldn't need anyone to protect him." I watched as my mother curtsied to the stranger. "He just looks . . . wrong. For a mage."

"It doesn't matter what he looks like—you are to stay out of the way. If you're not going to tend your duties, you can help me. I've got a million things to do, what with three of the cooks down with some sort of a pox, and Mother busy with the guest. Ysolde? Ysolde!"

I slipped out of the kitchen, wanting a better look at the warlord as he strode after my parents into the tower that held our living quarters. There was something about the way the man moved, a sense of coiled power, like a boar before it charges. He walked with grace despite the heavy mail, and although I couldn't see his face, long, ebony hair shone glossy and bright as a raven's wing.

The other men followed after him, and although they, too, moved with the ease that bespoke power, they didn't have the same air of leadership.

I trailed behind them, careful to stay well back, lest my father see me, curious to know what this strange warrior-mage wanted. I had just reached the bottom step as all but the last of the mage's party entered into the tower, when that guard suddenly spun around.

His nostrils flared, as if he'd smelled something, but it wasn't that which sent a ripple of goose bumps down my arms. His eyes were dark, and as I watched them, the pupils narrowed, like a cat's when brought from the dark stable out into the sun. I gasped and spun around, running in the other direction, the sound of the strange man's laughter following me, mocking me, echoing in my head until I thought I would scream.

"Ah, you're awake."

My eyelids, leaden weights that they were, finally

managed to hoist themselves open. I stared directly into the dark brown eyes of a woman located less than an inch from my own, and screamed in surprise. "Aaagh!"

She leaped backwards as I sat up, my heart beating madly, a faint, lingering pain leaving me with the sensation that my brain itself was bruised.

"Who are you? Are you part of the dream? You are, aren't you? You're just a dream," I said, my voice a croak. I touched my lips. They were dry and cracked. "Except those people were in some sort of medieval clothing, and you're wearing a pair of jeans. Still, it's incredibly vivid, this dream. It's not as interesting as the last one, but still interesting and vivid. Very vivid. Enough that I'm lying here, babbling to myself."

"I'm not a dream, actually," the in-my-face dream woman said. "And you're not alone, so if you're babbling, it's to me."

I knew better than to leap off the bed to escape the clearly deranged person, not with the sort of headache I had. Slowly, I slid my legs off the edge of the bed, and wondered if I stood up, if I'd stop dreaming and wake up to normal life.

As I tried to stand, the dream lady seized my arm, holding on to me as I wobbled on my unsteady feet. Her grip was anything but dreamlike.

"You're real."

"Yes."

"You're a real person, not part of the dream?"

"I think we've established that fact."

I felt an irritated expression crawl across my face— crawl because my brain hadn't yet woken up with the rest of me. "If you're real, would you mind me asking why you were bent over me, nose to nose, in the worst Japanese horror movie sort of way, one that guaranteed I'd just about wet myself the minute I woke up?"

"I was checking your breathing. You were moaning and making noises like you were going to wake up."

"I was dreaming," I said, as if that explained everything.

"So you've said. Repeatedly." The woman, her skin the color of oiled mahogany, nodded. "It's good. You are beginning to remember. I wondered if the dragon shard would not speak to you in such a manner."

Dim little warning bells went off in my mind—the sort that are set off when you're trapped in a small room with someone who is obviously a few weenies short of a cookout. "Well, isn't this just lovely? I feel like something a cat crapped, and I'm trapped in a room with a crazy lady." I clapped a hand over my mouth, appalled that I'd spoken the words rather than just thought them. "Did you hear that?" I asked around my fingers.

She nodded.

I let my hand fall. "Sorry. I meant no offense. It's just that . . . well . . . you know. Dragons? That's kind of out there."

A slight frown settled between her brows. "You look a bit confused."

"You get the understatement-of-the-year tiara. Would it be rude to ask who you are?" I gently rubbed my forehead, letting my gaze wander around the room.

"My name is Kaawa. My son is Gabriel Tauhou, the silver wyvern."

"A silver what?"

She was silent, her eyes shrewd as they assessed me. "Do you really think that's necessary?"

"That I ask questions or rub my head? It doesn't matter—both are yes. I always ask questions because I'm a naturally curious person. Ask anyone. They'll tell you. And I rub my head when it feels like it's been stomped on, which it does."

Another silence followed that statement. "You are not what I expected."

My eyebrows were working well enough to rise at that statement. "You scared the crap out of me by staring at me from an inch away, and I'm not what *you* expected? I don't know what to say to that since I don't have the slightest idea who you are, other than that your name is Kaawa and that you sound like you're Australian, or where I am, or what I'm doing here beyond napping. How long have I been sleeping?"

She glanced at the clock. "Five weeks."

I gave her a look that told her she should know better than to try to fool me. "Do I look like I just rolled off the gullible wagon? Wait— Gareth put you up to this, didn't he? He's trying to pull my leg."

"I don't know a Gareth," she said, moving toward the end of the bed.

"No . . . " I frowned as my mind, still slowed by the aftereffects of a long sleep, slowly chugged to life. "You're right. Gareth wouldn't do that—he has absolutely no sense of humor."

"You fell into a stupor five weeks and two days ago. You have been asleep ever since."

A chill rolled down my spine as I read the truth in her eyes. "That can't be."

"But it is."

"No." Carefully, very carefully, I shook my head. "It's not time for one. I shouldn't have one for another six months. Oh god, you're not a deranged madwoman from Australia who lies to innocent people, are you? You're telling me the truth! Brom! Where's Brom!"

"Who is Brom?"

Panic had me leaping to my feet when my body knew better. Immediately, I collapsed onto the floor with a loud thud. My legs felt like they were made of rubber, the muscles trembling with strain. I ignored the pain of the fall and clawed at the bed to get back to my feet. "A phone. Is there a phone? I must have a phone."

The door opened as I stood up, still wobbling, the floor tilting and heaving under my feet. "I heard a— Oh. I see she's up. Hello, Ysolde."

"Hello." My stomach lurched along with the floor. I clung to the frame of the bed for a few seconds until the world settled down to the way it should be. "My name is Tully, not Ysolde. Who are you?"

She shot a puzzled look to the other woman. "I'm May. We met before. Don't you remember?"

"Not at all. Do you have a phone, May?"

If she was surprised by that question, she didn't let on. She simply pulled a cell phone out of the pocket of her jeans and handed it to me. I took it, staring at her for a moment. There was something about her, something that seemed familiar ... and yet I was sure I'd never seen her before.

Mentally, I shook away the fancies and began to punch in a phone number, but paused when I realized I had no idea where I was. "What country is this?"

May and Kaawa exchanged glances. May answered. "England. We're in London. We thought it was better not to move you very far, although we did take you out of Drake's house since he was a bit crazy what with the twins being born and all."

"London," I said, struggling to peer into the black abyss that was my memory. There was nothing there, but that wasn't uncommon after an episode. Rapidly, I punched in the number.

The phone buzzed gently against my ear. I held my breath, counting the rings before it was answered.

"Yeah?"

"Brom," I said, wanting to weep with relief at the sound of his placid, unruffled voice. "Are you all right?"

"Yeah. Where are you?"

"London." I slid a glance toward the small, dark-haired woman, who looked like she could have stepped straight out of some silent movie. "With ... uh ... some people." Crazy people, or sane ... that was yet to be determined.

"You're still in London? I thought you were only going to be there for three days. You said three days, Sullivan. It's been over a month."

I heard the note of hurt in his voice. I hated that. "I know. I'm sorry. I ... Something happened. Something big."

"What kind of big?" he asked, curious now. He gets that from me.

"I don't know. I can't think," I said, being quite literal. My brain felt like it was soaking in molasses. "The people I'm with took care of me while I was sleeping."

"Oh, *that* kind of big. I figured it was something like that. Gareth was pissed when you didn't come back. He called your boss up and chewed him out for keeping you so long."

"I suppose I should talk to Gareth," I said, not wanting to do any such thing.

"Can't. He's in Barcelona."

"Oh. Is Ruth there?"

"No, she went with him."

Panic gripped me. "You're not alone, are you?"

"Sullivan, I'm not a child," he answered, sounding indignant that I would question the wisdom gained during his lifetime, all nine years of it. "I can stay by myself."

"Not for five weeks you can't—"

"It's OK. When Ruth and Gareth left, and you didn't come back, Penny said I could stay with her until you came home."

I sagged against the bed, unmindful of the two women watching me so closely. "Thank the stars for Penny. I'll be home just as soon as I can get on a plane. Do you have a pen?"

"Sec."

I covered the phone and looked at the woman named May. "Is there a phone number I can give my son in case of an emergency?"

"Your son?" she asked, her eyes widening. "Yes. Here."

I took the card she pulled from her pocket, reading the number off it to Brom. "You stay with Penny until I can get you, all right?"

"Geez, Sullivan, I'm not a tard."

"A what?" I asked.

"A tard. You know, a retard."

"I've asked you not to use those sorts of . . . Oh, never mind. We'll discuss words that are hurtful and should not be used another time. Just stay with Penny, and if you need me, call me at the number I just gave you. Oh, and, Brom?"

"What?" he asked in that put-upon voice that nine-year-old boys the world over can assume with such ease.

I turned my back on the two women. "I love you bunches. You remember that, OK?"

"K." I could almost hear his eyes rolling. "Hey, Sullivan, how come you had your thing now? I thought it wasn't supposed to happen until around Halloween?"

"It isn't, and I don't know why it happened now."

"Gareth's going to be pissed he missed it. Did you . . . you know . . . manifest the good stuff?"

My gaze moved slowly around the room. It seemed like a pretty normal bedroom, containing a large bureau, a bed, a couple of chairs, a small table with a ruffly cloth on it, and a white stone fireplace. "I don't know. I'll call you later when I have some information about when I'll be landing in Madrid, all right?"

"Later, French-mustachioed waiter," he said, using his favorite childhood rhyme.

I smiled at sound of it, missing him, wishing there was a way to magically transport myself to the small, over-crowded, noisy apartment where we lived so I could hug him and ruffle his hair, and marvel yet again that such an intelligent, wonderful child was mine.

"Thank you," I said, handing the cell phone back to May. "My son is only nine. I knew he would be worried about what happened to me."

"Nine." May and Kaawa exchanged another glance. "Nine . . . years?"

"Yes, of course." I sidled away, just in case one or both of the women turned out to be crazy after all. "This is very awkward, but I'm afraid I have no memory of either of you. Have we met?"

"Yes," Kaawa said. She wore a pair of loose-fitting black palazzo pants, and a beautiful black top embroidered in silver with all sorts of Aboriginal animal designs. Her hair was twisted into several braids, pulled back into a short ponytail. "I met you once before, in Cairo."

"Cairo?" I prodded the solid black mass that was my memory. Nothing moved. "I don't believe I've ever been in Cairo. I live in Spain, not Egypt."

"This was some time ago," the woman said carefully.

Perhaps she was someone I had met while traveling with Dr. Kostich. "Oh? How long ago?"

She looked at me silently for a moment, then said, "About three hundred years."

# PLAYING WITH FIRE

*The first novel of the Silver Dragons*

KATIE MacALISTER

**The heat is on . . .**

Despite her unique ability to protect herself by hiding in the shadows, May's on the run for breaking Otherworld law. And she's also in hiding from her demon boss, Magoth, who is absolutely determined to seduce her.

But then May meets Gabriel. The most gorgeously, broodingly, handsome piece of trouble you can imagine. Sparks fly – quite literally – when she discovers he's actually a shapeshifting dragon. And the passion that burns between them makes it look like he could be the one to take her out of the shadows for good.

That is, until Magoth orders May to steal one of Gabriel's treasures. And she really does have to decide if she's up to playing with fire . . .

Available as a Hodder paperback from March 2010

HODDER

# UP IN SMOKE

*The second novel of the Silver Dragons*

KATIE MacALISTER

## The sparks are flying . . .

Being held hostage by a demon lord is getting considerably chilly, especially when May Northcott's heart still burns for Gabriel Tauhou, the flaming-hot leader of the silver dragons.

Destined to be together and yet pulled apart . . . will there ever be a way to overcome what separates them without disaster?

Thankfully Gabriel has a plan to rescue his beloved mate. But it's risky – and would also force May to become a pawn in a very dangerous game involving hell, fire and all of humanity, just in order to secure her freedom.

She insists she'd do anything to be with Gabriel. But if the deal falls through and things get too hot, will she be able to withstand the blaze? Or will her life go up in smoke?

Available as a Hodder paperback from April 2010

HODDER